KAREN HEENAN

Coming Closer

Coming Closer

A Novel of 1930s Philadelphia

E-book ISBN: 978-1-957081-15-1

Paperback ISBN: 978-1-957081-16-8

Hardcover ISBN: 978-1-957081-18-2

"There will come a time when you believe everything is
finished; that will be the beginning."

— Louis L'Amour

Also by Karen Heenan

The Tudor Court
Songbird
A Wider World
Lady, in Waiting
The Son in Shadow
The Tudor Court Omnibus (ebook only)

Ava & Claire
Coming Apart
Coming Closer
Coming Together
Coming Home (Omnibus books 1-3, ebook only)
Home for Christmas (novella, ebook only)
French Lessons
Shifting Stages

Part One

1933

1

Ava

I rummage through Claire's underwear drawer, sorting by fabric even as I catalog the delicious colors: ice blue, orchid, butter yellow, ivory. A shocking black georgette slip with insets of handmade lace. One piece step-ins of peach satin with tiny bows at the straps. Bandeau brassieres in ballet pink crepe de chine with matching pants.

Pulling out a long, bias-cut slip in smoky lilac, I hold it against me, careful not to let my roughened fingertips catch on the satin. "Good lord, this is too pretty to cover with clothes."

"It's a negligee," she says, ducking her head. "There's a matching peignoir in the closet. With ostrich feather trim. Do you want to see it?"

I shake my head. "Something that lovely deserves to be seen."

"Well, it is." Claire's color deepens. "It's one of Harry's favorites."

It is my turn to blush. "I feel older and thicker by the moment." I fold the gown and put it back with the rainbow of shining fabrics. "But I asked for it. If I'm going to sew for these women, I need to know what they wear under their clothes."

"Most of them will have more substantial brassieres," she says. "Similar to what you wear, I imagine."

The idea of comparing my worn and faded undergarments to the magical assortment in Claire's drawer makes me smile. "I doubt it."

"And girdles," my sister adds. "I can't say I like them, but they do give a nice line, and they're better than corsets. Remember we used to try on Mama's corset while she was bathing?"

"I remember." Maybe I should invest in a new girdle. I have to start looking at myself the way I look at my customers, with an eye toward improvement. Before, it didn't matter. Daniel never minded, and I was usually pregnant, anyway. It matters now. Once this last baby is born, I will work on my appearance; I can't set myself up as knowledgeable about fashion looking like a coal miner's wife.

"You should cut your hair." Claire watches me in the mirror, reading my thoughts. "It's so pretty, but no one ever sees it, pulled back like that."

I touch the thick knot at the nape of my neck. I've worn it this way ever since motherhood claimed my time. There had been a brief moment of glory when Mama had done my hair in a grand pompadour for my wedding, but hairdressing took time I didn't have. A bun is neat and easy, and it can be taken down at night and braided for sleeping.

On rare occasions, I would leave it down. Daniel loved my hair.

Claire pulls a pin and the knot loosens. I sigh and remove the rest myself—it is better than being fussed over—and my hair tumbles to the middle of my back, dark blonde mixed with light brown. Daniel, in a rare poetic moment, once told me my hair looked like sunlight on a trout stream.

Combing it with her fingers, Claire bunches it up to chin level. "Here, I think," she says. "You've got a lovely jawline. We could have them put in a wave, too."

"I want to look like myself," I tell her, shaking loose and quickly twisting my hair back into its accustomed style.

"You will," she says. "Just newer. Modern."

I leave before my sister offers to make an appointment for me to have my hair done. She is right; I need to modernize myself if I want to be taken seriously, but although it may come to that, today is not the day to discuss such an undertaking. I need to get home before I embarrass myself. I make one final request, to distract her, and then depart.

Claire knows most of my life now, as I know hers. But I don't share the dark days, and this day has been dark since I got out of bed. Acknowledging the darkness makes it real; I would rather find ways to keep busy, to keep it at bay until the light returns of its own accord.

It doesn't last long, not most of the time. And if I'm honest, busyness is often not the best solution, but finding the time to be alone, to remember Daniel and allow myself the relief of tears, is almost impossible. The only part of my day available for mourning is after the kids have gone to school and before customers start arriving in the early afternoon.

Greeting them with red and swollen eyes will cause questions—or worse, sympathy—so I stuff my feelings down, burnish my sharp edges, and keep going.

My mother would be proud.

I have no sooner settled myself at the table with a cup of tea when the front door bangs, and voices, tumbling over each other, reach me in the downstairs kitchen. Only George and Toby this early; Thelma has a doctor's appointment, so she and Pearl won't be along for at least another hour. My eldest, Dan, is at work and won't be in until suppertime.

"Down here." Slow moving, I let them come to me.

They stream down the curved stairs, still arguing, kiss me on either cheek, grab slices of cake, and disappear again through the unlocked door of my workroom. The entire process takes less than two minutes, but I am as winded as if a tornado has blown through the house.

I finish my tea and shift to the sewing machine. Prudence Foster's latest commission won't sew itself, and for the next hour I disappear into my work. The girls come in at four, Thelma remaining upstairs with her homework while Pearl drifts down to check if I need help. A pot of stew is already on the back of the stove, and the dress is clipped to a hanger so the fabric can stretch before it is hemmed.

"How was school?" Pearl is a keen student and always has something new to share with me.

"So good, Mama." She pulls a book out of her bag: *Jane Eyre*. "Miss Rodney gave me this—she says she thinks I'll like it."

My girl inhales books the way her brothers eat cake. I am so proud of her I could burst.

"If it's something we'd all enjoy, maybe you could read it aloud in the evening," I suggest. "How was Thelma's appointment?"

"It was short today, but it was so nice we sat in the park after." She rummages again in her bag, and proffers a creased envelope. "This is for you."

While she gets on with setting the table, I return to my workroom and open the envelope. Max Byrne's report is brief, as usual, and begins, "My dear Mrs. Kimber."

Max Byrne is a doctor, and a friend of my sister's husband. Last year, when I was in the city, Claire convinced him to examine Thelma. I was shocked when he diagnosed her disability as rickets. The doctor at home had simply shaken his head, said she was crippled, and told us she would have to live with it.

Nine months later, my daughter is a different child. She still wears braces to correct the curve of her legs, but they have already been changed twice. The report offers some hope that by spring—perhaps—she can leave off the braces entirely. "Her progress has been exceptional," it continues, "and once this first year is up, Thelma may be better served with exercises to build her muscles, which cannot be accomplished as easily while wearing braces. I believe she would benefit from dance lessons, and if this is not something you would permit Mrs. Warriner to pay for, I can suggest several options for students from less well-heeled families."

I snort. Max Byrne and I are not that well acquainted, but he has an unerring ability to get under my skin. There was no need to mention my sister's willingness to pay for everything having to do with Thelma, from her treatments to her pretty dresses to these proposed dance lessons. I shove the letter into my apron pocket and listen to Pearl singing while I clean up the workroom.

Claire

After Ava leaves, I retreat to my sitting room to ease the inevitable tension in my neck any visit from her causes. We've been more comfortable with each other since her move to the city, but it's easy to misspeak and get her back up, and I spend most of our time together waiting for the other shoe to drop.

She left with two pairs of kid gloves wrapped in brown paper. Her hands are rough, she says, and she is afraid of snagging the delicate fabrics that are so in vogue, and that her clients will request. If the gloves help, I am happy for her to take them, but I'm not sure she didn't ask simply to distract me when I suggested she get her hair cut.

The gloves were in the attic, which is filled to the rafters with things no one has ever thought to discard. Not just my cast-offs, but things from my mother-in-law and assorted aunts and cousins—decades of dresses and hats, gloves and shoes, bags and furs. Ava was stunned by the plenty hidden away at the top of the house, and when I located the gloves, in the top tray of an old steamer trunk, she took them and made a hasty exit.

Despite her bravado, I know she is struggling. She and Daniel were so very nearly one person that I cannot imagine how she exists without him. I would be bereft if I lost Harry, certainly, but Ava and Daniel had paired off in their very first year of school. They survived so many hardships only for him to die in a pointless accident, when Harry and I had begged them both to come to Philadelphia and stay with us.

Now my sister and her children are here. The children seem to be adjusting, but I worry about Ava.

"Ma'am," comes a soft voice. Katie looks around the door, and my dog dashes in, yapping excitedly. "I thought maybe you needed this."

I expect more tea, but instead the door swings wide and my son staggers toward me on sturdy toddler legs. I drop to my knees, arms extended, and catch him when he falls into me, kissing the top of his head. Pixie circles, whining, his wet nose shoving in between us.

"Thank you," I say, looking up at her. "This is exactly what I needed."

After dinner, we take coffee in the living room. Harry smokes and casts occasional glances at the newspaper, while I put my feet up on the ottoman and replay the conversation with Ava in my head.

"You need another project," he says, breaking the silence. "You're brooding."

I come back to myself with a start. "What sort of project?"

Harry shrugs. "You've been at loose ends since Christmas. If you don't find something to occupy yourself soon, you're going to get under Ava's feet and there will be an explosion."

He's right, of course. For a long time, I was content, or at least comfortable, as nothing more than his decorative wife, but over the last year, I have outgrown the role. Prue Foster and I organized a Christmas gala for the city's orphans, and its success showed me what I was capable of.

Going back would make me feel like those gloves in the attic, folded away, waiting—for what? But I don't know what to do next.

I say as much, staring into my cup as if the brown liquid holds the answers. One thing I do know: I don't want to ruin my relationship with Ava by interfering too much in her life.

"What about continuing on with Prue?" he asks. "The gala got impressive results."

I've considered that, but what I enjoyed most, in the end, was the organizing, not the cause itself. The orphans never stopped making me uncomfortable, but that was my fault, not theirs. "Stella Good wants to start some programs for the children," I say. "It's not...what I want."

Leaning forward, he stubs out his cigarette. "For a while, all you wanted was a child."

I close my eyes. I did. Teddy is the center of my world, but how do I tell my husband that our son is not enough? "He doesn't need me every moment of the day. Look at Ava—she works, and she enjoys what she does."

"She also has no choice," Harry points out. "Five fatherless children and one more on the way, she's lucky to have a skill she enjoys."

It is illogical, but I am almost envious. No matter how difficult her life is, Ava has a purpose. I have yet to find mine.

Pearl

February 6, 1933

Whenever something new feels difficult, I remind myself that Daddy died because he couldn't change, and I find a way to adapt. Mama says I worry too much and I should remember I'm just a kid, but that's why I do it. I won't be a kid forever.

I want to be the kind of grownup who can survive when life goes sideways, like Mama. Everything fell apart for her in the last year, and yet here she is, in a new place, with a proper job, managing the way she always has. Not to mention another baby on the way. She gets cranky, but she's always had a short fuse. Daddy used to tease her about it, when he wasn't too tired or cranky himself.

In three months, I'll be thirteen. Last year, nobody remembered my birthday. Including me. Mama was in Philadelphia, bringing Teddy to Aunt Claire, and I was busy keeping house for Daddy and the boys, trying to make sure everyone had clean clothes and enough food and didn't kill each other before she came home. It was a lot.

This year is different, but if Mama asks, I'll tell her I don't need any kind of party. It's a waste of time and money we don't have, and besides, my birthday is so close to the end of the school year, I'd rather celebrate that.

Maybe that's what I'll do if she asks, tell her I'd like a party to celebrate my eighth grade graduation. Once I'm in high school I'll practically be grown up.

Claire

The door to Harry's office is open. "You've missed cocktails," I tell him. "Dinner in fifteen minutes."

"I'll be right there." He picks up an envelope from his desk, turning it over in his hands, then looks at me. "Does Ava have time to make you a new dress?"

The envelope is stiff and square, with some kind of seal. An invitation to something I will not want to attend. "If you make it worth her while. What is it this time?"

"It's the president," Harry says slowly, as if he doesn't quite believe it. "We've been invited to the inauguration."

My fingers tighten on the door frame as a sudden wave of heat washes over me. "Really?"

"Really. I got a separate note from Tyler Dawes with the details." At my blank look, he elaborates. "Ty was a classmate at Princeton. We've kept up over the years, mostly because we were two Democrats in a sea of Republicans. But now he's going to have a post in the new administration, and he thought of me."

I can't wrap my head around it. "Does he want *you* in the administration?" Will we have to relocate?

Harry smiles. "I doubt it. I've been out of the game for too long. But I appreciate the invitation, and Dawes said he could put aside two tickets to the inaugural ball. Will that make up for standing outside in the cold?"

"Will we actually get to meet President Roosevelt?" I am a bit dazzled by the president-elect—his patrician good looks remind me a bit of my husband, with a dash of movie-star glamor.

Giving the invitation one last glance, Harry tosses it onto his blotter and pushes his chair back. "I imagine so," he says. "Or at least the First Lady."

2

Claire

After dinner, Harry fetches the invitation so I can scrutinize it further, smiling indulgently at my excitement.

"The Inaugural Committee requests the honor of the presence of Mr. and Mrs. Harrison Warriner to attend and participate in the Inauguration of Franklin Delano Roosevelt as President of the United States of America." Seeing our names printed on the same page as the president's makes me dizzy again. "Special distinguished guests?"

He props his feet up. "Flattering the voters never hurts."

"What is the weather like in Washington in March?" I mentally begin packing. A good suit for day wear, with attractive but comfortable shoes for standing outside. A ball gown for the evening, of course. No doubt there will be at least one other reception...two cocktail dresses, the inaugural gown, three day looks, and two coats, cloth and mink. Hats and gloves for everything, of course, and shoes. And jewelry. My diamonds and what else?

I look up to find Harry smiling again. "What?"

"How many suitcases have you packed already?"

"I've lost count," I say loftily. "It's easy for you, men can wear the same thing to every event and no one notices."

My mother-in-law has been gone from the house since last summer, but her regular Thursday visit is a reminder of the dozen unhappy years I spent under her thumb. She arrives dressed as if for an outing at a fine restaurant, drinks a glass of sherry—doing her best to ignore Teddy, if he is downstairs—and then picks at her meal as though fearing it's been poisoned.

Thursday happens to be the day Mrs. Hedges experiments with new recipes, but she is an excellent cook, and even when the results don't appeal to Irene, they are delicious. I'm sure Harry doesn't notice.

We have exhausted the topic of the upcoming inaugural—Irene does not like the Roosevelts, Democrats, or progress generally—and I am enjoying a moment of peace when she begins again, on a different track.

"You heard about the Patterson boy's death?"

"Chiffy was hardly a boy, Mother," Harry returns. "He was five years ahead of me at school."

She purses her lips, unable to stand being corrected even by her son. "When I think of what he put his poor parents through…"

"Who are you talking about?" I am reminded of dinner conversations early in our marriage, when my husband and his mother would go on endlessly about people I'd never met. I didn't have the nerve then to interrupt.

"Christopher Patterson," Harry explains. "Old schoolmate of mine. Prominent family—his father was dean of Penn's law school, and a bank president." He takes a sip from his water glass. "There were five other children, and then Chiffy."

"He was a disgrace," Irene says swiftly. "Broke his poor mother's heart, the people he consorted with."

This is getting more interesting by the moment. Did he have a mistress? Had he cheated at cards? Irene's standards could turn on a dime. "What do you mean?"

Harry folds his napkin and puts it aside. "Chiffy followed his father into the law, but instead of going into banking or contract work, he became a criminal defense attorney." He cocks his head. "Along with being a notable drunkard and chaser of chorus girls. Somewhere along the way, his nickname changed over to 'Chippy,' because of the women he preferred."

Philadelphia society is full of formerly-eminent black sheep who've tarnished their family names, but these stories are surprisingly hard to find—no matter their personal feelings, families band together to protect their miscreant children from gossip. It is very unlike Irene to bring up anything this interesting.

"He represented murderers." Her voice is barely above a whisper. "Gangsters. Women of"—she searches for an acceptable turn of phrase—"women of no social standing. And he rubbed his parents' noses in it."

Katie collects our plates, impassive. I wonder what she thinks of these snippets of overheard conversation.

"Not really," Harry says. "He didn't care what they thought—which seemed a fair return for how little attention they paid him as a boy. The fact that his father disinherited him didn't seem to matter in the slightest. 'My father left me his good name. No son could ask for more.'" An odd, almost envious smile plays about his lips. "Last I heard, he was practicing law out of a phone booth in Broad Street Station."

"No one would rent to him. He was an absolute disgrace." Irene is always on the side of culling the herd.

"He didn't pay his rent," Harry says. "He never charged his clients."

"And you say he's died?" What a shame. Aside from scandalizing Irene, he sounds as if he would have been great fun at a party.

"Last week." Harry leans back so Katie can serve dessert. "The family didn't have a public funeral, probably afraid of who would show up."

"A tragedy." Irene pokes delicately at her layer cake before taking a grudging bite. "Such breeding, and he threw his life away on criminals and degenerates."

I look up, a sudden question arrowing into my mind. "Did Max know him?"

Harry breaks into hearty laughter. "Of course."

Ava

Claire has come and gone like a whirlwind, leaving behind an envelope of cash and the lingering scent of French perfume.

"I need a gown," she said. "Something amazing. Can you do it by the end of the month?"

"Of course," I told her. "But you've got twenty gowns in your closet already. I'm not saying no to your money"—the envelope was already in my hands—"but I don't want your custom out of sympathy, either. Is it impossible for you to wear a dress more than once?"

"Of course. But this is special." She informed me she and Harry had been invited to the inauguration in Washington, and showed me two pale green tickets to the inaugural ball. "So you see," she said, "I have to have something spectacular."

I scrutinize the tickets, registering that it costs five dollars to be admitted to the ball. It is both a lot of money and less than I would have expected for an event of such importance. "It's not going to be blue," I told her. "You and your damn blue."

"I like blue." Lashes flutter over eyes the exact color she would choose to wear. "But you know best. And I have a million things to do before then, so I'll leave it up to you. Let me know when you need me for a fitting."

I don't understand much about politics, but it seems to me the sort of dress I would normally make for Claire—bias cut and sinuous, to counteract her primness—would garner the wrong reaction in such a crowd. My sister must look like what she is, the beautiful wife of a prominent businessman, and her figure, while unavoidable, should not be on blatant display.

But fashion leans toward the form-fitting. I spend the rest of my work day thinking about it, making bad drawings, and finally haul myself out to the drugstore to surreptitiously look for inspiration in the rack of movie magazines.

And I find it, in an issue of *Silver Screen*—a profile of Joan Crawford, illustrated with photographs from several of her pictures, including last year's *Letty Lynton*, where she is clad in a gown that seems equal parts ruffles and attitude. I scrutinize the page for so long the druggist comes out from behind his counter and I reluctantly hand over ten cents so I can work out how to copy the dress without Mr. Terry's tactful cough intruding on my mental processes.

On Friday morning, I take the magazine to Mendel's. When I spread it open on the counter for the shop assistant to see, he holds up a finger and dashes to the back of the shop where the patterns are kept. Within minutes, he returns, triumphantly holding an envelope aloft. The illustration shows the same ruffled dress, albeit with a better neckline. While I do not want Claire to look too alluring, I refuse to put her in a Peter Pan collar, which only Joan Crawford could carry off while still managing to look blatantly sexual.

"I hadn't realized there was a pattern." But of course there would be; businesses exist to anticipate a need. "I've been trying to piece it together in my head."

"Is easier this way," the assistant says. "You will adapt it, yes, but the hard work is done for you." He looks at me with snapping brown eyes. "White? Or ivory?"

"Neither," I tell him. "And not black. What other colors do you have?"

Perched on the edge of my seat on the streetcar, I hug the bulky parcel of celery-green silk organza to my stomach and distract myself from my aching back by thinking of the marvelous dress it will become. It is the perfect color for Claire: spring-like and demure, capable of being worn equally well with flowers or diamonds—though I will suggest flowers.

Old Mr. Mendel cackled with delight at my choice of fabric. "Was a mistake," he wheezed. "The order, it was for dark green. I was going to send this back."

I purchased fully a third of the bolt, knowing it will take yards to duplicate those sleeves and the layers of shallower ruffles at the hem.

Having a pattern has taken some of the difficulty from the gown, but not all. The silk organza is intimidating in its fragility; from dressing Claire and her friends, I have become familiar with handling satin and velvet, but this will be a new challenge. I hope I am up for it.

"It shreds as soon as it's cut," I tell Pearl later, as my daughter stares consideringly at the organza. "It's going to have to be all French seams."

She wrinkles her nose, having no higher opinion of those tiny enclosed seams than I do. "What about the pinking shears?"

"I tried them." The clunky zig-zag blades cut neatly enough, but the fabric started to fray before I had more than handled it. "There's no choice."

"Then charge her more." Pearl shrugs philosophically, comparing the pattern to the magazine photo of Joan Crawford. "I like the pattern better."

"Me, too." I stand up and stretch, wincing. There will be time enough tomorrow to face Claire's gown.

Pearl

February 25, 1933

This might be the prettiest dress Mama has ever made, and she's made a lot of pretty things in the short time we've been here. I've been begging and begging to help, but she said no until yesterday. I knew she'd give in eventually. All those ruffles can't be hemmed on the machine, not even the electric one, and she hates rolled hems like poison.

The work has to be done at night, because of school, plus two days a week I take Thelma to her appointment after. Once the littles are in bed, we bring the extra lamp downstairs and spread the fabric out on the cutting table. Once I hem the ruffles, Mama will sew them on. It will save handling the fabric too much.

Even working as fast as I can, it will take three nights. The fabric is crisp and soft at the same time, so I'm able to crease it with my fingernail instead of using the iron. That's good, but also bad, because if I press too hard, it starts to fray.

It's the color of early spring leaves, a pale green with hope in it.

Mama worked on lining the bodice while I threaded a needle and made tiny, alternating stitches near the edge of the first ruffle, stopping every inch to draw the thread taut so the hem rolls under neatly. It's slow work, even with my fast fingers. I wish there was someone to read aloud to us the way I do when it's just Mama sewing.

By bedtime, I made it through the first pile of strips, which will become the sleeves. They're the most important, Mama says. If we have to rush, it's better for mistakes to happen at the hem, where they won't be as easily seen.

My head aches from focusing so hard and I want to get back to Jane Eyre, *but it will all be worth it. Something we made will actually be worn in the same room as President Roosevelt!*

Also, Mama says Aunt is paying a bucket of money for this dress because it's a lot of work in a short time. Trust Mama to take the romance out of it.

3

Claire

When I first left Scovill Run, I worked at a hotel in Scranton. In my innocence, I thought the Searle was the pinnacle of style and luxury. After my marriage, I learned the error of that belief, but as we mount the steps to the Willard and two smartly uniformed doormen grant us entry, a scene opens before me which makes even Philadelphia's Bellevue Stratford look shabby and tired.

Marble columns thrust upward to vaulted ceilings; graceful bowls of frosted glass hang from chains, casting diffuse light and making the polished floors glow. Potted palms shade scattered seating areas; ahead of us, the grand reception desk awaits.

My palms are damp inside my gloves. Why do I allow these places to intimidate me? I stand silently by while Harry signs the register, and follow him and the porter into the elevator.

Our room is smaller than I expect, though expensively appointed. The window is shrouded in heavy draperies that puddle on the polished floor. It faces the rear, so the sounds of busy Pennsylvania Avenue will not wake us—if I am able to sleep at all.

The porter stacks our bags and glances between us. "Someone will be up shortly to unpack for you."

I almost tell him not to bother; I am feeling too fragile to deal with strangers, but then I think of the wrinkles and creases inside those suitcases and smile politely. "Thank you."

Harry tips him and the door closes. "I'm sorry it's not a better room," he says, coming up behind me and kissing my neck. "It was the best I could manage at the last moment—Dawes's name got me this far."

I turn in his arms. "It's more than enough."

We have freshened up when it occurs to me. "What about your friend? Do I get to meet him?"

"He's here with his wife," he says. "I thought we'd go to their suite for drinks this evening and then down to the hotel restaurant, if that's all right with you."

"Of course." I smile brightly, but my insides quail. I have become accustomed to Harry's business acquaintances but this Tyler Dawes, college friend and political somebody—undoubtedly accompanied by a terrifying wife—will be something new under my personal sun.

A knock interrupts my thoughts and I open the door to a hotel maid. After giving instructions, Harry and I leave her to her tasks and go downstairs for lunch. Perhaps I will feel better once I've eaten.

After a short walk and a cup of coffee in a nearby café, Harry suggests venturing further down the mall. "I'm not certain the museums will even be open," he says, "but it would be a chance for you to see some new art."

On any other day, I would jump at the opportunity to immerse myself in paintings. "I'd like to go back," I tell him. "I'd love a nap and a bath before tonight."

"Your wish is my command." He turns us around. "Do you mind if I stay out for a bit?"

Perhaps it is terrible, but I do not mind at all.

Our clothes have been unpacked and are hanging, perfectly pressed, in the closet. I kick off my shoes, toss my dress over the back of a chair, and lie on the bed, my hands folded over my stomach. Why am I so out-of-sorts? I thought I was done being anxious at meeting new people, being judged for my unsuitability to be Harry's wife.

An hour of sleep restores me, and when Harry comes in later, I call to him from the blue tiled bathroom, where I am submerged in a cloud of bubbles scented with lily-of-the-valley.

He leans in the door. "Washing away your cares and woes?"

"Trying." I raise my shoulders. "I'm nervous about tonight."

Harry comes to sit by the tub. "There's no reason," he says. "Tyler is a perfectly nice fellow—far nicer than some of the people you've entertained in our house."

"It's not him," I admit. "It's his wife. It's always the wives."

"She can't be any worse than a Philadelphia society matron. Try to judge her by Mother's standards."

"By her standards," I question impishly, "or against her?" Irene is the most frightening woman I've ever met; Mrs. Dawes, however alarming, cannot be so bad.

"Whichever one works, darling." Harry squeezes my wet shoulder. "I'm going to start getting ready."

By the time the elevator opens on the eleventh floor, my anxiety is contained to a moth-like fluttering in my chest. I paste on a social smile as Harry knocks.

The door opens immediately. "Warriner!" The man is taller than Harry, with a lean, intelligent face. He ushers us inside. "Good to see you."

"Claire, this is Tyler Dawes," Harry says. "We spent four idealistic years at Princeton, dreaming up ways to save the world."

Mr. Dawes's hand is warm, his grip strong. "Those dreams didn't come to fruition, did they? I went into the law; you went into commerce. Neither one does a damn bit of good." He leads us to an elegant seating area. "Helen will be out in just a moment," he says. "She's still prettifying. Can I get anyone a martini?"

When I have a glass in hand, and the heady, comforting smell of gin in my nostrils, I retreat to the window while the men talk about the upcoming inaugural.

Far below, it is quiet, expectant. The kind of quiet that fills a concert hall before the music starts. The whole town seems to be holding its breath, waiting for the morning to arrive with the new president and a New Deal along with him. I have so much hope for Franklin Roosevelt and his plans; surely everyone in the District of Columbia shares my excitement. Around the hotel, so close to the White House that the roof is visible, the streets are filled with people—those like us, with tickets to the reviewing stands, others who will line the parade route to get a glimpse of the president and his wife, and those who simply live and work in this unusual city.

"You started without me?" The voice is clear, with an unexpected hint of the south. "Where are your manners, Tyler?"

"I knew you could catch up." Mr. Dawes circles his wife's waist with one arm. "Harry, you haven't met Helen, have you?"

Helen Dawes is possibly the most polished woman I have ever seen. Nearly as tall as her husband, she is thin to the point of being bony. Her dark red dress does not scream money; it says it very quietly and with authority. She wears her short-cropped brown hair in a mass of curls at the back of her neck, with a short fringe on her forehead. Her makeup is heavy but deftly applied, blurring her exact age from a casual observer.

She shakes Harry's hand, then zeroes in on me. I try not to visibly quail. "Tyler, she's charming!"

"You sound surprised." There is laughter in his voice.

"Darling, you've seen your friends' wives." She makes a face. "Of *course* I'm surprised." Taking my arm, she leads me toward the sofa. "So, Mrs. Warriner, tell me about yourself."

She is a woman, no different than Prue Foster, I tell myself. No different than me. I was terrified of Prue, and yet she is now my closest friend. "There's not a lot to tell, I'm afraid. And please, call me Claire."

It takes little time to become easy with Helen. Like Prue, she prefers those who can hold their own, rather than bend to the force of her personality. While I am not that strong, I can maintain the appearance of strength until I am comfortable. By the time we take the elevator down to the hotel restaurant, we are chatting like old friends.

"Where did you meet Mr. Dawes?" They make an odd couple with his New England energy and her southern languor.

"In New York," she says. "Not long after I graduated from Vassar. I was staying with friends and they took me out to Long Island for a party, where I met Ty. He called me two days later and courted me so persistently I just couldn't say no."

"You didn't try very hard." Across the table, her husband hides his laughter behind a drink.

"I know what I want," she says sweetly, lowering lashes beaded with mascara. "I didn't see the point in playing games." She turns back to me. "What about you, Mrs. Warriner? Where did you meet your husband?"

"He was a guest in the hotel where I worked." I sit back, waiting to be unmasked as an uneducated gold digger, unfit to sit at a table with graduates from Vassar and Princeton.

"I wanted to work, but my family wouldn't hear of it." She wrinkles her nose. "I made enough trouble that they sent me to college instead."

"Trouble?" I am gratified she hasn't inquired further into my meeting with Harry.

"No good Southern family likes a daughter who brings up Reconstruction at the cotillion." She lowers her voice, sounding distressed for all her bravado. "And we were a *good* Southern family. The fact that they let me go north to Yankeeland proves how bad I was."

"I didn't fit very well in my family, either," I confess, surprising myself. "They were content to stay where they were, but for as long as I can remember, I wanted to know what was in the outside world."

She smiles, relief clear on her face. "When I saw how much younger you were than your husband, I was afraid you'd be some fluffy little bunny and it would be absolute torture to spend the weekend with you." Putting a hand on my wrist, she says, "After the inauguration tomorrow, we're invited to tea at the White House. Could I convince you to come along?"

My mouth drops open and I shut it quickly, not wanting to look like a shocked schoolgirl. "Of course!"

Ava

I voted for Franklin Delano Roosevelt, but his election in November seems like a lifetime ago. It was the only second time I'd voted, and I might not have bothered but for a conversation between Claire, Harry, and Max Byrne, which made me look at the whole process, and my part in it, differently.

"It's strange to think that Aunt Claire is there right now," Pearl says, almost reverently. "It must be so exciting."

Patriotic music burbles from the radio, almost overshadowed by the impatient hum of the crowd. There is a spike in the noise, and then the excited voice of the news reporter begins to narrate what my sister must be seeing: the procession down Pennsylvania Avenue; the open car containing Hoover and Roosevelt; the car behind with their wives. I wonder what they would find to talk about.

The little boys grow restive and I send them outside, not wanting to miss the moment when Roosevelt takes the oath of office. I have never felt this involved in politics before. Is it because of Claire? Because we now live in a city, where politics seem more real? Or has my world splintered into so many pieces that I am willing to grasp at anything which might give meaning to my life?

A thunderous roar tears me from my thoughts: a salute of some kind. I have missed the oath. I lean forward, one hand on my belly. When the president speaks, the voice issuing from the radio is the voice of a rich man, similar to the voices I heard at Claire's Christmas gala, but his words are not what I expect. I listen, breathless, as he speaks to us—all of us.

"This great Nation will endure as it has endured, will revive and will prosper. So, first of all, let me assert my firm belief that the only thing we have to fear is fear itself—nameless, unreasoning, unjustified terror which paralyzes needed efforts to convert retreat into advance."

I cut a glance at Pearl and Dan; they are equally transfixed.

"More important," he goes on, "a host of unemployed citizens face the grim problem of existence, and an equally great number toil with little return. Only a foolish optimist can deny the dark realities of the moment."

Unexpectedly, my eyes fill. To hear our situation described in such clear and beautiful language—is it possible that, despite his background of wealth and privilege, he truly understands our struggles? The president goes on to detail his plans to alleviate the country's distress, and here my pregnant mind starts to wander, unable to focus on banking and policy. Dan will repeat it back later; he will remember and understand, or ask Harry to explain to him what he does not.

"For the trust reposed in me I will return the courage and the devotion that befit the time. I can do no less."

Pearl reaches across the davenport and takes my hand. Her eyes glisten.

"In this dedication of a Nation we humbly ask the blessing of God. May He protect each and every one of us. May He guide me in the days to come."

For a moment, we are silent. Then, Dan says what we are all thinking: "Amen."

Claire

After the oath of office and President Roosevelt's stirring speech, we return to the hotel to thaw out and have a quick lunch, then walk back to watch the parade. It seems to last forever, with military units, floats, marching bands and cars full of political figures I do not recognize. While my fur keeps me toasty, my feet have gone numb. After two hours, I tug on Harry's arm. "How long does this go on?"

"Until they run out of people." He looks down at me. "Cold?"

I nod. Left unsaid is my desire to rest and change my clothes, so I will be ready when Helen Dawes arrives.

"Let's go in, then."

Somehow I hadn't expected tea to include five hundred people, but there are easily that many bodies crammed into the state dining room. I needn't have worried about clothes; no one will see my black-and-white Molyneux dress in this crush.

"Will the president be in attendance?" Harry asks Mr. Dawes.

"It's not likely." He looks around. "Mrs. Roosevelt came back early, so she could be here—and from what I've been told, he'll look in here for a few minutes after he returns from the parade, but he intends to go straight upstairs to meet with his cabinet."

It seems fitting that he should want to go straight to work on behalf of the American people after such a stirring address. Bracing myself on Harry, I stand on tiptoe, but the First Lady is nowhere to be seen.

"I imagine he's exhausted," Helen says. "Did he really *walk* to the podium to take the oath?"

"Leaning on his son's arm. Polio, you know," he says to me. "The man can barely stand unassisted."

I'd heard something about an illness a few years ago, but he looked so vital in his photographs that I assumed a complete recovery. "Is it widely known?"

Mr. Dawes shakes his head. "Not outside his closest circle. Too many people would assume him incapable of thought, simply because his legs don't function."

There is a stir, and on the far side of the room, Eleanor Roosevelt stands framed in the doorway, followed by several women and a long-legged young man with the look of his father.

I watch the First Lady covertly, trying to formulate a description that will make Ava see her. Tall for a woman, with unfussy brown hair and a face best called striking. Those who don't care for her would undoubtedly call her horsy, and there is something equine in her long limbs and face; I can tell by looking at her she had been a gawky girl, unsure of what to do with her hands and feet. Her physical deficits are offset by a sympathetic gaze and a smile of infinite warmth. I like her immediately and refuse to leave until Helen Dawes arranges an introduction.

Mrs. Roosevelt is somehow both imposing and so homespun as to remind me of my mother. Her words, as she shakes my hand and welcomes me to the White House, are uttered in a voice as recognizable as the president's, and although there are several hundred people clamoring to speak to her, for those few moments, I am the focus of all her attention.

My next sighting of the First Lady is at the Washington Auditorium. We have been there for some time, dancing and talking to Tyler and Helen Dawes and others. The delay has allowed me time to see that—somehow—the ballroom is not full of gowns identical to mine. When Ava first showed it to me, I was petrified I would be one of dozens, but she assured me even if that were the case, hers would be better.

"Where is the President?" Voices rise around us as the White House party arrives. Mrs. Roosevelt is accompanied by a crowd of formally-dressed men and women, but her husband is nowhere to be seen.

"Still with the cabinet?"

"There were rumors neither of them would attend," Tyler Dawes says. "After the assassination attempt in Florida last month, who could blame them?"

Helen laughs. "What happened to 'nothing to fear but fear it-self'?"

"Perhaps that goes by the board when bullets are involved." He holds out his hand. "May I have this dance, Mrs. Warriner, before the tides carry us inevitably toward the First Lady?"

We share a foxtrot while my husband chats with Helen and another couple. Mr. Dawes is a skillful dancer, quick on his feet and watchful of the crowded dance floor. He spins me around so my ruffled skirts swirl around his legs. "Are you enjoying your visit to Washington?"

"I'm enjoying it very much," I tell him. "It's quite different from Philadelphia."

He cocks his head. "Particularly if you're in the same set that somehow produced Harry. He was always an outlier, even in college."

I want to ask what he means—Harry is the most conventional of men, perfectly at home in our social circle—but the music ends and we rejoin the others. One of the women looks at my dress with frank appreciation and I smile inwardly: Ava will have to be told yet again what a marvel she is.

She was right in her insistence that I wear flowers instead of jewel-ry. I brought both my diamonds and a pearl choker, but on looking at the dress hanging in the closet, Harry called the hotel florist and had a corsage of orchids sent up instead.

"You look like a bloom yourself," he told me when he pinned on the rich ivory blossoms. Their centers bore just a hint of blush. "These are icing on the cake."

It amazes me my sister is capable of intricate work like this, without having had any training beyond our mother's sewing lessons. My green organza is prettier than most of the gowns in the ballroom, and I have to assume it is also better made. When we encounter Helen Dawes, she looks me up and down with something like envy. "You look like an ode to spring," she says. "What an amazing color."

"Thank you." I have finally learned, with Ava's prodding, to accept a compliment. "My sister is a dressmaker."

"It's beautiful. I would have assumed New York." Asking permis-sion with her eyes, she reaches out and rubs the abundant ruffle at my shoulder between her fingers. "You look like a less avaricious Joan Crawford."

Mrs. Roosevelt leaves after an hour, but Harry and I dance until well after one in the morning and take a taxi back to our hotel to fall, exhausted, into bed.

4

Ava

I turn off Claire's sewing machine and pull the chain to turn off the light over my work surface. "Let's clear up now." I stand and stretch, my back crackling pleasurably, letting the edge of the table bear the weight of the baby.

Pearl's lap is spread with an abundance of pearl gray satin. "I'm almost finished," she says. "This fabric is so slippery."

"You've done enough for one day, baby." She is pale from indoor work; I wish I didn't need her help so badly.

"Can't I finish, Mama? It's just a few more inches."

I understand her desire well enough, and leave her to finish as I sweep up thread and scraps of satin from the floor. Tidying up is a habit from when I worked in the front room at our old house. Now I can leave it all out, go upstairs and sit with the family, or start supper. But I like to start fresh in the morning.

"Do you ever mind helping with this?"

"Of course not," Pearl says. "This is what I do."

"No, it's what *I* do. You won't have to do it, at least not forever." I don't want my girl to spend her life hunched over a sewing machine if she gets no pleasure from it. "Your granny and I did this because we had to."

"We still have to." She re-threads her needle and makes a tidy knot. "Don't we?"

"Yes." I tip the sweepings into the trash. "We do. At least I do, but right now, it's nice to have your help. But you're too smart to spend your life stitching."

"Aren't you smart?" Pearl stitches rapidly, barely looking down at the fabric.

"Not like you. By your age, I'd left school because we needed money. I had to work at something." I wipe the blades of my shears and hang them from their hook. "Sewing came easy to me, the same as it does to you, but that doesn't mean you have to do it forever. Have you ever thought about what you'd like to do when you grow up?"

"I hadn't, before," Pearl confides. "I thought if I could stay in school through eighth grade, that would be enough. Aunt Claire must have really been determined."

"She was," I say. "She wasn't made for a hard life."

"Like Thelma." Pearl carefully snips the thread and hands the dress to me.

"Maybe." I settle the shining garment on a padded hanger. "They look alike, I'll grant you that. But Claire always knew life would be easier because she was pretty, same as Thelma always knew things were going to be hard, because of her legs." I think of what Claire went through when she was around Pearl's age, and know she is stronger than I ever gave her credit for being. I push those thoughts away and put my hand on my daughter's shoulder. "But we were talking about you."

The house is quiet, the other children off on their own business. We go up the short flight to the back door and out into the tiny walled garden. Dan has built two benches and a table so we can eat outdoors, and I settle on one of them with a sound of relief.

"I want you to graduate high school. You may be helping me sew all the way there, but you're going to get an education. That's what your daddy wanted for you, as well." I turn my face up to the afternoon sun. The days are already getting longer; soon it will be spring, and the baby will be here. "It's important for a woman to have work she can do, because we never know what's coming. There was a long stretch when sewing was what kept us fed: first me and Granny, then you and me. Sometimes women's work is the only work available, but that doesn't mean things won't change over time. You don't have to be a dressmaker."

Pearl leans against the warm brick. She has grown; her school dress grazes her knees. I am thankful it has a good hem, so it can be let down again.

"I'd like—you know how much I love to read, Mama. I think I'd like to teach."

I have a vision of my daughter in a nice shirtwaist and a dark skirt, standing in front of a classroom. It warms me. "You would make a good teacher," I say. "I've watched you with the younger kids for years. It's not just that you're their sister, you have a way of handling them that makes them listen."

She picks at the surface of a brick, her face turned away. "I'd also...this is silly, maybe, and not as practical as teaching, but when I'm older and know more things, I'd like to write books."

Is it possible to be more proud of her? My dream changes from Pearl standing before a room full of rapt, impossibly clean children to a book jacket with the name "Pearl Kimber" on the spine. "If you can see that dream," I tell her, "you can make it come true."

Pearl

March 5, 1933

Listening to the president on the radio must have weakened something in me, because I would never have told Mama under any other circumstances about wanting to be a writer. But she didn't laugh like I expected, so maybe Mr. Roosevelt softened her up too.

It's something I've only begun to admit to myself since we came to Philadelphia. You can't have ambitions in a place like Scovill Run, they're ground out of you from the time you open your eyes to the way the world is. But here, just maybe I can be something more than Mama.

That sounds awful. I love Mama, and I'm so, so proud of her. I know she's still sad about Daddy, but she keeps those feelings to herself so we can all keep going. When he first died, she showed her upset, but it didn't last. It's not natural for her to show how she feels. I think the way Granny raised her, it was weak to show feelings. Aunt Claire's not like that. She laughs and cries as easily as Thelma. She gets tears in her eyes when she looks at Teddy. I'm sure she cried at the inauguration speech.

"Nothing to fear but fear itself," he said. Once upon a time, families had shields and mottos. If they still did, that would be ours.

Claire

The trip back to Philadelphia passes in a blur. Harry retreats behind a newspaper touting the accomplishments of the new administration thus far, while all the conversations I've had over the past three days—with Helen Dawes, Frances Perkins, and even Eleanor Roosevelt—whirl round in my head, drowning out the clatter of the wheels.

We had stopped at a toy shop before leaving so I could buy an enormous stuffed bear for Teddy. It sits beside me in the seat and makes me smile whenever I look at it. How he would have loved the parade—all the bands and soldiers and horses—but he is too small yet for such a journey. Katie would have had to come with us, otherwise I would have been looking after him the entire time and would have been prevented, like Cinderella, from going to the ball.

My disappointment at not being able to speak to Mrs. Roosevelt at the ball had been forgotten the very next day. Helen Dawes phoned early to ask if I would lunch with her, and after checking with Harry, who made plans of his own, I agreed to meet her in the lobby at eleven.

"Where are we going?" I compared my smart blue-gray suit against hers to make sure I was suitably dressed. "A restaurant?"

She gave me a tight-lipped smile, eyes crinkling with pleasure. "A luncheon for Frances Perkins," she said. "Our new Secretary of Labor."

A thrill passed through me at her words—that a woman could serve our government in a position of such importance when we have had the vote for just a few short years! It was a harbinger for how much women would accomplish in the future.

Despite the chill, it was warmer than inauguration day, and we decided to walk to the luncheon, continuing our earlier conversation as if we'd never been interrupted.

"Are you looking forward to living in Washington?" It would be quite a change from New York.

"In some respects," she said. "But it means I'll see my family more often." She rolled her eyes. "They've never come to New York, but Washington...well, Washington is almost the south." She stroked her fur collar with a gloved fingertip. "They don't like Ty, and I don't like people who don't like my husband."

"That's understandable." I had been afraid for years my family wouldn't like Harry, and so I had never given them a proper chance to know him—or for him to know them.

"After all," she said with a curled lip, "they don't have room to look down on anyone. My people *owned* people, at least until they were taken away from them. My mother's family hasn't quite accepted that they lost the war."

"How can it matter after so long?" I understood why it would matter to colored people—Ava told me both Mason and Esther Hedges's families moved north after they were freed—but surely a white family would have recovered more quickly.

"They took it personally," Helen Dawes said. "My grandmother grew up with slaves, and she lamented the loss of those good old days until the day she died." She blew out a breath, visible in the frosty air. "Thankfully, Tyler's people were lovely and welcoming, and by the time the children came, it was as though I'd always been there."

We talked then about our children—her girl and boy, both in college, and my Teddy, fourteen months—until we reached our destination. As our coats were being taken in the echoing marble reception hall, I thought to ask, "Have you met Miss Perkins before?"

"In New York," she said. "She worked for President Roosevelt when he was governor." Another merry smile. "Don't worry, Claire. You'll like her."

And I did. Miss Perkins—called thus even though she was married—was a calm, pragmatic woman who steadied me the moment we were introduced. When Mrs. Roosevelt joined our conversation a few minutes later, I barely flinched.

"Mrs. Warriner!" she said. "How lovely to see you again."

She remembered me! I restrained an absurd urge to curtsy. "I was pleased Mrs. Dawes asked me to come with her today."

"Mrs. Dawes loves to expand her circle of acquaintance," Miss Perkins said. "You'll find yourself involved in a worthy cause if you're not careful."

Helen reminded me of Prue Foster in her fearlessness; it was nice to know she was similarly well-intentioned. "I have a friend in Philadelphia who is awash with worthy causes."

"And are you involved in any of them yourself?" Helen picked a glass from a passing tray and looked at me over its rim. "Claire?"

"Not at the moment." My lack of activity is shameful. "No one has come up with anything yet."

Helen laughed. "You mean, no man?"

"Don't wait for a man to have an idea," Secretary Perkins chimed in. "You'll end up doing all the work and he'll take all the credit."

I looked between these powerful women, each so certain of their worth. "But where do I start?"

Mrs. Roosevelt put her hand on my shoulder. "Look around," she said. "Look around and find a need."

"I'm sorry?" I didn't think I heard her correctly.

"You've a brain," she said firmly. "And wealth to back it up, if I'm not mistaken." She raised her brows. "Find a need, then answer it."

"It's not that easy." I sounded like the old Claire, weak and unsure.

"It's exactly that easy," she said. "There's something under your very nose that needs doing, mark my words."

These women seemed to have all the purpose I lacked. "I recently helped to organize an event for three of the city's orphanages."

"An excellent start," Miss Perkins said. "No one ever takes into account that those children will grow up to be voters."

"I never thought of it that way." I took a sip of my drink, which turned out to be water in a champagne glass.

"You thought of them as human beings, which is even more important," Mrs. Roosevelt said. "It's only the jaded political class—of which I am regretfully a part—who see voters where others see people."

Something in the way she spoke made me feel as if a light had been switched on in my brain and it would grow brighter if I could keep talking to her. "I wish you weren't the First Lady."

"I can certainly imagine wishing that, but why would you?" Mrs. Roosevelt looked at me questioningly.

Blood rose to my hairline, and I spared a thought for how frightful I must look: red face, blonde hair, blue suit. "Because if you were an ordinary woman, I would very much like to be your friend." I looked at my feet. "That was tremendously inappropriate. I'm so sorry."

"Don't be silly, Mrs. Warriner." A wide smile brightened her face. "I wish more women would speak the truth. I would be honored to be numbered among your friends. Please do write to me at the White House and tell me how you get on."

It was an easy way to fob me off. She would receive a million letters every day, from women asking for favors, organizations wanting patronage. "Of course."

"Now, don't sound like that. I shall have a battalion of secretaries to sort through my mail, and anything personally directed to me will reach my desk."

Are they right, Helen Dawes and Mrs. Roosevelt and these other women? Am I capable of bold action? Can I do something to improve the world in which I live? It seems unlikely, as all I have ever done before this last year is attend parties and ask Harry to write checks for charitable causes, but their encouragement buoys me and I decide I should at least try.

After all, the orphans' gala was very successful. We raised more money than Prue Foster thought possible, and I had been responsible for a large amount of that fundraising. It had been a grand event, and I was dizzy with accomplishment at the end of it, but I don't want to do it again, and Stella Good and Marie Whittle are happy to take over for me.

What does Philadelphia need that I could possibly provide? Mrs. Roosevelt's words drain away and I am left with a void where my ideas should be. I rest my head against the stuffed bear's shoulder and let the swaying train lull me to sleep.

Ava

I cannot let go of what Pearl told me—she wants to be a writer of books! Mama would be so proud. Daniel, too, though he could barely read, pulled out of school too young to work in the mines.

Mama always said that a mother is only as happy as her unhappiest child. I can check Pearl's name off my list: it is obvious she will grow up to be a capable, happy woman. Dan will be all right, as well. He has a lot of his father in him, but he is more than a miner's son. I am curious what will happen with exposure to new things and new people in this city.

Toby and George are enigmas. Toby had been a pleasant enough baby, but when George was put into the cradle beside him, eleven months later, it was as if the second half of him had arrived. I wonder if they will ever separate, or if they will grow into adults who act as one. That could be intriguing or alarming, depending on circumstances.

Thelma is the true surprise. Despite her loveliness, I had never expected much from my younger daughter because of her physical limitations. But now, with those being resolved through Claire's interference and Max Byrne's treatment, she is like any other girl her age. And she is bright; I hadn't understood how bright she was.

As for Teddy, he is no longer my concern, though in my heart he will always be my son. But I don't have to worry about him. Claire and Harry will do their best and more. Any limits on Teddy's life will be his own, not things he didn't receive from others.

And what of this new little one, Daniel's last child? Who will he be?

I rub my palm over the increasing curve of my belly. "He would have loved you so much," I whisper. "And you would have loved him. He was a good father, he tried so hard." I stop short, wiping away tears, realizing I am making excuses to a baby who can't even hear me. "It was just too much. It was just too much, the world."

Loss sweeps over me. I sit on the stairs, a dust cloth in my hand, and let it come. Let him come to me in the only way he can, in memories so sharp they make my joints weak with longing.

It isn't the moments of joy I miss, or even the passion. It's the quiet times, sitting shoulder-to-shoulder on the porch step while he smoked, hearing his boots clomp up the stairs. The bed sinking as he dropped heavily onto the old mattress.

I miss the smell of cigarette smoke embedded in his shirts. I long for a basket of coal-blackened work clothes to somehow miraculously render clean. I miss his inability to put his mug back on the saucer. Though I do not dwell on it, I miss his physical presence. His few words. His wry glances. His hair, which would never stay slicked back because he couldn't keep his hands out of it.

God, I miss his hair.

Stupid, insignificant details compared to the level of my love for him, yet they are the worst of it. When we married, I knew there was a chance I would end up alone, but I also knew that having him—for however long—was worth that risk.

I recently took over the small bed, insisting that Thelma and Pearl sleep together, as sisters should. As Claire and I did, until my marriage. I miss Pearl's warmth, but she is a shallow sleeper and it wouldn't be long before she woke to find me weeping silently in the darkness.

The kids still cry, of course, and occasionally I let a tear slip in front of them so they won't think me cold. But I save my real tears for the night, when Daniel's absence from my bed feels like an amputation.

Grief isn't so much a state of mind as a physical condition, a weight like a sodden blanket or rock-loaded pockets, deadening emotion, making me move slowly through my waking hours. The only time I am myself is at the sewing machine, when I can either clear my mind to do what I do best, or test myself with some new challenge. There are many of those, for which I am thankful. Claire's ladies, as I think of them, take every magazine, see every movie, and envision themselves—with admirable confidence—in garments which do not suit their lives or their bodies.

I do what I can, adjusting patterns, cutting fabric to flatter, suggesting a more unyielding girdle beneath a clinging gown. And they listen, for the most part, trusting I need their money badly enough to tell them the truth.

Sometimes, after hours at the machine, I no longer remember his smile or the sound of his voice, his scent, or how it felt to be in his arms. It's too soon for this to have happened, surely; it's only been three months. Do I keep myself so willfully busy that I've forced him from my memory?

5

Claire

The glory of our return is almost immediately marred by a visit from Irene, who has no interest in Roosevelts, Democrats, or anything beyond the narrow confines of her chosen world, and who discourages any mention of politics on my part as unfeminine.

"I dined with the Ingersolls last week." She puts her hand over her glass as Katie attempts to pour. "The Pattersons were there."

Harry groans and does not refuse the offered refill. "You're incorrigible."

Her lips purse, as precisely as if they are drawn by a string. "I feel sorry for them, with that brother. The things people must be saying."

"Having said most of them yourself." Half the wine disappears in one gulp. "You're like the people who slow down to look at car accidents, Mother. Let poor Chiffy—and his family—rest in peace."

"Where is that girl?" Irene glares at her empty glass. "I met someone else interesting while I was there—"

"Enough." Harry drains his glass and pushes his chair back. "I have a call to make. Claire, would you mind taking Mother through for coffee?"

I rise more slowly, my pleasure that she has annoyed Harry tempered with the punishment of spending time alone with her. "Of course. Come along, Irene. Let me show you the new wallpaper samples for the hallway."

"She really got to you this evening." I brush my hair and tie a satin scarf over it to protect my fresh set, then switch off the vanity lights. A single silk-shaded bedside lamp provides a soft glow.

"I'm sorry I left you alone with her." He drops his robe on the bench and sits on the bed, stretching. "I feel protective of Chiffy, for some reason."

I sit beside him and lean my head on his shoulder. "He sounds a bit of a lost soul."

"He was both lost and the most grounded person I knew," Harry says. "He never fit in, and didn't want to. And once Chif dried out, he never looked back at his old life, or who he might have been if he'd stayed in the bosom of his family."

If his family was anything like the Warriners, I don't wonder. "When did you last speak to him?"

"A few years ago, it must have been." His eyes are far away. "We bumped into each other outside City Hall. He'd just come from court but he was wearing this ridiculous old coat and fishing boots, if you'll believe it. I tried to treat him to lunch at the Bellevue, but he had another appointment and slipped away."

I walk my fingers up the pearly buttons of his pajama top. "He sounds like he was a good man, even if he didn't do what was expected of him."

Harry stands, taking his buttons out of my reach. "He was," he says. "And even more, he was completely happy with his life, which is an enviable thing."

Ava

After the March bank holiday, after the president's first Fireside Chat on the radio, I look around and realize that, other than trips to church and fabric stores and meals with Claire, I haven't been outside the house since we moved in—certainly not for anything resembling pleasure. I count the money gradually building up in the jar in my workroom and make a decision.

"Why don't we go to the movies this weekend?"

A circle of open-mouthed faces stare back at me.

"I mean it," I say. "It's not likely there's something we'll all like, but maybe Dan can take the boys and Thelma, Pearl, and I will find something else."

There is a clamor as the kids realize I'm not joking. The reaction proves it is the right decision; how long has it been since they've had a treat? There was Christmas, but a treat for no reason is something different. Special.

"There's one called *42nd Street*," Pearl suggests. "It's a musical. Lots of singing and dancing."

Thelma sits up straight. "I want to see the dancing!"

Of course, she does. I silently curse Max Byrne for putting that idea into her head. I haven't spoken to Claire about lessons, because she'll agree like a shot and the lessons are something I would like to pay for myself, when I am able.

"Then it's settled." I look around, reaching over to tousle George's hair. "And you three pick out a cowboy movie or whatever you want. We'll go Saturday afternoon, after my fitting with Mrs. Mercer."

"Should we ask Aunt Claire?"

"We could," I say to Pearl, "but I'd rather it just be us."

"Me too." Thelma leans against me. "Just us."

Walking back to the house, I lean heavily on Dan's arm, the baby slowing my steps. It is tiring, walking on hard sidewalks instead of the dirt and gravel roads I am accustomed to, but there is less dust, even though the streets are clogged with cars and horse-drawn delivery carts.

"Did you have fun?" I ask, to get them talking. I need distraction for these last few blocks.

"Oh, yes!" Thelma tries to bound ahead, but her braces weigh her down as surely as I am weighted by the baby.

"Good." I call to Toby and George, scuffling as always. "Slow down, you two. How were your cowboys?"

Toby begins a convoluted explanation of the movie's plot, involving rustlers and outlaws, smacking at his brother each time George tries to get a word in edgewise.

I look at Dan. "I hope they didn't give you trouble."

"They were fine," he says easily. "I let them run a little and then clamp down." He offers me his father's smile. "This was good for them, Ma. For all of us."

For less than two dollars, including our extravagant automat meal, I have given my family the kind of outing we'd never had back in Scovill Run. Money does not yet grow on trees, but I vow to find a way to do this at least every other month. We need to do things as a family, or the boys will run so wild I'll never get them back.

Thelma starts flailing her arms in imitation of the dancers in the movie's finale. "Look at me, Mama," she cries, spinning and nearly hitting the lamp post that marks the turn from Pine Street onto Ringgold Place. "I'm dancing!"

Pearl

March 25, 1933

Today was magical. I don't know what gave Mama the idea, but I'm so glad. The boys walked over to the Mastbaum to see Tom Mix, while Mama, Thelma, and I went to see 42ⁿᵈ Street at the Boyd. Afterward we met at the Horn & Hardart on Chestnut Street and Mama treated us all to sandwiches! George and Toby insisted on putting in the nickels to make the doors open. I'm sure they could have done it all day. They could have eaten all the sandwiches, too, the greedy little pigs.

I don't think Mama's going to be able to get away with not giving Thelma dance lessons after this. She's been trying to tap dance in the kitchen since we got home, and Mama finally sent her to bed so we could get some peace.

Once I'm done writing, I'll go up. Mama's sitting with a cup of tea and I think she'd like some time to herself. Maybe that way she won't cry when she goes to bed.

Claire

Despite the fact that I was bubbling with enthusiasm when I returned from Washington, no new project has presented itself. Frances Perkins said blithely, "Don't wait for a man to have an idea," but I have no ideas, or at least none that strike me as worthy.

"I don't understand," I say to Prue over lunch. "I came home so excited, but I guess I'm just not like those women, because I don't know what to do with myself."

"Do you think Eleanor Roosevelt was born like this?" she asks practically. "With her upbringing, she wasn't trained to have a useful thought in her head. It all came later."

It makes sense when Prue says it, but Mrs. Roosevelt, Helen Dawes, Frances Perkins—all these women have such purpose, and I feel diminished in their presence. They are so sure of themselves and what they want to accomplish; I have days when I am exhausted by choosing a hat.

I have just come in from lunch when the telephone rings. "I'll get it," I call to Katie, who is upstairs singing to Teddy.

Max Byrne's voice is unusually subdued. "Would you mind if I left a few boxes at your house?"

"Of course not. What is it?" Not that it matters. There is plenty of space in the attic.

"Just some things from my office."

I think no more of it until he arrives an hour later, with two brimming cartons balanced carefully on his bicycle. Their contents—books and photographs, a packet of what look like letters—are oddly personal. "All this was in your office?" I ask. "Why?"

He lifts one shoulder. "I've been sleeping there for the last year or so. The hospital finally noticed, and it's their opinion that my salary is sufficient to cover bed and board elsewhere."

Max spends most of his waking hours either at the hospital or at one of his other jobs, but it is pointless to sleep in his office, unless— "Wait, were you *living* there?"

"Yes." He sets the boxes on the hall floor. "And, not surprisingly, they don't want one of their doctors taking up residence in the building." He sighs, momentarily deflated. "It was move out or leave entirely, which I can't afford, so Spencer's offered me his sofa for the time being. There's not enough room for the rest of this in his house."

John Spencer has a wife and three young children. Max is lucky to have been offered any space at all.

"You can't live like that."

Removing his hat, he runs his fingers through his curls, then jams it back on. "A lot of people are worse off, Claire. It was my decision to try to get away with sleeping at the hospital."

I shut the door and lead him down the hall. Katie glides downstairs, looks at us, and disappears to fetch tea—though I think Max would be better served with something stronger.

"Can I ask why you gave up your rooms?"

He drops heavily into an armchair and rests his hands on his knees. "Because I was hardly there, and there were so many other uses for the money. I don't need a landlady charging me for meals I'm never there to eat."

Max Byrne is in and out of orphanages and day nurseries all over Philadelphia, not to mention the migrant clinic he and Spencer run near the art museum. They pay for medical supplies but I always assumed his time was funded by donations. Max knows absolutely everyone, and is never afraid to ask.

I sit on the sofa, tucking one foot beneath me. "So you've been spending your own money on all these things?"

"I can only badger so long before people grow deaf," Max says. "I save my tap dancing for special occasions."

Katie puts a tray on the table and offers Max a quick smile before ducking out of the room.

"You can't stay on John Spencer's sofa." I add milk and two sugars to the cup and hand it to him. "Not when we have all this space."

His eyebrows lift. "And what will Harry say about that? Ava was family."

"You make it sound as if you're a stranger off the street. You've been his friend for as long as I can remember." It is a solution to his problem, and will cause us little inconvenience. "Honestly, Max, he won't mind at all—and you'll certainly eat less than Ava's boys."

He refuses, but I continue to work on him. Eventually his resistance crumbles like the coconut cake on our plates. "You're like water on a rock," he says. "You've worn me down."

"Good." A flush of victory straightens my spine. "Katie will make up the room, and when you come back tonight, you can bring your clothes. I assume they're in a suitcase under your exam table?"

Max passes a hand over his eyes. "Something like that."

The suitcase arrives later by messenger, and I carry it up to his room myself. Other than the boxes, it seems to be the extent of his worldly possessions.

Katie has dusted, run the sweeper, and made up the bed, and I re-arrange the sitting area to accommodate a table he can use as a desk. I had intended to put his things away, so he could come home to a tidy room, but when I chance upon a framed photograph of a girl, I put it carefully back and leave the boxes where they are. I don't want Max to think I was prying.

Harry is amused to learn we have another long-term house guest. "It's a good thing Mother moved in with Aunt Nora," he says. "Her rooms have barely been empty since."

"You don't mind, do you?" It hadn't occurred to me that he would. But a man's home is his castle, and Harry works very hard; Max's presence might be jarring. "He'll hardly ever be around."

"I'm more concerned about what your sister will say."

"I didn't think of that, until after I'd asked him." I can predict what Ava will say, which is why I don't plan to mention it until I have to.

"I may have to start calling you Maxine." Harry draws me close, and I shift until my head rests on his chest. "You've got your finger in at least as many pies as he does."

"Hardly." I look up at him. "And I'm far too fond of my comforts to do something as uncomfortable as sleeping on a sofa."

Ava

Dan left off bootlegging coal without a backward glance, but he is still a scrounger, trawling the alleys behind the houses of the wealthy and visiting areas of the city where vibrant secondhand markets thrive. His finds range from the lumber and fixings for my workroom to broken-backed books for Pearl and marbles for the boys to—amazingly—a painted wicker coach for the baby.

"The hood is cracked," he says anxiously, "but I thought you could make a new cover. Is there a way to waterproof canvas?"

"I think I can wax it." I know in theory how it is done, and if it will refresh this otherwise glorious vehicle, I will figure it out. "Did someone actually throw this away?"

He shakes his head. "There's an Italian neighborhood further south of here, with a big street market. Mostly they sell food, but this was on the curb and it only cost three dollars."

I flinch at the price but realize I can't pull a baby through busy city streets in the cart I used in Scovill Run, even if we'd brought it with us. "It's perfect," I say, and mean it.

6

Claire

Teddy and I often eat dinner in the nursery when Harry is out of town. It's like a picnic, sitting together at the little table with his stuffed toys in a circle around us. I usually read to him until he falls asleep, but I have plans this evening, and after we're done eating, I scoot back to my room to get changed. He calls after me, and I bring him to sit on the bed while I get ready, remembering how Thelma used to watch me dress during the months she lived with us. My boy is more active; he slides down and plunges into my closet. Half my dressing time is spent trying to keep him from wreaking havoc on my wardrobe.

The bell rings promptly at six. Marie's voice echoes up the stairs, greeting Katie and then fading as she goes into the living room. I put the last touches on my makeup and run lightly downstairs to meet her, Teddy protesting in my arms.

"Would you like anything to drink before we set out?"

Marie is on the sofa with Pixie. They look up guiltily, and the dog gets down. She makes faces at Teddy until he laughs. "I'm fine," she says with a last stroke of Pixie's head. "We can have tea there if we get thirsty."

Katie hands over Marie's jacket and I surrender my squirming child into her capable hands. He crows and reaches for her hair. The sound of his laughter follows us out of the house.

We drive across the bridge to the west side of the city, catching up on each other's lives. Marie has been in Boston since February, visiting family, and has not yet heard about my trip to Washington. Her eyes grow big when I tell her about meeting Eleanor Roosevelt and actually having a conversation with her.

"I didn't vote for her husband," she says, "but I think she's very interesting."

"You voted for Hoover?" I'm surprised; Marie is not particularly political, but after the orphan's gala, I thought she understood the dire straits of the poor. Voting for the man whose name had been given to the homeless encampments around the country is something I can no longer conceive of doing.

She gives a small shrug. "I didn't vote. I meant to, but my hairdresser's appointment ran late, and I almost missed my lunch reservation."

I hold my tongue. Two years ago, I would likely have given the same excuse.

We are barely through the doors of the Commercial Museum when we encounter a wall of dizzying scent. "Hyacinth," I say, inhaling deeply. "One of my favorites."

"Mine, too." Petite Marie stands on tiptoe to peer past the entry desk. "But look at the tulips!"

We pay our seventy-five cent admission and make our way into the Great Hall where the flower show is being held. Instantly we are awash in color—swaths of tulips, roses, daffodils, and hyacinth; piles of rock with artificial waterfalls splashing into ponds filled with thick, waxen lilies.

The hum of female conversation is nearly as overwhelming as the scent. The show closes tonight, so it is surprising the crowds have not yet died down. If anything, it is busier than I had expected. I look at the poster on the wall—two charming Dutch children in wooden shoes—and note that the show doesn't close until eleven.

We make our way through the crowded aisles, looking at displays by local garden clubs and horticulturalists, tree experts and landscapers, purveyors of fountains and garden statuary and weatherproof iron furniture. It makes me wish for a garden of my own, but we are here so Marie can get ideas for hers. Her family is moving to Bryn Mawr when renovations to their new home are complete, and she wants to get a head start on planning.

"I want an arbor," she says decisively. "A sort of temple."

"To what?"

"To music, I think." She rests her hand on the head of a statue: a cherub playing a set of pipes. "Can't you picture it?"

I could; that was the worst part. "Does Purvis know about all this?"

She smiles impishly, her brown eyes lit with amusement. "He will when he gets the bill!" Taking my arm, she tows me along until we reach a display of densely-planted roses. "Oh, look at these." The space is entered through an arch completely covered in shell-pink climbing roses, whose sweet fragrance is almost overpowering. Marie presses her face into the blossoms, then turns to me. "Aren't they perfect?"

An older man with a gardener's apron over his suit appears at her elbow. "These are New Dawn roses, ma'am. A fairly recent cultivar."

"Are they hardy?" Her giddiness drains away as she focuses on the dark green, serrated leaves. "In this area, I mean?"

He nods, taking in her enthusiasm and the quality of her fur-trimmed coat, calculating her value as a customer. "They were developed at a nursery in New Jersey," he says, pulling a card out of his apron pocket. "They have a long bloom season and are quite resistant to pests. I would be happy to discuss them further at your convenience."

Marie takes his card with a sound of satisfaction. "These will be perfect," she tells me. "When I get my—look, there's Geneva!"

At the sound of her name, a woman turns in our direction, a wide smile breaking across her face. Geneva Rowland was another one of Prue's recruits from the orphan's gala, but like Marie, she has been absent lately. We join her and, after greetings and compliments have been exchanged, make our way to the café for tea.

"What are you doing here?" Marie asks as we take our seats at a small table out of the worst of the crush. "I didn't know you liked flowers."

"Who doesn't like flowers?" She straightens her hat, which is decorated with cherries and an improbable bird. "I've started working with the Society of Little Gardens. We have a booth over on the other side, but I'm not volunteering tonight."

A waitress, clad in a frill-edged apron and matching cap, arrives with our tray. I lean to one side while she slides our order onto the table. "I've never heard of them."

"It encourages gardens in public places," Geneva says. "Have you ever noticed the poor don't have flower gardens or trees where they live?"

"I have." If they have any soil at all, they have vegetable gardens; children can't eat flowers.

"We donate window boxes, plants, and seeds to businesses, to encourage them to add a little greenery to their storefronts." She stirs sugar into her tea and takes a quick sip before continuing. "We've even started tenement gardens for children."

"I didn't know you were a gardener, Geneva."

She waves manicured fingers at us. "I sent my gardener to do my share. But I do like picking out flowers and deciding where they should go, and talking businesses into participating." She cocks her head and the bird's tail feathers brush Marie's cheek. "Weren't you looking for a project, Claire? We need more hands."

"I don't have a gardener to do it for me." I might not have found my purpose, but—no matter how worthy the Society may be—it is not planting flowers.

Ava

Three mornings a week, Dan's friend, Tommy Marinelli, knocks at the door and they head off to work together. The boys share the same awkward, rangy height, curly black hair, and deep brown eyes. If I didn't know the Kimbers came from Cornwall, and Daniel's mother was a Ryan, as Irish as my own mother, they could pass as brothers.

"I like that boy," I tell Pearl as she carries the breakfast dishes to the sink. "I'm glad Dan has a friend, even if it is through work."

"Isn't work where most grown-ups find their friends?" She slides the plates into the basin of warm water. "That's where all Daddy's friends came from."

I stop to think and wonder if that's why I have so few friends. Up until now, my life has been about raising my kids and sewing, all of which have kept me close to home. Claire and her circle have expanded my world, but other than my sister, I wouldn't call those women friends. The only friend I have in Philadelphia—aside from Max Byrne, who is an acquaintance and does not bear thinking about—is Esther Hedges, Claire's cook.

Later in the day, I pay her a visit. My sister is out, and when Katie lets me in, I head straight for the kitchen. The room is warm and smells of baking, and something inside me eases. Esther smiles at me. "Look at you, Mrs. Ava. That baby's getting bigger every day."

"Don't I know it." I shrug off my coat and pour myself a cup of coffee from the ever-present pot on the stove. "By bedtime she'll be even bigger."

It is a continuing mystery to me how my babies start the day small, and by the time I put on my nightgown they're sitting inches lower and what feels like pounds heavier. There's probably a scientific explanation for it, but it's not something I've ever heard.

Esther takes two cake pans out of the oven, and puts them to cool on the window sill. "Buttercream icing on these," she says over her shoulder. "Mrs. Claire's new favorite."

"I don't know why she isn't the size of a house." Only my boys show more appreciation for Esther's baking.

She tops up my coffee. "It's because she never stops moving. She's up with young Teddy before I've got breakfast ready, then she's either supervising the changes to the house, or out with one of her charities—unless she's having the ladies to lunch here."

It sounds exhausting, but not at all like work. Trust Claire to find a job which consists mostly of socializing.

A door closes above us and unfamiliar footsteps bound down the stairs. "Mrs. Hedges," a male voice calls, and I whirl around as Max Byrne skids into the kitchen. He stops short. "I'm sorry, I didn't realize you had company."

I slip off the stool, dusting crumbs from my skirt. "I'm hardly company," I say stiffly.

"True enough." He gives me a smile, then focuses on Esther. "I wanted to let you know I'll be out this evening, so please don't set a place for me."

She shakes her head. "You're as bad as Mrs. Claire," she says. "You never stop."

"I was an only child," he tells her. "I fear boredom more than any-thing." He reaches around me and snatches a bit of cake from the plate, leaving a crumbled edge that will have to be patched with icing. "Good afternoon, ladies."

He's gone before I can form the question. "Why is he here?"

Esther blinks. "Didn't Mrs. Claire tell you? He's renting your old rooms."

Claire

I should have told Ava about Max before she found out on her own, but I try to avoid my sister's volatile side. Anyway, it seemed unlikely they would run into each other. Her only regular appearance at the house is for Friday dinner, and that's the night Max goes to the migrant camp. She and the children would be long gone before he dragged himself home.

He is, despite his outsized personality, only a minor presence in the house. Most days he is gone before I wake up; Mrs. Hedges has taken to leaving a packed lunch for him in the refrigerator because he is often awake even before she comes downstairs. Katie tells me his rooms rarely need anything more than the bed linens changed. I had not expected him to be tidy.

The front door rattles as I wait for Stella to arrive for lunch, and I poke my head out of my sitting room. Max drops his hat on the hall table, running both hands through his curly hair.

"I didn't expect you home." Stella will be pleased; like most women—other than Ava, who seems immune—she blooms in Max's presence.

He checks his watch absently, as if unaware of the time. "I'm not. I just need to get something."

I follow him upstairs. "Mrs. Hedges told me you ran into Ava the other day."

"Are the wounds visible?" His grin is a bit unsteady. "You hadn't told her I was here?"

"You're not the only one she threatens to bite." I shake my head. "She's always been difficult. This whole situation has made her more stiff-necked than ever."

Max ducks into his room and emerges with several sheets of paper, which he folds and puts in his inside jacket pocket. "I can imagine." He pauses, his fingers tight on the door frame. "It's just, I'm rather fond of that sister of yours."

I widen my eyes, though I've known since their first meeting that Max fancied her. "Really?"

"Don't say anything," he says. "She'd buy a dog just to set it on me."

Ava is entirely capable of doing that. "She's her own creature," I tell him. "Give her time. If she decides to call off the dogs, she'll find a way to let you know."

He looks skeptical. "On her terms."

"On her terms," I agree. "Once you know what they are."

Pearl

April 12, 1933

I like Tommy Marinelli. I like him the way Jacky Polikoff used to like me. Of course, it's not mutual. He's sixteen, and so good looking. He doesn't have a girlfriend, according to Dan. Of course, Dan is good looking and he doesn't have one, either. They seem content to spend all their time together. Maybe because they have so much responsibility already, and give most of their pay toward keeping their families. Tommy has an older brother, but he's involved in something their mother doesn't approve of, so she won't take his money.

Tommy's uncle was a bootlegger and now Prohibition is over, Dan says he's a gangster, like in the movies, and Tommy's brother works for him. Sometimes he lies to his mom and says he worked overtime, but really he and Dan were off fishing and the money he gives her is from his brother. With three more littles at home, I can see why he wants that extra, and sometimes you can't tell mothers the whole truth.

7

Ava

A shadow moves across my work table and I look up in time to see a blue bumper pass the window. *Claire.* Our street is too narrow for parking, but my sister pulls her roadster up onto the sidewalk, even though I've told her she might cause some of my customers to have to walk in the street.

"They'll know it's me," she said, batting her eyes as if I were a man she was trying to impress. "And anyway, I never stay long when I have the car."

Letting herself in, she brings with her a spring breeze and a dizzying whiff of perfume. She blows a kiss in my direction, and reaches toward the chiffon-draped dress form. "That's lovely."

I roll it out of her way. "Same rules for you as the kids," I tell her. "Wash your hands before you touch anything."

"I'm not here to touch anything." She sighs theatrically. "I wanted to ask you to come over Thursday afternoon—I'm having some of the girls to tea, and it wouldn't hurt for you to meet a few more people."

Turning sideways, I show her my profile. "I don't think I'm quite presentable, not right now." I feel like a dirigible, dragging along the ground before taking flight. "I'd rather wait until the baby's born."

"You're always presentable." She sits on the edge of the upholstered guest chair, tucking her legs sideways, crossed at the ankles. Her kid t-straps are the same bottle green as her dress. It pleases me that she is not wearing blue.

I change the subject. "I stopped at your house the other day when you were out."

"Really? Katie didn't mention it." Claire runs her fingers through her blonde waves, a sure sign that she is lying.

"I didn't see her. I was downstairs." My friendship with her cook confuses Claire as much as it nourishes me. "Though I did run into someone else. Is Max Byrne living with you?"

A becoming flush creeps into her cheeks. "It's temporary. Honestly, he's hardly ever there."

"So I was just lucky?"

A small sound of frustration issues from her. "I do wish you would get over whatever you have against him. It's very difficult to have a friend you refuse to see, especially when he's done so much to help you. It's ungrateful, that's what it is."

When I fail to offer tea, Claire takes her leave. I shut the door hard behind her. I wish I had time to lie down, but the kids will be home soon and I have a million things to finish before the baby comes. Soon enough, I'll be off my feet for a few days and everything will fall on Pearl. I'm trying to make it as easy on her as possible, but it's hard to find the time or the energy.

At this stage in my previous pregnancies, Daniel would come up behind me and link his hands under my belly, taking the weight of the baby. It was both considerate and a form of intimacy in a time when my body was no longer comfortable with the more regular forms.

Rising up on my toes, I hitch my belly onto the padded back of the chair and the strain on my back decreases. Missing him comes out of nowhere, and I close my eyes against sudden tears.

When I suggest a walk after supper, Pearl insists that we all go. This close to my time, she doesn't like me out of her sight. We walk slowly down Pine Street and up Delancey in the blue twilight, admiring the grand houses. My eyes are drawn to the golden glow of the windows, the people inside leading their privileged lives. One triple window is more brightly lit than the rest, and as we pass, it opens and a flood of music reaches the street. We stand back out of sight, watching the formally dressed group around the piano. A woman drapes herself languidly over the instrument and light falls like honey over her satin back.

The sight freezes me, then I shake myself and walk on. It is times like this when the distance from my former life is most clearly felt. The only piano in Scovill Run was a rickety upright in the hall, and it hadn't been tuned in my lifetime.

Claire

The conversation with my sister bothers me throughout the day. Max's engaging presence at dinner makes me revisit it as I ready myself for bed. Why must Ava be so hard-headed where he is concerned? He's never done anything but be kind to her, help her—help Thelma in ways no one knew she could be helped. Her avoidance of him makes my life unnecessarily difficult, and hers, too.

I finish with my hair and snap off the lamp. The curtains block the light from the street, so Harry is no more than a dark smudge against the pillowcase. Getting into bed, I pull the cover up to my chin and turn to him. "Didn't you once tell me Max had been engaged? Years ago?"

"Yes." He rolls over to face me. "Why?"

"Just curious." I don't mention the photograph, which is nowhere on display and which I found, after vigorous dusting, tucked away in a drawer. "He never dates."

"He's got hopes of your sister." The words are nearly swallowed by a yawn.

"Not likely." I have the same hopes, but I don't expect them to come to fruition anytime soon—or at all, if Ava has a say in the matter. "We've known Max for years, and I don't recall him ever having a lady friend. He's always surrounded by people, but there's no one special."

Harry turns over again, and his voice emerges, muffled, from the pillow. "Maybe he's happy that way."

Maybe he is and maybe he isn't. But he's under our roof now, and that means I'll have a chance to find out.

Pearl

April 20, 1933

When I took Thelma for her appointment today, she was putting her socks and shoes back on and Dr. Max was writing his usual message, when he stopped and asked how Mama was doing. I said she was fine, because she wouldn't want me to say anything else, and also I don't know how she's doing.

But then I worked up the nerve to ask him what I've been worrying about. I told him after Teddy was born, Mama got sad and cried a lot and wouldn't get out of bed. She got over it, but Dandy and I are afraid it might happen again, and I don't know how we'll cope if it does.

The nicest thing about Dr. Max is he treats kids like they're adults. He doesn't laugh or say "don't worry." He actually TALKS.

He said he can't guarantee it won't happen again, but he doesn't think it will, because we've got Aunt Claire and Katie and her parents to help out. And him, too, if Mama will let him in the house. He asked if it had ever happened before Teddy, and I said no. Not that I knew of, anyway, and Daddy seemed as surprised as the rest of us.

Every birth is different, he said. Sometimes being afraid and worrying can be as hard as labor because the mind tries to shield itself from pain. I don't understand that but he looked so uncomfortable I didn't ask him to explain. Right before Teddy was born, Granny died and Daddy lost his job, so Mama probably had a lot of bad stuff on her mind.

According to him, it happens to a lot of women. Nobody quite knows why, which makes it hard to study. He looked almost mad when he said that, and then I knew he was, because he said since it's a woman's problem, they don't try very hard to figure it out.

I think Dr. Max likes Mama. And that's okay, because she'll never like him back (though it would be easier if she'd at least speak to him). She wouldn't do that to Daddy. Or to us. We're a family. It doesn't even matter that I like him, because we don't need anyone else.

Ava

"Is anyone home?" I pitch my voice so that Esther, stirring a pot on the stove, can hear me.

"Just me, my girl, and the baby." She cocks her head toward the stairs, where the faint sound of the Hoover can be heard. "You're safe. That nice doctor went out to work."

Dropping my hat and gloves on the table, I say, "Don't you start." I reach around her for a mug and help myself to coffee. "I heard enough of that recently from my sister."

"Enough of what?" Her smile gives her away. "Men as nice as him don't come around regular as streetcars."

I take a spoon from the drawer and sample the soup. "Needs more salt." Carrying my mug over to the table, I add, "Maybe I don't want to take the streetcar. Maybe I want to walk."

Esther picks up the salt, cuts her eyes toward me, and puts it down again. "And maybe you're wearing yourself out for no reason. Nothing wrong with putting your feet up occasionally."

This conversation is heading into territory I would rather not explore. "Where is the lady of the house?"

"Some meeting." She shrugs. "I can't keep up. She dashes in and out of here like she's being chased by bears. I just take down her schedule and cook food when they ask for it."

What lack is Claire trying to fill with all this frenetic busyness? She's got Harry, she's got Teddy—what else can she possibly need? I would love to have a fraction of her leisure time to focus on my kids, or to actually put my feet up for a change.

"Are they in for supper tonight?" I wonder if there will be time to have a word with my sister before they sit down to eat.

"They are," she says. "All three of them."

A cry echoes through the house and the Hoover ceases its roar. I resist the siren call of my son's voice, letting Katie go to him.

"Maybe I'll make an appointment." I don't have the energy to deal with Max, or Claire if she's going to be difficult.

Esther puts the lid on the pot, picks up her mug and joins me at the table. "You can't avoid that man forever," she says. "He lives here."

"And I don't," I return. "So it is perfectly easy for me to avoid him."

Her eyebrows raise. "By sneaking in the back door like a delivery boy."

I sink back in the chair. "I don't want to encourage him. Or Claire." It would take so little to get her back on that track. "I think she's trying to play matchmaker."

"*I* think she did a kind thing for a good man." She looks at me over the rim of her mug. "But you could do worse."

Not her, too. I stare down at my hands, smooth and pink from the lotion she sends over. "My husband is dead," I say. "I'm about to have a baby. Why does everyone think I'm on the lookout for another man?" I push the mug away, frustrated. "You don't understand—it isn't easy to replace someone who was a part of you. And I don't want to."

"Oh, I understand," Esther says. "I'm Mason's second wife."

"What?" I've watched them together. Their affection is clear, and of long standing. "When?"

"His first wife, she died three years after they were married." She sighs. "My boy, Tyrone, he was big and she tore real bad when he was born. When infection set in, they couldn't get a doctor to come."

"Your boy?" I wipe all thoughts of death in childbirth from my mind; it's too close to my time to think of things like that.

Esther nods. "Might as well be," she says. "Della, Mason's wife, she was my first cousin. I'd known him since I was your Pearl's age. He was a fine-looking man." She smiles again, girlish in her embarrassment. "I convinced him to let me take Tyrone."

"And he just let you?" I am endlessly fascinated by other people's lives, the drama hidden in plain sight.

She turns away, moves slowly to the stove to check on the soup. "He couldn't cope," she says simply. "He'd loved Della all his life, the way you loved your Daniel." Her back to me, she goes on, "I took Tyrone. My sister had a baby, so she fed him, and I did everything else." The wooden spoon turns in her fingers. "I did it for Mason, of course, but I also couldn't stand the thought of that bitty baby growing up without love, any more than I could the thought of his father living without it."

"And when did he ask you to marry him?"

Her mouth curls. "Never did," she says. "After six months he started coming to see Tyrone. By the end of the year, he would sit on the front stoop and take tea with me, and one night I just told him his boy needed a mother, and he needed a wife."

Will I ever understand people? Esther and Mason are the picture of devotion, and my friend hardly seems the sort to put herself forward and ask a man to marry her.

"We married on the first anniversary of Della's death," she concludes. "I named my first girl after her."

"But Mason loves you," I say stupidly. It does not seem possible that a man who truly mourned his wife could fall in love again so soon, no matter how young and pretty Esther must have been; she is an attractive woman still.

"He does now. Not so much then, but enough to make a start." She puts her hand over mine, a stretch for this woman who never forgets I am her employer's sister. "You'll never get over it, but your life will begin to grow around it until it becomes easier. And one day"—she squeezes my fingers and retreats again to the safety of the stove—"one day, you'll stop being angry. One day you'll realize you've done something without thinking of him first."

She breaks off, wiping her hands in her apron. "Listen to me, going on. You don't need my advice."

I take my mug to the sink, rinse it in silence. "When?" I ask finally. "When will that happen?"

Esther puts her arms around me and I let myself relax against her. "I can't tell you. But I promise you, that day will come."

A few days later, Harry's Packard stops out front and the boys tumble out. I open the workroom door and they skin past me, heading directly for the kitchen, though, if they've come from the Warriner house, it's unlikely they're hungry.

"Afternoon, ma'am." Mason Hedges emerges from the driver's seat. "I was asked to find out if you have anything going back for Mrs. Warriner."

I think of the blouse I should have finished by now, put aside to work on something more lucrative. "Not quite," I tell him. "Tomorrow."

He nods, then hesitates by the side of the car. "Mrs. Hedges told me you two talked the other day."

I would expect nothing else; I shared nearly everything with Daniel. "Yes?"

He rubs at a spot on the windshield, clearly uncomfortable. "I wanted to say...being happy is no disrespect to your husband."

I close my eyes, bombarded from all sides by well-meaning advice. "Thank you." I speak with more patience than I feel, because he has lost a wife and found a way forward. "But I'm not ready, not even to think about it."

He touches his cap. "Sorry if I overstepped, ma'am. Mrs. Hedges just wanted me..."

"It's fine." I cut him off, to put us both out of our misery. "Please let my sister know I'll drop her blouse off tomorrow afternoon."

8

Claire

Although I've been anticipating Ava going into labor for weeks, when it happens—when she stops short at the lunch table, a strange, inward-looking expression on her face—I am ill-prepared.

"That's it, then," she says, calmly finishing her tea. "Eat up, everybody, you're going to your aunt's after lunch."

"Is it time, Mama?" Pearl looks up from her soup, a sharp line appearing between her brows. "What should I do?"

"What you did last time." There is a hitch in her breathing. "We'll be fine. Claire's here."

An icy dart of fear pierces me. "I'll be no help."

Ava looks me up and down, acknowledging that fact. "You'll keep me company," she says, "while Pearl takes the kids to your house. And you"—she fixes her eyes on her daughter—"you bring Esther back with you. She'll know what to do."

"Yes, Mama." Pearl wolfs her soup and stuffs a piece of bread in her mouth. "What if she's not there?"

"She'll be there," I say. "But perhaps she could bring—"

"Do not bring Dr. Byrne," Ava orders. "Even if Esther vanishes in a puff of smoke right in front of you. We'll manage."

The children leave and Ava glances down at the table, then turns away and puts one foot on the stairs.

"Should I do the dishes?" She never likes to leave dishes in the sink.

"No," she says over her shoulder. "I need you."

She has obviously been anticipating the birth; a waterproof cloth is folded on the dresser, along with a few towels. Although Thelma told

me Ava has taken to sleeping in the smaller bed, she yanks off the quilt
and smooths the cloth over the big bed.

"Shouldn't you lie down?" I try to keep out of her way, and crack my
shin on the edge of the bed frame.

"Not yet." Hands pressed to her low back, she paces the narrow strip
of floor between the beds, then in and out of the bathroom. "Better to
stay on my feet. It shakes them loose."

I am ignorant of so much a woman should know. "Why did you ask
for Mrs. Hedges?"

She stops pacing. "Why not? She's my friend, and she's delivered a few
of her grandchildren."

Her friend? I think of the times I've come downstairs and found Ava
there, or seen them exchanging looks I didn't understand. How can they
be friends?

"Owww." Ava leans on the bathroom door frame, and something
splatters on the floor. "Damn."

"Are those your waters?" I always thought it would be a great gush of
liquid, but this is a small puddle.

"Yes." She takes her nightgown from its hook. "Put a towel over that,
will you? I'm going to get changed."

"Do you need help?"

She meets my eyes. "I've been undressing myself for thirty-odd years,
Claire."

Never have the few blocks between our houses seemed so long. I check
my watch repeatedly as we wait, while Ava's pains grow closer together.
She abruptly stops walking and takes to the bed. "They'd better get here
soon," she says, "or you're going to be delivering your nephew."

"Are you certain it's a boy?" I ask, rather than think about the horri-
fying possibility of helping my sister give birth.

"Of course." Her tone is waspish. "I'd know if it was a girl."

When I went home for Mama's funeral, Ava had been pregnant with
Teddy. She predicted he would be a boy because of how she was carrying;
after this many children, she should know, if anyone does.

"Have you thought about names?" I perch on the edge of the bed and
she takes my hand, seemingly unconscious of the gesture.

"Dennis," she says, naming the priest from Scovill Run, who'd nearly
been part of the family. "Or Gerald."

Gerald was our oldest brother, named after Mama's first husband. "Those are both nice."

"It would be Daniel, obviously, but I've already used that." She smiles tightly. "And Teddy."

"What about Jacob?" I do not mention Frank, our other brother, unloved by both of us.

"No." Ava stiffens, the cords on her neck standing out. She tucks her chin and makes a sound I can feel in my bones. The hump of her belly ripples. "We don't know that he's dead."

When the contraction passes and she flops back against the pillows, I surreptitiously shake my throbbing hand and ask, "Was Daniel with you for the others?"

She laughs. "Not a one. The first time, he wasn't back from the war. After, Mama always sent him away. It's not a time for men."

I would want Harry there, I think. I draw strength from him. "I don't know…"

"It's not their place," Ava says decisively. "A man will never look at his woman the same way again after he sees her like that."

I think of Max. "But what about doctors?"

"They're different," she concedes. I see from her face that another contraction is imminent. "Where is Pearl?"

"They'll be here soon." I hope I'm right. While I'm at it, I hope that Mrs. Hedges knows more about delivering babies than my thirteen-year-old niece and I do. In answer to my prayers, the sound of the front door echoes up the steps, followed by voices. "They're here!"

"Esther?" she asks. "Not him?"

"No." The voices are female: my niece and my cook.

"We're here, Mama," Pearl calls. "I'll start the water boiling."

I should have done that, I realize, and say so.

"Don't be stupid." Ava's face is red with effort. "You stay here with me. Pearl was there for Teddy. She doesn't need to watch this again."

Do I need to watch it? Already, witnessing my sister's pain is making me realize all the things I have been spared in my life; she is getting on with labor as if it is a commonplace occurrence, but I am horrified.

"How are you doing?" Esther Hedges sits on the other side of the bed, taking Ava's hand matter-of-factly. "That baby on his way?"

"He'd better be," she says through gritted teeth. "Because I'm tired of this already."

"It'll be over before you know it," Esther says, "and then your little man will be here." She looks up at me. "I brought some extra towels from the house, just in case. I hope that's all right, Mrs. Claire."

"Of course." I should have thought to ask Pearl to bring them.

"Don't worry," she says. "They're the ones from our rooms, not your nice ones."

"It doesn't matter." Why should my sister use the servants' towels?

"It does," Ava says clearly, and takes a breath. "I'm not getting blood and shit on your nice white towels."

Reproved, I shut my mouth, watching as Mrs. Hedges looks between Ava's legs and clucks approvingly. "I can see the head already."

"They get faster every time," Ava gasps. "I almost had Teddy in church on Christmas morning." She laughs, then winces. "The priest offered to clear the manger."

"Wouldn't that have been something?" Mrs. Hedges threads a towel through the iron bedstead and puts the ends in Ava's hands. "You pull on that now when it hurts, so you don't damage Mrs. Claire."

I have been forgotten, and wonder if I mind. All I've ever done is lose babies; Pearl has more experience in matters of childbirth. Closing my eyes, I push those thoughts away and think of Teddy, my sister's boy—my boy—in his nursery with Katie and the other children.

There is no nursery here. The cradle made by our mother's first husband is wedged in between the beds, with barely enough room to rock. "Are you going to use the small room upstairs for the baby?"

"This is the baby's room," she says when she is able to speak. "He'll move upstairs when he's older."

In the Scovill Run house, they were crammed in like chocolates in a box, but the situation was different then. The children arrived one by one, and Ava and Daniel learned to live with their growing family. How can my sister remarry with this full house? How would someone new ever fit?

Not that Ava has spoken of marrying again. She mourns Daniel deeply, but a woman without a man, even a woman with a respectable job, will not have any easy time of it. Once this baby is born, if I can convince her to put him on the bottle, rather than the breast, perhaps I can arrange a few introductions.

Max would be my first choice, but Ava has never been easy with him, even though he is the easiest man in the world, amenable to everything, and a doctor to boot. Although his salary always goes toward his projects, that would change if he had a family. He's also one of the few men I know who would be comfortable raising another man's children.

A howl brings me back to the present. Ava is leaning forward between her drawn-up knees, pulling with all her strength at the towel. Mrs. Hedges is stationed at the foot of the bed, watching, another towel close by. I shift closer to the pillow, to avoid seeing anything, until Ava elbows me in the hip and I move aside, in the way again.

Dan bounds up the front steps as I open the door. "Is she—?"

"She's had the baby," I say, drawing on my gloves, so tired I can barely stand. He tries to slip past, then stops. "Where are the kids?"

"At my house." Poor Katie had to deal with them all afternoon, in addition to taking care of her mother's tasks.

Torn, he looks into the house, then back at me. "I'll walk you home, Aunt Claire, and pick them up," he says. "They'll be wanting to see the baby." One last glance inside, chewing his lower lip. "Boy or girl?"

"Girl."

Dan is quiet, like his father, but it is a restful silence. Once inside, though, he shouts for the children and tells them the news. Bedlam reigns, and they charge out the door after him without a word of thanks. Even Thelma, who struggles to keep up, until Dan picks her up and takes off at a run.

Katie lingers in the hall. When they are gone, she takes my arm and leads me to my sitting room. "You look worn out, ma'am."

"I am." Her brown eyes are full of sympathy. "Your mother will be back soon."

"There's no need for her to rush," she says. "I have everything under control. Mr. Warriner called a few minutes ago. He won't be in until seven, so you have time for a bath and a quick nap, if you need it."

This is exactly what I need: someone to acknowledge my fraught state and understand I need coddling. I rest my head against her shoulder for the briefest of seconds. "That sounds blissful."

When Harry arrives, I am washed, dressed, fragrant, and nearly recovered. I greet him at the door and kiss his cheek, stepping back so Katie can take his case.

"I'm starving," he says, kissing me back. "Is dinner ready?"

"Will be in just a few minutes, sir," Katie says. "You have a drink with Mrs. Claire and it'll be on the table before you're done."

Harry smiles as she disappears to the basement. "I do believe our lives are run by that girl, and she's not twenty."

I sink into my chair while Harry mixes our drinks. "She gets it from her mother," I tell him. "Mrs. Hedges delivered Ava's baby this afternoon."

"Did she?" He turns, his face full of wonder. "A boy or a girl?"

"A girl." I take a deep swallow of gin.

"What's that?" Max pops in from the hall, tugging his tie straight. "Did I hear right?"

"Ava had her baby," Harry confirms.

Max grins like he'd delivered it himself. "That's wonderful!"

He asks, and I tell the news again: a girl, no name yet, Esther Hedges did it all.

"Then why do you look like you've been put through the wringer?"

For a moment, I want to slap him, then remember that only this afternoon I was planning his wedding to my sister. "I was not in my element," I say stiffly, wanting both of them to understand how difficult it was, watching Ava screaming and pushing, not to mention the mess. I told Esther to burn the ruined towels; I wish I could burn the memory of what I have seen along with them.

Ava

Just like last time, I awoke with back pains, and just like then, I thought, "Not today, baby. I have things to do." The pains subsided for a bit, but by noon they were back. The baby wanted to be born, and there was nothing I could do about it.

Claire was with us, but she looked nearly green with fear, so when Pearl took the other kids away, I asked her to bring Esther back to assist. When she arrived, the room grew calm, and by suppertime, I was holding a small, red infant to my breast, still marveling at Esther's words.

"It's a girl."

I had been so certain this baby was another boy; a replacement, somehow, for my lost husband. But instead I have a third daughter, with a fat curl of black hair on her forehead and squinched-shut eyes. They're blue, but I hope they will turn dark like his.

The kids, when they are allowed in, are happy.

Dan strokes the baby's satin cheek with a finger that, like his father's, will never be truly clean. "What about Lillie?"

"Or Danielle?" Pearl wants her say. "Lillie Danielle. For both of them."

I wanted a boy, but now, another thought strikes me, as clear as if the name appears in burning coals. "Her name is Gracie."

Their faces fall.

"How can you?" Pearl asks. "She's so beautiful."

Their suggestions are perfectly good, but wrong. I cannot explain my certainty that this baby should be named after the mine which claimed her father's life. "That's her name."

Pearl wipes her eyes with one hand while snuggling the baby under her chin with the other. "Why call her after something that took so much from us?"

"Maybe because of that very thing," I say slowly, trying to figure it out. "That part of our lives is over, and she'll never know it."

"It's a curse." Her voice shakes. "It will be a reminder every day of what we've lost."

I let her talk, closing my eyes while the baby is safe in her hands. Why is this name so important? Why can I not let go of my anger? I'm already losing him, in bits and pieces. Is the reminder the point?

"What about Grace?" Dan's calm voice slices through the drama-thickened air. "We'll know, but it wouldn't be such a burden for her to carry." He smiles. "Because someday she will ask."

"Grace," I agree. "Because we need it more than most."

Pearl

May 18, 1933

The baby is here, and just like that, we all move over one place in line. Thelma is so excited to finally not be the baby. I was afraid she'd be jealous, but she's not, not at all. Now her legs are stronger, she wants to be a normal little girl, and a normal girl has a baby sister and watches over her and teaches her to dance.

And Dr. Max was right. Mama seems like herself, at least so far. Only Mama in her normal state would insist on naming the baby after the Gracie mine. I got upset and Dan did, too, but there was no budging her. I can't imagine Aunt's reaction when she finds out. If I didn't know Mama had her reasons, I would think watching Aunt turn bright pink and sputter would almost be reason enough.

Ava

In the days that follow, I keep waiting for the long shadows to creep up on me the way they did after Teddy's birth, but they stay well back. I am unhappy—sometimes desperately so—but I am myself beneath the pain. The darkness does not seek me this time, and I am grateful.

The kids watch from the corners of their eyes, waiting to see if I become that strange, distant mother. I keep a cheerful face, to show they have nothing to worry about, that any distance is the normal exhaustion of a woman with an infant who requires feeding every few hours.

Despite her size, Grace has the lungs of an opera singer. When she wakes me in the night, I bring her down to the kitchen to nurse. The other kids need their rest—Pearl and Dan especially; the young ones will sleep through anything.

I pull the cord and the bulb flares into brightness. After all these months, I am still unused to the glare of electric light and I cover my eyes with one hand until they adjust. Sinking into the chair nearest the stove, I prop my feet on the fender and snug Grace in to my breast. She latches on, making small noises as she sucks, and I close my eyes and let my mind drift.

Normally, it is in these predawn hours that I am most vulnerable to the past, most fearful of the future, but tonight, those worries can't reach me. The kitchen smells of the roses that appeared on the front step the day after the baby was born. A long florist's box filled with a dozen pale pink blooms. There was no card. I assume they are from Claire and Harry, even though she denies it. "Wouldn't I have brought them myself, so I could watch you get worked up and yell at me?"

She has a point, but I know of no one else who would do such a thing. I stop wondering and enjoy the unexpected pleasure.

9

Pearl

May 25, 1933

Miss Rodney asked me to stay after school today. I was worried I wouldn't be on time to meet Thelma at Aunt's, but she only kept me a few minutes. She said she'd spoke to the principal about me. I was scared they were going to hold me back, but it turns out she's recommending I go to a different high school next year than where the other kids are going.

It's a school for girls who plan to go to college. I told her I didn't think I would be able to do that, and she said I should think again.

I wanted to tell Mama but when we got in, she was in the middle of making supper and then after that she had to finish a muslin for a fitting in the morning. I didn't want to give her anything else to think about, so I'll save Miss Rodney's papers until the weekend, when there's time to talk. We're supposed to be going to the movies again, but I'm pretty sure Mama will stay home with Grace and we'll go without her.

Maybe by the weekend I'll know how I feel. I should be excited. I am excited. But if I go to Girls High, I won't be able to walk Thelma to school, and she counts on me. It would almost be easier if they'd left me back instead, and given us another year of being together before things changed too much.

Ava

In the fog after Teddy, I failed to take notice of the more unpleasant aspects of recovery from childbirth. I remember them now: soreness not just below, but everywhere, as if I am one giant pulled muscle, and a steady trickle of blood, worse than my monthly curse, but not as bad as it has been with other babies; there was no tearing this time. Without Daniel, there will be no desire which would be painful in its fulfillment.

Without Daniel. My brain stops there, over and over. Daniel loved our babies, proof of our love made visible, and he had a soft spot for his girls. He would have been the first one to suggest naming this baby after my mother. I'm not sure how he would feel about my choice of name.

Grace is a good baby, an easy feeder, but she cries more often, and for longer periods, than I am capable of bearing. But I must bear it. School is not yet out and Pearl has played substitute mother too many times already. The baby's wails are so piteous, it is not difficult to imagine she knows herself to be half-orphaned, destined to never know her father's love. I will do my best to make up for that lack.

Holding her is the only thing that quiets her, but I can't sew with a baby in my arms, nor can I keep her on my shoulder when I'm doing handwork, for fear she will soil it. Being at my side in her basket is unacceptable—she opens her dark blue eyes, and then her mouth, filling the air with sound until I want to throw back my head and howl with her.

I have forgotten what silence is like. Because she needs me, I put my sewing aside until the afternoons, and take to the streets with the coach Dan procured. It is because of Grace that I finally begin to explore the city, its wide streets full of shops and traffic, its narrow alleys with rows of carriage houses being converted into garages, the short, stop-and-start blocks which lead to small, grassy squares or surprisingly large churches.

The variety of buildings is fascinating. Less than a mile from Claire's mansion—for all that she calls it a house, it is a mansion to me—there are squalid streets of tenements packed with recent immigrants from all over the world. I discover markets where I am the only English speaker, but a pretty baby goes a long way toward communicating with strangers, and often I come home with cheap fruit or vegetables snugged into the coach along with her.

I discover a little park further west which suits me better than the grand Rittenhouse Square. Fitler Square is a few easy blocks up Pine Street, and feels more personal: smaller, its trees heavy with bloom, it is a perfect place for me to hide away. Dropping gratefully onto a bench, I park the coach. Grace is sleeping, so I set it to bouncing gently with my foot and close my eyes, listening to the sound of traffic and the occasional clear voices of women coming out of the nearby apartment buildings.

Eventually, I find the rivers, both of them: the Schuylkill to the west and the Delaware to the east. The coach bumps over rough cobbles and smooth pavement as my baby and I absorb this new world. Grace likes the movement, and either sleeps quietly or makes small, interested noises, and I tell her what she cannot see from under the waxed canvas hood.

"This is Walnut Street," I tell her. "We're not far from your aunt's house now. There's a theater on the corner, it's playing something called *Lilly Turner*. Same name as your granny." I admire Ruth Chatterton's perfectly waved hair on the poster and sigh at the ruin of my plans for regular movie-going. "You're not going to be ready to sit through a movie for years." She coos, and I let her have my finger for a moment. "There's the big park, across the street. We'll go there next." There is a statue in one corner where all the nannies and young mothers gather with their charges; I like to sit there, among them but not one of them.

A young couple walks past, arm-in-arm. They have ice cream cones in their free hands, and I look over my shoulder. The ice cream parlor Max Byrne took me and Thelma to after her very first appointment is still there. It's difficult to remember that time clearly. So many things happened in those two weeks—giving over Teddy, learning that Max could help Thelma, leaving my little girl behind for an unknown period, explaining it all to Daniel and the kids.

It was a lifetime ago, and a whole different life besides. My eyes fill, and I push the coach rapidly across the street and into the park, where I can retreat to a bench and hide my shameful tears from the world.

Claire

I follow the sound of Teddy's piping babble and find him seated in a circle of toys, the patchwork dog Pearl made for him on his lap. The oversized bear we brought from Washington watches benignly from the rocker.

"Excuse me, Mrs. Claire." Katie slips around me, a damp washcloth in one hand. "All right, Mr. Teddy, let me clean that dirty face."

He stops mid-flow and tilts his face up to hers, waiting patiently as she wipes his cheeks and chin. When she finishes and tousles his hair, he returns to his conversation, of which I understand perhaps one word in ten.

"He's telling them toys all about our trip to the park yesterday," Katie says. "Isn't he such a talker?"

"Can you understand him?" Listening, I remembered my panic when I started French lessons and was not permitted to speak English in the class.

"About half the time." She shrugs. "It's not hard if you listen."

"It is for me." Why can't I understand my own son? I take one last look before I leave to visit my mother-in-law. "Can you find a way to get that dog away from him?" I ask. "It's filthy."

Katie's eyes widen. "It's his favorite," she says. "I take that away and he'll scream the house down. You know what babies are like, ma'am."

"Of course." I kiss Teddy's clean cheeks and take my leave, feeling nearly as squashed as if I'd been with Irene.

My friends have nursemaids or nannies who bring their scrubbed and handsome children out for inspection each evening, but whose constant care—to me—comes between mother and child. I hadn't wanted that for Teddy. Harry's upbringing made him cool and distant, despite what I knew his feelings to be. I didn't want that for Teddy, either.

Katie had seemed the perfect solution. She adored Teddy. I could have help when I needed it, and someone to watch him when I went out; it wouldn't do to take him to lunches or teas and hand him off to my hostess's nanny, no matter how much I wanted him with me.

When Thelma stayed with me, we were comfortable together from the start. I'd expected the same with Teddy, but it hasn't been that way, even after Irene's departure. He has reminded me, over and over, that I've never been around babies all that much. As the last of my mother's children, I was spared the raising of my siblings, and while I watched babies for our neighbors, a few hours in the afternoon was very different than having my own child.

I didn't think I'd have to learn to be a mother, but Katie's easy handling of my son has proved me wrong.

It is a gray afternoon. I was already dreading tea with Irene, and my interaction with Katie makes me even more low. To cheer myself up, I stop at Bonwit's and buy a new hat. It is a purchase even Ava will approve, a Eugenie hat in sleek, dark green velvet, slanting smartly over my right eye, with nary a flower or a feather in sight.

Alas, it does not go with my blue-and-white day dress, so I am lugging a violet-sprigged hatbox when I arrive at the Drake. Baxter greets me, and places the box on the foyer table. "Mrs. Warriner's other guest is already here," he informs me in his usual funereal tone, which makes me feel late no matter how early I might be. "They are in the living room."

The man seated across from my mother-in-law looks out of place, a too-large figure in a delicate dollhouse room. He unfolds from his chair, and I notice that his gray flannel suit is tailored to an athlete's body. His hair is black, the silver confined to streaks at his temples; a narrow mustache sets off finely-cut lips that curve into a smile as we are introduced.

"This is my daughter-in-law." There is more affection in Irene's voice than I have ever heard. "Claire, I don't believe you know Randall Francis Gardiner."

"I haven't had the pleasure." His hand swallows mine. Somehow it wouldn't surprise me if he kissed it rather than shook it.

"The pleasure is mine entirely. And please, call me Francis." Mr. Gardiner's eyes gleam, startlingly blue in his tanned face. A man who willingly spends a lot of time outdoors. "Squint has done well for himself."

"Squint?" His tone is ingratiating, but I don't like his words, speaking as if I am some prize to be won.

"A schoolboy nickname." Irene simpers. "Francis and Harry were at school together."

"All the way through Germantown Academy," he says. "But I went to Yale, and Harry went to New Jersey."

"Oh, you." She titters and gives Mr. Gardiner's bicep a light slap. "Princeton is as good a school as Yale."

"Perhaps." He brings Irene's fingers to his lips, and my earlier suspicion is justified. "But its location does it a great disservice."

We move to the dining room, a miniature version of what the dining room used to look like in my house, before I went to town and rid the place of every trace of my mother-in-law's tenure. The heavy furniture and velvet draperies block off any air from the open window, and a trickle of sweat makes its slow way down my back. I sit very straight, willing it to stop, to be absorbed into my girdle and not leave a mark on my rayon dress.

Their flirtatious banter is amusing, but I have no idea why I've been summoned. The reason becomes no clearer when I ask after Aunt Nora, Irene's sister, and learn she is in Cape May, readying her house for the summer season.

"I don't know why she insists on doing it herself," Irene says. "Surely that's what servants are for."

Not only did Francis Gardiner stay for the duration of my visit, he insisted on driving me home afterward, with a gallantry that managed to be both charming and set my teeth on edge. "You should have your own car," he said, leaning across me to open my door. "Tell Squint to buy you one."

"I have a car." I sucked in my stomach as his sleeve brushed against my ribcage. "I felt like walking today."

Mr. Gardiner tilted his head. "Your husband couldn't see the side of a barn," he said silkily. "You must have gotten awfully close to snap him up."

I slammed the door without another word and sprinted up the front steps, shaking with sudden, irrational anger. The door opened before I could touch the knob and Katie greeted me, taking the hat box as Pixie swarmed around our feet.

"Another pretty hat?" She peeked inside. "Oh, that's lovely, ma'am. And it's not blue."

"Won't Ava be pleased?" I stripped off my gloves and unpinned my current—blue—hat. "Is Mr. Warriner home yet?"

"Not yet. He called to say he would be late." She considered me. "But the doctor is here." She patted my arm. "If you've been visiting with the other Mrs. Warriner, why don't you let him make you one of those martinis?"

And so it was by the time Harry got in at seven, Max and I had each had a very strong drink and Irene's toxic influence had begun to dissipate. I wanted to tell him about my strange afternoon, but it no longer had the same urgency.

"Starting without me?" He kisses my cheek and reaches a hand toward Max.

"Can I catch you up?" Max nods toward the silver shaker, beaded with condensation.

Harry eases himself into his chair, massaging the bridge of his nose with his fingers. "I wish you would."

The room is silent while he drinks. Then he puts the glass down and tips his head back against the chair. "What a day."

"What happened?" It's not often Harry complains about business matters, at least not to me.

He looks at Max, not me. "Have you seen the papers?"

"Germany?" Max responds. "Or Washington?"

I haven't been paying much attention to the news, other than to look for references to Mrs. Roosevelt or Frances Perkins. A woman had also been appointed director of the U.S. Mint, which seemed another step toward progress. "What happened?" I repeat.

Harry reaches for his glass, realizes it is empty and drops back again. "Hitler," he says, sounding exhausted. "Ever since the Nazi party won power in March, worrisome things have been happening in Germany."

Max refills his glass. "Anti-Jewish laws," he explains to me. "Doctors and lawyers no longer permitted to practice, things like that. Jewish children no longer permitted to attend public schools."

Could the world not learn to live in peace? "How are they being educated, then?" I ask. "Are there other schools?"

"There may be," Harry says. "At least for now." He addresses Max again. "Today there was an article in the *Times* about a spate of public book burnings."

There is a little liquid left in the shaker; Max dribbles it into my glass and resumes his seat. "I thought you would be more disturbed about the banning of labor unions, honestly."

"I can hold more than one opinion, or one fear, at a time." Harry drains his glass again. "Any regime that fears books—fears culture—fears its own people—can very easily become dangerous."

They keep up their conversation through dinner. I participate when I can, but I know little enough of world affairs. It makes me feel, for a moment, like the dumb bunny Claire of a few years ago, but it is difficult enough to keep up with what's happening in Philadelphia. I will leave the world stage to the men, at least for the moment.

After we've finished, Max follows Harry into his office, still talking. I retreat to the living room with the latest Agatha Christie and wait for them. An hour passes and their voices continue to murmur behind the closed door. While I am enjoying Miss Marple's adventures in the British countryside, their absence reinforces what an unpleasant day this has been overall. Its only redeeming feature, thus far, has been my new hat.

I go to bed. Harry will come up when he and Max have run out of words, or they can talk until dawn. I have had enough for one day.

It is very late when he gets in beside me. "I'm sorry," he murmurs when he realizes I am awake. "I didn't mean to abandon you."

"It's all right." I am annoyed, but if he's willing to talk now, so am I. "I didn't get a chance to tell you who I met at your mother's today."

"No," he says, and yawns. "That's nice."

He is asleep. I roll over, punch my pillow in frustration, and join him.

10

Ava

The more clients Claire sends my way, the more I understand that I cannot remain the unadorned Ava Kimber of Scovill Run, with her shabby clothes and a knot of hair at her neck. As Ava Kimber, dressmaker, something must be done. I solve the problem of what to wear by stitching up a simple pale gray smock, a sort of uniform to put over my clothes while customers are visiting. The rest of me is not so easily dealt with.

Since our conversation earlier this year, Claire has offered time and again to take me to the beauty parlor where she has her hair done, but I will not accept charity in this instance. I wouldn't be comfortable there, anyway. On my walks with Grace I look for a place more suited to my budget, and when I find one, a few blocks south of our house, staffed by women who seem not too different from me, I make an appointment.

I choose a day when Claire will be out, and leave Grace with Esther, promising to be back as soon as I am released from whatever torture the salon has in store. I do not have the energy to face both the hairdresser and my sister's anticipation; her reaction will have to be enough.

The ten blocks to the beauty parlor seem like nothing, accustomed as I am to pushing the coach everywhere. I get there a few minutes early, give my name to a gum-popping young woman, and take a seat. The place smells like flowers, with a hint of something—rotten eggs?—beneath the scent. There is a stack of magazines in the waiting area, and I flip through them, not sure what exactly I will ask to have done.

"Mrs. Kimber?"

I follow the young woman through a curtain to a padded chair. "Miss Rose will be right with you."

Miss Rose is a tall woman of my own age with improbably black hair, and eyebrows dyed to match. I stammer when I explain what I want. "I make dresses for society women," I tell her. "I can't look like what I am."

One of those inky eyebrows raises. "Does it bother them?"

"It will." It has, I think, though their loyalty to Claire keeps them coming back. I sit very still as she takes the pins from my hair and lets it fall. I've always been vain of my hair, but there is no one now to take pleasure in it. I only remember it exists when I take it down to braid it for the night or brush it in the morning to put it up again. "Cut it off."

The young woman leads me to another chair and swirls a burgundy cape around me like a magician's assistant. I lean my head back as she washes my hair. Sitting and letting myself be fussed over is unnatural, and I have to force myself to relax. The floral scent of the shampoo she uses makes me smile in spite of my intention not to enjoy myself.

"Are you getting a permanent?" she asks. "It's a shame to cut all this off, but you'd look real pretty with curls."

"I don't know." I hadn't thought about a wave—I don't even know if I can afford one—but I don't want to waste the time saved by cutting my hair by dealing with curlers every day. "Would I have to set it all the time?"

"No, ma'am. Every few days, and pin curls if you're lucky. You have nice, thick hair." She wraps my head in a towel and leads me back to my previous seat. "Mrs. Kimber is going to have a permanent after her cut, Miss Rose."

I open my mouth to object, and shut it. I have money for emergencies, and while vanity is not an emergency, I decide to consider my new look an investment in my business. "Do what she says," I tell the hairdresser. When the shears begin dancing around me, I close my eyes. My head feels alarmingly light. Can hair weigh so very much? Am I bald? If I am, there is nothing I can do. I let out a breath and let Miss Rose work her magic.

The whole process takes longer than anticipated, and I hurry back to Delancey Place, not wanting to wear out Esther's goodwill. I take the long way around, duck down the alley, and let myself in through the kitchen.

"Well, look at you!" Esther is at the counter, stuffing a chicken. She pauses and wipes her hands on a towel. "Turn around, let me see."

I turn obediently, not used to this sort of attention. The women at the beauty parlor made a similar fuss, but they are paid to do that. And I had paid. Between the cut, the permanent, and what I hoped was a reasonable tip, my emergency fund is now short three dollars.

"How does it feel?"

"Lighter." I touch the fluffy curls at the back of my neck. "And it smells."

Esther smiles. "That wears off. Give it a day or so before you wash your hair, though."

That's what they told me when I complained of the sulfur stink; it was the ammonia in the waving solution. I use ammonia for cleaning, and it is strange to think my head was soaked in the stuff before they sat me under the hair dryer with another magazine.

"Where's the baby?" I ask, realizing Grace is nowhere to be seen. "Has Pearl come by and picked her up?"

"No, the doctor came home early, and that was the last I saw of both of them." She smiles, as susceptible to his charm as most people. "They're upstairs with Teddy. That man, he sure loves babies."

After several hours of being poked and prodded in a way foreign to every fiber of my being, I am in no mood for a confrontation with Max Byrne. I drop my bag and gloves on the kitchen table and stomp upstairs to retrieve my child.

They are, as Esther assumed, in the nursery, though not playing quietly. Max is on his hands and knees with Teddy on his back, making what Toby and George would insist are wild Indian cries but which, to my ears, sound more like a faulty teapot. Grace is on a blanket on the floor directly beneath him, and as Teddy kicks his sides, Max blows kisses against her neck, making her squeal.

It is a charming picture, I have to admit: my blond son, my dark daughter, both so happy. The sandy, rumpled man who is the cause of their happiness.

"What," I ask, "are you doing?"

He slides Teddy off and scrambles to his feet. Grace makes a small noise of complaint and he raises her carefully on his shoulder. "Esther had enough on her hands," he says. "I didn't want her to rock the chicken and stuff the baby, so I thought I'd—"

"Interfere." I wrest Grace from his arms and step hastily away.

His energy crackles like electricity. I narrow my eyes. How dare he have so much ebullience that I can feel it? I squelch my reaction, but there is a moment when every hair on my body stands at attention.

"If that's what you prefer to call it." Max smooths his shirt and straightens his tie. Neither have any relation to the suit jacket he shrugs hastily into. His eyes roam over me, taking in my hair, the touch of lipstick. "How have you been?"

"Fine." His lack of reaction makes me gracious.

"Kids doing well?" He catches up a newspaper from the chair and stuffs it untidily into his pocket.

"They'll be home from school soon." I leave the nursery, and he follows with Teddy, Katie having gone off to do her chores. Why is Claire never home in the afternoons anymore? How often does Teddy even see her?

We chat as we descend to the kitchen, Max asking about the kids' activities outside of school and nudging me again about dance lessons for Thelma once her braces are off.

"Maybe once school is out." I am too tired to argue. "She's certainly interested enough."

"I know." He laughs. "She tried to replicate the entire finale of *42ⁿᵈ Street* in my office."

Considering she'd done the same on our way home from the theater, I'm not surprised, but it pleases me that he enjoyed her performance. As Esther says, he really does like kids.

We reach the kitchen. I say a quick farewell to Esther, see Teddy imprisoned in his high chair so he can't help with preparations for supper, and pop Grace back into the coach. Max eases it out the door, then steps back.

"It was good to see you." He raises a finger to the brim of an invisible hat.

"You too," I say, and discover that I mean it.

Claire

After mass, I eat lunch with Ava and the children and walk home. I have no sooner settled myself with a book when the front door slams. Curious, I look into the hall and see Harry swerve through the living room doorway. The clink of glass reaches my ears. If he's drinking this early, lunch with Irene has not gone well.

"Harry?"

He turns, drink in hand. "Claire."

I nod toward the glass. "Is everything all right?"

"Fine." He puts the glass down and reaches for his cigarette case. "I took Mother to the Warwick after church and we ran into someone unpleasant, that's all."

As far as I'm concerned, the someone unpleasant had been Irene Warriner, but Harry's negative opinions are less pronounced than my own. Who could have gotten his back up so badly? "Do you want to talk about it?"

"Not really." Lighting his cigarette, he sinks into his chair and reaches for the Sunday *Inquirer*, dismissing me from the room.

At dinner, he is still out of sorts. Although the table has been set for three, Max has not joined us, and I half-hope he will arrive and lighten the atmosphere. When he does not, and we are on the verge of dessert, I ask again, "Do you want to talk about whatever happened today?"

Harry's eyes remain fixed on his empty plate. "We had almost finished lunch when someone stopped at our table."

"Oh?" Katie comes in and I pause while she clears. "Who was it?"

"Francis Gardiner." His voice is thick with something I can't identify. "He asked after you."

My mind flashes to that strange afternoon in Irene's apartment, Gardiner's excessive manners and snide words about Harry. "I met him at your mother's a week or so ago."

"So he said." I identify the tone: he is angry. "You didn't consider mentioning it?"

I think back. "It was the night you stayed up so late with Max. I tried to tell you, but you fell asleep, and by the next morning, it didn't seem important." Dessert arrives—a simple cobbler with fresh cream—but I am no longer as excited as I was when I saw the grocer's boy deliver fresh strawberries. "Are you upset I didn't tell you?"

"No," he says. "I'm not upset you didn't tell me, just that he did."

As if there is any difference between the two. "Irene said you were old school friends."

"We were not." He takes a bite of the cobbler. "We attended the same schools until college. Wolf Gardner is the reason I chose to go to Princeton."

"So your mother had that wrong."

His mouth curls, seemingly in spite of himself. "Mother could never abide losing any chance at a good social contact. Gardiner came from exceptional stock, but every tree has a weak branch."

Why did she invite me, then, knowing Harry's feelings? As far as I can tell, the whole point of my invitation was to make that introduction. "How is it that I've never met him before, if he grew up with you?"

"The whole family has been in London since the late twenties," he says. "The poor Brits."

As he visibly calms, I begin to enjoy the berries and cream, the light pastry. "What did you call him—Wolf?"

"School nickname," he says briefly. "We all had them."

Chiffy Patterson. I remember the dinner conversation about his former classmate. Wolf Gardiner. "What was yours?" I ask, curious if he will repeat the name Francis Gardiner told me.

He presses his lips together, shaking his head. "I don't remember."

I don't push. "Well, he seems house-trained. He must be, if he has your mother's approval."

"Mother's standards can be unpredictable."

"I've never found them to be." Her standards have been unattainable since we were first introduced, in my seventeenth year, where her expression of dismay upon understanding her son intended to marry me was quickly replaced with a genteel and long-suffering disappointment that has not shifted in more than fifteen years.

There must be something to Francis Gardiner if he has Irene's approval.

Ava

Pearl's voice reaches me as I climb the stairs. She is bent over the cradle, speaking softly to the baby. "...you'll never be hungry or have to wear clothes that were worn by four other people." She rocks the cradle slowly with her foot. "You'll miss all that, but it will be okay. You have us."

Listening to her, one thing is clear: any further conversation about her education is unnecessary. She will make the right decision without any help from me. I want her to go to this special school, even if it means I take on some of her chores. But I won't force her to go. I won't force any of them, even if it's for their own good. I spent my childhood feeling pressured and I swore, years ago, that I wouldn't do that to my kids.

Mama didn't do anything from unkindness. She needed my help. But things are easier now, and even when they aren't, I'm not going to let Pearl carry an adult burden while she's still a girl. She's bright, and that's her way out of this life. My kids are going to get every advantage that won't actively take food out of their mouths.

I make a sound so she has time to straighten her face. "Is she asleep?"

"Almost." She sniffs mightily and wipes her cheek with the back of her hand. "Do you need me downstairs?"

Yes, I want to say. "Is your homework done?" is what I do say.

"I have some reading to do, but won't take long." She looks at the window. "Let me help you while it's still light. I can read before bed."

11

Ava

By the time Pearl graduates eighth grade, we will have been in our house for six months. To celebrate these milestones, I tell the kids we'll have a party on the first Saturday after school lets out.

"Can I ask a friend?" Pearl wants to know.

"Of course." I moisten a section of hair, curl it around my finger, and stab a pin into it. I can't get used to sleeping in pin curls, so most mornings I do this and then wrap my head in a scarf while I sew. "Just let me know how many." It won't be anything fancy, but I can manage a cake or two, and iced tea, and I'm sure Claire will want to contribute something once she is invited. I might not even argue with her. The kids deserve a treat.

"Thank you, Mama." She hugs me quickly. "Come on, Thelma, we're going to be late for school."

"I'm coming." Thelma charges down the tight, curving stairs, her braces banging against the risers. "Dr. Max is going to take my braces off today!"

Pearl stops beside me. "You should come, Mama. It shouldn't always be me talking to him."

"Of course," I say again, without meaning it. "But I have to do the finish work on Mrs. Hanley's jacket before tomorrow. I trust you to report back."

Shrugging on a light sweater, Pearl straightens Thelma's hair ribbon, checks her buttons, and pushes her toward the door. "Mama, you have to come." The line appears between her brows. "Thelma is so excited—she

won't understand why you're not there." The look she gives me is pure
Mama. "And frankly, I don't understand, either."

Esther agrees to watch Grace again, so I wait for the girls at Claire's house
and we walk the short distance to Children's Hospital. Thelma chatters
excitedly, swinging my hand, and I acknowledge Pearl's rightness. How
could I miss this? I haven't been uninvolved in Thelma's treatment—the
drawer in my workroom table is crammed with dozens of Max Byrne's
written reports, some of them ornamented with cartoon drawings of my
daughter in her braces. I've read them over and over until I can recite his
hopeful, encouraging words by heart, but other than brief meetings in
my sister's home, we haven't spoken.

"I'm sorry," I say to Pearl over Thelma's head. "You shouldn't have
had to deal with all this by yourself."

She shrugs, smiling. "You're busy. I can't see to your ladies, but I can
do this much."

"True." I straighten my hat, hoping my hair will stay curled until we're
home again. "But you're right, today is special. And I should be here."

We go through the wide front doors, and I hang back as my girls
navigate the crowded lobby and lead me to the elevator. It's been a
year since Thelma's first examination. I was so out of my depth during
that entire visit, I don't remember the hospital at all, only Max's blithe
assurance that my girl was not the hopeless cripple the mining company's
doctor had diagnosed her as being, and with his help and Harry's money,
she would be able to walk normally.

"Should we go for ice cream after, Thel?" I ask as the elevator gates
rattle open. "Would you like that?"

"Can Dr. Max come, too?" She runs ahead of us to the office door, her
movements fluid beneath the clunkiness of her braces.

Pearl glances at me, then at her sister. "He probably has to work," she
says. "Let's celebrate on our own, just the three of us."

After a few minutes in the waiting room, Max ushers us into his office,
which no longer doubles as a bedroom—of course, since he lives with
my sister. His eyes register surprise at my presence, but his words are
straightforward. "How good of you to come. Pearl, let your mother take
your spot and I'll fetch an extra chair."

I cringe at being treated like a guest, but it is no more than the truth: my daughters, girls of seven and thirteen, have accomplished this while I hid myself away with my patterns and fabrics. I push the shame down; today is not about my feelings, but about Thelma's liberation.

Once seated in a hard wooden chair next to Pearl, I watch as Thelma hauls herself with difficulty up onto the exam table. Max waits, his arms folded, not approaching until she has settled herself with her legs extended in front of her.

"So, is today the big day?" he asks, putting one hand on the heavy metal hinge at her right knee. "Or would you rather keep wearing them? You'll probably miss them, once they're gone."

"No! Take them off!" Thelma erupts in giggles, leaning forward to grab his hand. "Take them off and burn them, Dr. Max."

The vehemence in her tone surprises me. She's hated wearing them, but it never occurred to me how tired my birdlike child must be of dragging all that metal around with her.

"Maybe we won't burn them," he suggests. His focus is wholly on her, as if we aren't even in the room. "Some other little girl might benefit from them, what do you say?"

"Fine," she says grudgingly. "Just not me."

Before he proceeds, he explains to us that this is not the end of Thelma's treatment. She will need to continue her exercises to build up the wasted muscle in her legs. "Let her walk Claire's dog after school," he suggests. "They'll both enjoy that."

"Pixie!" Thelma squeals, then returns to the subject at hand. "Now, Dr. Max! Now!"

"Okay, now." He undoes the top buckle; the leather there is tight and it fights me at bedtime, when my hands are cramped from stitching, but he works it with ease, moving through the next two buckles before lifting her leg and sliding the bulky contraption free of her shoe. She immediately starts to squirm and he closes a hand around her ankle. "Let me finish, will you?"

The second brace follows the first, and we all stare at Thelma's legs, thin and pale, lined with pressure marks from the braces, but straight. Straight, when they were once curved so badly it pained her to walk.

My breath catches. I've seen Thelma without her braces every night, but this is different. She's had a growth spurt lately and her legs are long; despite her pale Kovaleski coloring, she's going to have the Kimber height.

Max is grinning like a boy. He picks Thelma up under her arms and deposits her on the floor. In her candy-striped dress, ankle socks, and black strappy shoes, she looks like a doll waiting to be wound up.

"How does it feel, baby?" My voice breaks the spell.

She looks from me to Pearl to Max, and her right foot begins cautiously to tap. Then her left, and she spins away from the table, her small feet blurring as she attempts her dance routine for the first time without braces.

"It's like flying!" she shouts, twirling so her skirts fly out.

Pearl's hands cover her face. I wipe away tears, hoping no one has noticed.

But someone has. Max leans against the examining table, watching me watch my daughter. He's not wearing the smug smile I would have expected. Instead, he looks as proud and happy as we are—but of course he is, he's a doctor, he's done this. Why shouldn't he be proud?

And why shouldn't I be grateful? For all my complicated feelings about this man, he's done so much for my family, and asked for nothing in return, at least from me. He's been there for Pearl all this time when I've avoided him, he's coaxed Thelma through her exercises and the fitting of several sets of braces. He's restored my girl to a condition we never thought possible, and all he has ever asked of me is civility.

A crash drags me from my thoughts as Thelma bumps into the table and sends instruments and papers everywhere. Our laughter breaks the tension and allows me to shake Max's hand and thank him.

"It's been my pleasure," he says cheerfully, waving at Pearl to leave off cleaning up her sister's mess. "I hope I'll be seeing you all again soon."

I balk at that, and say only, "You live with my sister. It's not out of the question."

Pearl

June 13, 1933

I'd better get a good report for the end of the year, because otherwise Mama's going to skin me alive. She might anyway, because I invited Dr. Max to my graduation party.

Yesterday was Thelma's last appointment and Mama came with us. I didn't think she would, she's so silly about him. And I think he's silly about her, just a different kind of silly, the kind Mama doesn't like.

But it's ridiculous they don't get along. Life would be easier if they did, especially now he's living at Aunt's. I decided to chance it, and after we got downstairs in the elevator, I said I'd left my notebook upstairs. (I did, deliberately). When I went back up and got it, I asked him then. He said he'd come, so long as Mama's okay with it, and it wasn't quite a lie when I told him she said I could invite whoever I wanted. I'd like to tell Thelma, but I'm afraid she won't be able to keep a secret. If Mama doesn't know I invited him, she can't get mad. At least not until he shows up.

Claire

I pull in neatly to the curb and turn the key. My head is pounding; it took all I had to drive home, but I did not want to bother Hedges with retrieving the car in the morning. Gathering my bag and gloves, I get out, thinking of the martini that awaits me, and an eventual light dinner. When a tall man steps out of the shadow of the planter by the door, I jolt backward and my elbow strikes the side view mirror.

He holds up both hands as if to prove he is no threat and takes a few steps toward me.

"I'll scream." My voice wobbles. "Stay where you are. What do you want?"

"Clairy?" The voice is straight out of my past, the word a nickname for the clunky Polish Klara my father insisted on calling me.

It can't be. This man is *old*. His skin is leathery. His clothes—pants and a checked shirt—are filthy. A powerful smell wafts toward me. "Jake?"

He pushes his cap to the back of his head with the gesture I remember, and when he smiles, his eyes crinkle in a way that makes my own fill with tears. I hold out my arms, no longer caring how dirty he is. But he does. He steps back, his arms falling to his sides. "You'll never get clean, you hug me."

"I've got other clothes." I take his arm instead, find it thin and wiry inside his sleeve. "Where did you come from? Where have you been all this time?"

We are attracting attention. Our neighbors across the street come out their front door and manage to reach their car without ever looking at it. Mrs. Cantrell stumbles at the curb, finally turning away.

"Won't you come in?"

Jake looks at me, and then up at the house. "I don't belong in a place like this."

"Then why did you come?" I tug at his arm. The Cantrells glide past in their Ford and I offer a wave.

"Saw your picture in the paper," he says. "Your husband must be important, you got invited to all that fuss in Washington."

A small thread of worry—does he want something from us, because of who Harry is? But then, what does it matter? He's my brother, and I haven't seen him in twenty years. I want to give him things, the same as I do Ava.

"He knows people, that's all. Now, are you coming in?" The door opens. Because of the hour, it's Hedges, not Katie.

"You all right, Miz Warriner?"

"We're fine." One more tug. "Please come in."

He follows at last, and the door closes behind us. Standing in the marble-floored entry, he looks around, and says, "I can't sit down in here. We're better off outside."

I glance at Hedges, whose eyes are wide and questioning. "This is my brother, Hedges. Why don't you and Mrs. Hedges go up for the night, and I'll make coffee in the kitchen."

After a brief debate, Jake agrees the kitchen is acceptable, and I lead him downstairs. A pot of coffee sits ready on the stove and a cake dish and two plates wait on the table. Footsteps go hastily up the back stairs.

"This is good." He drops into the nearest chair, looking around. "I can't do much damage here."

"Please stop worrying." I take down two mugs and fill them with coffee. "Sugar? Milk?"

"If you've got them."

Jake is pleased to learn Ava is living nearby. "I'd like to see her," he says. "And Dan."

I tell him about Daniel, watching his face as he remembers our father and his own near-death the same day. "They're doing as well as can be expected," I say. "Ava and the children. They needed help at first, but she's proud. She wants to do it all herself."

"She always did." He smiles. "It's good you were able to help."

Hasty words bubble up, wanting to ask if Jake will allow us—allow *me*—to help him, but I push them down. Max has taken the rooms previously shared by Ava and the children, but there is a guest room standing empty. It is too soon, though; he won't accept an invitation to stay when I could barely get him into the kitchen.

"Will you come again?" I ask when he rises to leave. "I'd love for you to meet Harry."

"We'll see," is all he says. "I might be busy."

Doing what? I can't let him leave without some sort of guarantee. "Ava's giving a party on the last Saturday of the month. Please say you'll come with us."

My brother is gone before Harry gets in, back to wherever unsavory place he calls home at the moment. He wouldn't tell me, but I am afraid it is the museum camp or someplace like it. Judging by the looks of him, it's been a while since Jake has lived in anything resembling civilization.

Something must be done.

12

Ava

Voices echo off the brick walls, sounding so close they could almost be in the bathroom with us. The party is in full swing, the living room and back yard full of people. Two neighbor women, recent arrivals to the block, have come with their kids. One has a girl Thelma's age; I should go out of my way to cultivate her, for my daughter's sake.

At my insistence, the entire Hedges family is here, as well—not to help, despite Esther's offer, but as our guests. In addition to Tommy, Dan has invited Mr. Howe, the architect who owns our house. I hope he approves of the changes we've made.

Grace's head falls back, her lips separating from my nipple with a smack of satisfaction. Holding her to my shoulder, I maneuver to use the toilet, rubbing her back all the while.

"Now you'll go in your basket and be the center of attention," I murmur. "That's my good girl."

We have so much to celebrate—even more than I thought when I planned this party. Not just Pearl's graduation, but Grace's birth and Thelma's braces coming off. I flush the toilet and stop before the bathroom mirror, considering the still-unfamiliar sight of hair sweeping the back of my neck. Behind me is the bathtub, where I talk to Daniel. I stoop and lay a hand on its smooth iron curve. "You'd be so proud of them," I whisper. "So proud."

I never hear him the way I still hear Mama, but I know he's there, listening. Daniel wasn't a talker in life; I shouldn't expect him to change now, just because I want to hear from him.

When I go down, Pearl is opening the door to Prue Foster, Claire's friend and my first customer. I usher her downstairs, where sweating glass pitchers of iced tea stand on the table near the back door. "Is your sister here?" she asks, looking at the unfamiliar faces.

"Not yet."

Claire is rarely late, but Esther told me she was waiting for something and would be along soon. Waiting for something to bring with her, no doubt. Something she shouldn't be spending her money on, when I told her I wanted to do this on my own.

Claire

"If he doesn't get here soon, we'll have to go." Harry's newspaper is folded and put aside, his cigarette stubbed out in the ashtray. He has done all he can to amuse himself while I wait for Jake, and now he is waiting with me. "Ava will wonder what's keeping us."

"She won't think to ask when she sees Jake." I want this so badly, to bring him to the party, a gift even my sister cannot refuse. "He said he'd try."

"Try isn't yes," Harry says mildly. "Let's give him another fifteen minutes. Do you want to walk or drive?"

"Drive," I say, and then remember that our servants are already at the party and Hedges won't be available to find parking away from Ava's narrow street. "We can walk, I suppose. I'll put Teddy in the coach."

As Harry locks the front door, a shout makes us turn.

"I'm sorry," Jake says, jogging up to us. "I wanted to get cleaned up before I came."

He is freshly shaved, his hair wet. His shirt is patched at one elbow, but relatively clean. I pat his arm. "It's fine. We were about to walk over."

"Stay behind me," I say to Jake as I mount the white steps. "I want to surprise her."

"Do you think that's wise?" Harry parks the coach and hoists Teddy into his arms. "She's had enough to deal with. Perhaps a brother returned from the dead is a step too far."

"Nonsense." I open the front door. "Ava! Ava!"

She comes up from the lower level, wiping her hands on her apron. "There's no need to shout, sister. They'll hear you on the other side of the river."

"I have a surprise for you." I am unable to keep a smile from breaking across my face.

"What did I tell you about spending money?" She peers at my hands, which are empty save for my handbag. "What is it this time?"

I step to one side and Jake enters.

"Me," he says. "Hello, Ava."

The blood drains from her face and she is so still that she appears not to breathe. For a moment I worry Harry is right, then she throws herself at Jake, wrapping her arms around his middle. She pulls back, looking into his face and laughing.

I glance up, secure in my victory. "I think she's survived the shock," I say to my husband. "Let's take Teddy out back to see his cousins and leave them to catch up."

Ava

At some point I will apologize to Claire for assuming she would bring an expensive gift to the party. Though, when I think about it, if she hadn't brought Jake, she probably would have. Through the window, I look at him—dear, lost brother!—playing catch in the street with the boys, and my heart cracks open. There have been many changes in a year that started with desperate unhappiness. Closing my eyes, I say a quick prayer. I miss Daniel fiercely, but he would be proud to see how the kids are thriving in this new environment.

Me, too, for that matter. He always said I was capable of anything, but I'd have never discovered that in Scovill Run. I was too busy keeping us alive to attempt anything more. The last six months have been filled with new experiences. Terrifying, yes, but fulfilling too. We will survive.

The door opens again, and Thelma squeals. Pearl drags someone in by the arm. Her mystery guest. Curious, I stand to get a better look.

A gray hat is removed, and a familiar, curly head appears. Max Byrne stands on the threshold, a wrapped gift and a sprawling bunch of daisies in his hands.

I look around the room, at my children, my family. This is my life now. My future.

Is Max Byrne part of that future? He sees me, and his wary expression puts another crack in my heart. I turn toward him and smile, and hold out my hands in welcome.

Pearl

June 24, 1933

I volunteered to clean up after the party, but Mama said to forget it, that we would do it this morning. So I got up early to give her a break. I want to write about last night before I forget.

When I invited Dr. Max, I didn't know Aunt Claire was going to bring an even bigger surprise. She and Uncle were late, and Mama was getting fidgety, but then they showed up with an uncle I didn't know I had. Uncle Jake ran away when he was near Dandy's age and no one has seen him in twenty years.

He looks like Mama, the same hair and freckles, the same creases around his eyes from smiling. But he doesn't look like he smiles too often. He didn't spend a lot of time talking to us, mostly just Mama and Aunt, and he left before the party was over, without even saying goodbye. Dan was with him outside, and says he's been hoboing around the last few years. I'm not sure how he knows that, other than that he's skinny, and his clothes are patched, and because he ate as much as Toby but looked embarrassed about it.

So that's another new thing in Philadelphia. We have an uncle.

Dr. Max came, too. I'll write about him when I'm not so tired.

13

Claire

There is a letter on my desk with a Washington postmark. It has been there, unopened, for the better part of a week, taunting me each time I go into the room. Helen Dawes will want to know what causes I've involved myself with, what progress I've made. And what do I have to tell her? Nothing. Finding a cause is easier said than done.

When I finally tackle her letter, Teddy is with me in the sitting room, playing with some brightly-colored wooden blocks. His presence feels benevolent, protective, and I slit the envelope to face whatever is inside. Her handwriting is strong and angular, with no frills or nonsense. Her words are the same.

Dear Claire,

Hoping this letter finds you and Mr. Warriner well, and you up to your ears in some worthy cause which I cannot wait to hear about. Tyler has been devoting most of his waking hours to the New Deal, and while I support President Roosevelt with every fiber of my being, I've become quite tetchy about how rarely I see my husband!

At Secretary Perkins's suggestion, I have involved myself in an effort that trains young, unmarried women to become office workers. The time for domestic service has passed, and the typewriter is by no means the exclusive province of the male clerk. When business begins to boom again, as will inevitably occur (although not soon enough), women will fill many of the jobs formerly occupied by men.

Is that not only right? Women are always the organizers and administrators of the family, even if the man is the breadwinner. I believe bankers and lawyers and men of business like your husband will be shocked and surprised at how effective these new secretaries will be in organizing their lives.

I do not, as you might think, teach these young women Pitman shorthand or to use the typewriter. My skills do not lie in that direction. But I fundraise like a house afire, and there's not a man alive I won't ask for money to support my endeavors.

That's something I saw in you, Claire—a fearlessness you hadn't yet accepted in yourself. I hope you've come to terms with it and have found a focus for your energies.

Do write and keep me abreast of your news. I saw Mrs. Roosevelt only last week and she asked after you, and said that if we corresponded, I should feel free to remind you to drop her a letter.

Your friend,
Helen Dawes

Mrs. Roosevelt asked after me! I sit back in my chair, shocked by Helen's breezy words. She wouldn't make that up, so the First Lady must have actually said my name, which means I have been in her thoughts.

How astonishing.

Ava

Grace's feeding schedule means I have plenty of time alone in the middle of the night. This is both good and bad. I push down the inevitable thoughts of Daniel and replace them with practicalities like budgets and making plans for the future. Now that I'm more certain of my income, I want to take over the rent. It bothers me that Harry has been paying our way.

No one realizes how much energy it takes to be poor. It's not just work, if you're lucky enough to have it, but worry: how much will I get and how far will it stretch? Should I pay a bill or buy food? Mend those shoes again or buy cheap new ones that won't last? Good shoes will last, but they are out of reach when there are so many feet to be shod.

I check and recheck my figures, certain there must be a mistake somewhere. I was never good at arithmetic, but I have an instinct for numbers when there is a dollar sign in front of them. Poverty will do that.

But my calculations are right. I will be able to pay the rent at the end of July without Harry's help. It is unthinkable that I can support my family by sewing dresses, and yet it is true. Dan suggested I think of myself as a bootlegger. "You wouldn't make the money if the demand wasn't there," he says, and I am amused at the comparison.

When he and Pearl slip in through the basement door. I am surprised; it is after ten, and I thought they were upstairs, either in bed or in the living room. "What are you two doing outside?"

They approach, looking curiously at the columns of numbers. "Sitting on the step," Dan says. "The boys were snoring and when I came down, Pearl wasn't asleep either."

He turns a chair around and sits, resting his arms on the back. "What's all this?"

"Bills." I nod for Pearl to sit and turn the page around to show them. "That twenty dollars on top is the rent. That includes the light bill and the water." We have to supply coal and firewood, and I am already praying for an Indian summer. The next line is food, which is more than I would like, but there are a lot of us and I want the kids to eat better now that we can afford it. "Maybe next year we can plant a bit of a garden."

"Where?" Pearl asks practically. "The yard is tiny."

It is also mostly paved, which doesn't help. "Maybe you could build planters, Dan?"

"Maybe." His index finger, the nail chewed and broken, runs down the list. "This is a lot of money, Ma. Are we okay?"

"We're managing," I tell him. "Well enough."

"But it's all on you," he says. "You do nothing but cook and sew and take care of us."

Folding my arms, I look at him. "I'm a mother. That's what I should do."

"But you're exhausted," Pearl says. "And you toss and turn all night."

I do not like that she knows this. She wouldn't admit to hearing me crying, but she would tell her brother.

"It won't be forever," I say at last. "No mother sleeps well with a new baby." Raising an eyebrow, I add, "You should remember that, Pearl. You had charge of Teddy after he was born."

It is unfair of me to remind them of the low point when eleven-year-old Pearl carried the household because I refused to leave my bed and could not bring myself to use my son's name. I am grateful the price of Grace's birth is no more than ordinary exhaustion.

"It won't be," Dan agrees, straightening. "But you'll be no help to anyone if you get sick from working too hard." He lays his hands on the table and takes a breath. "You need to stop taking on extra work. I'm earning. Let me contribute more."

"Me, too." The line between Pearl's brows gives away her anxiety. "Uncle Harry says I could work in his office, filing papers."

"You're not going out to work."

"It would only be three days a week. Now school's out, I need to do more."

"No."

"Then what about Aunt Claire?" she persists. "She needs help looking after Teddy."

"She has Katie." Why does my sister need help with one small boy? I have a half dozen kids and would never think to ask for outside help.

"Katie isn't a nursemaid." Pearl plays her trump card. "If she can't manage her chores, her mother has to help, and Mrs. Hedges has her own work."

My kids are attacking me with love. I close my eyes, marshal my patience. "Fine," I say. "But not everything you earn. I've been looking into insurance—we would have had some for your daddy if he'd died working for the company. I want to get a small policy on myself."

It would give me peace of mind, knowing there was some security for the kids. If anything happens to me, I don't want Dan and Pearl to have to rely on Claire. She would turn her beautiful house into an orphanage, but it wouldn't be good for any of them.

It is some time before I can catch Harry alone. At first he refuses my request, but when I push, he presents me with a breakdown of what it has cost to feed and house my family since January. "I won't take a cent for the months you lived with us," he says. "That was an emergency, and you are family. I don't care if you pay any of this back, either, but you asked, and you deserve the truth."

It is a lot—one hundred forty dollars—but not more than I can conceive of paying, thanks to Claire and her women. I am more comfortable being in his debt than my sister's. "Thank you. I'll pay five dollars next month, and see how we get on."

Harry bows his head in acknowledgement. "I wish you wouldn't, but I understand."

It irks me that I can't have a bank account in my name—I have to have a man to sign for me, as if I am too immature to be trusted with the money I earn from my labor. Will it be my sister's husband again, or my son, not yet sixteen but apparently more responsible than myself, who signs on my behalf? I am expected to raise my children, yet I can't save money for them. I am expected to keep a roof over their heads but cannot sign a lease on my own.

"What is a single woman supposed to do?" I ask Claire, who has listened to my rant with sympathy but seemingly little understanding.

"Get married." Unexpected anger flickers in her eyes. "It's society's answer to every problem."

"I did that," I say. "Am I less of a person because I lost my husband? I can vote but I can't have a savings account?"

There is no logic that women were granted one right without the other, but perhaps keeping us from having control over our lives balances the risk of allowing us a voice in political matters.

Pearl

July 8, 1933

Mama says I can work outside the house this summer. I'd rather work in Uncle Harry's office, but I don't know if I'd be good at it and I can take care of Teddy with my eyes closed. Besides, I love spending time with Katie. This means I can do that and earn money at the same time.

Dan and I were sitting out back the other night and we got to talking. He can't stop thinking about hopping a train and going off somewhere. He won't do it, because we need the money he brings in, but I can see how much he wants to. Back in Scovill Run, he and his friends hopped trains up to Scranton and back, and then he and Daddy did it when they went to Washington, but I don't like to think about that time. I imagine he doesn't either.

I've read enough stories to know what Dan wants is adventure. So do I, but girls' adventures are smaller and closer to home. Like going to high school and taking care of Teddy instead of going into Uncle Harry's office.

Maybe next summer I'll be braver.

Ava

When Max arrived at the party, there had been no uncomfortable words; we simply picked up a friendship that had been, before, tentative at best, and built on it. He is a change from Claire, bracing and energetic, but without any desire to improve me, and this has caused me to relax my guard and willingly spend time with him.

Now, on Friday evenings, the kids eat supper at Claire's without me, and I accompany Max and his friend, Dr. Spencer, to the migrant camp at the art museum. Even though it can be difficult, I like going out there with them. It gets me away from the sewing machine and out from under my sister's eye. Now that it's gotten warm, my excursions with Grace are limited and this is the most fresh air I get all week.

When we are done, we walk back, stopping at the Swann Fountain to eat the light meal which I packed and left in the car.

Sitting on the edge of the fountain, Max balances his paper-wrapped sandwich on his knee. "You can't say I don't know how to show a lady a good time," he says. "One of these days I'd like to take you out."

"We've been out for hours." I take a hasty bite. These evenings aren't dates; they are simply helping where I can, and he is a part of that.

Max shifts almost imperceptibly, and yet his entire attention is focused on me, like a bulb with the shade removed. "I'd like to take you out properly sometime." His voice is soft. "For a meal at a restaurant, and dancing after. Do you like to dance?"

I've never danced with anyone but Daniel, unless it was a square dance where I was tossed between partners. "I haven't danced in ages."

"Perhaps it's time."

"I don't have the right clothes."

He smiles that easy smile, the one that says there hasn't been an obstacle invented he won't try to get around. Sometimes I wonder if he only sees me as a challenge. "You, of all people, can't complain you've no access to clothing."

I look up at him from under my brows. "What do you want me to do, wear one of my client's dresses?" I change my voice. "Oh, this spot, Mrs. Thorndyke? I think that's sauce from my supper with Max Byrne. You don't mind, do you?"

Max bursts into laughter, and that is the end of it. For now.

14

Claire

Max is careful with Ava, exhibiting a tenderness I had never seen out-side of his patients. The stronger elements of his personality—what I think of as his bull-in-a-china-shop quality—are subdued. It is probably this, more than anything, that irritates my sister.

I have my hopes there. Someday, in a hopefully not-too-distant future. Or more distant, if he spooks her again. A man like Max is exactly what Ava needs. He's as different as can be from Daniel, and anyway, their relationship—begun in childhood—could not be replicated by a man and woman in their thirties.

I don't like that he drags her along to his weekly trips to the camp, but Ava's absence means we have the children to ourselves for the evening. The younger ones play with Teddy until it's time for bed while the older children sit and talk with us. If Ava and Max haven't returned by eight—and they usually have not, staying at that awful place far too late—Pearl and Dan take them home.

How is it I can adore having my sister's children around, but shy away every time Prue asks if I want to drive out to the orphanage with her? Last year, when I first got involved with the gala, I thought asking people for money would be difficult, but that turned out to be the easy part. Seeing so many unwanted youngsters hurt my heart. Given the choice, I will find something that involves my mind over my emotions. I have learned enough about myself in recent years to understand I will be more effective if I do not want to bring every abandoned child into my own home.

Prue thinks I am being silly. "You go on and on about wanting a new cause to throw yourself into," she says, "and yet here I am with a ready-made one—which you already have experience with—and you won't do it. I don't understand."

"Marie and Stella are doing an excellent job, I'm sure." I hope they are; I've given them all my notes and donor lists from last year's event. "You don't need me."

"This is about you, not them." She smiles triumphantly. "You need occupation."

"And I will find it. But not there."

Pearl

July 22, 1933

Each week, Mama gives me a quarter back of my wages from Aunt. She says a girl my age should have some spending money. Yesterday I had an afternoon free and went to Woolworths by myself. I bought a yard of pale blue calico with yellow and white daisies sprinkled all over it, like the ones Dr. Max brought to the party. He said they were for me, but we all knew they were for Mama.

She thanked him, and her cheeks got all pink. He followed her downstairs when she went to put them in water, and when Toby followed, I didn't stop him. I hope I didn't make a mistake. There's no way she could be interested in Dr. Max, is there? I wanted them to be friends because it would make our lives easier but I don't want anything to happen between them.

Dandy says I should stop grousing, and let Mama do what she wants. I think he just wants to not be the only man in the house. If she got married again, he could go back to doing whatever it is boys get to do that girls don't. Which is almost everything.

I'm going to make myself a blouse. Maybe Tommy will notice me then. Probably he won't, but at least I'll have something new to wear when school starts.

Ava

I can admit to Claire that I am fond of Max. The rest is harder to explain, because it makes me sound unsatisfied with my life before we came to Philadelphia, and I wasn't. I miss Daniel like an amputated limb, but there are parts of this new life I have grown to appreciate and they would not be the same if I invited a man to share it with me.

I love my independence. Claire would say I've always been independent, but it's different now. Although Harry had to co-sign, the lease to this house is in my name. I have a business which is more than I could hope for, and less—yet—than I dream. My kids are healthy and growing and the light of my world.

And I don't want more of them.

A man like Max would want kids of his own. For all my achievements in this new place, they are fragile. Getting pregnant again—what would that do to my independence? To my energy? To the way these rich women view me?

People look at you differently when you have a lot of kids. They judge you. I deal with my customers primarily when the kids are at school, so it's never obvious how many of us there are in the house. They can't help but see Grace, but another baby would be too much.

Claire

We have just sat down when the front door opens. Moments later, Ava comes in. Without a word, she plucks Grace from her high chair and takes a seat with the baby in her lap. Max follows, sitting beside her. They are hours too early—it is usually eleven before Max returns from walking Ava home.

"You're back soon, Mama," Pearl says, before I can ask why.

"It's gone," Max says hollowly. "We drove up, but there was no one there. The police had driven everyone out and knocked down all the shelters."

"When?" Harry looks concerned. "I haven't heard anything about this."

The door opens and Katie appears. She takes plates from the sideboard, and slides them onto the table before Max and Ava, adds silverware, fills their water glasses, and departs.

Max shakes his head. "Not more than a day or two ago. John saw a cop on the street as we were driving back, and he pulled over to ask him." He takes a drink of water, and his expression says he wishes it were something stronger. "When he realized we were the ones treating the migrants, he told us to get lost."

Ava speaks up. "He wasn't quite that polite about it." She puts a hand on Max's arm. "Have something to eat. You won't feel better, but at least you won't be hungry."

He looks up, stricken. "We left the hampers in John's car!"

"I'm sure he'll drop them at a soup kitchen on his way home," she says, soothing him like he's one of her children.

The table falls silent as plates are filled, everyone either intent on their food or mulling over the news about the camp. It is a far cry from the usual rowdy Friday, where I allow conversation throughout the meal, something Ava discourages when they are at my house. My sister, who has adapted to far worse shocks, tucks into her dinner with little outward show of her feelings, but Max is visibly distressed.

"There must be another camp," I say, even though the idea of those places makes me uncomfortable. Then it occurs to me: if the camp is gone, then Jake, who I've seen only once since the party, may be gone with it. Or perhaps he'll take Harry up on his job offer if he has no other option. "Where do you think they've gone?"

His fork pauses halfway to his mouth, its load of mashed potatoes waiting to be consumed. "That's the question. There are always places to hide around the rail yards, but they drove out a lot of men. A hundred, maybe more."

"Maybe they left," Dan says quietly. "When they burned the Bonus Army camp, Dad and I got out of there real quick, and so did everybody else with any sense."

And just like that, Daniel Kimber is at the table. There is a sudden shift in all the children at the thought of their father, despite how painful that time must have been.

"But that was a temporary situation," Max says, not noticing the change. "You were never intending to stay, even if they hadn't driven you out. Some of these men had been there for six, eight months."

A bowl of fresh peas with butter makes its way down the table, and between them, George and Toby dump the contents onto their plates.

"You're not going to eat all that," Ava scolds. "Give some to your sisters."

"It's okay." Pearl pulls her plate back. "I like potatoes."

Ava

We walk home in the gathering dusk. I turned down Harry's offer of the car and Max's escort. It is a warm night, and clear, so the car is unnecessary; Max needs a stiff drink before bed, not more time pretending he is untouched by what happened.

Thelma leans against me while the little boys scuffle half-heartedly. Pearl pushes the coach and Dan lopes alongside. They are silent, but not from tiredness, I think; they, too, are disturbed by the destruction up at the museum, even though they hadn't seen it firsthand.

I had, and it is a sight I won't soon forget. It had been easy for me to view the camp as normal, to treat those wandering men as simply *men*. Seeing the tents and shanties flattened by trucks had sickened me. Hardier structures had been burned. Ragged streamers of smoke still drifted in the thick, warm air.

It was obvious that those who wrecked the camp did not consider these men to be people.

"Where are they?" Max was almost near tears; Friday evenings, for all their difficulty, were the highlight of his week. Dealing with these men made him light up in a way he never did when talking about his hospital work.

"Gone." Spencer kicked at a blackened square that burst upon impact, revealing itself to be a closely printed book, likely a Bible. "Somewhere the city won't have to deal with them."

We walked through the rubble, stepping over the scattered remnants of lives already diminished, and I thought of my husband, something I tried not to do when with Max. Almost a year ago, he and Dan had gone to Washington, hoping the government would give the veterans the money they were owed. That bonus would have set us up for the next few years, until the Depression eased and Daniel found work away from the mines.

Instead their tents were fired, their belongings destroyed. The men had been run down by horses and even tanks, sent by the president, driven by soldiers who had once been their brothers.

This was no different. Just another government more concerned with how things looked than how—or if—their citizens lived.

"God damn it." Max stopped, hands jammed in his pockets. At his feet lay a creased photograph, half embedded in the mud, a heel print obscuring the face. "There were people here—people who needed us."

There had been a man last week with a festering scar on his belly. Max tried to get him to go to the hospital but he'd spooked at the suggestion. "I'm not lettin' them get their hands on me," he said. "They'll cut me again."

"They won't," Max said. "They'll clean it, better than I can do out here, and give you something to keep your fever down." His hand darted out, brushing the man's forehead. "You should be somewhere indoors for a few days."

But the man balked, raising his hands and backing away. "No," he said. "No hospital. I won't be locked up."

"It's not jail—" But the man disappeared into the crowd, and Max couldn't follow him because he had other patients.

I caught up and took his arm. "They're not here, Max. He's not here." I held on until he looked at me. "We'll find them, but not tonight."

The wheel of Grace's coach catches on the uneven curb, and we stop while Dan straightens it.

"What will happen to them?" Pearl asks, her voice loud on the quiet street.

"I don't know," I tell her truthfully. "There's nowhere they could have gone, not all of them together."

"And they wouldn't have gone together." Dan's gaze is distant, seeing a different night, different men. "The whole point is to scatter them, drive them away like animals. Like we're not even human."

My son feels the same anger that infected Max, and he has experienced such treatment first-hand. Max, for all his upset, is a doctor, not the sort of man who would ever be targeted by police.

Claire

After my sister leaves, the men move to the living room and I take Teddy up to bed. When I return, their conversation has drifted from the camp to the latest news from Europe, which both interests and worries Harry. Max participates in the discussion, but it is clear his mind is elsewhere. When Harry offers to refill his drink, he looks up and says, "I wish there was a place where the migrants could be treated that wasn't on city property, where they can't be chased away."

It hits me then: the cause I've been searching for has been under my nose all along, as Eleanor Roosevelt said it would be. How had I not seen it when Jake first returned? I jump to my feet. "I'm off to bed."

Kissing Harry, and saying goodnight to them both, I retreat to our room to contemplate how to best fan the spark of my idea into a blaze that will give purpose to my life.

15

Pearl

August 7, 1933

I'm getting nervous about school. It's silly, since there's a month to go, but it's starting over again. Not that I had many friends last year, but they're all going to the local school. Girls High is all the way over on Spring Garden Street, way out of the way, and my going there will change everyone's schedule.

Mama said it was my choice, but I know she wants me to go, even though she'll have to cover some of my chores. I'll do extra on the weekend, and maybe take over cooking supper. I'll have to leave earlier in the mornings, too, so Thelma will have to walk to school with the boys, but she can stay with Teddy until I pick her up. It will work, I just feel selfish that I want it so badly. But Miss Rodney and the principal both think I can do it, and I don't want to let them down.

Ava

George is alone at the kitchen table, sucking up crumbs as neatly as Claire's Hoover. He and Toby have been inseparable since they were babies, but lately my younger boy is curiously unbothered by his brother's absence. I am glad he has found his own interests—though it was easier when I only had to wonder where one was, knowing they were together.

"Where are you off to?" I take his plate before he licks the design clean off the china.

He scrubs his fingers through his cropped hair so it sticks up like straw. "Firehouse."

"You're not getting under their feet, are you?" I shake off a vision of him being crushed under the wheels of an engine. "They're working, George."

"I know that." He gives me a sunny smile. "I'm gonna be a fireman when I grow up. They're letting me practice."

He vanishes soon after, and I retreat to the workroom to finish a job. The idea that my boy has chosen his future work, and it is as dangerous, in its own way, as his father's, rubs me the wrong way. This move was supposed to give my children safety.

Pearl startles me when she returns from the library. It is after twelve; the morning has gotten away from me. "Where's your sister?"

She places a stack of books reverently on the table. "Still at Aunt Claire's, playing with Teddy and Pixie."

We can't have a dog, but that doesn't stop Thelma from pretending Pixie is hers. While she loves Teddy, as often as not, he is an excuse to spend time with the dog.

"I thought we might take a walk," I say. "Do you know where this fire station is where George spends all his time?"

She nods. "It's down on Sixteenth Street, not far from the school."

"It might be nice to go and say thank you," I say, bringing out the cake I made while she was out. "For putting up with George."

Pearl grins. "And because you want to know where he goes every day."

"That, too."

It's a beautiful afternoon, so even pushing the coach, it takes only fifteen minutes to walk down Lombard Street. George, fueled by boundless little-boy energy, could do it in half that. We reach the school at the corner of Sixteenth Street, and I marvel at its four-story brick construction, the many windows to let in light. What a different experience this must be, to learn in a place that does not begrudge learning, or, for that matter, childhood.

Turning the corner, we soon arrive at the firehouse, a squat, two-story building with wide barn-style doors open to the air. Two men are seated on a bench outside, their legs stretched out before them. Water runs out the doors onto the pavement; someone is washing the engine. To my surprise, it is my son.

"George!"

He looks up, rag in hand. "I'm busy, Ma. I'll be home for supper."

One of the men unfolds himself and stands. "Can I help you, ma'am?"

I hold out my hand. "I'm Ava Kimber, George's mother. We"—I nod toward Pearl—"thought we'd come and make sure George isn't making a nuisance of himself."

The bucket clanks to the ground. "I'm not a nuisance," comes his truculent voice. "I'm working."

The man shakes my hand. "Lieutenant John Gallagher, ma'am. We like having him around, don't you worry."

The sun is in my eyes. Squinting, I look up at him. He is so tall that I can only make out his silhouette. "That's good to hear." I lead him to the coach. "I made this for you all, as a thank you for putting up with him."

He bypasses the cake for the baby, asking, with a quick sideways glance, "Do you mind?" He swoops Grace into the air. Her tiny feet kick and she chortles with joy. "George said you had a little 'un."

"Born in May." Something tugs at my heart, seeing Grace in the arms of such a big man. "And I've barely seen George since."

"That's about when he appeared." The second man joins us, shorter than the lieutenant, with slicked-back dark hair. "Joe diPasquale, ma'am." Another hard, all-encompassing hand. "He's a good kid."

George is standing in front of the engine, rag in one hand, lip stuck out a mile. "They're letting me work, Ma."

"Which is more than you do at home," Pearl says. George sticks out his tongue. "You haven't lifted a bucket since we moved in."

"Have too." He scuffs the ground with his foot, giving himself away. "Well, I would, but I'm here, right?"

The lieutenant cups George's head like a baseball. "You help your mama before you come here, understand?"

Silence from my son.

"Understand?"

"I will." Brightening, he looks at me. "Did you say cake?"

"For them, not for you!"

Cake is a magic word for boys of all ages, and some of the men at Ladder Five are barely older than Dan. They tumble up the steps behind us, and when Lieutenant Gallagher leads us into a big room overlooking the street, they scatter, fetching plates and mugs and setting the table as swiftly as waiters at a fancy restaurant.

"Maybe you could train him to do that?" I ask, placing the cake on the table. "And the dishes?"

"Will do, ma'am." The lieutenant hasn't yet surrendered Grace. She is as tiny as a kitten in his arms. "You hear, George? You're on chow duty for the next two weeks, until you learn to help your mother."

"Is this where you spend your time when you're not out fighting fires?" It's a pleasant room, with two large curtainless windows letting in the sunshine. A small table sits before one, with a checkerboard cut into its surface. Piles of red and black chips are stacked on the sill. A pair of battered armchairs, the sort Dan wouldn't even consider in his scouting of the city's trash, sit before the other window.

"Some of us live here full-time." It's the younger man, diPasquale. "My family doesn't have room, so it's easier."

"There's beds in the back," George volunteers. "Maybe I could live here?"

"And let Toby have the whole bed?" Pearl teases. "He'd get used to having you gone, and then where would you be?"

The cake is sliced and distributed, and we are given cups of strong coffee. I will surely be up late sewing, so I drink deeply and do not refuse a refill.

The firemen are interchangeable, except for the huge lieutenant—from their late teens to early thirties, they are rangy, fit men with skins reddened from constant exposure to the heat, and hands like baseball gloves. They all wear uniform shirts and ties, but they appear no more comfortable with formality than Daniel would have been.

Lieutenant Gallagher gives up the baby at last, but to one of the other men, allowing Pearl and me to enjoy unaccustomed leisure. Grace makes her way down the table, being kissed and dandled by each man, until she finally reaches me and I settle her on my shoulder. She is worn out by all the attention and falls asleep immediately; I tuck a napkin under her cheek so she doesn't drool through my dress.

For the first time I notice a small stove and icebox tucked into a corner. "You cook here?"

"We do." One of the young men stands and opens the icebox door. "It's meatloaf tonight."

"Yum!" George's eyes cut toward me. "Can I stay for supper, Ma?"

"But who does the cooking?" I shake my head at my son, unwilling to let him eat these men out of house and home.

"We do, ma'am," the lieutenant says. "We're like a family here. We all take turns, cooking, washing up."

"Laundry," another man says. "If we don't take it home."

"And washing the engine, until George got here."

The lieutenant escorts us back downstairs and settles Grace into the coach, tucking the now-clean plate in at her feet. "It was a pleasure meeting you, ma'am." He smiles. "And don't fret none about George. We've let him ride out with us on the engine once or twice, but he knows better than to come near the fire."

My son's promises mean little when he's interested in something. It is a matter of time before he comes home soot-stained. Still, it's better than coal dust. "Thank you for the coffee."

"Thank you for the cake," he says, waving us off and pushing the unwilling George after us. "Come back anytime."

Claire

The idea of a migrant clinic is the only thing that distracts me from worrying about Jake's whereabouts. It seems an enormous undertaking, to organize something that would replace and improve upon Max's makeshift Friday evening endeavors, but I am capable of an enormous undertaking; it simply needs proper planning. And with Max under my roof, I have someone available to whom I can put all the questions I write down in my little notebook in the afternoons when I would otherwise be reading or visiting.

"Say there was a clinic like the place you dream of." I look away so he can't see the excitement in my eyes. "What would it require? What would you want it to have?"

"An x-ray machine," Max says promptly. "And not a dinky one, something that can actually be used as a diagnostic tool." He chews his lip. "Three exam rooms."

"Why?"

"So the next patient is already set up when the doctor is free, and the waiting room doesn't get too crowded."

That makes sense. "What else? Think outside what you'd be given at a hospital."

"What's going on? Do you know someone who's planning something like this?"

I shake my head, and watch him deflate a bit. "No. It's only curiosity—for now. What would you want in a clinic to serve your migrant patients, if you could ask for anything?"

His eyes brighten. Max is never down for long. "Something to give them a little dignity. Showers. Donated clothing. Food. Not a full soup kitchen," he says, noting my alarm, "but things they can carry away. Bread. Cheese. Apples. Coffee and tea always on. Some of the men I treated at the camp hadn't had a hot drink in days, even during the winter."

He's given me a lot to think about, and I don't know if the idea slowly percolating in my brain has any merit—or if it would even be achievable.

The next night, I broach the subject with Harry. We have just made love and, like me, he does not fall asleep immediately after. I have spent the day trying to work out a plan of attack, but in the end, I simply say, "I think I've found a project."

"Excellent." He shifts so we are facing each other. "Tell me."

"A clinic," I say. "A clinic for the poor." He doesn't respond and I hastily continue. "Not something to replace the minimal services Max and John Spencer provided at the camp, but an actual clinic, staffed by doctors, who could treat all the poor of the city."

He is quiet for a while. The light curtains stir in the fan's gentle breeze. "That's quite a commitment."

"I know." I cannot do it alone, but I will find the right people to help me. "I could do it, Harry. With your support."

"What sort of support are we talking about?" He rolls onto his back, arms folded behind his head, prepared to listen.

I swallow. "Some financial, of course." I have to be honest; we are wealthy, despite the Depression, and I would be a fool not to take advantage. "But mostly what you've always given me, the knowledge that you believe in me."

"Then you have both, darling. And always will."

16

Pearl

August 14, 1933

Teddy is probably going to grow up like Toby and George, but right now I love him to death. And maybe he won't be like them, because he's an only child, and Aunt Claire and Uncle Harry will keep a tighter leash on him than Mama was ever able to with those two hooligans.

I'm not so sure lately, because Katie and I spend more time with him than she does. I get paid for four hours a day while she's out for lunches or meetings or sitting downstairs making lists. It's good, because sometimes he naps and then I can read the book I've brought with me. If Katie's done her chores, she comes to the nursery and keeps me company. She stopped school at thirteen but she reads nearly as well as I do, and she's gotten better in the time we've been reading together.

It seems funny to have a colored friend, and one who's older than me. There weren't any colored girls at my school, which is strange because there are lots of colored people here. Katie says they have their own neighborhoods and schools, and I guess it makes sense, because not everyone is nice to them. But who wouldn't be nice to Katie and Mrs. Hedges? Jesus said we were supposed to love everybody.

Claire

"Before you get too invested in this," Harry says over breakfast, "you need to find a location."

Does he suspect I was up most of the night making plans? Every time we discuss the clinic, it lights my brain on fire. And he is right—none of my castles in the air will be worth anything without a structure to put them in.

I take a sip of tea. "Where do you think we should look?"

"Good question." He puts his newspaper to one side. The subject engages him, if he's willing to forgo the morning news. "It can't be too central. The rent will be too high and too many people will be offended. That will be bad for donations."

"Too far away, and it will be difficult for me to get there—and you know Max is going to be involved. He can't be in two places at once, no matter how hard he tries."

Harry chuckles. "But he *would* try."

"He'll wear out the tires on his bicycle." I spread strawberry jam—a gift from Ava's kitchen—on my toast. "And then how would he get around?"

"Let me think on it." Harry pushes back his chair. "I'll give George Howe a call this afternoon and see if he knows of any suitable properties." Kissing my cheek, he disappears into the hall, and soon the door closes.

I don't want to rent; I want to own this clinic, the real estate as well as the idea. But I have no clue what a building would cost, and decide to go back to making lists and leave the finding of a property to my husband's judgment and experience.

When Katie brings my afternoon tea, she casts an eye at the state of my desk and squats to pick up a few pieces of crumpled paper, looking curiously at the lists of figures and equipment. "You starting a hospital?"

"Not exactly." I sketch my plan, tell her Max will be involved—a sure way to make her approve of the scheme—and say I am currently stalled until I find a location.

She pauses, laying a slender hand on the table. "Would you treat colored people?"

"Why not?" This is Philadelphia, not the deep south, the world Helen Dawes had grown up in and escaped. "The poor come in all colors."

"Not everyone will," she says. "Would you have a colored doctor?"

Are there colored doctors? There should be, but I honestly don't know if there are. "At least a nurse," I say, more certain that nursing is permitted for Negros. "It's early days yet."

She straightens my desk, flattening the papers and setting a book on top of them. "You could ask at Mercy Hospital, they always have nurses they're trying to place."

I look up, startled at this bit of information. "Where's Mercy Hospital?"

"Seventeenth and Fitzwater," she tells me. "My cousin Ebba goes there. I see her every Sunday at church, she tells me all about it."

The African Baptist Church is on Sixteenth and Christian Streets. I know that because Hedges once asked if he could drop Katie and Mrs. Hedges at church while he waited for me.

"Your cousin is a nurse?"

"Training to be," Katie says. "My Aunt Dora is fit to bust, she's so proud of that girl."

What difference is there between Katie and her cousin, other than the cousin stayed in school, instead of going out to work for people like us?

"Would you like to be a nurse?" I would not know to cope without her capable management of my existence, but I at least owe her the question.

Her nose wrinkles. "Not really. I don't like blood."

The poor girl. She'd seen plenty of it, when I'd miscarried the last time. "Do you miss going to school?"

"I'd be done by now, anyways," she says. "It don't much matter."

"You deserve more than this, Katie." I might not be able to cope with the orphanage children, but I could help individual young people when their problems presented themselves. "If you'd like to go back to school, or train for a different job, you just have to tell me."

She smiles then, and I feel as if I've been patted on the head. "Pearl, she goes over her lessons with me when she comes to watch Teddy. Sometimes she leaves me a book."

My thirteen-year-old niece has done more for my maid than I have. I am ashamed. "That's very good of her, but I should be doing more. Don't you have any ambitions, Katie?"

"To be like my mama, mostly," she says. "A good man, a job, healthy babies. That's enough."

I can't disagree, but is it enough, truly? For her, or for any woman?

Ava

"Where is George?" Pearl peers into the pot, then slams the lid down. "If he doesn't get here soon, we should eat without him."

"Dunno," Toby mumbles from the sink, where he is unsuccessfully trying to remove grease from his knuckles and under his nails. "I never see him no more."

"It would serve him right." Dan is already in his corner, Grace on his lap. "I'm starving."

The door bangs upstairs. That's an improvement; I've been trying to get him to stop running through the workroom, in case I have a customer. George's footsteps are followed by heavier steps. What on earth?

The stairs creak and George appears, followed by long legs in navy blue uniform pants. The legs keep going until they turn into the rest of Lieutenant Gallagher, smiling sheepishly over George's head. "Evening, Mrs. Kimber," he says. "I walked George home so he wouldn't be late."

"He is late." Toby glares at the stranger.

"I asked him for supper, Ma," George announces, heading for the sink. "Can he stay?"

I blink, surprised at my son's boldness. "I suppose. Don't you have plans, lieutenant? Family waiting for you?"

He takes the last step down into the kitchen, ducking his head so as not to crack it on the door frame. "I'm a bachelor," he says. "I live with my aunts, but they never know when to expect me, because of my schedule at the station."

"Well, then," I say, smelling a plot, "you're more than welcome to join us."

He is too big for the room. Trying to keep out of the way in a corner, he bumps first into a chair and then into the coat rack.

"Should I dish up, Mama?" Pearl asks from the stove.

The table is already set, but George takes another plate down from the cupboard and shoves it onto the crowded table. He looks around. "Can I get the chair from your workroom, Ma?"

"Don't call me Ma," I say automatically. "No, I'll get it."

"Let me." Lieutenant Gallagher lurches forward. "I'm putting you to a lot of trouble here."

I meet his eyes—blue, with pleasing creases at their corners—and smile. "Not at all, lieutenant. I'm not at my best today."

"You're well?" He lifts my heavy sewing chair like it weighs nothing.

"Just tired," I admit. "When Grace doesn't sleep, I don't sleep. And she's been very cranky lately."

"Please let me hold her while I'm here." He places the chair in the space George has made. "I love babies."

"So do I," I say lightly, "but I miss sleeping."

Lowering his voice, he says, "You have a beautiful family, Mrs. Kimber. My mama died when I was a just boy, and my aunts raised me after my pa went off to look for work. I'd have loved to be part of a family like this."

And for the next two hours, he is a part of the family. He listens to Toby and George squabble, questions Dan about his job with Mr. Howe, discovers Pearl likes to read and asks her favorite books, and tells Thelma she looks like the angel on a Christmas tree.

My kids are charmed, even Pearl, who usually looks askance at men, and I have warmed to the lieutenant in spite of myself. If only he wasn't so...large. He makes all our furniture seem tiny, all the doors and ceilings low. My teacups look like doll china in his big hands.

"Mrs. Kimber, do you mind if I smoke?"

"Not in the house." I gesture apologetically toward the workroom door. "The smell gets into the fabrics."

"Of course. I'm sorry," he says, abashed.

"I'll smoke with you," Dan volunteers. "We can sit out back."

We arrange ourselves on the benches, and Dan and the lieutenant light their cigarettes. I don't enjoy smoking, but the scent reminds me of Daniel. The conversation continues, the lieutenant telling us about life in the firehouse, and how many of the men now live there. "It used to be that way all the time," he says. "Now, it's because they don't have any other place, or their family can live more cheaply without them."

The way the men at the fire station stick together reminds me of the brotherhood of miners, and I say so.

"It's the same thing, I imagine," the lieutenant says. "You watch out for your brother, and you know he's watching out for you. It's the only thing that makes a job like this safe."

"But it's not safe," I say. "You're running into burning buildings."

"And you should see, Ma," George interrupts. "They smile when they run in."

Smile? I look questioningly at Lieutenant Gallagher, and he shrugs. "It's not a job for everyone," he says simply. "We do it because we love it."

Dan stands and stretches. "I need to go in. We start early tomorrow." He sticks out his hand. "Nice to meet you, lieutenant."

A few minutes later, George gets to his feet, yawning theatrically. "I'm tired. You coming, Toby?"

Toby looks at him. "I'm not tired."

George's face puckers. "You look like something the cat dragged in." He takes off, and Toby runs after him.

Thelma gets slowly to her feet. "I need to do my exercises. Will you help, Pearl?"

"Of course." She puts her hand on my shoulder. "And then I'll do the dishes."

Within minutes, the lieutenant and I are alone in the darkening yard. He looks at me. "They aren't subtle," he says, a laugh in his voice.

"No, they're not." I fold my hands in my lap. "Lieutenant, I don't know what George has told you, but it hasn't been that long since I lost my husband. I'm not looking to form a new attachment."

It is difficult to read his expression in the dim light, but he does not look surprised. "Understood," he says easily. "I thought it was too good to be true—a fine woman like yourself, with a beautiful family." He drops his cigarette, grinds it under his heel. "I hope you don't take it wrong, but I enjoyed myself this evening. It was nice, even to pretend."

I enjoyed myself, as well, but there is no point in telling that to this very nice man and getting his hopes up. "This won't change things for George?"

"Not at all," he assures me. "He'll make a good fireman in time. And until then, he's useful to have around the place."

The next morning, I catch George before he leaves. "What was all that, yesterday?"

He turns innocent blue eyes to me. "What?"

"Bringing the lieutenant home for supper." I cross my arms, give him my sternest expression. "He's a perfectly nice man, and he'll make some woman a wonderful husband, but it won't be me."

"Aww." His lip comes out, until he remembers that I hate sulking. "I like him, and I thought…"

"Whatever you kids have decided amongst yourselves," I say, "it doesn't mean I'm going along with it."

He looks at me again, and this time his eyes are filled with tears. "I just miss Daddy," he says. "Lieutenant John isn't him, but he'll do, won't he?"

I shake my head. "Don't you think the lieutenant deserves more than that, George?"

"I was thinking about us," he says, knuckling the tears from his eyes. "I'm sorry, Ma."

"I know you miss him." I hug my boy close; he is all elbows and hard edges. "So do I. I miss him so much I can't think about anyone else taking his place."

Lieutenant Gallagher is a good man. Mama always said it was easy to fall in love with a good man, and she married my father almost immediately after learning her first husband was dead. I can't be that way, even though it seems stupid not to. Lieutenant Gallagher has a steady job and decent wages, and he looks at my kids with the melting eyes of a puppy.

He must be dumbfounded by my lack of interest. Or perhaps not. He seemed intelligent enough to understand *why* I sent him away. Had I agreed to what George set up, there would be, somewhere down the road, a painful conversation where John Gallagher would tell me that he wants kids and I would have to say no. Even the Catholic church can't argue I haven't done my duty. I want to use my strength to mother the ones I already have, from the husband who can't be replaced.

Would John Gallagher understand that?

Would Max Byrne?

Pearl

August 19, 1933

George brought a fireman home for supper yesterday, the nice lieutenant we met at the fire station. He looked at Mama the way Toby looks at cake, and even though I didn't like his intentions, I almost felt bad for him, because it was obvious from the get-go she wasn't interested.

I talked to her later, once Grace and Thelma were asleep, and she was almost laughing about it, but it seemed like she felt bad, too. He was a catch, she said, and he hadn't expected to be thrown back. I asked why she wasn't interested, and she said there were a few reasons. She's not ready. He's not the right man. And because we're enough.

So maybe it will be all right. We'll stay like we are, and no one will come between us.

$$17$$

Claire

The first few buildings turn out to be unsuitable for one reason or another, but when Harry tells me of his latest discovery, I am unreasonably excited. This has to be the place! I've been putting out feelers for donations and have even received some, but at this stage, all my future efforts are contingent on having a physical location.

In addition to helping me actually find a spot, Harry has offered to donate the first six months' rent so the results of my fundraising can be put toward renovations and the purchase of equipment. When the project starts coming together, people will be more likely to take out their checkbooks. I cannot wait to get started.

Since Harry isn't available until tomorrow and I am compelled to see the building immediately, I ask Stella Good to come along. She is tentatively supportive of my plan, though she badgers me constantly to rejoin the orphanage project. Perhaps now, when the clinic becomes more real to her, she will give up asking.

We drive down Nineteenth street, passing Ava's block, and soon come to a prosperous colored neighborhood. Other than the skin color of the people on the streets, it looks no different than any other. Somewhere nearby is the hospital where I will inquire after a nurse for the clinic.

Philadelphia is a city of neighborhoods, for industry as well as residential living. Steel mills are located, for the most part, in Nicetown; knitting mills, like Harry's, in Kensington; and the breweries—before Prohibition shut them down—were located, most aptly, in Brewerytown.

Washington Avenue, a few blocks further south, has always been an odd mix. Running from Twenty-Fifth Street east toward the Delaware,

there are coal yards, steel mills, smelters, a furniture factory associat-
ed with Wanamakers department store, several textile manufactur-
ers, a cigar company, and the Curtis Publishing Company. Many of
these businesses have rail yards attached—for ease of delivery, obviously, but they are also places where the poor can hide themselves
away. A clinic in an area like this would be a blessing.

The street itself seems to be made mostly of overlapping tracks,
and I drive slowly until I can turn off at Twentieth Street. Half a
block further, then a right turn onto narrow League Street. The
buildings here are as hulking as those on the main thoroughfare,
but the buzz of machinery and traffic is drastically less. Only one
building, at the end of the street, seems active.

"Are you sure this is it?" Stella looks out the window uncertainly.
"I think I'll stay in the car."

I check the address against the slip of paper in my bag and open
the door. Her discomfort makes me brave. "This is it."

There are two buildings on the lot, as Harry said. The larger one
had been the sheet metal works, now moved to Easton. *Hoyt Steel* is
painted on its brick side in enormous block letters. The few windows
that face the front are either broken or covered over, and there are
boards nailed across the front doors. Despite the brightness of the
day, it is a bleak picture.

The smaller structure, set back off the sidewalk, once held offices
and a shipping area. In marginally better condition, its potential is
immediately clear. The open area could be used for patients—we
could set out benches for them to rest on while they wait to be called.
A few planters full of flowers never hurt anything. Maybe Geneva
Rowland and her garden club could help there. There is nothing
green in this part of town, not even trees, and heat rises from the
cracked and filthy pavement through the soles of my shoes.

The door is similarly secured, but the rectangular window is un-
covered. Peering through the smeared glass, all I can make out is a
cavernous dark space with a dim glow at the far end, where there
must be another window. "I think it will work," I call back to Stella.
"Come look."

"If you say so." She joins me, fanning herself with her hat. "Can
we go now? I'm sweating through my dress."

"So am I." There is an uncomfortable damp patch between my shoulder blades which I hope won't leave a mark. "Let me just look at the back."

I head down the alley between the buildings, and Stella follows, muttering. The structure appears in reasonably good condition, as far as my uneducated eye can tell. More windows would be nice, but altering the building might be too expensive. Perhaps we can add extra lighting.

At the end of the alley, a short stretch from the fenced rear of the factory on Washington Avenue, there is a loading area with a set of double doors and the small window visible from the front. One pane is broken and the window has been shoved up. I back away slowly, in case someone is watching from inside.

"I told you!" Stella whispers furiously as we trot back down the alley. "We shouldn't be here without a man."

"Well, Harry is in New Jersey." My original plan had been to wait for him, but I was too impatient. "And there's no one chasing us, see?"

"I don't care." She wrenches open the door and slides into the car.

I follow more slowly, putting the key into the ignition and turning it. The motor comes to life, but almost immediately, wisps of steam issue from beneath the hood. The car makes an odd choking sound and dies.

"Damn." I know little about cars, but that didn't sound good. "It's probably overheated."

"Aren't we all?" Stella glares accusingly at the dash. "Now what do we do?"

"I don't know." I raise the car's hood, flinching at its heat, and receive a face full of steam for my trouble. Slamming it shut, I wipe my face with my ruined gloves. "There must be taxis on Washington Avenue." I'm not at all sure why there would be, this far south. "If not, we'll find a phone booth and call for one."

I lock the car and leave it in front of what I hope will someday be the Philadelphia Clinic for the Deserving Poor, and we pick our way carefully over the broken pavement to Washington Avenue. The wide street is full of rail cars and trucks, with the occasional horse-drawn cart for variety. There is not a single private vehicle in sight, much less a taxi.

"Should we call the police?" Stella has gone pale. A reaction to the heat, or genuine fear at being in an unfamiliar place?

"They have better things to do." I look around, trying to decide which building looks most approachable. "I'm going in here to ask to use their phone. Do you want to come, or do you want to stay on the corner and look for a cab?"

"I'm not staying out here alone." She clacks after me in her high heels.

Rather than call for a taxi, I dial my mother-in-law's number, hoping Aunt Nora will answer. Baxter is usually at loose ends this time of the afternoon; he would be faster than a taxi. When she answers, I explain our predicament. "I'll send him right down," she promises. "Did you need to speak to Irene? She has company but I'm sure she'd come to the phone."

"No, please don't bother her." The last thing I need with sweat trickling into my undergarments is the frosty voice of my mother-in-law, letting me know I've foolishly put Stella and myself in an unsafe situation.

We retreat to the shade of an overhanging roof to wait for Baxter. Ten minutes pass, by which point I am ready to wring Stella's complaining neck; I'm feeling as patient as Ava on a bad day. I'm hot; my gloves are a total loss; and my hair did not benefit from an impromptu steam bath.

A horn honks, but the vehicle that pulls to the curb is a shining dark green Ford roadster, not Honora's staid Cadillac.

"Ladies, your knight in shining armor has arrived!" Francis Gardiner jumps out, clad in a fashionable summer suit and boater. His wolfish smile reminds me again of Harry's nickname for him.

"Aunt Nora said she was sending Baxter." I am in no state to deal with his flirtatiousness, not to mention my promise to Harry that I would have as little to do with the man as possible.

"Irene sent me instead." He gestures toward the gleaming car. "Isn't this better?"

It's a stunning car, but it has one seat. "The Cadillac would be more comfortable," I point out.

"I don't care." Stella nudges me. "Get in. I'm not going to be the filling in the sandwich, not when you dragged me down here against my better judgment."

"What is Squint doing, letting you wander around this part of town?" Gardiner opens the passenger side door and attempts to hand me in, but I manage without his help.

"It's not his fault." I leap to Harry's defense, but some part of me does appreciate being rescued, even though it is my car that has let me down, and not my husband. "My car died."

"Even so." He waits until Stella slides in next to me, then closes the door. Once he is settled, his leg pressing against mine, he pulls carefully into traffic. "This is no area for ladies as lovely as yourselves. Whatever were you doing?"

"Looking at a building." I shift to my right, and encounter Stella's warm, cushioned hip.

"Claire wants to open a clinic down here," she says. "I don't know why I let myself be railroaded into coming along."

"You look like an ice cream cone," Gardiner says. "Sweet, but quite melted."

Stella is dressed in head-to-toe pink, and does look a bit like a strawberry ice cream. I notice a few dark smuts on her skirt, and decide it is a suitable trade-off for how irritating she has been. Prue would have never carried on like a toddler because the car broke down—she would have undoubtedly flagged down a passing truck and bribed the driver to take us home.

Gardiner drops Stella off first, and I slide gratefully over on to her side of the green leather seat. "I can walk from here," I offer.

"Don't be ridiculous." His voice is like caramel—or am I still thinking about ice cream? "I will deliver you to your door like the precious cargo that you are. Those were my instructions."

That's quite a statement, considering Irene would prefer to drop me into the Schuylkill. I discreetly blot my hairline. "Do you see my mother-in-law often?"

He turns on to Delancey Place. There is a spot right in front of the house; I am going to have to ask him in.

"Every week or so." He shrugs. "My family is in London, and it's flattering, having a fuss made over me."

I hardly think he needs to look for fuss from a woman of Irene's age. In a better frame of mind, Stella would have been giggling like a schoolgirl.

This time I make certain to tell Harry about my encounter before I get distracted and he hears about it from his mother. His reaction is tempered by his distress that Stella and I were stranded. "I'll have

Hedges collect the car first thing in the morning," he says. "It probably overheated. It was a wretched day."

"It made a very sad noise when it stopped working." I put a hand on his arm. "I called for Baxter, you know, rather than a cab. Mr. Gardiner was visiting your mother again and she sent him to collect us."

I neglect to mention the cramped front seat, Gardiner's firm thigh, his tone while we drank lemonade in the living room as Katie watched surreptitiously from the hall. She has an instinct for when I'm uncomfortable.

"I'm grateful he came for you," he says, grudgingly, "though why Mother thought he was a better idea than Baxter, I'll never know."

"Aunt Nora intended for Baxter to come." I don't want her blamed for her sister's actions. I top off his martini with the last of the liquid in the icy pitcher. "I'm sorry I asked him in, but it seemed the least I could do."

Taking a deep swallow of his drink, Harry closes his eyes. "Don't worry, darling. I'm not upset. I can appreciate your instinct for hospitality while still loathing Wolf Gardiner."

"Pixie seems to agree with you." The dog had curled protectively at my feet, growling low in his throat every time Gardiner moved, and only resumed his normal, happy demeanor when the door closed after him.

That makes Harry smile. "I knew I liked that dog."

Ava

I settle the baby on my breast and lean back, glad to have a moment where I am doing nothing other than drinking tea and talking to my sister, who has dropped in unexpectedly. She is flushed, not quite herself; too many meetings, I diagnose, and not enough time with Harry and Teddy. She watches me, a strange expression on her face.

"What?" Grace tugs at my nipple, the hard ridge of her gums pressing against my tender flesh. She can't possibly be teething already.

There are milestones for babies: first tooth, first words, first steps. They vary, of course, but I know without thinking when Dan got his first tooth and when Pearl said "Mama." George never crawled or walked; he went from scooting on his bottom to chasing Toby around the room.

I will know these markers for Grace, but I missed out on Teddy's. I've questioned Claire, but she's uncertain, other than that his teething was long and painful to the entire household. How can she can be so detached when she wanted him so badly? He's thriving in their care, so I can hardly be critical, but I wonder sometimes if we were raised by the same woman.

"Feeding a baby like that." She glances at our son, playing with a pile of blocks in the corner. "It's one of the things I missed."

"It never stops." I don't think someone who has never had a baby on the breast can ever understand how my day revolves around feeding her or changing her diapers or putting her down for a nap, only for her to scream two minutes later because she is either hungry or her diaper needs changing again. The basket of mending makes me guilty; the bucket of diapers soaking out back makes me tired. "I don't know how I get everything done. I feel like I'm constantly chasing myself."

She listens, perhaps imagining the wreckage of her social life if she'd borne a child, and eventually shakes her head. "Can I ask—I've always wondered why were there no children between Thelma and Teddy."

"We occasionally got lucky." I remember that stretch of non-pregnancy with nostalgia, realizing it will always be that way, from now on. Once Grace is weaned, there will be no more babies.

"That gap always surprised me," she says, "considering the close spacing between the others." Her face falls, and she looks down into her cup. "Oh, I'm sorry, did you—"

"I did lose one, not long after Thelma." That loss isn't something I think about much anymore, though at the time it was unbearable, because I'd also lost Thelma's twin when they were born. "But mostly it was because Daniel was on nights. Lack of opportunity."

When Grace falls asleep on my shoulder, Claire lets herself out and I remain where I am, knowing one or another of the kids will be home soon enough. For the time being, I will close my eyes and enjoy the quiet.

Claire

Toward the end of August, a hurricane off the coast traps us inside. During several days of heavy rain, Harry retreats to his office, and I make lists of potential donors and catch up on my correspondence. With the clinic now well on its way, I am finally able to respond to Helen Dawes's letter.

Max goes out—people might stay indoors, but they don't stay well—and comes home drenched and discouraged each evening. I assume it's the weather getting him down, but when asked, he admits he is worried about the men who were evicted from the camp.

"The situation there was bad enough," he says, "but who knows where they are now? There's a lot of flooding in low-lying areas along the tracks, the kind of places where they'd hide out."

"I thought you were feeling deprived of my sister's company," I say, to lighten the mood, but his worry is contagious. None of us have seen Jake in weeks.

He gives me a half-hearted grin. "I can hold two thoughts at once. And I feel for the poor woman—trapped indoors with those wild Indians."

Ava

The house rings with the sounds of George and Toby playing a particularly bloody Wild West game. "Toby, if you scalp your brother one more time!"

"We ain't making no mess," he says. "Look, the blood's invisible."

"If you could make the sound invisible, I'd appreciate it."

Pearl and I drive ourselves crazy looking for leaks. Weather like this in our old house, water would have been coming in at least three places. It's almost a comfort when Thelma points out the dripping casement in the hall. Dan stuffs it with a rag, and promises to look at it when the storm passes.

"Surely three days are enough." Pearl rests her elbows on the sill and looks out at the street. It is raining so hard the houses on the other side are no more than shadowy outlines. "Dan, can you build us an ark?"

"No." He points to his brothers. "I'd have to put them on it. The house is small enough. On a boat, I'd throw them off."

I understand completely, and send them up to their room. "You can have all the gun battles you want, just stay upstairs."

Pearl and Thelma curl up on the window seat, one with a book, the other with her doll. I sit on the davenport with the mending, listening to the radio and rocking Grace's basket with my foot. Dan paces like a caged animal. His job is shut down because of the weather and leisure suits my boy about as well as it does me. After a while he yanks his jacket off its hook. "I'm going to Tommy's. I'll be back later."

"Take me with you!" Pearl jumps to her feet, her book flying. "I haven't been out of the house for days."

He shakes his head. "Nope. I'm going to enjoy the walk—alone."

Her face falls, and when the door slams behind him, she retrieves *Imitation of Life* from the floor. "Being a girl is no fun."

I shift over so she and Thelma can join me. "It can be," I say, "but not all the time. Why don't you read until I finish this, and then we can go downstairs and make a cake."

Thelma brightens. "And not give any to the boys?"

"Well..." I consider. "At least not until we've eaten our fill."

18

Claire

The next time I visit Irene and Honora, I fill them in on my plans for the clinic. Aunt Nora is enthusiastic—like Max, she's never met a worthy cause she doesn't like—and even Irene is strangely positive.

"Harry's donation is a few months' rent," I say, "but I'm going to have to come up with funds for the rest myself."

"What will you need?" Aunt Nora looks ready to reach for her checkbook, and I love her for it.

"The building needs work," I say. "It would anyway, but it's been empty for a while. We'll need equipment, medicines, furniture. And staff." Max and his friend, Dr. Spencer, will certainly volunteer, but I can't rely on them for everything. "So it will be a lot."

Aunt Nora rings, and when the maid appears, she says, "My checkbook, Anna. *Both* our checkbooks, as a matter of fact."

"Now, Honora—" Irene doesn't like to be managed, and she clings to her money like grim death.

"You can't take it with you, sister." Nora's expression tells me all I need to know about their relationship. "Might as well spread it around."

The maid returns with their checkbooks. Irene sets hers to one side. "Who's helping you with all this?"

"Harry, of course, and Max Byrne for what the clinic will need. And I'll ask Prue Foster. She's a wizard at fundraising. Other than that, I'm flying solo." Do I appear so incapable? "Is there someone you would recommend?"

"Hmm." She gives me a bright-eyed glance, her head cocked like a bird. "I'm not saying you can't do it, Claire. After all, you did a wonderful job for the orphans last year. But I don't think you comprehend how important this could be, how many people could benefit. You're going to need someone to help you steer this craft."

I had thought the same thing, but I'd never admit it to Irene, especially on the heels of such unexpected praise. "I'm sure I can manage."

The subject is dropped while we have late lunch in the stifling dining room. Mrs. Fell's cooking is no better than it was when she worked for us, and the meal is only bearable because Nora regales us with the plot of a slightly scandalous play she'd seen a few days prior.

"It sounds terribly fun." I smile at her, wondering how she can stand to live with her sister. Surely being alone isn't so bad.

Unusual for her, Irene does not throw a damper on our conversation. In fact, her expression is distracted and when she speaks, it has nothing to do with the topic at hand. "Do you remember Francis Gardiner?" she asks, studying her nails. "Such a lovely man."

"Of course." It hasn't been that long since she sent him to play knight in shining roadster.

"He knows everyone in this city, dear, despite having been away for so long." She smiles primly. "He could be a great help to you."

How can she be so dense as to promote a man whom her son dislikes so thoroughly?

"I don't know." Harry's opinion of Gardiner isn't likely to change because the man might be able to render assistance with the clinic.

She is already out of her chair, heading for the telephone table. "Why don't I call him for you? He lives downstairs, did you know? A nice little furnished apartment on the sixth floor."

When he picks up, she speaks to him, shrill and coy, while Nora and I nibble lace cookies and try not to smile. Is he busy? (He is not.) Would he like to come up for tea? (He would be delighted!) Is now a good time? (He is only not in the elevator because it would be rude to put down the phone while she is speaking.)

"He'll be right up," she says unnecessarily, stretching to catch a glimpse of herself in the beveled mirror. Patting her hair, she settles back into her chair; as much as she would like to let him in herself, it is more appropriate for Baxter to answer the door.

Francis Gardiner breezes in, bearing smiles and compliments and the scent of bay rum. His hair is freshly oiled and his mustache so meticulous it could have been painted on.

"Mrs. Warriner!" He kisses the air near my cheek, ignoring my outstretched hand. "I do hope your car is behaving itself these days."

"It's very well, thank you." Something about him rattles me: a disturbance, like the feeling in the air before an electrical storm.

Evans brings another cup and Irene nearly elbows her out of the way in order to pour.

It is embarrassing, watching her act no older than Pearl. I can't imagine my niece being this silly over a boy, and yet Irene, past seventy, is fluttering around him like a bride. Once she is certain he has everything he needs, she sits back and directs the conversation toward the clinic.

"Claire's been working very hard." She looks at me with approval for once. "It's not the project I would have chosen, perhaps, but it's a very worthy cause."

"Is *that* why you were on Washington Avenue?" he asks. "Do tell me more."

I fill him in on the migrants' camp and the loss of care caused by its closure. "Max Byrne and his friend, Dr. John Spencer, went out there every Friday evening for well over a year, and then it was broken up."

Gardiner nods. "I don't imagine the mayor wants something like that on the grounds of the museum, not after all the work that's been done to bring up the area."

"It's not his decision." I have thoughts about the way things are run in this city, but they are not proper conversation for Irene's lace-covered table. "And while there are other avenues—"

"The Salvation Army," he interrupts. "And I can think of several charitable organizations that have a doctor who occasionally treats the hobo class."

The hobo class! I begin to understand Harry's feelings a bit more. "Occasionally isn't good enough. I want to open a clinic that will remain in one place, where those who need it—men and women—know where to find it. Something that can't be shut down because it's inconvenient for powerful men."

Despite his irritating nature, Gardiner has several good suggestions about who to ask for funds, and offers to make a call to a banker friend about a line of credit. "If you think Harry will sign for it."

"Of course he will." I've put him on the board for that very reason. "Well, then that's settled."

We linger with Irene and Nora for an hour, and the conversation drifts to other topics. Gardiner is entertaining: sly and witty, knowing almost everyone despite having been out of the country for some years. When I stand to leave, he bounces up also. "No point in calling for the elevator twice," he says. "If you don't mind making a stop on the way down, Mrs. Warriner."

"Of course not." I button my jacket and tuck my purse under my arm. "Shall we?"

He does not ask the elevator operator to stop at the sixth floor, instead chatting all the way to the lobby and then following me through the glass doors and onto the sidewalk. "Allow me to walk you to your car."

"You already are." The autumn breeze tugs at my hat and I shove the hatpin further in, wincing as it grazes my scalp. "It's right there."

Max remains at the breakfast table after Harry leaves, nursing a cup of coffee. Mrs. Hedges has pointed out that the household's consumption has doubled since his arrival. "I like that man," she said, "but if I drank that much coffee I'd have the jitters 'til Tuesday."

"Something wrong?" I ask, pushing my empty cup away. One is enough for me, most days.

He shakes his head. "Just a slow start this morning."

"Not looking forward to going to the hospital?"

Another shake. "Not really. It's begun to feel pointless—our ideas don't seem to run on the same track anymore." He puffs out a sigh. "If they ever did."

I've known since the beginning that Max would put time in at the clinic, in the evenings or on weekends, the same as he does with his other outside work, but it strikes me now that having him there full time might be the answer to both our prayers. "Would you ever leave?" I ask. "For something else?"

He gets up and returns to the table with the silver coffee pot. I let him pour me another cup, then reach for the milk.

"It would depend," he says. "I feel useless enough in my current job. I'm not likely to find a paid position that would let me do the kind of work I want to do. But if I did—"

That's all the answer I need. "Are you sure?"

"What do you mean?" He stirs a little too enthusiastically, his spoon clinking sharply on my good china.

"I'd like you to work at the clinic."

Max blinks away the last of his sleepiness. "I was always going to dedicate some time to it, Claire. You needn't worry about that, whatever becomes of my situation at the hospital."

"Some time," I ask, "or *all* your time? I don't know if you realize the extent of my fundraising, Max. We can afford a full-time doctor, and I would love for it to be you. I can't think of anyone else who would do half the job you would. You're the reason I thought of doing it in the first place."

His face goes blank as he processes my words. "Run the clinic?"

"Yes." Excitement surges through me, and I want to grab his hand and drag him down to see the building, whose lease has now been signed. "Why do you think I've been asking you so many questions? Will you do it?"

"I don't know..." His voice trails off. An unusually troubled expression appears on his face.

"What is it?" I mentally go through my budget. "I don't know what the hospital is paying you, but if you're worried about the salary, we can afford at least three thousand. Possibly more."

He blinks. "It's not the money," he assures me. "And that's more than they're paying me—research isn't a profitable sideline to have gone into—but it's more than I'm worth since my heart's not in it."

I put my napkin aside. "Then what is it? You'd be absolutely perfect for the job, Max, you know you would."

"I'm already living in your house," he says quietly. "But to work for you, as well? I don't want to be a total charity case."

"It's not charity!" I want to shake him, but settle for clasping his arm. "I want this clinic to succeed, and I can't think of anyone better to make that happen." Giving him my best coaxing smile, I add, "I'll pay you enough that you can give us rent. Will that make you happy?"

"You're incorrigible." He laughs. "I suppose it will. I don't know what was wrong with me—I don't care what people think. At least not most of the time."

"You care what my sister thinks." That's what he means, but I don't understand how Ava has suddenly entered this conversation about his prospects.

"I do." Max rubs the back of his neck. "I'm pleased as punch she's finally warmed up, but I'm not sure how she'll take to me working for you."

If that's his worry, then his plans for her have gone further than I could have hoped. I decide to push a little. "With the kind of salary the clinic could pay, Max, you could think about your future. Don't you ever want to settle down, have children?"

My words fall into an uncomfortable silence. He finishes his coffee and puts the cup gently into the saucer. "Of course that's what I want," he says. "You see how I am with kids. But I can't have them, so it's easier not to think about it."

"You can't?" It is hard to be delicate when my curiosity is aflame.

"I can't." He pauses, then elaborates. "I was engaged once, but it ended. It's better to not disappoint anyone else."

Like the girl in the picture, whose name—Daisy—Harry had recalled after much questioning. She saw, I think, the promise of Max's profession, but also a young man so bowled over by her beauty that he would grant her anything. Is that why he is so adamantly anti-status, with his gauche clothing and refusal to live anywhere respectable, and his insistence on treating those that fashionable society prefers to forget?

What kind of woman would let Max go because of something he couldn't change? She was young; maybe she regretted her decision when not every man who came down the pike was like him.

"You should find a way to tell my sister that," I say carefully. "It might matter."

He looks confused. "Why?"

I hold back a sigh of impatience. "Because she's had *seven* children, Max. And she might be afraid that a new man—should she even *consider* marriage—might want his own."

Pearl

September 5, 1933

Today was the first day of school. I'm so tired I can't see straight, but I'm also really excited because it feels like the start of a whole new life.

When I got there this morning, I was so scared my knees knocked together. I'm glad my new dress is long enough to cover them. There were so many people there! Not only girls, but teachers, men and women, more than I thought one building could hold. I asked about the library but didn't have time to get there today. Maybe I'll save it as a treat for a bad day. I'm sure I'll have those, because I can already tell that while my grades in English and history got me here, I'm going to have to work really hard to catch up on arithmetic. It's like a foreign language.

Also, there are colored students in the school! I couldn't wait to tell Katie, but she didn't seem that impressed. I guess because she couldn't finish school, it doesn't matter. I think it's good, though. The world is full of a lot of different people, and we should meet as many of them as possible before we get too old and set in our ways.

Ava

George drifts in through the downstairs door. "Hi, Ma."

"You okay?" He is earlier than usual; I hope he hasn't worn out his welcome at the firehouse.

He shrugs and hands me a note. "The lieutenant sent me home."

I open it.

> *George is running a fever. I sent him off home before we all catch it. Gallagher.*

Wonderful. "How are you feeling?"

"A little tired." My son wouldn't admit to being tired, even if he was asleep on his feet. "And my head hurts like I've been out in the sun."

"Have you been out in the sun?" Where is Toby? Are they both sick?

"I went straight to the firehouse from school."

I put my hand on his forehead: hot. When I tilt his head up, his face looks puffy. "Go get undressed and hop in bed. I'll bring you up a cold drink in a few minutes."

He doesn't complain, which is worrisome, but clomps away, his feet heavy on the stairs. It's nearly four, so hopefully Toby will be along soon—whatever one of them has, the other is likely to get.

When I take George's drink upstairs, I find him already asleep, which decides it. I hate asking for help, but I don't want the boys to miss more time than necessary this early in the school year. Slipping out through the front door, I go down to Mr. Howe's office to borrow the telephone and dial Claire's number.

Katie answers, and I tell her my plight. "Mrs. Claire isn't here, but Dr. Max just came in. You want me to send him along?"

"Yes." I've scarcely seen him since the camp was broken up. "And if you run across Toby, send him home."

Max arrives within the hour, one hand on the shoulder of a glassy-eyed Toby. "I told Claire to keep the girls overnight, just in case," he says. "I picked this one up at the garage. Whatever George has, he's got it, too."

"Wonderful." I have two jobs that need to be finished by the weekend; I could use Pearl now, not tomorrow. "George is already in bed. Go on up, I'll be there in a few minutes."

He looks at the pile of satin in my lap. "Stay here. I'll come back down after I've examined them."

I nod and turn back to Lavinia Thorndyke's latest commission, which is to be worn at to son's engagement supper on Monday evening. I'm thankful I've made enough dresses for her by now that I can finish this without another fitting.

By the time the stairs squeak under Max's footsteps, the skirt has been basted to the bodice and it's on the dress form. Something isn't quite right, but I can't decide what it is, not yet. I'll work on Mrs. Norris's evening jacket until the answer comes. A least that can be run up on the machine, so I can manage that without Pearl's meticulous handwork.

"It's mumps." Max comes around the turn of the stairs. "I'll contact the school tomorrow, let them know they've probably got an outbreak on their hands."

"You're sure?" My heart sinks.

He leans against the door frame, watching me. "Where's Dan?"

"At work." I look at Grace in her basket by the sewing table. I can't risk her getting sick. "He'll have to take the baby to Claire's when he gets in."

"Have any of them had mumps?" he asks. "Dan, in particular?"

"No." Despite the conditions we'd lived in, they'd been healthy kids. "Why?"

A strange expression crosses his face. "He can't be around the boys until they're no longer contagious."

"Why?" I am not willing to lose my son's help during what will undoubtedly prove a trying period. "He's best at managing his brothers."

"Because," Max says, "I imagine you'd like to be a grandmother someday. Mumps can sterilize a young man."

"What about George and Toby, then?"

"They're safe." He rubs his chin. "The risk is higher if you've passed puberty."

I press my fingers to my forehead, then push away from the table. "Thank you for the warning. What about the girls?"

"You might want to let Thelma stay on with Claire," he suggests. "She's not at risk in the same way, but you don't need another sick little one. Pearl is old enough to help, and the boys will be on the mend if she picks it up next."

I don't want Pearl getting sick because I can't manage. "She stays with Claire, too," I tell him reluctantly. "I'll figure it out. I won't have her missing school, and she'll be a help with Grace—they'll have to put her on the bottle if I'm not around."

He nods, understanding. "Then I'll come by as often as I can. Leave a key under the flowerpot out front, that way I won't disturb you if you're resting."

The idea of Max Byrne letting himself into my house is disquieting, but his schedule is unpredictable, and I would rather accept his help than disrupt my daughter's education. "Thank you," I say. "I will."

19

Ava

The next three days pass in a blur of exhaustion—and another storm. Toby and George are feverish and achy more than sick, but their sore throats will not permit solid food and that makes them cranky. George's neck and throat swell to the point where his brother calls him pumpkin head, making him cry. At the end of my patience, I shout at both of them and escape downstairs to work on Mrs. Thorndyke's dress.

It is coming along at last, the difficulty with the bodice resolving as I stared at it, clutching a cup of tea, sometime in the middle of Thursday night. I picked out the basting stitches, made a small adjustment, and fell asleep with my head on the table until the boys woke me ringing the bell Claire had sent over.

Max comes and goes, sometimes while I am asleep. His notes, left on my sewing table, are brief and say things like, "The boys are improving. Back later," and "Take care of yourself."

Pearl

September 14, 1933

We're still at Aunt's, stuck inside because of the weather. I should go home and help Mama, but that would leave Katie with Thelma and Grace to look after, in addition to Teddy and I can't do that to her. Even with the rain, Aunt is in and out so much I can't be sure she wouldn't forget there was a baby in the house.

Anyway, it gives us time together. We've been going over my new math book, and Katie is quicker with numbers than I am, at least until I tried to explain algebra. She says if it's numbers it makes sense, but once there are letters involved, it goes all fuzzy. I kind of agree with her.

I told her I want to be a writer when I grow up. She says she doesn't have ambitions like that, but I think ambition is a good thing, because it makes us try. If we fail, we'll keep trying. Otherwise we just live and do the same things over and over and think that's life. That was how we lived in Scovill Run, all of us. Even Mama. But she's changed, and so have I.

Ava

The boys somehow sleep through the worst of the storm, though the windows rattle loudly enough to drown out the radio. Each time I look in on them, I check the hall window, but Dan's repair has held. I retreat to the workroom, stitching by the lamp until my eyes burn with tiredness.

It is after eleven when Max knocks at the door. He is soaked through, refusing to come in until he has shaken the worst of the water from his hair and sopped through all the kitchen towels I have on hand.

"I was just thinking how nice it was not to have to mop up water," I say, as a puddle forms around his feet. "You can't stay like that, but I don't have anything for you to change into."

He knuckles water from his eyes. "I had a landlady when I was in college," he says. "She had boys, and when they complained about getting wet, she always said"—and he breaks off and gives me an apologetic grin—"they were neither shit nor sugar, and not likely to melt."

I laugh in spite of myself. "I'll keep that in mind."

He removes his jacket and drapes it over the back of the chair. "Have you had any rest?"

"Some," I lie. "The boys are asleep."

"Bad evening?" He grabs a few sheets of the newspaper I use for patterns and places them on the chair before sitting. "You look tired."

I look awful is how I look. I've barely had time to wash and my hair hasn't seen pin curls in days. My blouse feels sticky, and my eyes are gritty from lack of sleep. "Thanks."

"You're doing the work of three people, how else should you look?" He crosses his legs, sets one foot to bouncing. "It's time for you to get some sleep. I'll sleep in Dan's room in case the boys need anything."

I am tired enough to allow him to stay, but I can't take his advice. "No sleep for me," I say. "I've got an order to finish."

"Whoever it is, they'll understand."

"Mrs. Thorndyke will *not* understand, not when she doesn't have her new dress for Monday."

"Oh." He nods. "She's a special case."

She's a special customer, that's what she is. Despite her demands and constant, mosquito-like whining, she keeps coming back. I have made more clothes for her than anyone but Claire and Prue Foster. "I should probably cancel the order and let her hate me. I'm going to make a mess of it anyway, as tired as I am."

"You will not cancel," he says firmly. "Vinnie will run that mouth all over town and hurt your business. Do you want me to put on a pot of coffee? I'll check on the boys and then come back down and keep you company while you work."

With his constant chat to keep my eyes open, I make enough progress in the next three hours to allow a break. "Upstairs," I say, levering myself out of the chair as my low back protests. "I need a soft surface."

He pours the last of the coffee and brings the mugs while I prop myself in the corner of the davenport and put my feet up. That lumpy old piece of furniture has never felt so comfortable, and if I was alone I would probably fall asleep right there. Instead, I continue our meandering conversation.

"How did you find out about the mumps making boys sterile?" I turn the mug in my hands. The coffee has long since grown cold, but I don't have the energy to warm it.

"Medical school."

"Of course."

His mouth quirks. "Not in the way you think," he says. "Are you tired?"

"Exhausted," I tell him. "But I don't think I can sleep."

Max takes a mouthful of coffee and makes a face. "Well, then, let me tell you a bedtime story about four medical students, some dirty postcards, and a microscope."

I do not hear more than a few words when suddenly he is tucking a blanket around me. "I must be losing my touch," he says. "Usually my stories keep people awake."

Closing my eyes again, I try to smile at him, but sleep takes me and I wake in the morning to bright sunlight and that damned bell, echoing down the stairs.

Claire

Between my schedule and the hours they spend at school, I hardly notice the children's presence. Max is gone most of the time. I hope nothing is wrong at the hospital. He promised he would look in on Ava and the boys each day, and I haven't seen him often enough to confirm that he has. In some respects, the last thing Ava needs is his presence—she has a natural immunity to charm—but if he doesn't stop by, she will be alone. I would go over myself, except there is never enough time, and I don't want to bring sickness home to Teddy.

Instead, I focus on my fundraising plans. The finances involved in the creation of the clinic flummox me. When I stare too long at the columns in the ledger, my brain hurts.

I keep scrupulous track of each contribution, the giver's name, and, in brackets, my opinion on whether or not they can be persuaded to donate further. Harry's generosity will take care of the rent, but we need funds to renovate and equip the building, and even afterward, it is going to take sustained effort to keep the clinic afloat. Salaries will need to be paid, medicines and supplies purchased. A general fund will need to be established for unexpected expenses.

What have I gotten myself into?

From watching Prue, I understand the organizational aspects and how these things work. There must be a board of directors—with myself, obviously and Harry, because I need a man's name on the bank account.

Max, because he'll be the one to run the clinic's day-to-day operations. Prue because she's always keen to add her name to another charitable endeavor. Marie or Stella? Both are willing volunteers, but I'm not sure if I can count on them long term, especially since Marie moved to the suburbs.

I need a treasurer. Prue refuses, saying rightly that her talents lie in arm-twisting and charm, depending on who she is speaking with. Stella blanches, using as her excuse that she can't even keep to her dress allowance. "I exceed it every month and Fred gets so cross!" Marie says the same, plus her relocation to Bryn Mawr makes her inconvenient.

If only Ava had time! But time is the one thing my sister does not have, even if she were willing to help out. I can think of no one better suited to teaching me how to stay on a budget.

There is one who would be willing to serve, but as soon as Francis Gardiner's name pops into my head, it is followed by Harry's angry voice, saying he doesn't even want me speaking to the man. But why should Harry get to control who I speak to? *He* won't do the job, he's already told me so. And Gardiner comes from a banking family; he was involved in the stock market before the Crash. Certainly he could manage some simple bookkeeping.

Before I come to my senses, I pick up the telephone and dial the number on his card. He answers on the third ring

"Claire, how lovely to hear from you." There is a smile in his voice. "You've made the sun come out!"

Since it's been raining for three days, any mention of sun is almost laughable, but when I look out the alcove in the direction of the front door, weak light spills across the polished hardwood floor.

"I wondered if you'd be free for lunch one day this week." It feels strangely like I'm asking him on a date. I add hastily, "I have a business proposition for you."

"I'm free today," he says, "if you haven't eaten."

"I haven't." I think guiltily of Mrs. Hedges's very nice consommé and salad.

"Then let me take you to the Viennese Tea Room." He is brimming with enthusiasm; it is difficult to believe he and Harry are of an age.

"I invited you," I point out. And although dining at home would be more discreet, there would also be more talk than if we were seen dining together in a restaurant. "It should be my treat."

He laughs. "We'll discuss it over lunch. Shall I pick you up?"

"No!" I don't want him coming to the house in case Katie makes an offhand comment in Harry's hearing. "I have to drop something at my sister's. I'll meet you at the Bellevue in an hour."

"I'll be waiting." Another smile through the telephone wires and he is gone, leaving me with a dead line and a most important question: what to wear?

When I pass through the glass archway into the Viennese Tea Room, no more than a few minutes late, I am breathless from rushing.

My choice, after trying on and discarding a half dozen outfits, is a recently-purchased suit of dark gray wool flecked with sapphire. Its fitted jacket has wide lapels, one of which I have ornamented with a diamante brooch. Underneath is a silk blouse in my favorite ice blue. The suit says I am a serious woman who wants to talk business, but the blouse, which brings out my eyes, adds a flirtatious element which Gardiner will no doubt appreciate.

He rises smoothly from the small, gilt-edged table and kisses me on both cheeks. I'm not certain how I feel about that, but his cologne distracts me and before I know it, I'm seated across from him with a menu in my hands.

I make a pretense of studying the card's offerings before putting it to one side. "I think I'm too distracted to eat."

"Nonsense." He takes a sip from his water glass and gestures for the waitress, who appears from behind a white-streaked green marble column. "Why do ladies always say they're not hungry?"

"I'm not, truly." I've been one of those ladies, though, among women. We monitor each other's plates like Pixie waiting for scraps, looking to see who will be the first to break and show hunger.

The waitress waits patiently for our order. I allow Gardiner to convince me that a plate of tea sandwiches will not be difficult to consume. It hardly seems sufficient for a male appetite, but he assures me it is plenty.

I wonder briefly if we are both ordering a second meal rather than admit we've already eaten.

Once the tea is delivered and poured out, I explain my predicament. "I wouldn't, of course, expect you to take on the duties of treasurer," I say, fully intending he do exactly that, "but if you could give me some guidance before I get in too deep, I would appreciate it."

His dark eyebrows raise, creasing his otherwise smooth forehead. "I'd be honored to help you, Claire, but I admit I'm surprised—Squint should have taken this on, and gladly."

"He offered," I say, "but this is my project, and I don't want to keep running to him for help." Instead I have run to a man my husband detests; thankfully, Gardiner does not look for logic when he can find flattery instead.

As the waitress places our sandwiches on the table, he gives me a winning smile. "Then let me be your knight in shining armor, as well as your treasurer. I don't suppose you brought the books with you?"

"Of course not." I look at the plate of sandwiches and select one. "Perhaps one day later this week we can go over them."

Gardiner raises his teacup in a salute. "I look forward to it."

Ava

When the door closes, I sigh with relief. The dress is gone, swaddled in tissue and folded into one of those white cardboard boxes Claire insists I use. They make a nice presentation, but I hate having to buy them.

The stair creaks. "It's okay," I call. "The coast is clear."

Max comes down the last few steps in his sock feet, his shoes in one hand and an errant soup bowl in the other. "I put the boys out back to keep them quiet," he says, rinsing the bowl in the sink. "I was more afraid she'd notice I was here."

It's the first time they've been downstairs in five days. That they are playing quietly tells me they're not completely back to normal, but Max assured me they're no longer contagious and simply have to take it easy.

I yawn and stretch. "She sent her driver in for it. Getting out of the car would involve making an effort."

"And our Vinnie doesn't do that." Max walks through the kitchen and looks around my work room. "Is it always this chaotic?"

Not having swept for two days, the floor is adrift with thread and bits of fabric. At one end of the cutting table, the scraps from Lavinia Thorndyke's dress are bundled carelessly with the newspaper pattern pieces I made for her alterations. The muslin gown hangs limply around the neck of my dress form, a sad comparison to the recently-departed gold satin number.

"Not usually," I tell him. "But if you mean it when you said the kids can come home today, I might save it for Pearl. I'm pretty sure Claire didn't make her do housework."

My kids can come home. I am thankful that work and the boys have kept me busy, because otherwise I would have been frantic with missing Grace, who has been weaned to the bottle, whether or not I am ready.

Max has been an enormous help, and not only with the boys. His inconsequential chat kept my mind focused when I was almost stupid with tiredness. When I cut an organza facing incorrectly and nearly cried, he pushed me gently into my seat and pinned the pattern to a fresh piece of fabric, making sure this time to cut on the fold. Watching him handle my scissors and pins, those exclusively feminine items, was oddly stirring.

"You have to let me pay you."

"No." He gives me that disarming smile and for some reason—most likely exhaustion—I see his fingers, curled around my shears. "I don't think so."

I take a breath, hold it so I don't lose my temper. "But you've done so much—stopping in at all hours, sleeping upstairs with the boys." I rub my temples. "What do I owe you? Don't go giving the bill to Claire."

He straightens his tie. "Would you consider a barter?"

"I suppose." What is he driving at? Does he want me to make him a shirt that isn't ugly?

"Have dinner with me." His smile is triumphant. "That's what I want."

"That's ridiculous." I've already told him I won't go out with him.

"It's what I want," he says again. "Or I could tot you up a bill that would make your head spin—two patients, multiple house calls, aspirin, soup, ice cream. Sewing. Completely out of bounds, that last bit." He smiles again. "Dinner?"

"Fine." Part of me is actually pleased to give in, but I'm damned if I'll let him know. "But nothing fancy."

"Do you think I can afford fancy?" His laugh is contagious. "When my patients refuse to pay for my services?"

Pearl

September 18, 1933

We're going home tomorrow when we get in from school. Dr. Max came in last night, in a jolly mood, and said the boys aren't catching anymore. I'm so glad. Nice as it is, I'm tired of Aunt's house. I've had nothing to do but play with Grace and Teddy and sneak books off her shelves.

Thelma would stay, I think, because Aunt lets her dance in the nursery when the babies are awake. She'll dance anywhere, it's like getting those braces off turned her into a whole different girl.

20

Ava

The dark green front door opens and my sister appears, ushering someone out. "You've been an enormous help," she trills. Her tone reminds me how she charmed every man in Scovill Run without looking seriously at any of them. "I don't know how I'd manage without you."

The man is facing her, so all I can see is an expensive camel hair coat and the gleam of brilliantined hair. "You'd find some other willing volunteer who finds you irresistible," he says. "Men like me are a dime a dozen."

"Well—" Seeing me, Claire breaks off. "Ava! This is Francis Gardiner, our treasurer."

I put out my hand. "Pleased to meet you."

"The pleasure is mine," he declares, taking my hand and keeping hold of it. "So you're the talented sister."

I assume Claire has been singing my praises again, and smile faintly, not liking his over-familiarity. "I'm a dressmaker, Mr. Gardiner. Nothing special about that."

"I doubt that. You are yet another member of a very special family." He drops my hand and turns back to Claire. "Until our next meeting."

"That's Friday, with the entire board," she says, waving him off. "With a luncheon afterward."

I follow her indoors, looking back over my shoulder. Francis Gardiner stands beside a small green roadster, watching us.

"So tell me about John Barrymore there," I say when the door shuts behind me. There is something disquieting about the way he looked at her. "He's a bit on the slick side."

"You sound like Harry!" Claire's cheeks are pink.

Does she actually believe this man's flattery? He's the type who would compliment a lamp for its shape if there were no women in his vicinity. "Doesn't Harry like him?"

"Not at all." She leads me into her sitting room, and since she leaves the door open, I know Katie has been warned to bring tea. "They were at school together and their opinions of each other...let's say they're not the highest."

I settle a satin cushion against my low back. "And you don't mind going against his wishes?"

"When did you ever listen to anyone?" Her bright laughter fills the room. "I'm doing what I need to for this clinic to work. Harry's busy, and Francis Gardiner seems to have all the time in the world at his disposal, so I'm taking advantage of it."

But is he taking advantage of her in some way? I often wonder, even now, if Claire realizes how lovely she is—that bit of cluelessness attracts the sort of man I believe Francis Gardiner to be. I decide to involve myself a bit more in my sister's pursuits. Claire might not listen to reason, but if I think this Gardiner is stepping out of line, knowing Harry dislikes him makes me feel better about voicing an opinion.

"Are the boys feeling better?" she asks, once tea has arrived.

"They're back to their normal selves," I tell her. "George told me this morning he was going to the firehouse after school."

"Maybe he's looking out another fireman for you." She smiles impishly.

I take a sip of tea, add a bit more sugar. "I think he knows better than to try."

Claire pushes a plate of cookies toward me. "What about a doctor?"

"No." She's obviously found out how much time Max spent at the house and it has gotten her hopes up again. I do not mention his invitation, or my acceptance. "Leave it, Claire."

"Well, if not Max," she says, her eyes brightening with challenge, "there are several very nice men I could introduce you to."

"Why do you want me to remarry so badly?" I ask. "We're doing fine."

"Wouldn't you like to do more than just get by?"

"Of course," I say truthfully, "but I won't get married again just for that."

"Then what about the children? Don't they deserve two parents?"

I narrow my eyes at her. "Harry's twenty years older than you. He'll likely die first, unless I kill you. Are you going to go out and find another man, to give Teddy a father?"

"No!" She flushes. "No man could replace Harry."

I put a hand on her arm. "Then why won't you understand that Daniel can't be replaced? If I choose to be with someone else, it has to be when I'm not trying to fit him into the hole Daniel left in our lives. Max—or any man—deserves more than that. And until then," I say, emphasizing each word, "I am managing."

Pearl

October 4, 1933

I like Girls High more than I ever thought I would. I hadn't made close friends at my old school, but at least I knew people. This was a school full of strangers, or so I thought.

And maybe it is, but they're enough like me that I'm not worried. Even the rich girls. Some will judge me for my clothes or where I grew up, but most of them just want a good education and don't pay that kind of attention. They want to go to college, these girls. They're good at math, and some of them spend their lunch hour in the chemistry room doing extra experiments.

I've made two friends now, Peggy and Hazel. Peggy is pretty, with dark hair and long legs, and Hazel is more like me, with brown hair and lots of freckles. Peggy wants to be a teacher and Hazel says she's going to be a lawyer like her father.

Peggy's mother is dead and she and her four brothers live with her aunt while her dad works somewhere out west. He sends money, but she hasn't seen him since she was ten.

Hazel is an only child. I wonder what that's like? She says her parents pay too much attention to her and she'd like to have brothers and sisters but her mother couldn't have any more kids after her.

I can't spend as much time with them as I'd like because they don't live close (Hazel is dropped off every day in a car like Uncle Harry's), but we eat lunch together every day and we've already decided when the school year is over, we're going to meet on the first Saturday of every month and go to a movie.

Claire

Jake comes and goes from my life, with no rhyme or reason to his appearances. He is working in one of Harry's factories, but he won't tell me where he's living. Now that the camp is gone, I assume it is indoors, as he is clean; the factory manager wouldn't likely allow him to work in the state he'd been in before.

Other than his maddening refusal to answer my questions, he is very nearly the sweet brother of my childhood. Yet there are times when there is a flicker—or more than a flicker, if I'm honest—of someone else. He'll say something unkind, then pass it off as a joke. It throws me, but then a moment later he grins and is my Jake again. I shrug it off, knowing he has had a far different life than mine.

When he shows up a few days after the Kimber children have gone home, I again offer him the guest room, and he again refuses. "It's enough that your husband's given me a job."

Is it? We have more than we need, and it hurts when he turns down my offers of help. "But where are you staying?"

"That doesn't concern you, Clairy. It's good enough for now."

"But we have plenty of space." I can't understand why he refuses to accept help.

"I won't live here." His big hands are on his widespread knees, his face angled away from me. "I won't let you turn me into someone else." His tone chills me through; it is so very nearly the same as when he told me, as children, that he was leaving because of Mama's insistence that he go back to the mines.

"I don't want you to be anything but my brother," I say. "That's all."

"That's what you think." He looks up, and his eyes are bleak. "But I see what it's done to Ava, trying to be what you need."

What has it done to her? And how does he know so much about our sister?

"Jake, I just want you to be happy. I'm so pleased you're here, in a place where you're safe and well cared for." Even before he reacts, I understand I have spoken to him like a child. "I don't mean it that way—but I missed you so much. You have to forgive me if I go a little overboard."

He heaves himself to his feet. "You can't turn me into someone different," he says with evident reluctance. "Not even with all your money. I'm a grown man. You need to realize that."

"I don't want anyone different." I wrap my arms around his middle and rest my head on his chest. "I just want my brother."

We are still in the kitchen—the only room where he is comfortable—when Ava and Dan come to pick up Thelma. Ava greets Jake like she's seen him last week, which makes me wonder if they have spoken frequently enough that his words about her should bear weight. She pours herself a cup of coffee and sits, heaving a sigh of relief, while Dan plops Grace in Teddy's chair.

"I was trying to persuade Jake to move in," I tell her, hoping she will agree with me.

He makes a face. "And I was telling her that I wouldn't."

"Don't push." It is Ava's standard response when she thinks I'm going too far with a good idea. *Don't push.* It is infuriating.

Dan clears his throat. He is nearly as silent as his father, and in the same way, people listen to him when he speaks. "Why don't you stay with us?"

"Where?" I ask. "You're already packed in like sardines in a can."

Ava looks between our brother and her son. "There really isn't room," she says reluctantly. "Otherwise..."

"He could have my room," Dan volunteers. "It's not much, but you wouldn't have to sleep with the boys."

I expect Jake to refuse, the way he's turned down all my invitations, but he appears to consider it. "I wouldn't want to put you out," he says finally.

"You're not." Dan drags his fingers through his black hair, looking very like his father. The expression on Ava's face tells me she sees it too.

"There's space in the boys' room, I just took the storage room because I get up early and I don't like to disturb them."

Jake nods. "I get up early, too. This job he got me, I have to catch an early trolley to get there."

So wherever he is living, it's not near the Kensington factory. It is gratifying to know, even though it no longer matters.

"Well, that's settled." Ava drains the last of her coffee. "When would you like to move in?"

Pearl

October 10, 1933

Mama said she was sorry about Dan's room, but he's the one who offered it to Uncle Jake. We can always use the money. I feel bad because Dan's earning full wages working for Mr. Howe, and yet he's back sleeping with the boys after having a space of his own, even if it is a cramped, made-over storage room.

He said not to worry, but I've noticed he stays out later now. Having Uncle Jake around gives Mama another grownup to talk to, which is nice, but he wakes Grace up almost every night with his crashing and banging. No one is perfect and we should be glad to have another relative, but I wish he was more considerate about the baby. He's not the one who has to get her back to sleep.

Even though Uncle Jake makes her laugh, Mama still looks sad. I know it's because she misses Daddy and maybe even our old life in Scovill Run, but I don't know how to help her, or even if I can. Sometimes I miss him so much I can't breathe, and it can only be worse for her.

Sewing and the boys' constant troubles are a distraction, but it's not enough. Aunt wants to get her involved in that clinic thing but Mama says she's got plenty to do without all that. And she does. But also I think Aunt is matchmaking. If I said I don't approve, she'd tell me I was being selfish, that Mama deserves to be happy. And maybe she does, but Aunt doesn't get to be the one to decide.

Ava

The inside of the car smells of my sister's perfume, and I instinctively look behind me.

"I made her get out," Max says. "It took some doing, though."

I sink back against the seat, putting my handbag on the floor by my feet. "Thank you."

He smiles over at me. "She's more excited about this outing than you are, by the looks of it."

"I agreed to have supper with you." I sigh. "And now somehow it's turned into a trip to New Jersey."

"A trip to the *shore*," he corrects. "But I've downgraded it to lunch, so you really don't have to worry about fancy now."

No, but I have to worry about what to say to him during the long drive ahead of us. How long does it take to get to the shore? I try not to show my excitement. I've always wanted to see the ocean, but organizing all of us to take the train would have been extravagant, and I could never just go on my own.

This—this *lunch* with Max Byrne—is somewhere in the middle. It's not as selfish as going by myself, but there are layers of meaning attached which I choose not to look too closely at, right now.

He's a good driver, not as distractible as Claire. If he sees a pretty hat or a pretty woman, he doesn't call my attention to it. Soon we are over the bridge and driving through small towns and densely packed pine woods. The air inside the car is chilly, but I have a sweater and it doesn't occur to me that I could ask him to turn on the heat.

Nearly two hours passes before Max turns to me and says, "Put your window down."

I look at him. The wind will spin my hair into a bird's nest. "Why? We'll be there soon enough, won't we?"

"Just do it. You can close it again if you want."

I crank the window down, and he does the same. The wind in my face is cool and moist, and even though I cannot yet see the ocean, I can smell it. I shoot a glance at Max and find him grinning like a boy.

"You can put it up now," he says. "I wanted you to smell it."

We drive through the town and park on Seaside Avenue, a short block from what Max calls the boardwalk. I have by now seen magazine photographs of the wooden sidewalk running along the sand, shops and restaurants on one side and the ocean on the other. This seems to be at the far end, where the boardwalk curves. I look at him for direction.

"This way." He nods to the right. "We can walk up toward the piers, so you can see what all the fuss is about."

I walk beside him, our footsteps sounding hollowly on the planks. Although the boardwalk is crowded with people, the air filled with music and the shouts of children from the varied amusements, my eyes keep turning toward the ocean.

"I thought it would be blue," I say. "But it's gray."

Max steers me smoothly toward the railing, where we lean to look across the sand. Even on this October Saturday, the beach is crowded with families, seeming not to care that the breeze is tilting their umbrellas and whipping their kites frenziedly skyward.

"It's changeable," he says. "Like you."

He wants me to respond, so I keep silent, watching the waves and the kids running in and out of them, shrieking and squealing. The fresh, salt air fills my lungs and expands my chest. I take a deep breath and it feels like the first breath I have taken in almost a year.

"Are we going to stand here all day?" I nudge him. "I thought you were going to feed me?"

His face brightens. "I thought you'd never ask! There's a café about a block along that I quite like—nothing fancy, I promise."

"You seem very familiar with this place." I sidestep a group of boys Toby and George's age, tearing along the boards.

"I haven't been here in a few years, but I used to take the train down regularly," he explains. "It was a cheap way to get away from the city after too many days at the hospital."

Why did we not take the train, if it's so cheap and easy? Borrowing Claire's car will give her an involvement in my business that I don't want to encourage. Now she will know precisely what time we return, and it will only add to the list of questions she will ask when she happens to drop in on me tomorrow.

The café is as promised, a narrow, unassuming place whose front windows look toward the ocean. We are seated in the back, at a small corner table. I would suspect it was by request but the place is crowded and we do not look like a couple who require a dark corner.

Max is entertaining, regaling me with stories of his years at medical school, pranks played on fellow students, and his previous trips—usually solo—to Atlantic City. I find it intriguing that someone so ebullient, so constantly involved with his fellow man, needs time alone. I listen, contributing little, and enjoy the meal in spite of myself, glad it is food I understand. But I have to wonder: while my hamburger and French-fried potatoes are delicious, they hardly seem worth such a long drive.

Afterward, we take to the boardwalk again, passing scores of tiny shops, some shuttered for the season, others which look as if their last good year had been before the Crash. Atlantic City is an odd mix of shabby prosperity and the sort of forced gaiety that caused the orchestra to play on the deck of the Titanic as it went down.

"Do you want to go in the water?" he asks.

I look down at my practical shoes, my ankle socks. "No," I say. "This is fine."

After a few more minutes, he suddenly takes my arm and leads me toward the car. "There's someplace else I want to show you."

"Where? I thought we were going to walk some more?"

He says nothing, and I'm still asking questions when he turns the car down a narrow road. We bump along the uneven surface, then stop. The car is surrounded on all sides by the same high grass that marked the dunes in Atlantic City.

"Where are we?" I ask suspiciously.

"A few miles south," he says. "Near Ventnor. It's quieter here. I thought you might want fewer people about."

I think that might be what *he* wants, but I open the car door anyway; it's easier than arguing with him, and I can handle myself. He's right; there is nothing here but the sound of the waves. The shrieking kids, their watchful, calling parents—all have disappeared. High above, a gull screams and is gone.

There is a path through the grass, invisible from the car. Max goes first, making a path, and I follow. After a moment I call to him, "Wait."

He turns back, sees me wrestling with my shoes and offers his shoulder to lean against. "Sand in your shoes sounds romantic," he says, "but it's not much fun."

He leads me across a narrow strip of sand to a stone jetty thrusting into the rough water. I look at him dubiously and he holds out a hand. I ignore him, tucking my shoes under my arm and hauling my skirt up so I can clearly see where I am walking.

When I bump into him, I realize we have reached the end of the jetty. I step to one side, and my knees almost buckle. There is nothing in front of me but the gray-blue ocean, all the way to the horizon. All the way to Europe, as far as I know. The water meets the sky in a hazy blue line.

We have left the sand behind. The water is on all sides, splashing and lapping at the jetty as the waves come in. Spray peppers my arms and face. The roar of the ocean, with no human noise to compete, fills my ears and I sink down abruptly on the rocks.

It is an insistent sound, leaving no room for anything else. Daniel and the kids disappear, scoured away by the waves. Claire, my financial worries—even Max, whose tweed shoulder is just in my periphery—none of them exist for the moment. There is only the ocean. I don't know how long we sit there; when I finally come back to myself, I am chilled through and his jacket is around my shoulders.

Embarrassingly, my cheeks are wet, and I try to wipe them without being noticed. When I think it is safe, I turn, and catch the expression on Max's face. He is as moonstruck as an adolescent boy, and my response is automatic, shattering the ocean's spell. "What are you looking at?"

"You," he says simply. "I'm thinking that I'd like to kiss you, except you'd probably use my head as a beach ball."

His honesty strikes a chord. Where else has all this been going, if not to this moment? "You could try," I say. "I'm not armed."

He shifts closer, his smile uncertain. "You could take me apart with words and your bare hands, and you know it," he says. "But I'm willing to risk it."

21

Pearl

October 14, 1933

Today Aunt took us to the movies. It was The Bowery, *plus Laurel and Hardy and a Mickey Mouse cartoon. We all enjoyed it, even Thelma, except she complained because there wasn't any dancing. Mama would have liked it, but she and Dr. Max went to Atlantic City to have lunch.*

I don't understand driving all that way to eat a meal when they could have had a perfectly nice time at the automat with us. They left after breakfast in Aunt's car and didn't get home until dark. He didn't come in, which was a shame, because I would have liked to have seen if he was as flustered as Mama.

For all that she says we need to knock off the matchmaking because she doesn't want to get married again, I think Dr. Max has other ideas.

Ava

It is barely daybreak when I make my way down the twisting stairs to light the stove. Dan will be up soon, and I need time to get myself together before facing his all-seeing gaze.

I'd dreamed of Daniel again, the second time this week. Maybe some-day I won't remember the exact color of his eyes, or the way his hair fell across his forehead, or his bony wrists, and then I will be free. But that day has not come, and likely never will, because every day I see his image in our son's face. It's not fair to either of us that Dan has grown to look more like his father every day. There is a looseness to my boy which Daniel never had, but in his height, his careful movements, the watchful intensity in his eyes, he is Daniel all over again.

It is a lot to bear. He would, I think, prefer not to so closely resemble the man he both loved and fought so fiercely, the same as I would prefer not to be reminded of my loss, especially early in the morning before my defenses are properly in place, but there is nothing either of us can do about it.

I sit with Grace and wait for the stove to heat, listening to the quiet. Mornings are different here. If I get up at five, I can have the birds, but traffic starts early—first the milkman, and then our landlord's workers are on the job by seven, repairing other houses on the street. But the distant thrum of the breaker does not run beneath these ordinary sounds, and the only siren is at the local fire station. When it wails, I don't automatically look for my loved ones.

As I put the coffee on to boil, I wonder what Daniel would have thought of this place. He'd never wanted to live in a city, never wanted to be beholden to Harry or anyone else for his existence—and yet our existence had always hung, precarious, on the whims of the Scovill Mining Company.

Here, at least, we have options. If my dressmaking business fell apart tomorrow, I could find other work cooking or cleaning or serving in a shop. Dan has his building job, but he is capable of learning a new trade, if he had to. The younger boys already see no limit to their futures.

What saved us, I have come to understand, is the ability to bend. In my stiffness, I very nearly broke and took my family down with me, but I learned in time. We cannot stop the buffeting winds, but it is our choice whether we lay down before them.

A thud echoes down the stairwell; Jake is up. No matter how often I tell him to be quiet in the morning, he makes more noise than all my kids combined. A few minutes later, remembering, he creeps down to the kitchen and takes the mug I hold out, curling his hands around it and drinking silently, leaning against the wall.

My brother is almost as uncommunicative as Daniel. He speaks more, but says less. I know nothing about how he lived during those long years we were apart, and he's not inclined to share; if it wasn't for the children, and my loyalty to a brother driven away by Mama's hardheadedness, I would have vetoed Dan's invitation.

Toby and George like Jake, because if he's around, and sober, he's willing to play ball with them in the street or head down to the Schuylkill to go fishing. I appreciate that; the younger boys are at an age where Daniel's lack is sorely felt. Harry dotes on them, but I don't think they understand the depth of his affection. Jake is not particularly affectionate, but he is *there*.

It is different with the girls. He calls Thelma doll baby and dances her around the living room, but rarely acknowledges her beyond that, and his interactions with Pearl are prickly. She is suspicious of strangers, for all that he is family, and I don't blame her.

Dan says little, but he is the one who offered up his room to an uncle he barely knew, and that shows enough family feeling for me.

"Jesus, these early mornings." Jake grunts, setting the mug aside. "See you tonight."

"Supper at six," I call after him, knowing he'll be late.

Dan is on his heels, and though he is no lover of mornings—no boy his age is—he kisses my cheek, drinks his coffee, and quickly puts his lunch together while I make him toast and an egg. "Later, Ma," he says. "Pearl's in the bathroom. She'll be down in a minute."

"Good." I sit back by the stove, hoping for a few more minutes of quiet before the rest of the kids join me. My thoughts are uneven, matching my emotions. We got back from the shore not long after suppertime, but I am not accustomed to driving, nor being in crowds, nor being alone with a man.

I had tried my best to convince myself we were simply going to lunch, but yesterday was more than a meal. He'd remembered, from more than a year ago, my disappointment at not seeing the ocean, and had taken me there. When the crowds on the Atlantic City beach kept me from enjoying myself, he'd given me my own private ocean.

And he'd kissed me. That is something else I've tried not to think about. Claire will tell me any day of the week that he likes me, but it was different seeing it plain on his face, the tentative touch of his fingertips on my jaw as he leaned in to kiss me.

He is only the second man I have ever kissed.

Is this another kind of bending—to experience these feelings with someone new, a man who, while kind and caring, is not my husband, and who will never make me boneless and stupid with desire? Not that I'd given him much opportunity, pulling away after a moment and asking whether we shouldn't get on the road before dark. Max regarded me with his usual good humor, a trace of my lipstick on his lower lip, and agreed it was time to go.

Claire

The voice on the other end of the line is not quite familiar. I recognize the faint southern accent in time to save myself from sounding stupid. "Helen, how are you?" I drop my gloves on the table and settle in for a chat. "How is Mr. Dawes?"

"I'm fine," she says. "Ty is, too, what little I see of him. The president keeps everyone busy."

"If half of what we read in the papers is true, I don't know when anyone in the capital gets any sleep."

Her rich laugh fills my ear. "I'm not sure either."

It's good to hear from her; once I got over my fear of responding to her letter, a healthy correspondence has sprung up between us. Helen's missives are full of Washington gossip and stories of the impressive people she's met in her position as the wife of one of President Roosevelt's inner circle. Far more interesting than anything contained in my own pale blue envelopes, which relate nothing more interesting than Teddy's latest accomplishments and my efforts to acquire funding for the clinic.

I try not to think of that, focusing instead on a smear on the glass of the framed print of the Eiffel Tower. I rub at it with my finger, then stop as Helen shares the reason for her unexpected call.

"I'm in town, Claire—in Philadelphia, if you'll believe it—and I must see you. My train doesn't leave until four."

"I'd love to," I say, my plans to meet Stella going by the wayside as easily as Teddy drops a toy for another, more interesting one. "Why didn't you tell me you were coming?"

"It was just supposed to be a flying meeting," she says. "But I finished early, and now I'm all yours. What if we meet at one, at the tearoom at the Bellevue? I remember the darling little sandwiches from the last time I was there."

I check my narrow gold watch. Half past eleven: I'll have time to cancel with Stella and change into something nicer. I can't have lunch with Helen Dawes wearing an ordinary day dress. "I'll meet you at one," I tell her. "I'm looking forward to it."

"Me too, darling. I want to hear all about your clinic so I can tell Mrs. Roosevelt."

We stay at the lunch table until Helen's fear of missing her train makes us dash to the car. I drive full speed down Broad Street to the station and pull to the curb before the doors. Helen slides out, adjusting her fur collar her fur coat up around her ears. "This was divine, Claire. I'm so glad you were available."

"So am I." I lean over and we clasp hands before she sprints inside. Closing the door, I maneuver into the busy Market Street traffic and head for home, then remember that there is a donation of linens waiting for me at Snellenburg's. If I'm quick about it, I'll be home before Harry—the last thing I want, after such a nice day, is for him to chide me for being late for dinner.

Ava

"There's a new man at the garage," Toby announces at supper. "He's going to teach me how to change a tire."

I shut my eyes for a moment, imagining my nine-year-old son squashed under an automobile. I worry about the boys—the younger ones, mostly, though Dan comes in for his share of concern. Toby and George are so opaque it's difficult to find a way in. They are all appetite and noise and dirty clothes; it's hard to remember they have thoughts and feelings they don't share with the rest of the family, and possibly not even with each other. Over and over, I vow to spend more time with them, and then a dress order comes in, or they don't come home until their food is on the table, and any conversation is pushed aside for a later date. I'm afraid one day I'll look up from my sewing to discover they are men, and already gone from my life. If Toby is excited about becoming a mechanic, I can't pour cold water on it.

"Well, that's fine, isn't it? You're learning a lot there."

"Yep." He grins at me, displaying a gap where he's lost another tooth—when? "And I thought maybe he could come to supper."

Pearl snatches up his empty plate and stacks it with the rest. "Don't start that again."

"What?" His lip comes out.

"You know what." She glowers at him from the sink. "The same business George tried with that fireman."

Is that what this is about? George seems to have backed off, and I thought Toby was entirely too involved in his own world to follow his brother's example. "You don't need to find me a husband," I say with exasperation. "If that's what you're doing."

"But Mama..." Toby bites his lip and looks down.

"Aren't we doing okay?" I ask. "Is there something you need?"

Around the table, the kids all shake their heads. "We thought you'd like one," Dan says. "You're lonesome."

"How can I be lonesome in this madhouse?" I look around. "I've got all of you."

"It's not the same," Pearl says. "You had all of us before, plus Daddy." She glances again at Toby. "Not that you should rush into anything."

While she puts the dishes to soak, I mull over how to handle their interference. I don't want to discourage them from talking to me, but the last thing I need is more matchmaking. Claire is more than enough in that department, and I'm trying hard not to think about Max. "Come on," I say. "Let's get this out in the open."

They troop up the steps behind me, waiting as I sink down on the davenport and then crowding in around me. The old piece of furniture creaks under our combined weight, and Dan gets up and leans over the back, his hands on my shoulders. It's the same pose Daniel would have assumed.

"Your daddy isn't replaceable." I tell them. "This family doesn't need two parents, not so long as I'm earning enough to keep us afloat. I'm not getting married again for financial assistance."

Pearl takes my hand. "That's good, Mama."

"Dad can't be replaced," Dan says over my shoulder. "But it might be nice for you to have another adult in the house."

"I have your aunt and uncle, if I need grownup conversation. And Uncle Jake, when he's around." I look over at the boys. "By the way, would one of you rub some powder into the board outside his door? That squeak is driving me crazy." Dan avoided it when he got up, but Jake doesn't have the same awareness and every day it sounds like he's deliberately tap-dancing on that creaky board.

Undeterred by my attempt at distraction, George sighs heavily. "I wanted you to marry Lieutenant Gallagher."

"And I wanted Dr. Max," Thelma responds pertly. "It sounds like we're not getting either of them."

"No, you're not." I pull George in against me, just to feel him struggle. "So don't get their hopes up."

"See, Thelma," Pearl says. "I told you so."

"I thought you wanted me to like Dr. Max?" I look at her keenly.

"Not that much!"

I sigh, remembering what it was like to be her age, and let the matter drop.

She takes the little boys downstairs to help with the dishes, and Thelma follows. Dan vaults over the back of the davenport and plops down beside me. The springs twang alarmingly. "Sorry if we pushed, Ma."

"You mean well." I can forgive him anything. "But I'm not ready. I'm not sure I ever will be." Since it's the two of us, I add something else that is as clear to me as the irreplaceability of my husband. "And any man I married would want kids. I'm not having any more babies."

Dan slides down further, propping his feet on the fender. "Dr. Max can't have them."

"What?"

He tilts his head my way. "He can't have them. He had the mumps when he was in medical school. That's why he wanted me out of the house when George and Toby got sick."

I remember Max's insistence that Dan stay with my sister, and a story I missed by falling asleep. Was that what he had intended to tell me? It isn't something I can ask—he told Dan in confidence, or at least with the expectation that the information wouldn't be repeated.

But it removes one more barrier between me and Max Byrne, and I'm not sure I like that at all.

22

Ava

At the beginning of November, on a chill day when snow sifts from a pale gray sky, an envelope drops through the mail slot. I pick it up, turning it over curiously. We rarely get mail.

"It's from Father Dennis," I tell the kids, and they crowd around.

The priest in Scovill Run had been like a member of our family. He'd come to town not long before my mother had arrived from Ireland to find her husband dead and buried. Father Dennis buried many more family members—my brother; my father; my mother. My husband. He is a good man, but there is pain attached to his memory. I hesitate to find out what he has to say.

But the kids have closed in, asking for news of their old home and so I open the envelope, scan the few lines written on what appears to be a blank page torn from a book.

"He's well," I say, "and sends his regards, as does Father Anton. Trudy is still at the rectory." I read the last line and stop, biting my lip. "And he thought we should know, there's been a collection." I swallow. "A stone is being raised in the cemetery on the anniversary."

The anniversary of Daniel's death, which I can't bring myself to think about, much less say. The anniversary of nearly losing my eldest son. Of the death and maiming of men and boys as familiar to me as my own family.

"I wish we could be there." Pearl is perched on the arm of the davenport, wearing her good blue school skirt. Her sandy hair falls forward, obscuring her face.

"Do you?" I can't think of anywhere I'd less like to be. The idea of a public celebration of private grief makes me want to curl into a ball.

She slides off. "I don't want to go back for good," she says, "but it's like visiting Granny's grave. I miss that, too."

I had never seen my mother's grave after it was filled in, nor the pink granite stone Claire and Harry bought to mark it. I do not want to see another monument to mass death with my husband's name on it; there were already several such stones in the St. Stanislaus cemetery, including a memorial to the collapse that killed my father. I avoided them all.

"I wouldn't mind going, either." Dan's voice is troubled; his relationship with his father had just been mended before they were trapped together underground.

"Well, we can't afford it," I say flatly, departing from my years-long script of 'we don't need.' I certainly don't need to go, but we couldn't afford the fares anyway and I will not ask Claire for money to attend a memorial service when the one we attended before we left town was sufficient, and painful enough.

Pearl

November 4, 1933

Father Dennis wrote that they're putting up a stone at St. Stan's for Daddy and the others. I made the mistake of saying I'd like to go and Mama's face was a picture. We'll never agree on cemeteries. I used to visit Granny on my way home from school and tell her about my day and how we were all doing. It was a comfort.

A memorial stone wouldn't be as personal, and Daddy's not underneath it anyway because the company wouldn't bring them out. But I'd like to be there. Plus I could see Father Dennis and Mrs. Metzger.

Mama put the letter away and dragged the boys upstairs to get cleaned up. Toby looks like he has potatoes in his ears again. Dan took the letter down and looked at it, then put it back. He hasn't said anything but I know what he looks like when he's thinking.

Claire

We receive a letter from the priest from Scovill Run, informing us they've somehow raised money for a monument to the men who died last year, and inviting us to attend the service. I consider asking Ava if she'd like to go, but decide not to volunteer to get my head bitten off. No doubt Father Dennis has informed her. If she wants to go, she'll tell me.

I mention it to Harry over breakfast. He is not surprised by the news. "I knew they were doing it," he says, when I ask. "I sent them a check several months ago when the old priest wrote to me."

"He didn't write to me." I pleat my napkin between my fingers, feeling obscurely offended that Father Dennis, who makes me uncomfortable because of his ties to my past, has contacted my husband without my knowledge.

"You're not the money man." His newspaper crackles as he turns the page. "He knows who to ask for these things."

Soon after, Harry leaves for work and I go up to play with Teddy before heading out, wondering how much he donated to the memorial. I have no clear idea how much money we have—Harry has never refused me anything, but then, until the clinic, my wants have always been relatively in line with those of a normal wife.

That he is not only helping to fund the clinic, but also to memorialize my sister's husband fills me with an almost uncomfortable sense of obligation. Harry is self-contained, always, but there is more to him than meets the eye. His voice rarely rises above conversational levels, and I have never, in all our years together, heard him shout. His suits of gray or navy pinstripe are conservative, especially when contrasted with Max's garish wardrobe. His hair and nails always look freshly trimmed, though I rarely know when he has been to the barber.

He gives little away. I'm not sure if it's by choice, because of his business, or if it's all he knows; when we first married, I waited for passionate declarations of love, but they never came. He loves me—that is clear, after all these years—but his upbringing stifled any capacity for spontaneous outbursts.

I am emotional enough for the two of us, but I have learned to sit on my feelings and present a smooth and pleasing surface to the world. Harry is right; it does make things easier.

Pearl

November 7, 1933

Ever since we got here, Dan's been good, not sneaking off and riding the trains, but today he told Mr. Howe that he wanted to go to the memorial and was given Friday and Monday off so he can travel back to Scovill Run. It's funny, he never went to church. He still doesn't. But he says he needs to be there for this. I can't wait to see how he breaks the news to Mama. She's so soft on him, she won't get mad the way she would if I insisted on going.

I wish I could go places with no one looking at me. Dan said sometimes when he hopped trains there were girls, but not many and they usually dressed like boys to keep themselves safe. I would do that, but he'd never take me. He acts grown up, but Mama still scares him.

Ava

Dan came in from work today, bolted upstairs, and returned within minutes wearing his oldest clothes and carrying a bulky sack over his shoulder. "I'll be back Sunday night or Monday," he said briefly, helping himself to a slab of bread once he'd checked to see there was enough. The bread disappeared into the sack, along with two apples.

"Where are you going? Does Mr. Howe have you working away?"

He stopped, staring at me as if considering what to say. "No," he said finally. "I'm just going somewhere."

He was gone before I could challenge him further, and as I tried to follow, George and Toby streamed in through the door, blocking my path.

"He's hopping a train," Pearl says quietly, beneath the boys' clangor.

"Why?" I thought those days were over, now he has a job, but a boy his age still wants adventure. "What about work tomorrow?"

"He got time off." Pearl is well informed about her brother's plans. "He won't get in trouble."

I shake my head and drop back into my chair. I hate thinking about him jumping on and off trains, dealing with the kind of men who ride them. I have nothing against those men on principle, only that they might view my son as a target for the kind of casual brutality which exists among men everywhere.

"Don't worry, Mama," she says. "And anyway, Uncle Jake's with him."

Has my household lost its mind? "Why?"

She shrugs. "That's what Dan wanted to know when he volunteered to go with him. Why?"

"Where are they going?" It was the one question I hadn't thought to ask.

"Oh, Mama." Pearl's pale eyes fill with tears. "Don't you know? They went home."

Over the next three days, I cook and sew and go to the store and eat supper at Claire's house, but a part of me is always absent, wondering how my son is managing. Did they get on the right train? Have they made it safely to Scovill Run? Were they in time for the service?

How surprised Father Dennis will be to see Dan after a year and Jake after twenty. He'll have some stern words for my brother, no doubt, about his desertion of Mama and the rest of us, but he'll end by taking them to the rectory, where Trudy will feed them and give them a bed.

I walk the unpaved roads in my mind, feel the vibration of the breaker through the soles of my shoes, hear its constant rumble. See the black dust embedded in every crack and crevice. Is the mine even operating these days? They were cutting shifts and letting men go even before we left. If he and the others had been working, instead of bootlegging, with no safety inspections and insufficient equipment, maybe my husband would be alive instead of under that damned mountain.

I was right to stay home. Even thinking about it makes my chest tight. When Thelma asks me a question, my voice catches in my throat as if I've inhaled the filthy air of home.

Dan will tell us about it, and that will be enough. I can't go back.

Claire

November 13, 1933

Dear Mrs. Roosevelt,

You may not remember me, but we were introduced by my friend Helen Dawes last March at the inaugural tea and again at Secretary Perkins's luncheon the next day.

You were kind enough to tell me I should write to you when I found a worthwhile project in Philadelphia. It has taken some time, both to determine what was needed and then how to go about achieving it, but I would like to tell you about my plan for the Philadelphia Clinic for the Deserving Poor.

Until this past summer, there was an encampment for homeless and migrant men near the Philadelphia Art Museum. When that camp was broken up, a doctor friend made clear to me how great a need there was for medical treatment that did not shame those who cannot afford private physicians and might only seek hospital care as a last resort for injuries and ailments which could have been readily cured if they had sought treatment sooner.

I have obtained a lease on a building in South Philadelphia, employed one full-time doctor and have two more who will volunteer their services. Currently, I am searching for nurses who come from the same communities as our patients so they will feel more at ease.

It has been an all-consuming project, but the clinic is scheduled to open in mid-March. I want to thank you again for the inspiration you provided, without which I might never have attempted such an undertaking. If you are ever in the Philadelphia area, I would be honored to give you a tour.

"Ma'am?" Katie's soft voice interrupts me. "They're all here. I've poured tea, but I'll hold off on bringing anything else out until you call."

"Thank you." I re-read my words, then put the letter aside. Who am I to think Eleanor Roosevelt would even be interested in the clinic? She has so many worthwhile causes to choose from, and people from all over the country clamoring for her attention. What makes me special?

Every seat at the dining table is filled, mostly by women, all dedicated to bringing the dream of the clinic to fruition. Max can't be with us; the hospital has a claim on his time for a bit longer. But Francis Gardiner is here, seated in the middle on the right side, his back to the buffet, with Stella Good on one side and Prue on the other. Marie is across from them, and there are three other young women, recently added to the board as secretary and fund-raising mercenaries under Prue's command.

"Thank you all for coming." It strikes me again: all this is down to me, my idea. My doing. As easily as I came up with it, it could all vanish, if we don't get it right. I take a deep breath. "Shall we begin?"

Ava

Late Monday afternoon, Jake breezes in, full of tales of their travels, mimicking Father Dennis, and telling us how the town has deteriorated since he left.

"Ran away," I interject.

"Whatever." His eyes crinkle, refusing to accept criticism. "The mine's still going, somehow. You couldn't get me back there if you held a gun to my head."

"Me either." Dan takes a deep swallow of tea. He has been quiet since their return. Not sad, exactly, but there is something bruised about him; going home wasn't as easy as he thought it would be. "I took some pictures, Ma. I'll drop the film off this week."

I'm not sure I want to see them.

Jake goes outside with Toby and George, and the girls run upstairs to change—they had just returned from Thelma's dance lesson when

Jake and Dan arrived. My son stays at the table, turning his mug in his long-fingered hands, so like Daniel it unnerves me.

"How was it?"

"Hard," he says. "Seeing his name on the stone."

"You took a picture?"

My son raises his eyes to mine. "Someday Gracie will need to know where she came from."

His use of the name I wanted to give my daughter, which he and the others vetoed, catches me unawares. "You're stronger than I am," I tell him. "I couldn't have done it."

Dan gets up, pours more tea, bounces between stove and table with his father's nervous energy. "Seeing it...it brought it back. It should have been me."

Pushing him into a chair, I say, "I loved your father, more than I have words to tell you, but you are my son." My eyes burn with tears I refuse to shed. "I've coped with losing him. I couldn't have survived losing you."

"But you've got other kids." His expression is bleak. "Dad could have done more for you all than I have."

"Like what?" I take his hands. "If you'd been killed, nothing would have changed. I hate that I didn't push him harder to leave. It wasn't his fault—it was all we knew, and change was more frightening than the risk of what could happen." I swallow hard, push down on a truth I don't often acknowledge. "He would never have left, and your brothers would have grown up and gone into the mine or started bootlegging themselves. Your sisters would have no education. Grace"— I break off, thinking how it had been after Teddy's birth—"she might not have survived."

And I would have had one more grave to avoid: my son's, which I could not have borne.

I swore I would never let my kids know about these fears. I don't want Dan to think badly of his father, but I also don't want him to make the same mistakes. We're living in the change Daniel and I were afraid of, and while it is frightening, what's ahead is so much better.

"Never, ever wish you'd been in his place." My voice wobbles alarmingly. "I couldn't bear it."

My son pulls me sideways and rests my head on his shoulder. "I didn't know, Ma. Don't cry. I don't know what to do when you cry."

This makes me laugh. "Get used to it," I say, wiping my eyes with my sleeve. "Women cry. And it's not always because we're sad. Sometimes we're angry, and we don't know how else to show it. I've spent my life angry. It's finally fading and I don't know what to do with the space where it lived. I feel empty—losing your dad and my anger at the same time makes me wonder who I am now."

It is strange talking to my son as another adult, but he has always been there for me, and this is a conversation I am not comfortable having with Pearl, and would never try to have with Claire.

"You filled a lot of it with work." He pats my head and sits me upright, pushing my mug toward me. "And what about Dr. Max?"

"What about him?"

His smile is one-sided. "He'd like to take Dad's place."

A hot wire of the old anger runs up my spine. "He's a friend," I say shortly. "And even if it ever became something more, he'd never take your father's place."

"You can't be alone forever."

I sigh. "When am I ever alone?"

23

Claire

The meeting runs late. When Harry comes in, Max on his heels, everyone is in the front hall, preparing to depart. Harry's manners are flawless as he greets the women, but after they dash to their waiting cars, he focuses on the man hovering possessively at my shoulder. "Gardiner."

"Warriner." With a twitch of his lips, he takes up his hat and is gone before further pleasantries can be neglected.

"Darling." I stand on tiptoe to kiss his cold cheek. "How was your day?"

"Better before I saw him." Turning away, he takes off his hat and coat. "I thought I told you I didn't like him?"

"You did. But he's been an enormous help." My stubborn streak rises. "I don't understand what your problem is with Francis Gardiner. Every time I mention his name, you get that look on your face."

He turns away, but not before I've seen quite a different expression. "What is it?"

"I had lunch with Mother today," he says. "She all but told me you're having an affair with him."

All the blood drains from my head, leaving me dizzy. "You don't believe her, do you?" Another thought. "She's the one who introduced us."

Harry pauses in the living room doorway. "It would be so easy," he says. "You're never here. Even when you're here, your mind is elsewhere, and whenever I ask how the clinic is going, it's all him him him."

The dizziness turns to numbness. I can't feel my fingers. "Because he's involved." I reach for the banister, rather than his arm. It seems wrong, right now, if he is thinking I could possibly be sleeping with Francis Gardiner. "I talk about Max all the time, too—you don't think I'm up to anything with him."

One brow raises. "Max doesn't look at anyone but Ava. And you must know, Wolf Gardiner doesn't care if the clinic succeeds or not. He's in this for reasons of his own."

The effects of our disagreement linger through dinner, and show no signs of fading over drinks afterward. Eventually Max makes a tactful exit, and before his door closes upstairs, Harry raises the topic again.

"I don't know why you're being so difficult," I protest. Francis Gardiner has been nothing but useful, no matter my husband's personal feelings. "And if Irene actually insinuated that, she's wrong."

"You have to cut him loose." He places his glass on the mantel. "That's all I'm going to say, Claire."

"But—"

He is gone before I can finish, his footsteps thudding on the carpeted stairs.

I look in on Teddy—snoring in his bed—and walk tentatively into our room. Harry is standing at the window, ready for bed. His suit hangs neatly on its valet, while his watch, cufflinks, and coins are on the dresser. Even angry, he is neat.

"Nothing is going on with Francis Gardiner." I sit before the mirror and unscrew my earrings.

He drops both hands on my shoulders, lightly. "I know. But I can't stand the man, Claire. And if I overreacted because I wasn't expecting to see him in my house, I'm sorry. I won't have him here again."

"What am I supposed to do?" I slip from beneath his hands, picking up my brush and drawing it roughly through my hair. "He's the treasurer. He's involved in every aspect of the clinic. I can't get rid of him."

Harry takes a breath, holds it while he gets his temper under control. "If you need assistance with financial matters, you have only to ask."

"When?" I cock my head. "While you're reading the paper in the morning? While you're at the office? Maybe during dinner?" I cover his hand with mine. "I'm not complaining, Harry, I'm simply pointing out we have limited time together and I hate to waste it talking about money. How could I extract him, anyway—even saying I wanted to?"

"Let me offer an alternative way of thinking, Claire. You have the same connections as Wolf Gardiner, and they're more honorable. Do the work yourself." He meets my gaze in the mirror. "Don't attach his name to something that is so important to you. You'll end up disappointed."

"If he's so bad, why did your mother involve him?" I turn from the dressing table, the brush hanging loose in my fingers. "Especially if she thinks I'm capable of being unfaithful. She's the one who more or less insisted I take him on."

He shakes his head wearily and lowers himself to the mattress. "Mother is a law unto herself. I don't know what she has in mind, but I doubt it's your best interests."

I remember his words when Irene calls the next day asking if I have time to meet her at Snellenburg's to buy a gift for her maid's upcoming birthday.

"I'm sorry, I'm already tied up." Why should she need help buying a birthday present for Evans? Does she think of me as the same class as that pathetically loyal woman? I doubt it—she probably considers Evans to be a step up on the social ladder.

"Oh, what a shame." She almost sounds sincere. "I thought perhaps since you have such a close relationship with that Katie, you would be able to help."

I cast a quick glaze around the hall, lowering my voice just in case. "I'm embarrassed to say I've never given her a gift."

"You're employing her entire family. That's gift enough." Irene hesitates. "I'm sorry you can't join us, but another day."

"Us?" Has she roped Aunt Nora into this expedition?

"Francis Gardiner is escorting me." She giggles. "It was he who suggested you come along. He'll be so disappointed."

"He's a grown man," I say, thinking again of Harry's words—and Irene's ugly insinuation. "I'm sure he'll get over it."

Ava

It is after Thanksgiving before I decide what to do about Dan's film. After Betty Nichols's fitting is done and she skips off to her next appointment, I take off my smock and freshen my lipstick. It's a cold day but there's no wind; if I wrap Grace well, the walk to Market Street will do us both good.

Woolworths is crowded and I am reminded, when shoppers rush by with rolls of brightly-colored wrapping paper, how close we are to Christmas. I refuse to think about that right now. I march up to the counter in the camera department and present Dan's receipt. Two minutes later, I exchange money for a fat envelope.

"Aren't you going to open them?" The counter girl blows lipsticked kisses at my baby. "Most people can't wait to look."

I shake my head. "I'm picking them up for my son." It's not exactly a lie. Whatever those photos contain, I don't trust myself to look at them in public.

The kids straggle in from school and I hand Grace off to Toby. "Keep her alive until Pearl gets back," I say over his objections. "I have a headache and I'm going to take a bath."

It's not my usual time, but the boys won't think about that. Pearl will start supper when she gets in, while I see what my past has to offer. As the tub fills, I sit on the toilet lid in my slip and open the packet. Count the stiff edges. There are twelve—a dozen opportunities for pain. Steam fills the tiny bathroom. Despite my lack of clothing, I crack the casement window over the backyard and a thin wedge of frosty air drifts over my lap.

The first photo causes an instinctive flinch. The breaker, skeletal and black against a pale November sky. Next, the muddy crossroads at the center of town, with St Stanislaus off to the right. The church doors are open, and two priests guard the entry. In spite of myself, a smile tugs at my lips.

It fades quickly as I thumb past the next three photos: the headstones of my father, mother, and youngest brother, Teddy.

Dan must have started walking then. The sixth photo is of a long row of shabby double houses ranged on either side of an unpaved road. Ours is at the far end. I strain to make out the details, but I don't have to. The next photo is taken straight on, showing the sagging porch rail and the front window, still cracked. A bare patch on the roof needs shingling; whoever lives there now has a bucket in the front bedroom.

I am hunched over, bent almost double in an effort to protect myself. I straighten and turn over the next picture, sucking in a breath to see my friend Trudy between Fathers Dennis and Anton, her grandchildren posed in front of them. She looks tired but happy, with a bit more flesh on her bones than when I'd last seen her. Something good, anyway.

My guard down, the next photo strikes like a blow. An upright slab of granite stands alone in the church cemetery. The photo was taken from a distance, but I am certain, before I look, that the next one will be close enough to read the names. Not only Daniel's, but men I've known all my life from school and church, their brothers and sons.

I am crying now without realizing, fat tears dripping off my chin and wetting the front of my slip. The water thunders into the tub, drowning out all sound, and I let go, sobbing out the pain and worry and grief of the last months.

When my tears subside, I force myself to look at the next photo. It should be the most distressing—taken from outside the fence, it shows Father Dennis standing in front of the monument. The frame is filled with black-clad mourners, families and friends of those men sacrificed to the greed of the coal company. Somehow it doesn't hurt as badly to see the monument on its own.

I could have gone to the service. Claire would have lent me the money. Even now, looking at the photo, I know I wouldn't have survived it. People think I'm strong, and maybe I am, but often it's because I avoid the things that will undo me.

One left. I turn it over, not knowing what to expect. It is a photograph of our house on Ringgold Place, Grace's coach parked out front, light pouring from the front windows.

"He's a good one," I murmur to my dead husband. Dan has brought me full circle, showing plainly that the past is past and this—now—is home. I put the photos carefully into the envelope and set them away from the tub. Dropping my slip and underclothes onto the rag rug, I slide into the hot, fragrant water, and close my eyes.

Claire

Despite Harry's ultimatum, I cannot bring myself to cut ties with Francis Gardiner. That means I must find another venue for our meetings, to avoid any chance of another encounter between them. Prue volunteers her house, but I don't want to rely on any of my girlfriends, nor do I want to meet in a restaurant—that would make it look like I *couldn't* do it at home. Finally, I ask Irene if we can hold the next meeting at her apartment. I was curious how she would respond, after what she'd said to Harry, but she is more than happy to offer up her dining room, along with Mrs. Fell's lace cookies.

"It will be more convenient for Mr. Gardiner," I say, trying to provoke her, as Baxter takes my things. "Having the meeting here."

"It will." A delicate pause. "He visits quite often."

She wears mauve crepe with lace at the neck, an outfit more appropriate to a garden party than a December afternoon. While she told Harry that I was interested in Francis Gardiner, I'm almost certain if he arched one of those black eyebrows, she would be on him like a shot. The idea makes me shudder.

"Let's get you some tea, dear," she says, misinterpreting. "It's quite nippy out there. I do hope you didn't walk this time."

"No, I drove." I follow her to the living room, where we will wait for the others. "Is Aunt Nora here?"

Irene seats herself and waves me toward the sofa. "Not at the moment." She rings for tea. "But she'll be back before the meeting is over, I'm sure."

Harry's aunt is one of the few people in his family I've ever warmed to, and it irks me that she always seems to be gone when I stop in, as if Irene shoves her out of the way.

"So Mr. Gardiner is a frequent visitor." I wait for Evans to clear the door before I look up at Irene. "Interesting, as Harry seems to think I'm the one...entertaining him."

Her cheeks redden beneath their precise spots of rouge. "Harry's always been the jealous type," she says. "I told him he was overreacting, but you know how men are."

"Hmm." My husband shows jealousy as frequently as he overreacts. "Well, *however* he got the notion, I do hope you'll discourage it in the future."

"Of course, dear." She takes a small sip of tea. "Though frankly, book-keeping seems a waste of his talents, if you ask me."

Pearl

December 11, 1933

Today I am a woman. That's what Aunt said when I stopped at her house after school and told her I was bleeding. I wadded up toilet paper in my pants in the girls' room and walked very slowly and carefully. Spring Garden Street never seemed so far away before.

She thought maybe Mama hadn't told me about the curse, but I've known since last year. Granny hadn't said anything to her and she thought she was dying, and she didn't want me to be scared. Why would Granny not tell her, if this happens to every girl eventually?

It's not so bad, I guess. My back hurts and I feel like one of the boys punched me in the stomach, but Aunt gave me a belt and pads, not flannels like Mama uses, and then Mrs. Hedges made me a cup of chamomile tea and I put my feet up and read one of Aunt's books until it was time to go home.

Claire

The doorbell rings, and soon after Katie appears in the doorway. "It's your brother, ma'am," she says. "He's here with a delivery from Mrs. Ava."

"Tell him to stay put." Since he moved in with Ava, Jake rarely comes to the house anymore. If she has chosen to use him as her errand boy, I will take full advantage. "I'll be right there."

Katie vanishes upstairs with my dress box while Jake and I go into my sitting room. He is not as resistant to being indoors as he once was, though he looks doubtfully at the chair and brushes the seat of his pants before sitting.

"It's fine," I tell him. "Just sit, and we'll have tea. Do you want something to eat?"

He shakes his head. "I'm good. One thing about Ava, she keeps you fed."

"I'm sure that's not the only good thing about living there." I am amazed they found space for him in that crowded house, but once upon a time I would have considered it a palace. "Is it?"

"Hmm." He shrinks back as Mrs. Hedges delivers a tray with tea and a plate of still-warm cookies. "It's noisy."

"You should be used to that," I say, pouring tea and gesturing for him to add cream and sugar to his liking. "Look how many of us there were."

Jake dumps sugar into his cup and stirs vigorously. "It's not the kids, it's that ever-loving sewing machine. It's worse than the breaker, going day and night. I can hear it on the third floor."

"You used to hear an actual breaker. You *worked* on the breaker." I snap a cookie in half and take a bite. "And you can't complain about her sewing machine—it's how she makes her living."

"Right." He gulps his tea and drops the cup back into its saucer. "Because she sews for you and your friends. She should get a real job."

I bite my lip before I say something I'll regret. "It is a real job, and it allows her to be home with her children, which is what she needs. So what if my friends and I ask her to make dresses for us? Her work is excellent and we pay her accordingly."

"Right," he says again, and pours another cup of tea. "You do it for her."

The room is stifling. I run a finger inside my collar. "Of course," I say. "She's my sister."

My brother falls silent as he finishes his tea. "You think you're helping," he says finally, tucking a few cookies into his shirt pocket, "but you're just making things worse for her."

"What do you mean?" Jake likes to show his independence but there is no reason to be cruel.

"Only way you can do your lady bountiful routine is if we stay poor." His mouth twists. "She's afraid of losing all that work, so she tells you what you want to hear. Remember the fuss she made at the party? I guess she never told you she saw me last year."

"No..." I cast my mind back, try to remember when that could have happened. "At the camp?"

"Where else?" Jake snorts. "We ain't likely to meet at one of your fancy society parties."

Ava had said nothing. I remember when she'd come in—it was late, and I was awake because I'd had words with Irene. We'd talked briefly and gone to bed. How could she have seen Jake, after almost twenty years, and not told me?

"Why would she do that?" Tears build behind my eyes and I blink furiously, not wanting to look weak in front of him.

"She was protecting you." Jake puts a hand on my arm. "The same as I'm trying to do. You don't make it easy on us."

I pull away. "I don't need protection," I flare. "Not from you, not from her."

Not for the first time, I wish my sister had a telephone. But this is a conversation that must occur face-to-face. I snatch up my bag, shove a hat over my freshly set hair, and slam the front door, not bothering to ask Hedges to drive me. The blocks between our houses pass in a blur of rage. It begins to spit rain as I reach Pine Street and I pick up speed, turning into Ringgold Place at a near run.

Down the street, around barrows of building supplies and stacks of bricks—will George Howe *ever* finish these houses?—I clatter down the shallow stairs, almost tripping over the umbrella stand set out to drain.

"Ava!" I push open the door and stop short. My sister is on her knees, pinning a hem for Betty Nichols, who is balanced on a stool with one hand braced against the wall.

"Didn't you see the sign?" Ava speaks through a mouthful of pins.

Turning, I note the square of cardboard tacked to the door. 'Please knock.'

Betty looks down from her perch. "I could have been in my scanties, for heaven's sake."

"But you weren't," I spit. "Calm down. Ava, I need to speak to you."

A pin glides through black satin, then another. I wait. She takes the final pin from between her lips and inserts it. "In a minute, Claire. Go on through to the kitchen." She stands, offering a hand to Betty. "Let's get you out of this. Carefully, so you don't snag your stockings."

They vanish behind the screen. I go into the kitchen and throw myself into the nearest chair and steam as I listen to her chat with Betty. Finally, the door opens.

Ava does not look pleased. "Even George knows to use the upstairs door when I'm working. What is so important that you can't knock?"

"Quite the fond farewell." I ignore her reprimand. "I'm not sure I've ever gotten that level of affection from you. 'So nice to see you, Miss Nichols. I'll have this ready next week, Miss Nichols,'" I mimic. "Betty Nichols is a bitch and you know it as well as I."

Her eyebrows raise. "Miss Nichols isn't the only one. What's gotten into you?"

"Jake," I say, my voice suddenly shaking. "He told me."

She sits down across from me. "Told you what?"

"That you saw him last spring, when you were here."

"Damn." Ava is quiet for a long time. "I gave him your address, but I didn't think he would come. It seemed easier not to get your hopes up."

I push my chair back, unable to stay seated. "I'm sick of everyone protecting me! He doesn't want to upset me. You don't want to get my hopes up. Am I so fragile?"

Ava covers her face with one hand. "You might find it hard to believe," she says, exhaustion in her voice, "but your feelings weren't my first concern. If I had told you, and if you got upset, *I* would have had to deal with it." Her hand drops, revealing wet eyes. Her eyes are wet. "I had just given up my baby. I didn't have the strength for my feelings and yours too."

24

Ava

I have been dreading the holiday season, and now that it's almost upon us, I am no closer to being ready. The kids will have presents—small ones—but I can't justify a tree or decorations beyond paper chains and whatever greenery Dan scrounges and gives to Pearl to put up around the house. Though I'd rather not, we will have supper on Christmas with Claire and Harry and enjoy their tree and whatever extravagant gifts they've bought for the kids.

There is another orphans' party on Christmas night, though Claire was not involved in the planning this year. As soon as they learn about it, the kids insist on going. I'm sure it costs money to get in, but I will let my sister take care of that. I'm getting better about closing my eyes to her excesses.

The society women of Philadelphia apparently all require something new for the festive season, and I am busy until the night of the twenty-third. I have done the unthinkable and told my customers I will not be available on Christmas Eve because I am spending it with my family. There was some grumbling, but their orders were completed on time, and even though I would prefer to sleep in, on the morning of Christmas Eve, I am up early to start preparations for our supper.

"I like splitting up the holiday," Pearl says, drifting into the kitchen with her hair in its stubby night braids. "Spending Christmas Eve here, and then going over there tomorrow."

"I like it, too," I confide. "I only need to cook one meal."

She pours herself a cup of coffee and perches on the edge of the table. "Aunt doesn't have to cook any."

Though I have never said anything, I'm sure my perceptive daughter understands why I'm skittish about spending Christmas with Claire. It will be Teddy's second birthday and the anniversary of Daniel losing his job—two events that changed our family forever. Last year, when we were living in their house, it was easy to sneak into the nursery before anyone else was up and spend time with him. Now that he's older and talking a mile a minute, I can no longer risk it. I am his aunt now, and I accept that, but at Christmas, I will always miss my baby.

Claire

My holiday preparations have been slipshod because I've been wrapped up with the clinic. Mrs. Hedges has ordered and prepared all the food. She is as trustworthy as Katie, even if I'm not always comfortable with her because of her friendship with my sister. Harry suggested we shop for gifts for the children, but I put him off, needing to fit in one more meeting. When it fell through and I called his office, he wasn't here, so I ended up telephoning an order in to Wanamakers instead. It was disappointing—we'd had such fun shopping for them the last two years—but it couldn't be helped.

Ava stubbornly refuses to spend Christmas Eve with us, so I reluctantly ask Irene. Aunt Nora has gone to her daughter's, but Max is there, and Irene is surprisingly agreeable. She is also surprisingly well-informed about the clinic's progress, and tells me, when Harry is out of the room, that she's invited Francis Gardiner for drinks later in the evening.

"He's all alone, poor man," she says, "what with his family in London. I feel for him."

I've never known Irene to have sympathy for anyone, and it reminds me of how flirtatious she was on the day she introduced us. Gardiner speaks of her as an amusing old woman, but is it possible she sees something more in their relationship? Is my mother-in-law making a fool of herself? I can only hope.

She leaves at eight, with barely concealed impatience. Max goes for a walk, tactfully informing us that he'll be going straight up to bed when he returns.

I'd put a bottle of champagne on ice earlier and, with coupes filled to the brim, we settle in before the fire to exchange presents. In addition to a book I knew he wanted, I found a lovely set of cufflinks—gold with striated onyx stones. His main gift for me, as always, is jewelry, this time a pearl and emerald bracelet that will look lovely with my green organza. The second package is flat, similar in shape and size to the one I gave him. Harry has never given me a book before.

I tear the wrapping paper and uncover a blue, leather bound volume with my initials embossed in gold. Opening it, I realize it is a 1934 appointment diary.

"For all your meetings," Harry says. "You've outgrown that little social calendar on your desk."

"Thank you." The light from the fire catches on his lenses. Without seeing his eyes, I'm uncertain that he's serious. My constant busyness has worn on him, and he's not been shy about letting me know. I take a sip of champagne and turn to a safe subject—Teddy—and how I am looking forward to Christmas morning, now that he's old enough to understand. "Last Christmas feels so long ago," I say. "So much has happened."

"To everyone," he agrees. "Teddy's growing up, and Ava and the children have started a whole new life." He pauses. "And you've started a business."

"Does it bother you?" I ask, knowing it does, in some way I don't yet understand. "The clinic?"

Harry takes my hand, holds it firmly on his thigh. "If you're happy, Claire, then I'm happy for you."

"I'm happy," I murmur, moving closer on the sofa. "But I could be happier." Tilting my head, I kiss him, feel the swiftness of his response. It's just as well Max is going straight up to bed. We'll already be there by then.

Pearl

December 26, 1933

Yesterday was perfect. I can hardly remember last year, so much happened at the same time, but I'll never forget this Christmas. We had Christmas Eve at home, Mama and Uncle Jake and all of us kids, and it was almost like the old days, except for Daddy. Uncle Jake can't take Daddy's place, but he tried his best—singing carols along with the radio and carving the goose that Mama splurged on. Thelma asked why we hadn't invited Dr. Max for supper and Mama stopped cold, like it hadn't even occurred to her. He was probably with Aunt, because I don't think he's got family of his own.

I know Mama was worried about presents, same as always, but it was fine. I got a new skirt, a pretty dark gray that will go with my two school blouses, and Thelma got a new dress. She's in the same state I was a few years ago, growing out of everything, and my old clothes aren't fit for the ragbag. The boys got cheap toy cars, but they were happy with them. Dandy got another roll of film for his camera, since he used his last roll going back for the memorial service.

Mama's best gift was for all of us. She took one of Dandy's photographs of the memorial stone and had it made bigger and put it in a frame. Now it sits on the shelf with the other family photos, and Grace will understand about it from the time she can ask questions.

Since she's so little, all she got for Christmas was a rattle, but she didn't care. She spent the whole night on my lap or Mama's, looking from side to side to see what was going on. When we sang Christmas carols, I swear she laughed.

The next day, we ate a huge meal at Aunt's house and Dr. Max was there. Afterward, we went to the orphans' party at the hotel again. My little sister who used to be scared of her shadow got up on stage and did a dance for everyone.

Every time I miss our old life, something happens to make me realize that, except for Daddy being gone, this is so much better.

Ava

I don't recall such a year for extreme weather in my life. Maybe I was too busy to notice back in Scovill Run, but I'm busy now and the torrential rains of August and September and that queer black blizzard in November, where dust from the Midwest was seen as far north as New York, are impossible to ignore. Christmas was cold but clear, but the day after, as the kids and I stumble out of bed, bleary-eyed after our late night, several inches of snow cover the ground.

Toby and George want to go outside immediately, but I make them eat breakfast and then see that they're well wrapped up, knowing they won't come home until forced by their empty bellies. They push past Jake, who is clearing the steps and sidewalk. Dan disappears a few minutes later, muttering something about visiting Tommy, and eventually Pearl takes Thelma out to make snow angels in the street, leaving me by the fire with Grace in my lap.

At some point, she has grasped my finger and now she is solidly asleep. "Grace," I whisper, tugging gently. "Mama has things to do." Her grip flutters, then tightens, and I give in. She is my last baby, and someday she'll be too big to want to sleep like this.

It is strange to have no paid work waiting for me. I'm not worried; there are several jobs coming after the new year, and this bit of leisure gives me time to work on something for myself.

My new life requires an unusual amount of clothing. Claire tactfully suggested I have a new dress for evenings at her house when people outside the family will be present. I object, on principle, and let her convince me that my green print dress cannot be the only garment I'm seen wearing by potential customers.

"I don't want to spend money on myself," I tell her. "The kids are growing, and all the boys are going to be out of their pants by spring. And no"—I stop her before she can interrupt—"I'm not letting you buy me a dress, or cloth for a dress. There has to be a limit, Claire."

Her pretty brow puckers. She's never liked to be thwarted. Then her eyes light up. "What if you took something no one wanted?"

This suggestion involves another trip to her attic. I'm grateful that unused things don't get thrown away in the Warriner household—our home, after all, is furnished with their castoffs. The attic would be a wonderland if the waste didn't bother me so. There are trunks and wardrobes stuffed full of abandoned garments, all of which could be taken apart and turned into wearable clothing.

"Here's my wedding dress," she says, bending over an open trunk. "I made sure it was well packed so my daughter could wear it someday."

I stop her before she can take it out, remembering clearly the heavy ivory satin and lace gown that had caused so many hard feelings. Mama was hurt because it was store-bought, and Irene had proclaimed it excessive and inappropriate for a courthouse wedding.

"Maybe Thelma will wear it."

"Maybe." She sighs. "I've got fifteen years' worth of clothes up here, and that's not counting what Irene left behind—and who knows what else there is. There must be something you can use."

I sort ruthlessly through the collection, turning resolutely away from beaded fringe dresses from the twenties, deflated Victorian bustles, and white work summer gowns. When I bring out an abundance of black taffeta, I hold it up for her to see.

"This will do." The long skirt falls into deep folds from what I can already tell is a too-small bodice. "There are yards of fabric in this."

"You don't want black. It looks like mourning."

"Why shouldn't I wear black?" I close the wardrobe and pick my way carefully across the littered floor. "All the mourning I've done in my life, I've never yet had a black dress."

Pearl took it upon herself to deconstruct the original dress, neatly opening seams and pressing the fabric flat, leaving me with yards of excellent quality silk taffeta—more than I need for a skirt, but not enough to remake the bodice.

"What are you going to do for the top, Mama?"

I shared my idea—to dye all the leftover satin from my various jobs into a uniform shade and make a new bodice. "Do you think that would work?"

She squealed with delight. "I can run to Woolworths tomorrow and pick up a box of dye. Black?"

Despite wanting a black dress, I didn't—not entirely. "It has to be dark," I said, "to make sure it matches. Try for charcoal gray, if they have it."

Rit did indeed make a dark gray dye, and the various remnants of white, ivory, yellow, rose, and pale blue satin are now close enough in color as to be indistinguishable. I have made the bodice with full bishop sleeves with high, tight cuffs and collar from the remaining taffeta. A small dish on the mantel holds faceted glass buttons, my sole purchase other than the dye.

Grace slumbers in her basket as I put the finishing touches on the dress. Compared to Claire's elaborate gowns with their ruffles and feathers and lace, I look like a widow, but I feel as glamorous as Jean Harlow. I've sewn a multitude of luxurious fabrics for others; I'd never thought to wear them myself.

The snow continues, day after day, finally stopping on the last day of the year. No sooner have the flakes ceased than the Warriners' Packard pulls up outside. Hedges knocks, presenting me with a note from Claire.

> *The weather has canceled everything, boo! We're having a small gathering tonight to ring in the new year. Only people you know. Please come.*

I am desperate to get out of the house, but am I that desperate?

Hedges smiles broadly. "Mrs. Claire says if you agree, I should pick you up at eight."

I emerge from the bathroom in my underwear to find my daughters sprawled on the bed, waiting to help me get ready. I slip the dress over my head—it is still warm from the iron—and they dive to do up the buttons, oohing and aahing at the crisp hand of the fabric. The skirt flutters around my calves and I twirl to make them laugh. Pearl insists on doing my hair and Thelma donates a rhinestone clip Claire gave her. A few stones are missing, but my hair is thick enough that no one will notice.

"Now perfume." Pearl offers up her cherished bottle of Blue Waltz, another gift from my sister.

I dab a bit at my throat. "I feel like Cinderella going to the ball," I say. "I hope the Packard doesn't turn into a pumpkin."

Despite Claire promising I would know everyone, I am nervous until I walk into her living room and recognize all the people there. I am no longer intimidated by Prue Foster, and the other women are familiar, though I don't recall their names until Claire introduces us.

"Is that the dress from the attic?" she asks under the hum of conversation. "It's amazing!"

I smile; for the first time I don't stick out in a crowd of her friends. It is a good feeling.

The men, including Max, are gathered around the liquor cart. Alcohol is legal again, but Prohibition had never been the law of the land in this house.

"Do you want champagne, Ava?" Harry offers a glass filled with golden liquid.

"No." I shake my head. "Tea's good enough for me."

Claire looks stricken. "I gave them the night off, after Hedges picked you up," she says. "But I can go downstairs and make some. If you really want it."

"Champagne will be fine." My look tells her I'm not happy, but I can pretend to drink it and then pour it off into the flowers.

Max breaks away to join me. His drink is already half empty. "You look stunning this evening."

Heat rises to my face and I look away. "Thank you."

"Have you been railroaded into demon rum?"

I consider the shallow glass in my hand. Tiny bubbles cling to its sides and pop on the surface. "Asking for tea means Claire would apparently have to chain herself to the stove for the rest of the evening."

"And we wouldn't want that." Max touches the rim of his glass to mine with a tiny chiming of crystal. "There's nothing too demonic about champagne—they call it giggle water, if it makes you feel any better."

"It doesn't." I raise the glass, sniff, take a tentative sip. The flavor—tart yet sweet, and those bubbles—is like nothing I've ever tasted.

"Well?" He looks at me expectantly.

"It's all right." It's actually quite delicious, but I can't say that, not when Mama raised us strict temperance because of what drink had done to our father.

The champagne eases conversation. I talk to Mrs. Foster and the other women, sharing complaints about the snow and the cabin fever we've all suffered since Christmas. Max's eyes are on me frequently, and when I finally finish my drink, he is there to offer a refill.

I drift toward the window. The street lamp casts a circle of light over the piled snow, and I shiver and take a healthy gulp, letting the bubbles fizz against the roof of my mouth.

"You're getting the hang of it."

Max is at my elbow. My breath catches as the air around us suddenly turns thick. Can he sense it, or is it just me? I turn away, briskly rubbing my arms, trying to make the feelings go away, and from the corner of my eye catch sight of the dreadful check of his suit. "Do you pay extra for those awful clothes?"

That hadn't been intended for his ears, but he throws his head back and laughs as I clap my hand over my mouth. "I'm sorry—"

"Don't be." He wipes his eyes. "You're the only person over the age of eight who's ever had the nerve to ask."

"I should go." It's nearly ten, and I never promised I would stay until midnight. I remember then that Hedges has the night off, and I will have to walk home in my new dress and my best shoes. My sister passes and I catch her arm. "I need your galoshes. I didn't think to bring mine."

"You're not leaving already?" She gives me a sad face, but her eyes are already on someone across the room.

"I want to be with the kids at twelve." They should be long asleep by then, and me with them, but Claire always accepts excuses involving the kids and she fetches her galoshes with no further argument.

"I'll walk with you." Max hands me my coat and shrugs into his own. "It's late to be walking alone."

"I don't mind." The champagne has made my head fuzzy, truth be told, and I need fresh air.

He opens the door, letting in a blast of cold, and takes my arm. "Neither do I."

Most of the sidewalks haven't been cleared, and there are few people on the streets at this hour. I'm grateful for Claire's boots but feel bad for Max.

"Don't you have overshoes?" I ask, as he slips and rights himself by grabbing hold of a lamp post. His leather shoes are already stained with wet.

"Somewhere." He guides me over a hump of snow on the corner and we walk in the street, where the snow has been flattened by traffic. "I was in such a rush, I didn't think to get them."

The cold has dissipated the effects of the champagne, but my cheeks flush anyway. "You're getting cold and wet for no reason."

His gloved hand reaches for mine. "For a very good reason." We turn onto Ringgold Place. "I enjoy your company, and I didn't want you walking alone on a night when there might be drunkards on the street."

I step over a pothole caused by a recent delivery of building supplies. Someday they will finish working on these houses, but not yet. "Aren't they all in Claire's living room?"

He laughs again and leans against the iron railing of my steps. "Not all, no." His lip curls "Forgive me if I'm a little careful of you."

"You don't need to be." I put one foot on the step. The lamp in the front window shines on his face and for a moment I forget my widow's dress, my widowed status. "But thank you for walking me home."

"My pleasure."

He hesitates, then takes a step toward me. "I can't get close enough to be close to you, Ava." One hand comes to rest on my arm; I feel his fingers through my coat and the satin sleeve beneath. "Why won't you let me in?"

"It's not that easy," I say, trying to convey in those few words everything I still have to get past, that I like having him close until I don't—or until Daniel's presence in my thoughts makes me feel unfaithful. "I wish I could."

Neither of us move, and then we both do. I pull away first, my heart pounding. "Goodnight, Max."

"Happy new year, Ava."

Part Two

1934

25

Pearl

January 1, 1934

Mama kissed Dr. Max last night! I shouldn't have been looking, but Dandy and Uncle Jake were both out and I was hoping one of them would come home because I was bored. I wasn't expecting Mama so soon.

Toby and George were horrible all night. They wouldn't listen to me or go to bed and their scuffling got Grace crying. I know she's teething and can't help it, but there was a point where I couldn't bear to hear her scream and actually screamed myself, not that anybody could hear me.

But back to Mama. She and Dr. Max came up the street real slow, talking, and then they stopped out front. I backed up so I could look down at the steps without them seeing me. They weren't talking then, just looking at each other and then all of a sudden they both leaned forward. Their noses bumped. It looked awkward, but then they tried again and it seemed to go better because they did it for a while.

Ava

Jake shambles into the room and drops into the nearest chair. His hair is matted from sleep and he is unshaven, but he is at least dressed; I have insisted on that. "I saw you last night."

"So?" I put a mug down in front of him and turn back to the stove where I have a pan of eggs going for the kids' breakfast.

"You looked like a whore."

From his voice, it's clear that Max and I weren't the only ones drinking last night. I'm glad he didn't confront us then, when I was fuddled by champagne; it would have been even uglier than it is about to become. He's seen me with Max before—they've even eaten at the same table on the rare occasions Jake has come home on time. Jake even remembered him from the camp when they met at Pearl's party, and they had a quiet discussion in the corner of the garden.

Once, when I complained about my brother's drinking and his unpredictable hours, Max suggested I give him a bit of leeway until he became accustomed to living with us. "The kind of life he's had, it damages some men," he said. "All men, but some more than others. He's doing the best he can."

I think about that, and then I don't. Hands on hips, I swing around to face him. "You forfeited any right to an opinion about my behavior when you abandoned our family."

He starts to get up, then drops back, rapid movement not suiting his hangover. "What would Dan think?"

"What are you implying?"

He does get up then, slamming the chair back against the table hard enough that his coffee sloshes. "I'm not implying anything. You were making a spectacle of yourself in the middle of the street."

The kids are moving around upstairs; I have to shut this down quickly, before they walk in on us and want to know why we're fighting.

"The only person out on the street last night, besides us, was you, staggering home drunk from wherever you were." I glare at him. "You're no picture of virtue, brother, stinking of whiskey and cheap perfume every time you have a dollar to your name."

"You get your money on time." He stops at the bottom of the stairs. "What I do with the rest is no business of yours."

I narrow my eyes. "And what *I* do is no business of yours."

With a thunder of footsteps, the kids stream past him into the kitchen. "Mama, Dandy says we're going to the park for a snowball fight!" Thelma squeals. "Can we go?"

I look from my brother to my son, who is already more of a man than his uncle. "Hasn't he already said you're going?"

Claire

Friday dinner is always early. On our own, Harry and I would sit down at half-past seven, but Ava likes the younger children in bed, or at least at home, by eight, so even though there is an empty seat at the table, we dig into roast beef, potatoes, green beans, and another experimental jellied salad.

Every dish on the table is scraped clean, but the jellied salad stands alone, with two small slices missing. I point my fork toward it. "Has everyone had enough?"

The affirmative chorus—even from Harry—convinces me this is yet another dish not to be repeated. Eventually I will find a recipe they will eat.

"Where's Dr. Max?" Thelma asks for the third time. "If he doesn't get here soon, we won't see him."

"If you don't, you'll see him tomorrow," Ava says, patient with her daughter's adoration. "He probably had things to do."

"When does he not?" Harry asks. "Katie, would you bring in dessert?"

There is room aplenty for chocolate cake. My nieces and nephews tear into it like they're starving, and I shake my head at Ava. Her expression says plainly that I should know better; the children accept Jello as a sweet, not mixed with vegetables and served warm alongside a roast.

The front door opens before we have finished, and voices float in from the hall: Katie, her voice high with concern, Max, and another man. I push my chair back.

John Spencer appears in the doorway. "Sorry to interrupt," he says. "I'm just delivering Max to his room. I'll be out of your way in a moment."

Ava stands. "Why can't he deliver himself?"

We're thinking the same thing, that Max has overindulged, and his friend has escorted him home. It's unusual, but given the amount of stress he's been under with his job and the extra work of setting up the clinic, I wouldn't blame him.

An uneven step, and Max joins Spencer in the doorway. His face is bruised, and his left arm is strapped to his chest. "Good evening, everyone," he says casually. "Don't mind me. I had an altercation with an automobile on Oregon Avenue."

Ava sits down again. "You're hurt."

"A bad sprain, that's all." He smiles, but there is pain behind it. "I swerved to get out of the way of a car and either I hit some ice or the tire caught in the streetcar track, I'm not sure which. I'll take an aspirin and be off to bed."

"You will not," Spencer says firmly. "You've got a mild concussion, my friend. I don't want you sleeping for a few more hours."

Max looks impatient. "I'm fine, John. I'm not dazed, I'm perfectly coherent, my movements are coordinated—except for this thing on my arm—and I'm tired. I worked a long day, and I want to go to sleep."

Spencer looks at us. "Will one of you take responsibility for this reprobate? I'd like to get home to my wife."

"Of course." I take Max by his good arm and lead him to the table. Gesturing toward the cake, I ask, "Can I interest you in a slice?"

He nods, sulky as a small boy not being given his way. "Did I miss one of those godawful jellied things? That's one benefit to being late."

The children burst into laughter and the moment lightens, for most of us. I sneak a glance at Ava. Her face is white, the napkin twisted in her hands. Before long she gets to her feet. "We should let Dr. Max get some rest. Let's head on home."

They leave with Dr. Spencer, and Harry and I sit in the living room with Max for another hour, until he convinces us to let him go to bed.

Once the holidays were behind us, Harry offered to speak to several of his associates, to warm them up for me, but I remembered his earlier words—that this is my project—and shake my head. "Although I would appreciate their wives' names, if we're not already acquainted."

The men of Philadelphia might hold the bank accounts, but the purse strings, especially for charitable donations, are held by their wives. I start organizing luncheon parties, inviting two or three women at a time plus one of my friends—Prue, Stella, or Marie—to back me up. Any more and it would devolve into uncontrollable chat and I would never be able to speak my piece.

I always begin by talking about the camp, which most have heard of, and Max's involvement, which they have not, but are also not surprised.

"Those men make me uncomfortable," Agnes von Thiel says. "Hanging around on street corners doing nothing."

Because of Jake, I want to jump to their defense, but instead I tell the truth. "I'm uncomfortable most of the time, too. But they need help." I appeal to their common sense. "We can't fix the Depression—we can't make a world where these men can return home and pick up the lives they had before the Crash—but this is something we can do." I tell them how the men live, in train yards, abandoned warehouses, shacks knocked together from scrap wood deep in Fairmount Park. "It's not an easy existence, and it's hard to stay well without good food and dry clothes and a roof over their heads."

"But a clinic, Claire. Dealing...medically with these people. It feels..."

"Well, *I* won't be dealing with them." I laugh lightly. "That's what Max is for. And wouldn't it be nice, for his sake, to actually have the bulk of his do-gooding in one place, instead of pedaling that ridiculous bicycle all over the city? You heard he nearly broke his arm last week?"

They laugh, and I feel a momentary shame for poking fun at someone so good. But he would be the first to make fun of himself, if it got these women to hand over a portion of their dress allowance.

"Would it be just men?" Prue's real concern is always with children.

"Of course not." My original plan hadn't included women and children, but what was a plan for if not to be flexible?

Katie appears silently with another plate of cookies and a fresh pot of tea.

"The deserving poor," I say enthusiastically, after she leaves, "come in all ages, all sexes, and all races. I'm looking into finding a colored doctor."

Lillian Penn-Slater's teacup stops halfway to her lips as she considers the appalling thought of a dark-skinned physician. "Oh, Claire, I think that's going too far, don't you?"

I give her my best smile. "That's going to cost you extra, Lillian."

When they leave, I turn to Prue with a victorious smile. "They should be good for at least five hundred, don't you think?"

She throws herself down in Harry's chair, kicking off her shoes and settling her stockinged feet on the ottoman. "Apiece, if I'm not mistaken," she says. "You've gotten very good at this, Claire."

I start to demur and instead drop onto the sofa, laughing helplessly. "You've taught me well. And this is my third luncheon this week, so I'm getting a lot of practice. I have an interview with a reporter from the *Inquirer* on Monday. I wish you could be there for that."

"You'll manage splendidly." She covers a yawn with a manicured hand. "Now, if you offer me something stronger than tea, I'll help you make up the guest lists for the next three lunches."

Pearl

January 8, 1934

I'm the biggest fool in the world. This whole last year I've been so turned around and I couldn't see it. After supper tonight, I was doing the dishes and Dr. Max came down and picked up the towel. I said I didn't need help, that he should be careful of his arm, but he started in drying like he hadn't heard me. Then he says, "I thought we were friends."

My throat closed up. Finally, I stammered something but then I ruined it by breaking a plate because I was in such a tizzy. He picked up the pieces and while he was doing that, he started talking.

He said it was me who got Mama to accept him, but ever since then, something's changed. He said it's the same thing that makes Mama take a step back every time they go forward, that we're worried letting him in will change our family. He doesn't want to change anything, he said. He just loves Mama.

Tears were running down my face and dripping into the sink. I never expected him to understand what I was afraid of. And is he right? Does Mama worry about that, too? When I could speak, I said I was sorry.

Dr. Max sat me down before I broke anything else and said, "There's nothing wrong with being afraid of change."

And that was what did it. I wrote in this diary at the beginning of the year that Daddy died because he couldn't change and that I would always find a way to adapt. If I can't find a way to adapt to Dr. Max, then I haven't learned anything. For all my fine words, I've spent most of the last year scared. Of changing schools. Of working for Uncle Harry. Of losing my family because of someone who only wants good things for us.

When I say my prayers tonight, I'll close my eyes and tell Daddy that we'll never stop loving him, but maybe there's room in our hearts for someone else. After all, he and Mama never loved us any less when they had another baby.

Ava

The front door rattles and opens partway, interrupting our quiet conversation. Jake slides in, bringing a blast of cold air with him. He sheds his coat and hat, hanging them any which way on the wooden rack. "Wicked out there."

"Where were you?" I ask. "You missed supper."

Normally, it's difficult for me to stay mad at Jake—he turns so quickly from anger and suspicion to the laughing brother he was before Tata's death—but our last disagreement has been hard to forgive. When I look at Max, I hear Jake's words, his use of Daniel as a weapon, something I won't tolerate from Claire or my kids, and I cringe. The little boys love him, and Dan seems to appreciate not being the only man in the house, but I'm not sure how much longer I can live with him.

"Out and about." He nods to us, his eyes narrowed, and disappears up the stairs, leaving behind a waft of cigarette smoke.

I press my lips together until the temptation to speak subsides. The happiest times in my life—my wedding and the birth of my kids—happened without Jake, because he left our mother alone with three daughters to care for. With that behavior, he doesn't get to sit in judgment of anything I do.

"I don't think he likes me." Max tips his head back, smiling at the ceiling. He doesn't care.

"He's protective." So are the children, but if anything, they encourage Max's frequent visits. "Don't mind him."

"I don't."

It is comfortable, sitting on the davenport before the fire. Too comfortable. The house feels empty without the constant hum of the kids' activity. I put my knitting on the table and reach for a truck Toby left on the floor. That boy will be the death of me yet. I put it on the mantel, next to the vase with Max's latest flowers, and catch a glimpse of him when I turn. The look on his face is not difficult to interpret. Flustered, I straighten the vase and throw an errant petal into the fire, hoping he'll look away.

"You know I'm in love with you." Max never minces words, even when he should.

"I know." Neither do I.

One corner of his mouth turns up. "I think you'd rather I weren't."

"I would." My eyes go to his arm, so nearly broken in that accident. I remember leaving Claire's house and seeing his mangled bicycle leaning against the house. What if the car had struck him? What if he'd hit his head, instead of taking the brunt of the fall on his left side? He's not going to stop riding his bicycle everywhere, and I'm always going to have to worry about something going wrong.

I'm not sure if I have it in me to worry about another man. It's hard enough keeping track of all the kids, and wondering what bump or bruise or upset they're going to bring home next; letting Max into my heart is a level of risk I'm not sure I'm ready for.

Don't borrow trouble from tomorrow. I squelch Mama's voice before the words are fully formed. Sometimes worrying is the right thing to do. I don't return to the davenport—it would be too easy to fall together with its sagging cushions—and sit on the window seat, patting the space beside me. "I do care about you—"

"Stop! Stop!" He holds up both hands. "I can hear the 'but' coming."

"But," I say gently, catching his wrist and bringing his hand to the cushion between us, "you deserve more than I can offer."

The dying fire crackles companionably; on the other side of the glass, sleet hisses. Upstairs, the kids are asleep. The silence lingers while his hazel eyes look deep into me, past my words and into the secrets I've left unspoken.

"Shouldn't I be the one to make that decision?" He links his fingers with mine; his hand is warm. Smooth. Not the hard hand of a laborer, which has always felt like manhood to me.

I take a deep breath and slide my fingers free. "You deserve more than a tired woman with too many kids who will never stop loving her dead husband," I say bluntly. "I care about you, more than I expected. More than I'd like, if you must know. But I'm not whole, Max. And you deserve someone who is."

He takes in my words, and soon, with visible effort, he's found his equilibrium. Any hurt is concealed behind a crooked grin. "Then I should say goodnight." He picks up the muffler the girls knitted him for Christmas, winds it around his neck. The difference between Pearl's tidy rows and Thelma's uneven stitches is clear from across the room. "Before I wear out any goodwill I've built up."

"Wait for this to slack off a little." I hadn't expected him to bolt for the door. I might not want his love, but I enjoy spending time with him. "Jake's right, it is wicked out there. I'll put the kettle on."

"It's time for me to leave you in peace." Reaching out, Max brushes his knuckles against my cheek and something unexpected flutters low in my belly. "It was a nice dream, while it lasted." He pauses on the doorstep. For a moment, I think he's giving me the opportunity to change my mind, but instead he says simply, "Leave your faucets running tonight, so the pipes don't freeze."

Once he is gone, the house feels even emptier. That flutter nags at me, reminding me of our day at the shore, when he kissed me by the ocean and I felt the first stirrings of attraction for a man who wasn't Daniel Kimber. It's not right, letting Max have all these feelings I can't reciprocate. He's already had his heart broken once, according to Claire, by the deplorable Daisy. I will not allow myself to be the next woman to hurt him.

I cast a glance at the vase, seeing the flowers as if for the first time. Daisies. In the middle of winter. Does he favor them because they remind him of her? Or are they a way of proving to himself that he no longer cares? Or does he simply like them?

The fire is almost out. I hold my hands toward the flames until they warm. Inside, I am chilled through. Before I go to bed, I turn on the kitchen tap, leaving it to slowly fill my biggest pot. I do the same with the bathroom sink and the tub, then use the cold as an excuse to crawl into bed with Pearl and Thelma.

26

Claire

Something is wrong between Max and Ava. I know only because he asked if I would tell him when she was coming for dinner so he could arrange to be out of the house. How have they managed to mess this up?

"I thought things were going well."

"So did I," Max said. "I don't want to talk about it. Just give me a heads up, if you can."

Ava was similarly tight-lipped when I high-tailed it over to her house later that day, having asked Prue to handle a donor meeting. She was in the chilly workroom, doing something complicated and beautiful. When I asked her point blank about Max, she shook her head. "I don't want to talk about it."

"That's what he said."

She looked up, and there was a weariness in her eyes I hadn't seen since Daniel's death. "Then listen to him, if you won't listen to me."

And so I have, scheduling my sister's appearances, leaving notes for Max and wondering—to the point where Harry plugs his ears—what happened to the match I so carefully promoted.

"They're perfect for each other," I say again, nestling against Harry's shoulder. "I don't know what went wrong."

He reaches over to turn off the bedside lamp. "Maybe they are," he says. "But Ava's been through a lot. Maybe the timing isn't right, even for perfect."

"I know what she's been through." He doesn't understand how much I want their relationship to work, how I want to believe in a romance that is more than young love. "But she's throwing happiness away with both hands. Max is good for her, and he loves the children. How many men are willing to take on another man's children, much less six of them?"

Stifling a yawn, Harry says, "Your sister doesn't need someone to take on the children. She's managing."

I know that, too. But I can't imagine managing is enough.

Pearl

January 20, 1934

The worst of the weather is over, but the house is still cold, especially the basement. I don't know how Mama sews down there all day, my hands would fall off. And if it's this bad here, people must be freezing solid in Scovill Run.

Mama's been roasting potatoes for Dan and Uncle Jake to put in their pockets when they leave for work. It keeps their hands warm and then they can eat them for lunch. I want to ask her to do the same for me, but I'm being a baby. School is indoors, and I eat my lunch in a warm room. Uncle Jake is inside, too, but Dan is outside for most of his work day and he comes home with his fingers stiff and red. He says it could be worse, because he could be unemployed. Or underground. He'd rather work for Mr. Howe and get frostbitten fingers than lose another one on the breaker, and I don't blame him one bit.

Ava

Thelma has been poking along on the same bit of patchwork since Thanksgiving. Hand sewing is slow, of course, but I will not trust her tender fingers with either of my sewing machines, and anyway, this is how I learned my stitches, and how I taught Pearl.

"How's it going, honey?" I lean over to check her progress.

"Fine." She covers it with her skirt. "Don't look at it."

I sigh. The kids have all been touchy lately, sensing my upset if not actually noticing Max's absence. "I just want to—"

"I don't like sewing!" Thelma throws the quilt square on the floor. "It's boring and I'm tired."

Pearl snatches it up. "Thelma—"

She is too hard on her sister, I think, listening to her lecture. Pearl has always had to be older than her years; now that life is a little easier, I wish she could relax and be a child, but she is no better than I am at changing the habit of years. I was like that with Claire, resentful because Mama let her shirk the chores I did without complaint. I don't like seeing it repeated in the next generation.

I turn on the radio, effectively drowning out their squabble. Un-luckily, the song is from *42nd Street*, the movie that started Thelma's obsession. She slides off the davenport onto the patch of bare floor by the stairs and starts to dance.

Pearl snaps it off. "I thought you were tired."

A final flourish and Thelma curtsies to an invisible audience. "I am," she says. "Of sewing."

"Sit down and finish your square." Pearl's voice is dangerously quiet.

"Why? Aunt Claire doesn't." Thelma throws herself onto the end of the davenport, ignoring her needle. "She dances and goes to parties and goes shopping. She doesn't sit and sew all day like a drudge."

"Your aunt knows how to sew," I tell her, wondering where she learned that word. "We both had to do it when we were young. She still can, she just doesn't."

When my little girl smiles, her resemblance to my sister is even clearer. "Then I won't, either."

"Aunt stopped sewing when she was old enough to get a different kind of job." Pearl is angrier than I am at her sister's obstinacy. "No one gets a free ride in this family."

It hurts to realize she has taken on this belief to the extent she'll reprimand her beloved little sister. "It's all right."

"It's not all right, Mama." Pearl bites her lip, then blurts, "You're too easy on her, because of how her legs used to be. But she's fine now." She swipes her hand across her eyes and I recognize tears of frustration. "You can't have one rule for one child and another rule for the rest. It's bad enough that George and Toby don't bring in any money. At least they're learning skills. Thelma needs to learn properly, to help you when I'm old enough to get a job outside the house."

"I'm going to be a dancer," Thelma says placidly. "And if you don't stop yelling at me, I'll never give you free tickets to my shows. You'll have to pay to see me, like everyone else."

Claire

After a late dinner, I suggest cocktails in the living room before bed. Surprised, Harry agrees, and I excuse myself to check on Teddy while he mixes our drinks. After I peer in at our sleeping son, I whip off my clothes and change into the lilac satin peignoir set which is Harry's special favorite. Taking the pins from my hair, I run a brush through it, softening the waves as I hope to soften up my husband.

He looks up when I swish into the room, the feather trim quivering with every movement. "You do know how to make an entrance, darling."

"I'm trying to make up for not being around." Instead of sitting, I rest one hip on the arm of his chair, letting the soft satin brush against his shoulder.

"It happens." He touches the rim of his glass to mine. "I've certainly gotten over-involved in my work. I just never expected it from you."

It hurts that he expects so little of me, but I understand; for years, I was nothing more than an ornament with a heartbeat. Now I am a wife and mother and businesswoman, and I'm not always certain how to fit it all into one day. I have neglected him, and he has every right to be annoyed.

"How is it going?" he asks, knowing I won't be able to relax until I've gotten the latest news off my chest. "Are you on schedule for the opening?"

"Almost," I tell him, sliding off the chair and beginning to pace. "Donations have been coming in steadily"—I don't tell him how many of those donations have come by way of Francis Gardiner—"and all that's left is to finish the structure and buy the x-ray machine."

He nods approvingly. "You're a marvel." Taking a sip of his martini, he adds, "I can't believe Max is so insistent on hospital-quality equipment in a clinic of that size. No one would expect it."

There it is again: the faint sting of disapproval, the attitude that the clinic won't add up to much. "It's very important to him," I say. "And to me."

"Well, don't expect people to fund something they don't understand the use of—they're fine with the poor being treated and kept off the streets, but they won't pony up money for what they consider an extravagance."

I'd already discovered that. Even Aunt Nora had raised an eyebrow. Draining my glass, I put it on the table and return to the arm of Harry's chair, lifting my hand and letting the feathers tickle his neck. "You'll help, won't you? It's not so very much."

He goes so still it feels like I'm caressing a statue. "I'm not a bank, Claire."

"I never said you were." I slide down and stand before him, feeling like a child called on the carpet. "But you believe in this project. I thought you'd want to help."

"I believe in *you*," he says with a shake of his head. "And I've contributed all I'm going to. This is your project. If you want it as badly as all that—badly enough that you've neglected our son and barely said two words to me about anything other than the clinic—you'll find a way." He pushes himself up from the chair and steps carefully around me. "I'm going to bed. It's been a long day."

I remain downstairs for a while, emptying the shaker and fuming in my now-pointless finery. Drinking does nothing to improve my mood, and when I wake in the morning and find Harry already gone, and a headache pounding in my temples, I want to cry from sheer temper. I resist and go down to breakfast, hoping coffee will dull the pain.

Max is there, polishing off a plate of eggs. He greets me cheerfully and I grunt in return.

"Not too spiffy this morning, eh?" His smile is brighter than the sunlight streaming through the windows. I blink at him. "Neither was Harry. What did you two get up to last night after I went to bed?"

Dropping into my chair, I close my eyes and wait for Katie to pour the coffee. "Just toast," I tell her, and when she has gone, I add, "He said he won't pay for the x-ray machine."

"Was he supposed to?" Max mops his plate with a piece of toast. "I thought that's why you were fundraising?"

"It is, but we don't have enough." I tell him of the difficulties I've encountered: the structural work the building required before we could start renovations, the price of supplies, the cost of even George Howe's discounted, off-season labor. Paint. Furnishings. Equipment. "It goes out as quickly as it comes in."

"Then we need to find another way." He nods decisively. "That's all."

It's easy for him to say. He's not the one running all over town, being forced to charm old women and stuffy businessmen into doing something charitable for their fellow citizens. I've drunk more cups of weak tea, sat through so many lectures about personal responsibility and bootstraps for people without boots that I could scream.

"It's not that simple." I spread butter on my toast and then drop it back on the plate. Eating is too much effort. "Everyone's given already."

"Then find another way. I won't harass my friend, no matter how badly I want that damned machine." He levels a glance at me. "And from the look of him this morning, you shouldn't harass him either."

"I didn't."

But I had. He'd already helped me find the property and paid the rent, and I treated him like a walking checkbook. Maybe he'd reacted badly, but so had I.

"What about a party?" he suggests. "A gala, the kind of exclusive affair people fight to get into. Charge enough for tickets and the price of the machine will no longer be an issue."

All I want is to go back to bed until I can think of a way to apologize to Harry. "I don't want to plan a party. I'm wrung out."

"You're hung over," he says reasonably. "Let Prue plan it. She's a whiz at these things, and if her name's attached as something more than another donor, you'll get all the right people."

"I don't know..." My head is pounding. If he doesn't stop talking, I *am* going to cry.

"A hundred dollars a head." He grins. "One-fifty for a couple. The rich will be cheapskates and pair off, and you'll be swimming in cash."

$$27$$

Ava

The cold has lifted and all the kids, except Pearl, are out of the house—Thelma is with Teddy, Dan with Tommy, and the boys wherever they get to these days. She and I have retreated to the living room, where I darn a basket of socks without heels and she lets down the hem of her school dress, both of us comfortable in front of the fire.

"I wish Dr. Max would come around."

My daughter has been nibbling around this subject for days, to the point that I regard her with the same glare I would give my sister, or Max himself. "I thought you didn't want me to be nice to him."

"I didn't, then. But now I do. And he likes you." Pearl raises her eyebrows. "Not even you can control how people feel."

She bends over her stitching, and I look at the neat part in her hair and wonder when my little girl grew into someone willing to give advice to her mother. When I was her age, I felt like an adult, but I wouldn't have dared tell my mother what to do. It's good that Pearl is comfortable enough to give me her opinions, but I don't have to agree with them.

Max Byrne can like me—love me—or not. It isn't my business, so long as he keeps his distance. He's been as good as his word. I limit my visits to Delancey Place, but he is never there at the same time. When we come for supper, the kids ask for him, straight out, and Claire says, "He's trying to give your mama a little breathing room."

"Don't put it all on me," I say crisply. "And this does not need to be discussed now, Claire." I don't know what the kids thought about me and Max, but they'll get over it soon enough, if they're not reminded by her bringing up his name all the time.

Weeks go by. I have almost convinced myself that I don't miss him. But for a big city, Philadelphia is like a small town—most people don't stray far from their neighborhoods. A chance meeting will happen eventually; I want to be prepared.

But I am not. When I encounter Max on South Street, coming out of a bakery with a string-tied white box, something lurches in my chest. He stops short and nods a greeting.

"How are you?"

"Fine." He smiles, but it doesn't reach his eyes. "You?"

"Fine. Running a few errands." I gesture toward the packages nestled around Grace in the coach.

"Esther and Mason are visiting their son," he says. "I offered to pick up dessert."

"She told me the other day there was a new baby."

Max comes closer, but it's Grace he bends to see, crooning and running a finger along her cheek. "She looks well."

"We're all well." I don't know why I want to convince Max that I don't miss him, when what I really want is to let him pull me close so I can rest for a moment. I am struck with a dart of disloyalty. How can I want this with anyone but Daniel?

"Who's a beautiful girl?" Grace squeaks with pleasure and struggles to free herself from the cocoon of blankets. Her brown eyes—her father's eyes—are open wide.

"We have to go."

Pearl

February 10, 1934

Someday I'm going to be old enough to be told when things happen in this family. Dr. Max hasn't been to see us since the ice storm, and he's never at Aunt's house anymore when we come for supper. I tried asking the other night, but Aunt said Mama needs room to breathe, whatever that means, and then changed the subject. When we got home, I tried to talk to Mama, but she said it was time to read to the littles before bed.

At first, I didn't want Dr. Max and Mama to get involved, but now that he's gone, I miss him. It was fun when he was around, playing cards in the kitchen or taking a turn walking Grace when she howled with her teeth coming in. I don't understand what happened.

I wonder if they had a fight? He's the easiest man in the world to get along with, even for her, so that's hard to believe. And we all like him. Dr. Max isn't Daddy, but no one could be. I hope Mama didn't stop seeing him because of that.

Claire

In all the years of our marriage, Harry has never raised his voice to me. When he is angry, he goes quiet until it passes. This evening, without Max, has been very quiet. "Is everything all right?" I ask, when we move to the living room. "You didn't have a lot to say tonight."

"Perhaps I've grown accustomed to dining alone." Harry sets his drink on a coaster, so the table isn't marred with a ghostly ring from its moisture.

"That's not fair," I say, stung. "I've been in for dinner every night this week." Sometimes late, but I'd made it home, leaving work unfinished or a meeting going on as I dashed out.

The silver cigarette case gleams in his hands. He offers one to me and I shake my head. "Something has to give, Claire." He strikes a match. "Before we do."

His words send a chill through me. "Do you want me to stop? We're so close."

"No. I'm proud of what you've accomplished—of who you've become." The flame pauses, flickering, in mid-air until it reaches his fingertips. Shaking it out, he drops it into the ashtray and tips my face up to his. "I wish you had some sense of proportion. You throw yourself into these causes so wholeheartedly you forget there's anything else."

"I don't forget—"

"Very well." He lowers his hand, retrieving his cigarette and successfully lighting it this time. "You put off, until later. And by the time later comes, you've got another list in your hand. Teddy's almost stopped asking for you. Did you even see him when you got in tonight?"

"Of course." I do not mention that he was already asleep. I'll look in on him again before bed, and spend time with him after breakfast. I'm not due to meet with the board until ten.

Pearl

February 17, 1934

Last week, Peggy introduced us to a girl from one of her classes. Her name is Helen, but she said to call her Lenny. We took to her right off and now she sits with us at lunch. Most of the time she's studying, but when she's not, she makes us laugh.

She wants to be a teacher. That's what most of the girls plan to do, but Lenny also spends a lot of time up on the roof, where the horticulture club has set up a greenhouse. She told us all plants have Latin names and Peggy said it must be like learning a second language. Lenny gave her a look and said English is her second language. Her family is Russian, which is no surprise with a name like Sharamatew, but she's got no accent at all.

She's as blunt as Mama, but I'm used to that. And we have one thing in common. We're both trying to become something different than what life marked us out to be.

Ava

As if we all don't have enough to do, Claire has decided to throw a party to celebrate the opening of the clinic. They apparently need more money and she didn't think she could ask people unless she gave them something in return. I don't understand how paying to attend a party is getting something, but there are many things about Claire's world that I don't understand and I'm probably better off not knowing.

Somehow, I convinced her she didn't need a new dress. Maybe I'm shooting myself in the foot, but I'm tired. She made the mistake of telling me she hadn't worn the Letty Lynton dress since last year at the inaugural, so she can wear that and look stunning and I'll get more orders for dresses I will hopefully have the energy to fulfill.

I'm in a funk lately. It's not the same as the dark time after Teddy was born, thank God; I'm just exhausted and want to be alone, except that when I am alone, I don't like my thoughts and then I hunt down one of the kids to keep me company. Thelma's gone back to being a sweetheart again, practicing her dancing in the kitchen and talking to me through the door, or coming in and sitting quietly, letting Pearl teach her something more interesting than quilt blocks. She's quick to learn when she's not bored, but I don't like seeing her get sucked into the business. I'll be happy when Pearl doesn't have to pitch in.

Worst of all, Claire wants me to come to this party. If I'm not making her a dress for this circus, why on earth does she think I would be willing to attend? I survived that Christmas party two years in a row, but the kids were there to occupy me. Max also ran interference, wearing the same ridiculous elf suit he'd worn the year before. I can't allow myself to find it endearing that he will go to such lengths to entertain children he doesn't know. Maybe he simply enjoyed the opportunity to be a child again himself. I have few memories of a carefree childhood; if I did, perhaps I would also want to relive them.

That's another problem with Claire's party: Max will be there and there is no way for me to avoid seeing him.

Claire

The clinic opens in less than a month. The sheer weight of expectations—my own and everyone else's—presses down on me like a boulder, and although I would like to retreat to my bed and lose myself in contemplating the Renoir, I ramp up my efforts, scheduling more luncheons and dinners, one of which is planned for this very evening.

I dread it, even as I check in with Mrs. Hedges to make sure everything is under control. Perhaps I can squeeze in a nap between now and five o'clock.

"Do people really like these things?" Her brown finger hovers over the magazine photo of another jellied salad. "Or do they pretend they do because it looks so fancy?"

"They like them," I assure her, hoping our guests have more sophisticated palates than my nieces and nephews. "Can you make it?"

She looks affronted. "Of course I can. It's not all that different than the other ones. I wanted to make sure you were serious, that's all."

Harry comes in from work as I spin through the hall. "Claire!" He catches my arm. "The Garretts can't make it tonight."

I stop in my flight, already rearranging the seating. "Why not?"

He takes off his hat, and I slide his overcoat from his shoulders. "Not sure. Garrett called as I was leaving, they caught me at the elevator with his message."

"Well, that leaves us with the Ingersolls and the Sibleys." This is my last effort with some of the old guard and Harry has agreed to be at his most helpful and convincing.

He turns. "Didn't Mrs. Ingersoll call earlier?"

"I haven't heard from her."

"I saw Philip at the club at lunch." He shakes his head. "Some sort of family emergency. Something about their son..."

My dinner for eight has become an intimate dinner for four, and I've never been all that comfortable with the Sibleys. They are more Irene's generation than mine, in both age and temperament.

"So it will be the four of us," I say brightly, and kiss his cheek. "Lovely. I'm going up to spend some time with Teddy and then get changed."

Half an hour with my boy lifts my spirits, and when I return to my room to change into the dress laid out on the bed, I am almost looking forward to the challenge of sweet-talking Sarah Sibley.

"Ma'am?" Katie looks in. "You had a call while you were with Mr. Teddy."

"Yes?" I tug a fresh slip over my head. "Why didn't you come and get me?"

"She said not to bother." Her hands twist together. "It was Mrs. Sibley, ma'am. She's unwell."

Turning so she can't see my face, I pick up my dress. "Thank you for letting me know."

"Do you need help getting ready?" She lingers in the doorway.

"No," I say shortly. "You'd best go down and let your mother know Mr. Warriner and I will be dining alone."

After the door closes, I toss the dress aside and throw myself on the bed. Three cancellations with the flimsiest of excuses—something has abruptly transformed us into social pariahs.

Not us. Me. Harry has done nothing wrong. His single deviation from the life that had been planned for him was to marry me, and that was far enough in the past to no longer matter. Or was it? Had I, in my pursuit of funds for the clinic, unknowingly made some misstep or offended the dignity of some prominent matron? I rack my brain but cannot recall anything that might have brought about a coordinated response of this magnitude.

When at last I go downstairs, Harry is seated by the fire, another Chesterfield in his fingers. "So we're all alone," he says, and turns in my direction. "Which is a shame, because you look stunning."

I force a smile and sit on the arm of his chair. "Are you not reason enough?"

"I am appreciative enough." He takes my hand. "And I can't say I'm disappointed. The last few months, this house has felt like Broad Street Station."

28

Ava

"Why did I agree to go?" I moan to Pearl, who sits across from me covering buttons with small circles of fabric. "I never enjoy this kind of thing."

"It's not about the party," she says placidly, wrapping thread around the gathered fabric and knotting it. "It's for the clinic. This is more important than the orphans."

That's another thing I don't want to consider—my sister's success in wrangling this clinic out of thin air. For all that I have made fun of Claire's love of dresses, they have become my mode of survival, and it is daunting to realize, yet again, that there is more to my sister than her glossy exterior. Her philanthropy makes me feel small and not very intelligent. Grousing about the party makes it easier, somehow, to bear it.

"I don't have anything to wear."

Pearl bounces up, scattering buttons everywhere. As she collects them, she says over shoulder, "We can make something in between our other work, so long as it's not too complicated."

I draw myself up and pronounce, "I am not a complicated dress woman," but somewhere beneath my words is a smidgen of excitement. A new dress, not something made over. Sliding from behind the table, I pull the box of patterns toward me. They are all dresses I've made before, with notes written across the stylish ladies depicted on the envelopes. None of the elongated women resemble me in the slightest; most of them are slender enough to make Claire look dumpy.

"What about this one?" I hold up an envelope. "Or maybe this." I place them side-by-side on the cutting table.

Putting the buttons aside, Pearl considers both patterns. "This one has an awfully low back, remember?" The envelope drawing shows the front, with its relatively modest neckline, but I remember it drops dramatically in the rear, with a large bow over the wearer's bottom.

"Hmm. I'm not sure if I need decorations back there." I imagine a bow spanning my hips and shudder. "No, I don't think so."

"It could work," she says. "But you'd have to raise the back to cover your girdle—this was for Miss Nichols and she doesn't wear one—so it would hang differently, wouldn't it?"

I imagine Betty Nichols's reaction if I turn up at the party in the same dress. She might even be wearing her steel gray version with its butter-yellow bow, so if I do use this pattern, I will have to be careful she doesn't note any similarities. Then again, she's three inches taller than me and at least five inches narrower around the hips. She would never conceive we could wear the same dress.

Neither can I, but I've made similar gowns for Mrs. Foster and Mrs. Thorndyke and they were happy with the results; if Lavinia Thorndyke can look good in bias cut satin after four thumping boys, so can I.

I'm not brave enough for the gown with the bow. I page through the fashion magazines Claire regularly delivers and draw Pearl's attention to a more modest gown I think will suit me and will not take too long to put together. Made of contrasting colors, the dark skirt comes to a high point in the front where the two overlapping bodice panels wrap around, tying in a simple knot in back. It is not too low in either direction, and though the panels drape gracefully at the shoulder, there are no set-in sleeves to contend with.

"What about this?"

She takes the magazine and backs away, holding it out to look from it to me. "This is really pretty, Mama. It's not fancy, but..."

"But I'm not fancy. It's okay to tell the truth."

"It's not fancy, it's *elegant*."

By the end of the day, Pearl has gathered together newspaper for pattern pieces and retrieved enough muslin from previous dresses to cut out an abbreviated form of the gown once the pattern is made. "That way we can fit it to you before we cut into your good fabric. When are you going to go shopping?"

I hadn't thought that far ahead, lost in a fantasy of dress-up as if I am no older than Thelma. Coming to my senses, I say, "I shouldn't go. Or if I do, I can wear my black dress."

Pearl pulls back, a skeptical look on her face. "It's money you're worrying about, isn't it?"

"When is it not?" I rearrange the newspapers on the table. "It's not a necessary expense."

"It is!" She takes the pieces away from me. "How many women are going to be at that party who might not have heard of you yet? If you're there, wearing one of your dresses, you look successful. Rich people like success."

She is right. It is because of the expectations of the wealthy that I have cut my hair and started to wear makeup. Not being pregnant for the first time in ages, I've also splashed out on a proper girdle. Its Lastex panels are more comfortable than my old corset, and they will hold my abundance in check beneath the unforgiving sheen of satin.

Claire

I had enjoyed our solitary dinner, but it was difficult to keep from wondering what had gone wrong. "I'm sure it's a coincidence," Harry said more than once, seeing my expression. "It's February. People get sick. Things come up."

"I'm sure you're right," I said, poking the jellied salad with my fork. Mrs. Hedges had been correct; it was visually appealing but tasted terrible. "But all three couples?"

Max came in at ten, and I left the men to have a drink and went up to bed, hoping the next day would bring some needed clarity.

In the morning, the failed dinner party no longer matters because this is the day Barrington Leech's article will appear in the *Inquirer*. I wait impatiently while Harry reads his sections of the newspaper over breakfast, tutting about the latest worrisome news from Germany.

Finally, he pushes his plate aside. "I'm late," he says, gathering up the paper. "See you tonight."

I tilt my cheek for his kiss. "Leave the society page, will you?"

Pouring a second cup of coffee, I retrieve the pages, hoping that the gala has been given proper coverage. We haven't sold nearly enough tickets to afford the x-ray machine. As a matter of fact, I haven't sold any tickets in almost a week.

A photo of Harry and me dominates the front page. I read the first line—*Prominent Socialite's Brother a Vagrant?*—and it doesn't make sense. Then it does, and I skim the next lines with my heart in my throat and my stomach threatening to return my breakfast to the damask tablecloth.

> *Any member of Philadelphia society who has recently made a contribution to Mrs. Harrison Warriner's proposed clinic has no doubt heard the heartwarming tale of the project's inspiration: the prominent hostess wished to alleviate the suffering of the men living at the notorious encampment behind the Philadelphia Museum of Art. What is not so widely known is that the brother of the clinic's patroness was, until recently, a denizen of that very same encampment.*

Not a single word of my long conversation with Barrington Leech is present in the article. Instead, it is paragraph after paragraph of innuendo, ending with the infuriating conjecture that the funds collected are intended to pay off my embarrassing brother and send him far away. There are actual quotes from Jake, along with a photograph.

Where have these lies come from? I recounted the entire history of the project to Mr. Leech—I even drove him down to look at the building, which, less than a month out, still resembled a construction site. He knew the names of the other women involved, and that Max's treatment of those "denizens of the camp" had been the inspiration for the clinic. I close my eyes against a sudden dizzying nausea. It's not just wrong, but ludicrously so—no one could possibly believe it.

Except they do. Our empty table last night is all the proof I need. Word of the article was leaked, as anything salacious always is, and society has closed ranks against me. The people whose money I need to support the clinic will give no quarter because there is a shadow of truth to the story: my brother did live at the camp, and if asked, I would have to admit it.

How did Mr. Leech even discover Jake's existence? And why would my brother talk to a reporter? I cover my face with my hands. Tears leak through my fingers. Why hadn't I asked for the page before Harry left? He always knows how to handle things.

I can call him! I bound out of my seat, then remember Hedges is driving him to New Jersey. He will be out of reach until he returns tonight. Distantly, the phone rings, and then the door opens. Pixie scurries in and tries to climb in my lap, whining urgently. "Mrs. Claire," Katie says, "it's Mrs. Foster."

The dog at my heels, I leave the shelter of the dining room for the telephone alcove. It somehow feels exposed and dangerous. "Hello?"

"What were they thinking, publishing such rubbish?" Prue's fury is audible through the telephone line.

"I don't know." I steady the wobble in my voice; it will not do for her to know I've been crying. "There's not one word of my interview in the whole thing."

"There's not one word of anything but filth. It's all lies!"

"You've met Jake," I remind her, curling the cord around my finger and rubbing Pixie's head with my other hand; attuned to my emotions, he will not leave my side until I am calmer. "He did live at the camp before he moved in with Ava."

Who knows where he had lived before that? Thankfully the article hadn't explored Jake's past, only mine; I shudder to think what it would be like if he'd recounted the twenty years apart from his family.

"I'd forgotten," she says, "but that has nothing to do with you, anyway. It's just going to be hard to explain to the women who take Leech's words as gospel."

With a sigh, I tell her about our absent dinner guests, and we agree that at least one of them had advance notice of the article. My brother's unfortunate situation has been turned against me, and while it is hurtful enough personally, it may well spell doom for the clinic.

"I haven't moved a ticket all week." Prue says. "You?"

"No." A cold finger of doubt. "Do you think this story has been out there longer than a few days?"

A pause. "Well, we'll find out. We don't have a lot of time for damage control." The line crackles and she continues, "I'll make some calls this morning, try to get a few more people on board before they have a chance to read the paper."

The likelihood of success is small. For all her clout, even Prudence Foster can't convince Philadelphia's elite to support a charitable endeavor that has been sold to them as a combination of extortion and sisterly guilt. I retreat to my sitting room, shutting the door firmly behind me. My desk is littered with lists and proofs of the gala invitation. I shove it all aside and spread out the front page of the society papers again to look at my brother's picture and wonder—why?

Ava

After the children are in bed, I make my way back to the workroom to finally unwrap the fabric I purchased this afternoon. When Pearl came home from school, she took Grace and said firmly, "Don't come home until you find something perfect."

"I'm making an evening dress," I told Mr. Mendel and his shop assistant. "For myself this time."

The old man smiled and pushed back his skullcap, mussing his thinning gray hair. "For yourself, Mrs. Kimber? That is not something you do often, I think."

"It's a charity event," I told him. "I'm going as a walking billboard."

Mr. Mendel got down with some difficulty. "Then let us go and find something."

I was shocked; I'd never seen him move off that stool in all the times I'd been in the shop. He directed traffic and offered opinions, but he never came out from behind the counter and left the heavy brass cash register unattended.

"Not velvet, I think," he said, leading me toward the section of the store where bolts of dressy fabric shimmered in the low light. He looked at me critically. "Satin."

"Satin," I agreed. "But rayon, not silk." The dress was an investment, but I wasn't going to spend more than I could make back.

A sigh, and a slight detour to the less costly fabrics. While they were not the best he had to offer, there was a riot of color that any candy store would be proud to claim. I closed my mind to most of them, looking exclusively at the practical shades.

"Not black?" he asked, looking at me closely.

"No." I already had the black dress I'd remade for Christmas. "I need color, but nothing showy." I proffer the page I'd torn from the magazine. "This, but not in black-and-white."

"Blue," he said. "To go with your eyes."

After all the times I pushed Claire to choose other colors, she would laugh herself silly if I showed up in blue. "Let's see what you have," I said, willing to be convinced.

I chose navy for the skirt—it was close enough to black that I didn't think of it as blue—and I was considering whether I wanted ivory for the bodice when Mr. Mendel tugged a bolt loose from the end of the row. The satin caught the light from the hanging bulbs and I gasped.

"This is what you need," he said, and handed it to his assistant. "Is a remnant." He smiled broadly. "My gift."

"I couldn't accept it."

"Consider it an investment." He returned to the counter while the satin was cut. "You are good customer."

"You've always been so kind, Mr. Mendel." The sky blue satin shimmers on the counter, a color so pure it hurts my eyes to look at it. "And now this. Thank you."

His fingers tap the keys of the register, totaling up the rest of my purchase: navy satin, organza, thread. He takes my money, sorting it neatly into the cash drawer, before saying, "We understand each other, I think, Mrs. Kimber. We know quality when we see it."

Claire

The next day, things are no better. Harry is gone before I am even awake, a note on the breakfast table saying simply, *"Have a good day. I love you."*

"That's all well and good for you," I grumble, not even bothering to smile at Katie as she brings my plate. "How early did Mr. Warriner leave? Did you see him?"

She shakes her head. "I didn't, ma'am, but my mama said he called for the car at half past six."

I spent most of last night crying on his shoulder or into a number of increasingly damp handkerchiefs. There had been no mention of meetings today, so I assume he can handle no more of my sniveling. I wanted him home this morning, because during the night it had come to me—how to solve the mess I was in. His mother is the key. Irene has more power in this city than I can ever hope to possess; along with her cadre of equally old, equally wealthy women, she could ruin anyone who forgot their place or put a foot wrong. Just as easily she could save me, and reverse the damage done by this vindictive reporter.

And by my own brother.

I will think about him later, I decide. Right now, I have to focus on Irene. When I call, Evans informs me my mother-in-law is at home. From her sly tone, I know she's read the article, probably sniggered over it in the kitchen with Mrs. Fell.

"Claire?" Irene's voice, reedier than usual, comes over the line. "How are you?"

"As well as can be expected." From habit, I pat my hair, checking for the stray wisps that she never fails to point out.

There is a creak as Irene sits at the telephone table. "I saw the paper. How are you bearing up?"

I swallow hard. Sympathetic Irene is something new under the sun. "Not well," I confess. "No one is returning my calls, and we haven't sold a ticket to the gala in over a week."

"Shameful." She clucks. "That reporter should be horsewhipped."

"I admit to having had the same thought."

"What does Harry say about it?" Irene asks. "He knows the editor. He could probably have the man fired."

My gaze, flighty as I feel, darts around the hall. "He hadn't said much," I tell her, ashamed of my husband's lack of outrage on my behalf. "He seems very distracted."

Another cluck. "Men and their business. If they didn't provide for us so well, there'd be no purpose for them."

Hearing Irene criticize her son, even obliquely, is more shocking than her sympathy.

"I don't really know how he can help," I begin. "But *you* could."

After fifteen minutes, I put the phone down, utterly wrung out. Mrs. Hedges appears at the end of the hall, a dust rag in her hand: polishing while Katie is occupied with Teddy.

"Can I bring you some tea?" she asks. "Or coffee?"

I shake my head. "Right now, I don't think straight gin would be enough."

Upstairs, I take off my day dress and stand before the closet in my slip, trying to decide what a supplicant would wear to prostrate herself before a powerful benefactor. I choose a simple black dress with a white collar and cuffs, which I last wore at my mother's funeral. Gloves. A neat black hat with a small veil.

I do not look like a woman with a vagrant brother, extorting cash from the wealthy to assuage her guilt.

Taking a deep breath, I peek into the nursery. Teddy is sitting on the carpet, building a tower of blocks while Katie sits in my rocker, reading aloud to him. They look up at my entrance.

"I'll be gone for an hour or two," I say. "Off to visit Mrs. Warriner."

"I hope she can help, ma'am." Katie's gaze is full of warm sympathy, and I remember how she once put her arms around me, when I lost my last baby, and how good that felt.

"Thank you." I start to speak to Teddy, then change my mind. He is so accustomed to my comings and goings that he has gone back to his tower.

"Mrs. Warriner is in the living room," Baxter says, funereal as always. "Mrs. Ramsay has gone out."

So I am to face Irene alone. She probably invited me because her sister isn't here to provide a buffer. But no buffer is needed. Irene is gracious and empathetic, squeezing my hand once or twice and denouncing Mr. Leech until I feel sorry for him, despite his iniquities.

"I'll start making calls tomorrow morning," she tells me. "I have the orchestra tonight—I'll be in the Sibley's box—and I'll put a word in Sarah's ear."

"Mrs. Sibley has never been interested in donating." I'd tried twice before the abortive dinner party, but she is made of stronger stuff than the young women of my set and the malleable wives of Harry's associates.

"Not yet." Irene gives a chill smile. "But she will. *And* she'll buy two tickets to the gala." She pats my shoulder, stepping back so Baxter can help me into my fur. "Have faith."

"It's so kind of you to help." I don't like being under obligation to Irene, but here I am, thanking her. "I know we haven't always seen eye to eye."

"Don't be ridiculous." A more familiar Irene appears for a moment. "This reflects on my family, not just yours."

I ride down in the elevator, my head ringing like a church bell. I need two aspirin and my bed, that's what I need. Why had I been stupid and left the car at home? It wasn't that cold, but I no longer felt like walking.

As I cross the lobby, a dark and glossy head rises like a seal from behind a folded newspaper. "Claire!"

Francis Gardiner moves like his joints have been oiled, I decide, as he bridges the distance between us with a barely visible movement.

"Mr. Gardiner." Irene has taken every ounce of strength I have left; I do not have energy for the mental gymnastics required by a conversation with him. "This is unexpected."

He brings my gloved hand to his lips. "I do live here."

"Upstairs," I return, pulling my hand free. "I wouldn't have expected to encounter you in the lobby."

Gardiner smiles. How can a minor stretching of the lips convey so much? "Alas, my bachelor life is such that I was prolonging the inevitable trip to my lonely rooms by reading the paper."

I flinch; any mention of newspapers is raw after my conversation with Irene. "I won't keep you, then."

"No, please do." He tosses the paper aside. "How tactless of me to have mentioned it."

So even he knows of my shame! Somehow that bothers me more than a stranger knowing. "I don't wish to discuss it."

"Of course not." He offers his arm and I take it reluctantly, letting him guide me through the doors and onto Spruce Street. "Would you permit me to buy you a cup of coffee?"

"No, thank you. Irene has already filled me with tea and recriminations."

"Now, she's not so bad." He gives me the grin that surely inspired his nickname. "I find her quite charming."

"That's because she likes you." Despite my refusal, he appears to be drawing me toward a tiny tea shop on the corner. "I don't have time to stop."

He opens the door. "Really? Are you off to some big society shindig this afternoon?"

The sheer cruelty of his words makes me stumble and he takes my arm and leads me to a small table in the corner. By the time I have caught my breath, the waitress is bringing a tray with two cups of coffee, a pitcher of milk, and sugar.

"That was unnecessary," I say after a restorative sip. "Irene says this will all blow over."

"I'm sorry." He is close enough that his sleeve brushes mine. "I wanted to spend a few minutes with you, and I didn't know how else to get you to agree."

"Does being unkind generally work?" I narrow my eyes in my best imitation of my sister.

Gardiner lapses into silence and I drink my coffee and try to settle my nerves before he speaks again. The shop is busy for this time of day, and no one is looking at us, but my skin prickles as if I am being watched. My unease grows when Gardiner takes my hand, removing my glove one finger at a time and dropping it on the table, before turning my palm so it faces up.

"What are you doing?"

He put a light finger on my wrist. "Your pulse is racing."

I jerk away from him. "Well, it's not because of you," I say, even though it is. There is always a respectful distance in the way Harry touches me, but Gardiner is more straightforward, and I briefly wonder if he dominates every encounter this way.

"A man can dream."

"I have enough to deal with right now," I tell him, drawing in a shaky breath. "I do not—you need to behave."

"Behaving is no fun." When he smiles, I can almost see the twitch of whiskers. "But I'll stop. I wouldn't be able to forgive myself if you cried."

Though my eyes are stinging with tears of frustration and anger, I say contrarily, "I don't cry easily."

He touches my wrist again, fingers trailing lazily toward my palm. "That's probably for the best. I can't bear to see a woman cry. I always want to kiss her until she stops."

<h1 style="text-align:center">29</h1>

Ava

Three busy, satin-filled days pass before Claire's absence registers. When Pearl comes in from school, I look up from my work to ask if she's seen her aunt.

"She's upset about something. She wouldn't tell me, but Katie gave me this and said to show you." She hands over a folded section of newspaper. "It's horrible. Is it true?"

"Let me read it first." I spread it out on the cutting table, careful not to smudge the satin.

It's an article from the *Inquirer*, a few days old now, accusing Claire of misleading people into donating money for a clinic when she really intended to waltz off with the funds to set our brother up in a new life. There is a posed photo of Claire and Harry at some event, and another of Jake, smiling cockily for the camera. He is quoted as saying that his sister promised him a job and a house away from Philadelphia if he cooperated with her plan. He sounds as if his conscience has been overcome, but I know better.

"Is your uncle home yet?" The newspaper blurs before my eyes; I do not think I've ever been this angry.

"No." Pearl leans against me. "It's not true, is it?"

"Not a word of it." I clench my jaw. "Your aunt has been planning this for months, ever since that night Dr. Max and I came back and told her the camp was gone."

"Then why would Uncle Jake say those things?"

I shake my head. "I don't know. Yet."

Jake does not return by suppertime. Dan said he left early in the morning, quietly for once.

"I'm going upstairs before we eat," I tell them. "Keep an eye out and let me know if you see him coming."

His small room is untidy, looking more like the scene of one of the younger boys' Wild West games than the bedroom of a grown man. It smells like a man, though—the mixed odors of cigarettes and unwashed clothes hang in the air. A shirt hangs from the top drawer of the chest, and when I jerk the lower drawer open, a near-empty brown bottle rolls to the front. I look at the label and drop it into the pocket of my apron, disgusted.

"Pearl's keeping watch," Dan says, appearing in the doorway. "What are you looking for?"

"I don't know." I won't put my suspicions into words until I have proof, because I want to be wrong. "Is there anywhere he could hide something in here?"

He edges past me and shoves the bed away from the wall. When he tugs on it, the baseboard below the window comes away. We both see the bundle of bills tucked in the space behind it.

"That," I say hollowly, "is what I was hoping we wouldn't find."

I leave the kids to clear up. "I need to go visit your aunt."

"Can I come?" Pearl asks. "I'll do the dishes when we get back."

"No, me!" Thelma tugs my arm. "I want to see Teddy."

"Teddy will be in bed," I tell her, "and your aunt and I need to talk about grown up stuff." I meet Dan's eyes. "If your uncle comes in, tell him I want to talk to him."

I have hidden the money in the coal bin, where no one but Toby and George would think to look. Three hundred dollars, an amount Jake could have never saved with his habits. Either he extorted it or he was paid off. I'm not sure which is worse, or if I care.

When I arrive, Claire is in the living room with Harry and Max. I wait in the hall while Katie fetches her. "We'll need tea," I say, as I lead Claire into her sitting room. "With lots of sugar."

My sister smiles when she sees me, but it is only reflex: there is no happiness in her. The delicate skin around her eyes is shadowed, her eyes red-rimmed. "How good to see you."

"Why didn't you let me know?" I wait until she sinks into a chair, punching a pale green cushion with unwarranted fervor.

Her eyes flutter closed. "It's all been too much—and I've been so busy trying to reverse all the damage."

I'm concerned about the clinic, of course, because it's so important to her, but I'm more concerned about the Judas in our family. "What about Jake?"

"Honestly, I've been trying not to think about him." She covers her face with her hands. "It feels like such a betrayal."

"That's because it is." His return had made Claire so happy, but it was uncertainty about who he might have become that kept me from telling her I'd seen him last year. "I wish you'd told me sooner."

"I couldn't." She sighs, looking completely exhausted. "I've scarcely had a chance to breathe. Prue has been talking to people for me, and so has Francis Gardiner. Stella, too. Even Irene has gotten involved. If you can imagine, she's been the biggest help of all."

"That old bat?" I can't imagine she would do something to help Claire, but then again, any scandal affecting Claire would affect her son. "What about Harry?"

Her face crumples. "He said I'm blowing it out of proportion, and it will all pass." She stops speaking as the door opens.

I smile up at Katie and nod for her to put the tea on the table. "We can manage."

"Yes, ma'am." Her eyes dart between me and Claire, concerned. "I'll say goodnight, then."

"He's probably right?" I pour Claire's tea and, without asking, dump in three spoons of sugar.

"Maybe." She takes the cup. "But I want him to stand up for me. I'm his wife, and I've been accused of stealing from our friends. This could ruin everything."

I'm sure Harry isn't disregarding her feelings. "What does Max have to say?"

"Oh, you know him!" Claire looks nettled. "He's in one of his unbearable moods where nothing can touch him. It's infuriating."

I know that mood, and am as willing to dwell on it as Claire is to think about Jake's treachery. "Maybe they're right. What's Irene done?"

A faint smile touches her lips. "More than I expected. If she vouches for me, no one will continue to believe those terrible lies. She's talked several donors into staying with the clinic—one was on the verge of asking for his money back. And Prue sold four tickets for the gala this afternoon." She reaches over and adds more sugar to her tea. "Maybe it will work out."

That doesn't solve the issue of our brother. I set my cup aside. If I drink any more, I'll be up all night. "How could he?"

"I don't know." Tears creep into her voice. "And saying I was embarrassed to let him live here, when I could barely even get him through the front door."

"He also failed to mention he was living with his other sister." I am angry all over again, seeing Claire's reddened eyes and knowing what she's been through. "So he's not without a roof over his head."

"It hurts, that's all." Claire's lip trembles and her blue eyes fill with more tears. "It hurts, Ava. He hurt me."

"I know." I pull her close and hold her as if she were no bigger than my Thelma, suffering a similar hurt. "I know."

She buries her face in my neck and sobs, her thin shoulders shaking. The stress of the last few days has hollowed her out, made her insubstantial in my grasp. "He's my brother. All I wanted was for him to love me."

"I know," I say again, rubbing the spot between her shoulder blades and trying not to mind the wet patch she's making on my shoulder. "And he does, I'm sure he does. He's just...broken, Claire."

It's true. I'd sensed the same bitterness in Daniel when things fell apart. He fought it, but if he'd lived, he might have become like Jake—I saw flashes of it when he'd fought with Dan and when I came home after leaving Thelma with Claire. Knowing this makes me soften a bit, but I have made up my mind. Claire, and the sanctity of my home, are more important than my damaged brother.

"I have to go," I say at last, and she takes a shuddering breath. "Make sure the kids go to bed. Will you be all right?"

"I will." She sniffs and I give her one last hug. "Thank you for checking on me."

"That's what sisters are for, remember?"

I walk home in the dark and bitter cold, remembering a similar walk on New Year's Eve, glad at least there is no ice to slow my journey. If I had asked, Harry would have happily rousted Hedges to drive me home, but that would have been only slightly less upsetting than Max offering to escort me. Or not offering.

The factory lets out at five and the streetcars run every fifteen minutes, but Jake rarely makes it in before nine. Sometimes it's even later, and twice he failed to come home at all, prompting Dan to grumble that he would take his room back if his uncle didn't intend to make use of it.

Once the kids are in bed, I retreat to the workroom to finish sewing snaps on the side of my dress, fiddly work best done in daylight, but the light of the unshaded hanging bulb will have to do. The faint echo of bells reaches me through the narrow window. I count eleven, and a few moments later the front door opens and the floor creaks over my head.

"Jake?"

The footsteps stop, hesitating at the junction of the stairs. Up or down? At last, he makes his choice, and soon his feet, then his legs come around the turn of the steps. Finally, he appears in his entirety. "You're up late," he says, non-committal.

"And you're home late." I raise my brows. "Where have you been?"

His expression darkens. "Do I need to account to you for my comings and goings now, Mother?"

I bite the inside of my cheek and put down my sewing before I ruin it. "You're a grown man," I agree, "but it's my house you're making free with, disrupting everyone with your comings and goings."

"Don't you mean Claire's house?"

I stop short, my lecture derailed. "No," I tell him. "*My* house."

Jake sits heavily on the padded bench and it groans at the abuse. "Come on, Ewa." It's our father's voice I hear, drunk and sneering. "You don't expect me to believe you pay for this place out of that frippery work you do?"

"It's Ava," I spit. "Or have you forgotten, Jakub?" I wave a hand at my work space, hung with two finished dresses and more in progress. "Yes, this frippery work, as you call it, pays the rent. And buys the food."

I shove my chair back and stand in front of him. "Your food, too, as a matter of fact."

"I do my part." His tone is sullen.

"So does Dan," I remind him. "And Pearl. We all do our part here." I sit beside him. "I won't put up with tantrums from you any more than I will from Toby, and I won't be lied to, either.

He tips his head back against the wall. "And who's lying to you?"

"You are." I take a breath. "And you lied to the reporter. Do you know what that article has done to Claire?"

"Nothing can touch Princess Claire," he says. "She lives like the Depression doesn't exist. It makes me sick."

I used to think the same way, so I am gentler with him than I'd intended. "She does what she can. This clinic of hers—it will help a lot of people, people like you *were* before Harry got you a job."

"*Gave* me a job." He pushes up from the bench and retreats to the kitchen.

I follow, glad to have him away from my dresses. "It's the same thing."

"It's not. And the sister I remember wouldn't say it was."

There's a pot of tea on the table. I hold my hand close to its side. Warm enough. "The sister you remember was a kid. A lot has changed since then, for all of us. Claire's rich. I'm widowed. You're...whoever you've become. You're certainly not the brother I remember." I meet his eyes. "Not if you can do that to Claire."

"What did I do?" he asks. "So I talked to some reporter. Big deal."

"You took their money."

"It's only money," he says brusquely. "It's not like it came out of her pocket."

"It's not about the money." I shouldn't have to explain this to him. Mama always said loving Jesus was easy; it took a true Christian to love Judas. "It's the betrayal."

"I don't get why she's all worked up over that damn clinic." His expression is pugnacious, challenging me. "It's not like she's done anything. She's a rich woman taking credit for things other people have done."

My mind goes to his assumption that I need help with the rent; he cannot conceive that women are capable of making things in their own right. The tiny kernel of truth in all this is that Claire is trying to be more than a rich woman, and his actions have made her look and feel like a fraud.

"She'd have given you the money, if you'd asked."

He jumps from his seat, understanding his stash is no longer secret. "It's harder for me. I can't do what you did."

"Really? Why?"

"Because I have pride," he says with a shrug. "And I won't throw that away and let her hand me things until I no longer recognize myself."

My sympathy shatters into a thousand pieces. "So you accept money from a stranger to destroy your sister's reputation instead?"

His head jerks around. He'd never imagined that he could hurt her. "Fine," he says, "I'll go over there and make nice, if you think it'll help."

"You will not," I say. "You won't mean it and you'll just get her hopes up. This is like something Tata would have done. I always thought better of you."

"You barely know me. You and Claire want to put me in a box. I've never liked boxes, that's why I've been on the road so long. I could have stayed upstate, but they wanted too much from me."

"Who wanted what from you?" A nasty suspicion is forming in my mind.

"Family."

"You had family, other than us?"

He shrugs. "I don't know where they are now. Not where I left them, I know that much. She said if I was going to come and go as I pleased, she was going back to her folks."

I think of how good he is with my boys and I am suddenly sure that somewhere, there is a wife and at least one son. And he walked away from them the way he walked away from Mama and us. "So you abandoned everything when it got hard."

"You wouldn't understand. If Daniel was here, he'd tell you."

"I told you before, you don't get to use him against me." My hands curl into fists. "Do you remember where pride got Daniel? Dead, that's where. Just like our father. Harry offered him a job, probably at the same place where you're lucky enough to work, but we were too proud to take it."

Jake watches me pace and says nothing.

"Pride killed Daniel as surely as the mines. It left me without a husband, my kids without a father, and all of us without a home. If Claire *wasn't* generous, we'd have nothing." I take a breath, try to calm myself. "She means well, Jake. She just wants us to together again."

"I'm here, ain't I?" His chin juts, reminding me of the boy whose loss we'd mourned. "She'll get over it, same as you will."

The sneer is back. I duck into the alcove where the coal bin lives and come out with the bundle of cash in its rubber band and throw it on the table. "I won't 'get over it'," I tell him. "And neither will Claire. It's time for you to move along, brother."

He looks at the money, then picks it up and counts it.

"It's all there." I stop again, my mind made up. "I won't put you out at this time of night, but you've worn out your welcome. You will pack your things and tomorrow morning, you'll take your money and get out."

Pearl

February 20, 1934

I was tucked back in the window seat with a book when Uncle Jake came in. I know Mama wanted to talk to him, but there's something more than what was in the newspaper. I hate not knowing, but Dan told me he'd fill me in later on what he knew.

Uncle went past without seeing me, but Mama called from the basement and he stopped, then went down. They were quiet for a while, then he actually yelled at her and she got that tone in her voice that says "watch out." I don't think he knows about that, though, because he kept shouting.

I came closer to listen, thinking it would be nice for once to know more than my brother, and Uncle Jake almost knocked me down, he came up so fast.

"Damn kids," he said, and kept going, stomping up the steps and slamming the door of his room. Grace started crying, of course. Mama didn't come, so I brought the baby down in case she needed distracting. She was sitting at the kitchen table in the dark. Just sitting there. I can count on one

hand the time I've seen Mama absolutely still. The workroom light was on, so I could see a little. There were tears on her cheeks.

She told me Uncle Jake will be leaving in the morning. I asked was it because of the article and she said he took thirty pieces of silver to betray Aunt Claire, and she wasn't having it.

"Never betray your brothers and sisters. Never. Walk away from them, if you have to, like I'm doing with Jake, but never betray them."

Claire

"I saw Howard Sibley at the Union League today," Harry says. "It seems he and Sarah are feeling better and would like us to come for dinner next week, to make up for canceling on us. Are you up for it?"

"If you like," I say listlessly. Personally, I wish Sarah Sibley had been carried off by her fictitious malady, which hadn't kept her from attending the orchestra with Irene.

"Howard has been considering a venture into plastics," he says. "So it might be a boring evening for you, with us talking business."

"Oh, to hell with your business!" I burst out, surprising myself. "That damned article has turned my world upside down—half our donors think I've embezzled the funds to set Jake up in a cushy new life—and all you can talk about is business! The clinic is hanging by a thread and where have you even been lately? Not supporting me!"

Tears brim and I furiously wipe them away, realizing for once in my life they won't help my cause or the torrent of accusation that pours from me, now that I've started.

"Busy with work, not caring I'm about to lose everything I've worked for!" I take a breath. "This could ruin everything, don't you realize? They could all demand their money back and I won't have it because I've spent it on the renovations, but they'll think I've stolen it—"

A sob breaks through and I press my fist to my mouth to stifle it. I'm not ready to cry yet.

"They won't," Harry says, his voice mild. "Or they won't now."

"What do you mean?" I ask from behind my fingers. A hiccup escapes me.

"People believe what they're told, until they're told something more believable." His smile is the tiniest bit smug. "No one will ask for their money back."

"You mean you've been—" Blood rushes to my head until it pulses with heat, as I contemplate that I have been berating my husband for ignoring me while, behind the scenes, he has been making everything right.

"Yes, among other things." He pats the cushion beside him and I sit, not letting myself lean against his starched white shirtfront; I don't trust myself yet.

"The article."

"Yes, that damned article, as you said. Not what any of us were expecting." He rubs his shadowed jawline, his fingers making a sandpaper sound. "I spoke to the editor as soon as I found out about it—not the day it came out, for which I apologize—but the next morning."

"Irene thought you should have had the reporter fired." I do, too, but I will let his mother take responsibility for the suggestion.

"Did she?" He tilts his head back, considering. "Interesting. I don't want Leech fired—he did his job, as he saw it. He had a run-of-the-mill society story and he was offered something far more interesting to supplant it."

"But it isn't true!" I've spent the last week saying it to one person or another. "It isn't true."

"But it *was* convincing." Harry raises an eyebrow. "At least superficially. And I didn't ask for his job because I wanted to know where he got the story, and who connected him to your brother."

"He's gone, you know." Ava told me this afternoon he'd disappeared again. "Jake."

"I'm not surprised." He leans forward, lights a cigarette. Offers it to me. "He made a pretty penny off all this."

I refuse, then, as his words register, reach for it. "He was paid to say those things about me?"

Harry lights another cigarette for himself. "Would you rather he'd done it for free?" He circles me with his arm, snugging me against him. "I don't think there's any real malice in him, Claire, but he's not the brother you loved as a child. He's had twenty years of hard living between then and now. We can't judge him."

I draw smoke into my lungs and hold it, remembering the conversations with Jake where he told me he couldn't live up to my expectations. It sickens me to think I might have pushed him into this.

A question occurs to me. "Whose money was it?"

Harry stiffens, so slightly it could almost be an inhale. But I know my husband's body and its movements.

"Harry?"

"The reporter paid him," he says, stubbing out his cigarette. "For his story."

"But it wasn't the newspaper's money?" I drop my cigarette into the ashtray and catch his wrist in my fingers before he can busy himself with anything else.

"No." He turns and takes my hands. "That's why I've been so quiet these last few days. Once I found out who was behind all this...I needed time to figure out how to handle it. How to live with it."

I'm afraid I know what he is going to say. I pray I am wrong.

"It was Mother," he confirms. "She knew about the interview, and she called the paper to offer a better story. She gave them Jake's name, told them where to find him, and then paid to have him confirm the lies she fed the reporter."

This is so far beyond what I thought she was capable of that I am speechless.

"I truly think she has gone insane." He leans forward, kisses me on the forehead. "I'll make it right, Claire. You don't have to worry. But I can't talk about it yet." His lips linger at my hairline. "It's too painful."

30

Claire

Harry is gone by the time I come down, and Max might as well be, for all the attention he pays to the outside world. "I don't suppose you have a sign painter among your varied acquaintance?" I sit across from him. "You know everyone."

"What for?" Max shovels in scrambled eggs, barely looking up.

"Because the renovations are almost complete and the building has yet to acquire a sign." I stifle a sigh.

"I think so." He washes the eggs down with coffee, rakes his fingers through his curly hair, and pushes his chair back. "I'll call in on him today and let him know what you're looking for."

"You remember what it should say?" I'm proud of the name I'd come up with. Even Barrington Leech had praised it, before the story of my brother overtook any mention of the clinic by name.

"Of course." Max grins. "Leave it to me, Claire."

He is barely in the house for the next few days, finishing off his time at Children's Hospital, organizing supplies and donations, and keeping up his other volunteer activities. When I finally catch him, trudging up the steps one night after eleven, he pauses on the landing. His eyes are heavy-lidded with exhaustion but he musters a smile. "Did you see it?"

"See what?"

"The sign. It looks fine, doesn't it?"

"I haven't been there yet." I draw my quilted silk robe closer, wrinkling my nose at the smell of smoke on his clothes. "I'm driving down in the morning."

"You'll like it," he assures me with a yawn. "O'Brien painted it on the front window, and then he got out the ladder and did it on the brickwork at the side of the building."

Most of the factory buildings in South Philadelphia had names painted on them, usually in ten foot letters. Our building is smaller than those, but it was thoughtful of Max to tie the clinic into the neighborhood.

"I'm looking forward to seeing it." I take his shoulder, push him toward the stairs. "Go to bed."

The next morning, I'm out early—ahead of Max, for once—because I'm excited to see Mr. O'Brien's artistry. As always, the streets are crowded with vehicles, and I have to wait for several minutes on Washington Avenue because a stalled truck has blocked the intersection and no one is willing to give way in the opposite lanes. When I finally turn onto League Street, the clinic is hidden beyond the taller buildings but it soon comes into sight. I slow the car, unable to believe my eyes.

Under the roof's peak, in large white letters—not ten feet tall, but near enough—it says *The People's Clinic.*

What happened to *The Philadelphia Clinic for the Deserving Poor*? I remember Max's expression when he'd heard the name and understand exactly what happened. It wasn't what he had in mind, and when I foolishly gave him the opportunity to change it, he couldn't resist. I continue up the block and park, already knowing what I will find on the front window: the same blunt prescriptive in gold letters, outlined in black.

It has a ring to it, I admit. Just not the sort of ring I had in mind.

I dig into my handbag for the key. The lock sticks and I have to nudge the door with my hip. I add it to the mental list of things Mr. Cullen must deal with before we open.

I flip on the lights, and the waiting area blooms into brightness. While the examining rooms are hospital green at Max's request, this room is a sunny pale yellow, almost identical to my sitting room. The ceiling is white, and that, in combination with the many hanging lights, makes it a bright and cheerful space—a far cry from the filthy abandoned building it had once been, and an even further stretch from Max's outdoor clinic.

Just inside the door are rows of wooden benches where patients can wait. I had wanted padded seats, but then, remembering Jake's refusal to sit anywhere but the kitchen, I chose something plainer so people don't have to worry about dirtying the furniture.

There is a desk in the corner where a nurse will sit, taking down the patients' names. Beyond are three examining rooms, a room for Max's cherished x-ray machine and, through a door at the back, a separate area with showers and racks and shelves filled with donated clothing.

Other than the purchase of the x-ray machine, the only section of the clinic as yet unfinished is the small kitchen. It was part of the original plan, but Mr. Cullen had been unable to find a stove suitable for the purpose until recently, and it is due to be delivered and the kitchen finished by the end of the week.

"I don't know why you think you need that." His tone made it clear that I was being silly. "It's a medical clinic, not a restaurant. What's next, a soda fountain?"

"Dr. Byrne treats his patients like human beings." I was getting better about sticking to my guns and not being embarrassed about it. "That might involve offering them tea on a cold day."

"We can't have a gas line run, you know." His ham-pink face grew bright with frustration. "The city service doesn't extend here."

"Then think of something, Mr. Cullen."

He stalked off, grumbling, but two days later an invoice arrived for a three burner Coleman camping stove. It used gas canisters and would fit handily on the enameled counter alongside the cast iron sink. Men like to grumble, but with proper handling, they generally get where they're needed in the end.

We need mugs and plates and basic flatware. My first thought is Wanamakers, but that is a waste of hard graft. I'll see if Pearl wants to go to Woolworths; we'll buy them out and maybe I can sneak a little treat in for her while we're shopping. She's growing up. Ava tolerated the perfume at Christmas, but she might have my head if I buy my niece a tube of Tangee.

I stand in the center of the waiting room and imagine it bustling with patients, a nurse in a neat white uniform, Max and his friend Dr. Spencer conversing seriously in a doorway.

It strikes me then—really strikes me—that I have done it. I have created this from nothing, from a daydream on a train and a desire to do something besides be a pointless ornament. I wonder if Mrs. Roosevelt will ever read my letter, and if she would consider visiting the clinic if she happened to come to Philadelphia. That would be an achievement for Irene to read about in the newspaper.

Pearl

March 17, 1934

Mama's gone off to the party looking like Cinderella. It was so wonderful to see her actually wearing something as nice as what she makes for other people. It's more simple, of course, but Mama's not a fuss-and-ruffles type. She thinks she's too big, or too old. Too something that isn't true. She could carry off anything, if she wanted to.

Dan and I are at home with the kids. He's twitchy, but I told him there's no way he's going out and sticking me with the little ones for hours. Maybe we should have taken Aunt up on her invitation and gone to her house, except then we would all have to get home again, and Mama said she might be late. Knowing her, she'll probably be early. It wasn't even half-past ten on New Year's Eve when she came home, and that was with Dr. Max walking her.

He's bound to be at the party tonight, since he'll be working at the clinic. I wonder if he and Mama will talk, and if they'll be able to patch it up. Whatever it was.

Ava

I don't understand how or why Claire enjoys these events. Within minutes of passing through the doors to the Warwick Hotel ballroom, she is off, flitting from person to person, doing what she needs to do. At least with the Christmas parties I'm safe behind a table, pouring eggnog. As a guest I feel simultaneously exposed and lost in the crowd.

When Harry stops to speak to someone, I make my excuses and retreat to an empty stretch of wall near the drinks table. From there, I can watch the crowd to my heart's content and count the women wearing my dresses. Including my own and Claire's green inaugural gown, there are five: Lavinia Thorndyke, sleek in black satin; Geneva Rowland in rose velvet with candy-colored chiffon sleeves; and Prue Foster, wearing the first dress I made for money, purple satin with a harlequin drape.

Aside from my simple blue gown, this party is an advertisement for my business. Seeing my dresses on these rich women, holding their own against the best Philadelphia retailers have to offer, fills me with pride. The nagging tension in my neck begins to ease. This is my achievement, the work of my hands and many, many nights of worry and planning. We will survive here, in this new place. I have made sure of that.

The room is filled with couples: dancing, laughing, speaking quietly with their heads together. As any couple, rich or poor, might, at an event such as this.

I miss that.

I have made sure we will survive, but just as surely, I have made certain I am alone.

The music stops abruptly and Harry mounts the shallow steps to the stage and taps the microphone. "None of you came here tonight to listen to me," he says, "but I do have something to say. It concerns my wife, and her purpose in organizing the clinic." Claire's head whips around; whatever this is, they haven't discussed it in advance.

The faces around me are avid with expectation of repudiation or disgrace. Across the room, Irene is smiling broadly, her arms folded across her sunken chest.

"Right before we left to come here, we received a telegram." He reaches into his breast pocket and retrieves a slip of buff-colored paper. Opening it, he reads, clearly and for effect, "President Roosevelt and I wish to offer our sincere congratulations on the opening of The People's Clinic. We are so very proud of you." A pause, and his eyes move slowly around the room, seeing what I saw. "Your friend, Eleanor Roosevelt."

There is a moment of silence, then wild applause. I join in. Claire's hands are over her face, her ruffled sleeves shaking with the strength of a month's worth of emotion. The article has been wiped from the public memory by a few well-chosen words from the First Lady, and Harry's impeccable timing.

He steps back and offers the stage to his wife. Claire kisses him, to more applause, then comes to the microphone. The white flowers at her shoulder match the sprays on either side of the small podium. Everything in this world is deliberate, calculated to convey an impression. It's something I need to study, even as I question its necessity.

"Ladies and gentlemen." Her voice is steady; you'd never know that a moment ago, she was crying. "On behalf of The People's Clinic, I want to thank you all for coming.

"Most of you have already contributed to the building or equipping of the clinic, and I thank you for being gracious enough to write yet another check to be here tonight." There is a murmur from the crowd. She takes a visible breath and leans in. "Though I've been told some people will do almost *anything* to be seen at the right party. I hope you all get your pictures in the paper tomorrow."

Their laughter surprises her and pinks her cheeks. "I won't take up any more of your time. The person you really want to hear from is Dr. Max Byrne, who will head up the clinic and who can speak about it much more intelligently than I ever could." She beckons to the man standing behind her. "Max?"

Max is at the bar, talking with great animation to Prue Foster's husband. The coupe of champagne in his hand sloshes when he waves to illustrate his point. He is flushed, smiling. A good man, happy in his work.

It's easy to fall in love with a good man.

My mother's voice catches me by surprise; I haven't heard her in a while. As always, she speaks the truth I need to hear. I take a deep breath, focus on Max. *You can stop pushing, Mama. I hear you.*

It's a long way across the ballroom. I fight the urge to flee as I sidestep dancers and accept a glass of champagne from a passing waiter. What is it Harry calls it? Dutch courage? I knock back the entire glass and the bubbles rise to my head.

When I reach Max, he is tipping down the last of his drink. I put my hand on his black sleeve. "Max."

His fingers tighten on the stem of the glass. "Ava."

"It was a good speech," I say inadequately. I envy his passion; he is so full of energy and enthusiasm about the clinic venture.

He shrugs. "I'm full of words," he says, quoting me to myself. "It's not difficult."

I lower my head. "I'm sorry." All the things I'm sorry for swirl in my mind, but I can't voice them—if I start apologizing to this man for all the times I've wronged him, we'll be in the same spot when the band goes home. "Would you like to dance?"

Max puts the glass carefully on the table and turns to me. "I thought you'd never ask."

I step into his arms, anticipating a reminder of Daniel and all the times we'd danced together, but it is different with Max. His grip is inquiring, allowing me to decide how close I want to be held. Daniel's arms had never asked; they'd simply taken, because I was his and he knew it.

For a moment the ballroom fades away and the grubby, poorly-lit hall in Scovill Run rises around me. The man holding me is no longer at eye level, but a head taller, his chin brushing my temple. Tears burn and I blink them back.

Daniel is gone. Max is here. And he does not deserve to be held to a standard he will never meet.

We dance for a long time, silent, getting used to each other's rhythms. "This has to be heading toward something," he says at last. "Not keeping company on the sofa of an evening or having dinner at your sister's."

I wet my lips. "What do you mean?"

"You know what I mean." His patience with me is enormous. "When I told you I was in love with you, you couldn't get me out of the house fast enough. I'm not made of rubber, Ava." His warm breath tickles my ear. "I won't bounce back forever."

"I was scared." I look into his eyes. "When you hurt your arm, I realized how much I cared. I wasn't sure I was ready for that again."

He spins me around, maneuvering us between the other couples and into an alcove protected from view by tall potted palms. Another deliberate choice; people need the occasional discreet corner. "And are you ready now?"

"I want to be." All I can offer him is honesty. "But I can't guarantee how quickly I'll get there."

"I can wait." He pulls me close, until we are concealed behind the palms. "So long as we're heading in the right direction."

"We are." My hands are on his chest, though we've stopped dancing, and so I take the opportunity to lean in and kiss him.

31

Claire

The evening is almost over. I return from the ladies' room and encounter the astonishing sight of my sister on the dance floor in Max Byrne's arms. It makes me as happy as Mrs. Roosevelt's telegram. Before I reach our table, Francis Gardiner appears before me and bows, a bit too correctly. Over his shoulder, Harry's expression is thunderous but he doesn't intervene. Whichever choice I make, there will be talk. In the end, I offer my hand and let him lead me out for a foxtrot.

Gardiner is as good a dancer as I would expect, and when I return, breathless, after three dances, Harry's expression is no brighter, and there are several more butts in the ashtray.

"What's the matter?"

He doesn't look at me. "You know I don't like him."

I sit down, arrange my wrap around suddenly chilled shoulders. "I never expected you to be the jealous type."

He presses his lips together. "And I never expected my wife to act like a fool over a man who isn't worthy of shining the shoes of those migrants you've made the clinic for."

"But he's helped me get the clinic." I sit up very straight. "And I'm grateful."

"I've also helped you," he says, his voice low. "So has Max. So have a hundred other people here tonight."

"And yet you're only angry at one of them." Across the room, Gardiner leans on the bar, a drink in his hand. Watching us. He is not a nice man, but I won't stand for Harry telling me what to do, not when he's done less to help me with the clinic than Francis Gardiner.

"Because I know him." Harry polishes his glasses on a napkin and shoves them back on his face. "And it might interest you to know he's married."

I conceal my surprise. "That's of no interest to me, either way."

"It interests me," Harry says. "He's never had a relationship that could even vaguely be termed decent."

"Well, we don't have a relationship." I smooth my white evening glove where it has been creased by my bracelet. "We're business associates."

"I don't waltz with my business associates." I've rarely seen this level of outrage in Harry, not even when a business deal has gone wrong. The closest I can remember is the time his mother criticized Teddy.

"You don't have any female business associates."

I sound no older than Thelma, and far more petulant, but it makes him smile—a small smile, but my husband is visible again. "If I did, I'd have the sense not to try to seduce them on the dance floor."

I reach across and take a puff of his cigarette. "He doesn't mean anything by it."

"I doubt that." He covers my hand with his. "I've known Wolf since I was six years old. He was slippery then, and he's slippery now. Do you know how he ended up in London?"

Taking a sip of my champagne cocktail, I look over the rim of the glass. Gardiner has turned away. I try to remember what Irene told me about his background. "The bank transferred his father. The whole family moved."

"That's the story they decided on," Harry concedes. "But it's not what happened."

"So then why did he go?" He may not like Gardiner, but it isn't like him to get personal. "What did happen?"

His chin drops to his chest as he debates what to tell me. "It was before the Crash," he says. "Wolf was working for an investment firm, doing some...questionable deals. He was lucky—he usually is—but this time he played fast and loose with the wrong person's money. He hadn't covered his tracks, assuming everything would go as planned, but when it didn't, old Baird Sibley—Howard's father—refused to cover for him."

"What happened?" Gardiner is watching us again; this time I turn away.

"His father had to bail him out and pay back the money he lost. It was close to a hundred thousand dollars, from what I heard. Because of the respect people had for old Mr. Gardiner, it was swept under the rug, but he arranged for a transfer and the whole family left for England soon after. The expectation was Wolf would stay there, keep his messes on the other side of the pond."

It strikes me that, in addition to knowing her son's dislike of Francis Gardiner, Irene knows all this, and yet she made sure he was thoroughly enmeshed in my business. This, on top of her duplicity with the newspaper reporter, makes me look at him with new eyes.

"Do you know why he's come back?"

Harry looks into his empty glass, then pushes his chair away from the table. "I'd rather dance with my wife than talk about him. Once the clinic is open and you have time to take a breath, I'll tell you the whole sordid tale."

Pearl

March 18, 1934

At church this morning, I thanked God for the miracle He sent us. Mama went to the party for Aunt's clinic last night, grumbling all the way, but she came home with Dr. Max! I was asleep, but I woke up when I heard them talking down on the step, and then I heard him laugh. It was private-sounding, not like his usual laugh at all, and I cracked open the window the tiniest bit. I couldn't hear much, only that it would be hard for him to wait until Monday to see her.

When Mama came upstairs, I made a show of waking up and asking if she needed help getting out of her gown, but she said no and went into the bathroom. Even though it was late, she turned on the water and by the time she got out of the tub, I was asleep again.

Ava

I should know better than to drink champagne. It always gets me into trouble.

Not trouble, not really, but when Max and I left the Warwick—he insisted on walking me home, although he was the guest of honor—I knew putting him off again would be impossible. We will be a couple, and I will have to deal with both my sister's and the kids' happiness.

I'm not unhappy myself, but I hate letting my private life be picked over by people, even people I love. Max seems to understand. After he came for supper tonight and we sat up late like we did before, he said it was in my hands, how I wanted to let people know, but he hoped I wouldn't keep it a secret for too long.

"You're too wonderful to keep under my hat," he said, as we kissed goodnight. It was a light caress, not like the kiss we'd shared on New Year's Eve, but there was intent behind it. If we spent too much time together, we'd end up fooling around on the davenport like a couple of kids, and that's the last thing I want, imagining Pearl coming downstairs to warm a bottle for Grace and finding us in a position needing no explanation.

She seems to know, anyway. When I came in from the party, she woke up very conveniently and offered to help me undress. I said no because I couldn't face her questions. In the brightly lit bathroom, I brushed my hair and scrubbed the makeup from my face. I removed my gown, putting it on the padded hanger I'd left on the back of the door, and then I tackled my underwear. Released from the confines of my girdle, my stomach quivered like one of those monstrous jellied things Claire likes to serve. I've lost most of the weight I gained with Grace, but my skin will never be tight again in my lifetime, any more than my breasts will stand up on their own.

I don't compare myself to Claire—her slender build is so different from mine that we may as well be different species. She has never borne a child, and it sometimes seems I've never stopped. Stretch marks gleam silver along my sides and above the waist of my pants, proof I have birthed a near baseball team in my time.

Daniel loved my pregnant body. He could make me feel beautiful until the last weeks, when I lumbered around like a cow ready to drop a calf. Nothing could make me feel good about myself by that point. He once told me that pregnancy softened my sharp edges, by which he no doubt meant my tongue.

It has gotten no less sharp with age. Max made it clear he wants me, despite the awful things I've said to him, and that, more than anything, makes me realize I can't avoid the future simply by hiding from it.

Claire

The car is near to overflowing: Hedges, of course, is at the wheel; Max, Harry and I are already in the back seat when Ava appears, and we make room for her. Katie, bouncing with restrained excitement, shares the front seat with her father and a pair of hampers. When we slow to a stop in front of the clinic, the painted letters on the window are almost hidden behind a milling crowd of shabby men. I looked closely at them until Ava tugs at my arm.

"He won't be here," she says softly. "Celebrate your achievement and forget about him."

"Easier said than done," I mutter in return, but I get out of the car and hand the key to Max, standing back to watch as he opens the door.

"Come on in," he shouts. "Take a seat, and someone will be right with you."

That is not precisely accurate; the nurse can't start until tomorrow, but we didn't want to put off the opening. I sit at the desk and take down names and vague descriptions of ailments, while Ava assists Max in the examining room. Harry mingles with the men, chatting amiably, and Katie lights the stove and puts water on for tea.

John Spencer arrives at noon and Harry leaves, taking Katie with him so her mother doesn't have Teddy and Grace for the entire day. Ava takes over the tea station, then helps several men find clothes in their sizes and produces a sewing kit from her purse to sew on buttons and patch shirts. The men linger, smoking like chimneys and drinking gallons of tea.

When we leave at four, the doctors stay behind for a final two hours. I ease myself into the back seat of the Packard, my back protesting, and slide over so Ava can join me.

She wrinkles her nose. "We smell like an ashtray."

I take a shallow breath and taste smoke in the back of my throat. "No wonder they all cough like that." I arch my back, trying to loosen the tightness caused by being too long on my feet. "I want a bath."

"Me too." Ava stifles a yawn behind her hand. "Except I might drown."

The sky is gray outside the car windows, the sun nearly down. It is tempting to go straight to bed after my bath, but I can't—Max will be home at seven and I want to hear his thoughts. I'm sure Ava does as well.

I have no idea how they came together at the party, if it was a chance meeting or if he stalked her across the ballroom until she gave in and danced with him. Nor do I care. It is enough that they have reconciled. I watched them today, their interactions matter-of-fact and fond, and my hopes are once again high.

"Why don't you use the tub in the hall bath?" I suggest. "That way you won't have to go home. And once we're all clean and pruney, we can sit by the fire and have a drink until the men get home."

"I need fresh clothes," she points out. "And the kids are in from school by now. I can't abandon Pearl. She's got homework. They all do."

Hedges clears his throat. "I could drop you ladies off and pick them up, Mrs. Ava. Miss Pearl could bring a change of clothes for you and they could do their schoolwork in the kitchen."

Ava is too tired to argue and, thus managed, we stumble from the car and make our way upstairs to sink into a bliss of hot water and scented bubbles.

Ava

Judging by the crowd this morning, The People's Clinic is as necessary as Max and Claire believed it would be. I took the day off to help out—there was no nurse for some reason—and ended up spending a day with Max that felt like one of our camp visits, just indoors and with far more cigarette smoke.

Most of the patients were men, which was to be expected. I'm sure once word gets out, there will be more families taking up space in the cheerful yellow waiting area. In addition to the standard run of cuts and sprains, skin disorders, and nagging coughs, the men were also in need of Katie's tea and cookies, and more than a few of them took advantage of the donated clothing stored in the back room. I'm not sure whose idea that was, but it was brilliant. The weather is cold enough that a coat or scarf might be what prevents these men from coming down with a cough, or pneumonia.

Claire and I leave around four. The crowd has started to die down, and John Spencer is there to keep Max company and give him a ride back to Claire's after they lock up. On normal days, he'll bicycle back and forth—a long ride, but nothing he can't manage, considering the way he tools around this city.

All I want is to go home, but Claire suggests a bath at her house, then supper, and I can't resist. I emerge from the tub having rinsed away the strain of the day, the smells of smoke and soup and poverty, and find clean clothes laid out on the guest bed.

Shrugging off Claire's robe, I reassemble myself: pants, brassiere, girdle, stockings. The armor that encases me and makes me presentable. Pearl selected my green print dress, the one Claire bought when I came to her with Teddy back in 1932. It's showing wear but is more than good enough for a weeknight meal.

When I go in search of my sister, I find her in her bedroom. "The kids downstairs?"

"With Mrs. Hedges," she says. "Doing their homework."

I smile. "And eating cookies."

"Probably." She is attempting finger waves with her damp hair, with little success. I take over, running the comb through her water-darkened strands and anchoring the waves with pins. As short as her hair is, it will dry quickly. "Do you think it went well?"

"I don't see how it could have gone better." I drop onto the bed, leaning back on my elbows. "It was like clockwork, even without the nurse."

"She'll be in tomorrow," Claire says. "It was a shame, but I didn't want to put the opening back by a day, not when we'd advertised it."

A rumble reaches our ears. With the carpeted steps, it can only be several children pounding upstairs at the same time. They arrive in the doorway—Pearl, holding Grace; Thelma, with Teddy; George and Toby locked in what appears to be mortal combat. Seeing us together, they stream in and throw themselves on the bed, and the topic of Philadelphia's poor is put aside until we sit down to eat.

It's after nine when Max drives me the few blocks to the house. Because it's a school night, Dan and Pearl have already taken the kids home. Grace remains with me, bundled into a shawl on my lap. Max is unusually silent, and when he parks Claire's car outside my door, he covers a yawn with his hand.

"Tired?" I don't see how he can't be; I'm exhausted, and I was there for just a few hours.

"Yes, but also wide awake." He takes my hand, careful not to jostle the sleeping baby. "This is what I was meant to do, Ava. Why I went to medical school in the first place."

The excitement in his voice is contagious. "You think the clinic will succeed, then?"

"Of course." His fingers tighten on mine. "It's exactly what was needed."

His warmth creeps up my arm and I fight it the best way I know how, by being difficult. "But there are other clinics, aren't there? Why is Claire's so special?"

Max cuts a glance at me. "Because it's not linked to a church or a larger organization, like the Salvation Army, for one thing," he explains. "The men don't want to feel like charity cases. This place, well, they can pretend like it's a normal medical facility."

"While you get on with doing what you do best." It's useless; I can't be cold with him, not when he's fizzing like a Fourth of July sparkler.

"Exactly." He lets go of my hand, then leans toward me and cups my cheek. "Now kiss me goodnight so I can go home and fall into my bed like the conquering hero that I am."

32

Claire

The phone rings in the hall. I pick it up and am immediately punished for not waiting for Katie to answer it.

Irene's voice is thin, tentative; she sounds her age. "Do you have a moment?"

I haven't spoken to her since the gala, where she had the sense to stay far away from me. She's called twice in the last week, but Katie has been instructed to tell her I'm unavailable. "Not for you, no."

"But, Claire..." She sounds near tears. "I can't manage without Harry."

"You don't need to," I assure her crisply. "Just without me. That should be no hardship for either of us." It feels good to be honest after all these years.

There is a long silence. "Then he hasn't told you?"

"Told me what?" I'm not going to let Irene spin me another of her fairy stories. "What lie do you have for me now?"

"It's not a lie." She sighs. "Ask Harry, if you don't believe me." There is a sound of swallowing. "He won't see me. Won't speak to me." An outright sob. "My son has cut me off."

If this is true, then he hasn't told me everything—and it's too personally hurtful to Irene for her to lie. But I remain wary; she's fooled me before. "What did you expect?"

"Not this." She has gotten control of her voice. "I thought when I apologized, he'd...well, perhaps not forgive me, but at least soften a little."

"He's a grown man, Irene. I'm not likely to be able to influence his decisions."

"I think you could," she says. "He listens to you in a way he never listened to me."

I press my lips together. "I'll tell him you called," I say at last. "He can do what he will with that information." I take a breath and let slip a little of the fury I've held back for so long. "But he deserves better than you."

A choking sound, almost as if she's laughing. "I always thought that about you, and look where it's got me. Perhaps we should let him think for himself."

I pass on Irene's message, and several more she has left with Katie; I have taken to avoiding the telephone. "She's going to keep calling until you deal with her."

"She's been dealt with," Harry says. "That's why she's calling."

He's speaking in riddles, and I tell him as much. "Up until the last few weeks, your mother has been such a part of our lives I couldn't turn around without tripping over her, and yet this past Sunday, you actually went to St. Patrick's with me and the children."

"I enjoy spending time with them." He fiddles with the knot of his tie, unwilling to look at me. "And they behave there."

"Fear of God, Ava always says." I'm not willing to let him off the hook so easily. "Did you go to church with us because you're avoiding your mother?"

"More or less." Harry sighs heavily. "You might as well know the truth, or at least some of it."

I move from my chair to a spot next to him on the sofa, snuggling in under his arm, in the hopes that my presence will make it easier for him to speak. "Tell me. All of it, preferably. You did promise."

There is a long pause, and finally he says, "Mother didn't introduce you to Wolf Gardiner with the intention of helping you to succeed, you must know that."

Somehow, even after the debacle with the newspaper, I hadn't wanted to believe her capable of such deception. She'd been supportive, for once—the clinic was a more public project than she would have chosen, she said, but she congratulated me on my philanthropy on more than one occasion. I blossomed under her unaccustomed praise, and when she suggested Gardiner as a solution to my problems, I took it as a sign that I had finally gained her approval.

"But he did help," I say slowly. "If making the clinic fail was her intention, she didn't succeed. And after the article, she even helped me. After you confronted her, I assume."

Harry looks at me then, his eyes bleak. "She doesn't care about the clinic." His voice is ragged, and for the first time in years I notice the difference in our ages. "What better man to throw at you, in the hopes your head would be turned, than someone I've loathed for decades?"

I don't know how to convince him that his suspicions are just that—suspicions. The fact that she had no compunction about using Gardiner, so long as it achieved her goal of damaging me, brings a surge of anger so abrupt that my temples pound.

He rubs his mustache. "There's no other explanation."

There are several, all of which go back to the fact that I've never been good enough for her son. We go to bed without speaking further of the matter, but Francis Gardiner—and Irene—could fit in the space between us.

Irene has never liked me, but to set me up hoping I would disgrace myself, hoping Harry would reject me—is she truly willing to bring down the scandal of divorce upon her own family, not to mention hurting her son? Is there anyone she could have chosen to wave in front of me who, if I had taken him up on his offer, would have hurt Harry worse? She never understood her son's choice, but I've done my best, since my marriage, to become as presentable as any girl from Irene's social strata. I speak well, I look better, and I've even presented Harry, albeit unconventionally, with a son.

And it's clear now that in her eyes, it's never been enough, and it never will be.

Pearl

April 4, 1934

Hazel gave me The Great Gatsby *for my early birthday. Aunt wouldn't let me read her copy because she said it was too grown up. Mama said I can read whatever I can understand, but I can't nag Aunt for her books, so I put in a reservation at the library. When I mentioned it to Hazel, she gave me hers after the Easter break wrapped in tissue with a pink hair ribbon.*

I can't wait to read it so I can tell Aunt what I thought and also that I'm absolutely not too young to read it.

Ava

I have always thought of clothing as functional, but I don't make functional clothes now; I make beautiful dresses for rich women. They have everything, but there is always a need in them for more. To look better. To look better than someone else. To minimize a feature no longer her best. To draw the wandering eye of a husband who pays the dress bill but doesn't pay enough attention to her.

These women, for the most part, have less than I do. They've got money, but only because of the men in their lives. They don't have a skill that could support them through hard times. If their menfolk lost their fortunes tomorrow, they'd be in line at a soup kitchen wearing their fancy dresses and pastel gloves, because there isn't a one of them who can even sew on a button.

"When do you think you'll have it ready?" Mrs. Thorndyke steps off the stool, moving carefully to avoid the pins in her hem.

I unhook the back and let the dress puddle around her feet. "It should be ready by—"

A wail issues from the kitchen, where Grace has been sleeping behind the partly closed door.

"Please give me a moment." I haul myself up. "She quiets down fast."

The baby's face is screwed up as she readies herself for a lusty crying session. I slip past and get the bottle that has been waiting in warm water and pop it into her mouth.

A shadow falls across the basket. Lavinia Thorndyke, clad in only her slip, stares at my daughter. "What a darling baby," she says, leaning down. "She doesn't look like your other children."

I suck in a breath. "She looks like her father," I say. "And my oldest boy. I don't believe you've seen him."

"I'm sorry," she says, and the eyes she turns on me are liquid with tears. "That must be difficult...at times."

"At times," I concede. "But other times it's good to feel he's still with me."

Mrs. Thorndyke nods, and strokes Grace's cheek with one finger. "Mr. Thorndyke is my second husband. I lost my first in the influenza epidemic." She licks her lips. "He survived the war to come home and die of the flu." Caressing Grace again, she concludes, "We weren't blessed with children. There wasn't time."

She has four sons now with Parnell Thorndyke, but I've seen inside her now, to an empty space maybe even she doesn't often peer into. "I'm sorry that happened to you," I tell her. "Grace is a comfort. I wish her father could have known her."

Lavinia Thorndyke straightens, blinks her eyes hard. "'Wish in one hand,' my mother always said. It doesn't get us far, Mrs. Kimber." Her gaze fastens again on her dress. "Now, when do you think you'll have that finished?"

Pearl

April 15, 1934

I don't know what I was expecting from The Great Gatsby. *Not what I got. Also, if there really are people who are that rich, Aunt and Uncle don't have as much money as I thought.*

Mr. Fitzgerald made me see everything with his writing and I want to read it again to understand how he did that, but I didn't like any of the characters. Not even Nick, who told the story. I wanted to shake him and say, "If you don't like these people, why are you spending so much time with them?"

I told Aunt I read it and she shook her head. I asked her why Gatsby kept on chasing after Daisy when she was married, and she said men are mysterious creatures. Then I asked if she thought Daisy had gone to bed with Gatsby when they were younger. I think that shocked her. But if they didn't, it would be like Gatsby had created a fairy tale in his mind about a woman he'd barely known and to me that's worse than bed.

Aunt also told me that she and Uncle met Mr. Fitzgerald and his wife in Paris! I made her tell me all about it, and ended up being late home because of it. But I don't care, I'm almost always on time.

Daddy never talked about the war, but he did tell me once that he and his friends went to Paris on leave and it was the most beautiful place he'd ever seen, except for when he came home. I hope that was because he missed Mama, because there was nothing beautiful about Scovill Run.

Claire

"What's going on with Irene these days?" Ava asks. "I saw her at the party, but she was keeping her distance."

I've hesitated to tell her, because the truth is so awful, but I can't keep her in the dark. She'd find out anyway, somehow, and then I would have to explain myself. "She was behind that newspaper article."

"That bitch!" Her eyes spark. "How did Harry take it?"

"He was the one who figured it out." Because there are certain things even my sister doesn't need to know, I don't reveal the extent of his hurt. She's sure to understand, anyway, but she will be tactful enough not to probe. "She also involved Francis Gardiner in the project in the hopes I would take a liking to him."

"That slick bit of business?" Ava laughs. "I don't think so."

I wish I'd taken her opinions more seriously at the time; if I'd added them to Harry's dislike, perhaps I'd have saved myself some heartache. "Irene thought it would work. Do you know, she's older than Mama was when she died." I smile crookedly. "She's going to outlive us all, from sheer spite."

"Probably." Ava's gaze goes distant. "I miss Mama."

I'm so shocked my sister has admitted to having an emotion that at first I don't know how to respond. Finally, I say, "Me too."

"I wonder where we'd all be if she was alive."

The question sounds idle, but there's something Ava wants to say. "What do you mean?"

She looks down at her knitting, a long twist of gray wool spiraling over her lap. "We'd probably still be in Scovill Run."

"Do you think so? Even with Daniel?" I never know if I'm permitted to mention his death, and it is easier to be delicate with words than face my sister's wrath.

"Mama wouldn't have left." She grumbles exasperatedly and unravels a few stitches. "It was all she knew."

"She knew Ireland, and she left," I remind her. "And you wouldn't have been able to stay in the house, so what else would you have done?"

Ava's lips turn up. "She'd have probably stayed behind to keep house for Father Dennis and let us come to you."

"Do you think?" Because I left home at seventeen, Ava had known Mama far better than I had. "Wouldn't she have missed the children?"

"Of course. But she never wanted that town to beat her."

I blink at this thought. "Is that how you feel?"

"Sometimes." Her needles begin to click again. "I gave up."

"How exactly were you supposed to fight them? And why would you want to?" I lean over, put my hand on the scarf growing from her needles. "You *won*. You escaped. You saved your children."

She looks up, the light on her face, and I wonder if this is the first time she's thought of it that way. "I suppose."

"Dan would be in the mine," I say bluntly. "Facing the same fate as his father, and ours. Pearl wouldn't be in high school. She'd be cleaning houses or sewing until her eyes went, like Mama. Thelma would be a cripple." And Teddy wouldn't be mine. If I hadn't gone home for Mama's funeral, Ava and I wouldn't have reconciled to a point where I felt comfortable asking for her baby.

"And Teddy," she says, reading my mind.

"And Teddy," I agree.

"But I still miss her."

"I hear her sometimes. Not her ghost," I say hastily, not wanting my sister to think I'm crazy. "Her words, things she would say." I glance over, and Ava is staring at me, frowning.

"So do I."

Pearl

April 20, 1934

There's been a ton of orders lately. It seems like every lady in Philadelphia wants Mama to dress her. There are really only about six regular customers, including Aunt, but there are always new ones, who admired a dress and asked where it came from.

I don't mind helping, even though Mama says I have to put my schoolwork first. I do, but I can think about my assignments while I'm hemming or sewing on snaps. Those things are boring and repetitive, but that's why I like them. I can think about my own things and not mess up.

And I keep remembering, even when it's hard here, there's a lot less to do. I miss my chickens, sometimes, but I don't miss taking care of them. Or working in the garden and canning for endless sticky days every summer. Cooking and laundry never stop, but there's time to breathe now.

I took ten cents out of my savings today and bought a bar of Cashmere Bouquet soap. Hazel uses it and always smells so good. It would be nice if it faded my freckles, like it says in the ads, but I'm not hopeful. Hazel looks like someone spattered her with paint and she uses it faithfully.

Anyway, I'll smell good and maybe Tommy will notice. If he gave me a compliment, I think I'd die happy.

33

Claire

The board meets at my house for the first time since the opening of the clinic. Because it is the full board—which includes Francis Gardiner—Harry has asked me to speak on his behalf. Max is also missing, unwilling to be away from his patients, and so I am left with a half dozen women and Gardiner, who dedicates himself to amusing them. It is infuriating, and because of what I now know about him, it is difficult to keep quiet when he disrupts our business.

At last we are finished and I usher everyone out, grateful to my bones it is early enough that I will have time to recover before Harry gets home. I have no sooner turned away from the door than the bell rings again.

Gardiner stands on the step, an abashed grin on his face. "Forgot my pen," he says. "Can't have that."

Katie appears with the offending fountain pen, and he tucks it into his inside pocket but makes no move to leave.

"Is there something else?" My mind is full of thoughts of lilac bubble bath. "I have to—"

"I'll just be a moment." He slips past me and heads into the living room. "Squint's not going to be home for a bit."

"I do wish you'd stop using that silly schoolboy nickname." I've asked him at least a half dozen times by this point. "School was a long time ago for both of you."

He gives me a slow smile. "I suppose your husband always refers to me by name."

"It's not as if you come up in conversation, unless I'm filling him in on board meetings." Harry does call him Wolf, and it suits the watchfulness, the faint aura of danger that lingers like the scent of cologne. But I don't say that.

"Which he never attends." Gardiner sits in Harry's chair and swings his feet up onto the ottoman. "I'm beginning to think he's avoiding me."

I take a seat across from him, pointedly not making myself comfortable. "Unlike you, my husband has a job."

"Whereas I'm more of a kept man." There is something unpleasant in his smile. "You can say it."

Katie pauses outside the open door, then moves on. A decision has been made: if Gardiner is to be offered additional refreshment, she will not be the one to do it.

"What are you talking about?" I'm so weary I can barely string words together, but I don't know how to get him to go without ordering him out of the house—which would make future meetings uncomfortable. "I don't have time for word games."

"It's not a game," Gardiner says. "Word or otherwise." He crosses his ankles, appearing to admire the shine on his shoes. "I don't have the kind of money to carry on like this, as I'm sure Squint—sorry—*Harry* has told you."

"Then how—?"

He has the grace to look abashed. "If there's a game afoot, it's not mine. Irene's spent a pretty penny these past few months, keeping me in comfort and style, not to mention providing all my contributions to the clinic." The wolfish smile returns. "Not that it hasn't been a pleasure, spending all this time with you, but I wouldn't have bothered on my own dime."

He stretches to put his hand over mine, and I pull away, repelled.

"It has been useful," he continues. "I'll grant you that. Your seal of approval has gone a long way toward rebuilding the bridges I've burned in this city."

"My seal of approval?" He speaks as if I have power—which means Irene believes I have power. That's an odd thought.

"You may not be the old guard, but this new generation—the up and coming, the nouveau riche, the well-intended society do-gooders, they trust you. And now they trust me." He somehow becomes larger in his clothes. "Irene's done me a good turn while she was having her fun."

"I've never known Irene to do a good turn for anyone but herself, and Harry," I say. "Why would she go to that much trouble for you?"

"Because she can't stand *you*." Gardiner quirks a brow as if this should be obvious—or that, even being obvious, I would have anticipated my mother-in-law procuring someone to seduce me away from her son. "And other reasons."

"Such as?"

"You've seen her," he says lazily. "She might have been a terrible wife to Squint's dear old dad, but she's convinced herself she'd enjoy it, if I would ever look at her. As if that dried up old woman could be anything but a ticket for my future."

I had, for a moment, almost felt sorry for him—allowing himself to be used in such a way to regain his reputation—but he is no better than my mother-in-law. Worse, in a way, because Irene used the tools available to a woman. Gardiner has more in his arsenal than manipulation.

"You will withdraw from the board of the clinic," I say shakily. "Or I will remove you myself."

"What if I don't want to go?"

How would my sister deal with him? I take a deep breath, summon my inner Ava. "If you fight me, I'll tell everyone what you're up to."

"That would implicate Irene, and by association, your husband." Confident, he leans back in the chair. "You'd never do that."

"You don't know me very well," I say. "I would do it in a heartbeat, and Harry would back me up."

Ava

"This has to be heading toward something," Max said on the night of Claire's party, the night when I decided to let him into my heart. We have edged around the topic, ever since, as I try to discover what that truly means. I love him—I'm almost certain—but can I allow myself to love him? Will I be able to lay my ghosts once and for all, to let him into not just my heart, but my family? Our home?

The kids—even Pearl—are thrilled to have him back. He's an easy presence in the house, but his presence reminds me, over and over, that Daniel is an absence. Each time we are together, my mind goes to—*if only he were here.*

But he is not. I have raised my kids without excessive sentiment, so none of them will ever voice that painful thought aloud. The least I can do is follow my own guidelines.

Max, for his part, adores the kids and speaks to Dan as an adult, the man of my house. This makes me happy; I want no one sidelined by this budding relationship, and Dan must be handled delicately. He thinks about going off with Tommy or his other friends, riding the rails and having stupid, dangerous, boyish adventures, and I don't want anything to push him into acting on those desires.

"The kids come first," I tell Max. "If you want me, you have to understand that. I won't ask you for money—I can support them myself—but you have to know before this goes any further."

His face, tense from whatever he was afraid I would say, softens into a smile. "I would expect nothing else. And you don't have to carry the whole burden. You've gone it alone long enough. I'm happy to contribute to their upkeep or anything else they need."

Something rises in me, and I push it down. I'd prefer to do it myself; I'd always expected I would have to. "It's good to know I can count on you."

"Always." He catches my hand and brings it to his lips. "Always, Ava."

I exhale. "That's settled, then."

"Then you'll marry me?"

Max's eyes are bright, and I hate to dim that light even slightly. "Maybe," I say. "There's one thing I'd like to do first."

He looks confused. "Before we tell everyone?"

"Before I accept." I put my hand over his. "Do you think we can borrow Claire's car again?"

"I'm sure we could." He smiles uncertainly. "What did you have in mind?"

"I'd like to go back to Atlantic City." I meet his eyes. "And spend the night."

Pearl

May 2, 1934

As I get older, and read and learn more about people, I wonder who my father really was, and what his world was like. There had to be more than the mine and worry and his family. I know he loved us, and somehow he loved that job, but what else was in his head? I am more than my family and school. I'm my stories and my ambitions and my love for my family and Katie and my fear for what Dandy gets up to when he rides trains. Did Daddy have all that? Did the life he lived ever let him be anyone other than husband-father-miner? Did he even know himself?

Claire

It is a perfect late spring day, too beautiful to spend at the clinic, where I drop in a few times a week to admire its efficient functioning, get under Max's feet, and set the nurse to muttering. Perhaps Ava might be willing to play truant and take a drive through Fairmount Park with me and Teddy.

If she had a telephone, I could call, but a telephone, according to her, is an unnecessary luxury. When she marries Max, that will change. A doctor needs to be reachable in case of emergency. No matter. I will drive over and haul her bodily out of the workroom, if I have to.

I dress quickly, zipping myself into a white dress sprinkled with poppies and sliding my feet into matching red t-straps. The sound of the bell echoes through the house, followed by Katie's light footsteps. Voices reach me, and I tuck my purse under my arm and head downstairs.

Francis Gardiner waits at the foot of the steps, with Katie before him, not quite blocking his way. "There she is!"

I look from him to Katie. "It's all right. Mr. Gardiner isn't staying." We go into my sitting room and I stand at the desk. We haven't spoken since I dismissed him from the board. He looks a bit tired, his usual brilliance dulled. "Why are you here?"

"Squint has won the day." He gives me an odd smile. "I leave the field a vanquished man."

I don't rise to the bait, not wanting to give him any more attention than he deserves, and watch as he lowers himself into my reading chair. He leans forward with his elbows on his knees. "I've got one foot on the boat already."

"You're leaving?" I clasp my hands so I don't fidget.

"I've no choice." His mouth twists. "I'll take the train to New York tonight and sail for London when my father wires the funds."

Without Irene's help, he can't even leave the country; the best he can do is lose himself in New York until his parent pays his way. I almost feel bad for him.

"What did you expect?" My tone says I am done with him, but anger requires more energy than I currently possess. "Lying to everyone, playing her game." I offer my hand. "I wish you well, I really do."

He takes it and pulls me toward him, so I nearly stumble. "You could come with me," he says. "We could start fresh in Europe—you told me you love Paris."

For a moment I am stunned, then I choke out something resembling a laugh. "You've changed your tune. I thought I wasn't how you would have chosen to spend your time?"

His fingers tighten around my wrist. "Do you think I wanted this? Irene sold you to me as a stupid little floozy who'd bewitched her son with whatever she had between her legs. And now I'd like to find out, because you've bewitched me, too."

I am shocked by his crude language, and by the knowledge they are Irene's words, Irene's thoughts he is repeating. "You should leave."

"Claire." His voice is ragged. "Come with me. What do you have here?"

I snatch my hand away. "A life," I say with simmering rage. "A home. A son. A husband."

Gardiner draws me close, his arm like an iron bar around my waist. "Irene's house," he says against my neck. "Irene's son. And your sister's boy, from what I've heard. You can bring him, I don't care."

"Let go of me." I push against his chest. It's like shoving a piece of furniture.

He tips his head back, looking down at me. "You're not very convincing." One hand, the fingers spread wide, slides down the thin rayon of my skirt and cups my bottom.

For a moment I freeze, remembering something years in my past, another big man who laid hands on me and laughed when I pleaded for him to let me go. Remembering what happened next. Francis Gardiner is no rapist, but the cold panic spooling through my veins isn't logical. I squirm in his grip, getting one hand loose, and slap him across the face. He releases me abruptly and I step backward, trip over the ottoman, and sprawl on the carpet.

One hand to his reddening cheek, he stares at me. "That seems...excessive."

I scramble up, smoothing my skirt. "I asked you to go."

"And I said—"

The door opens. Hedges leans into the room. "Did you need me to drive you somewhere, sir? Mrs. Claire asked you to leave."

Gardiner doesn't look at him, but at me. "Well, there went my bonus."

I smooth my skirt again, wishing my emotions were as easily tidied. "What do you mean?"

"Irene would have given me a lump sum if I could have taken you away from Harry." His voice has changed; now he is all business. "I don't suppose you'd consider disappearing for a day or two, so the old bitch would cough up the money?"

He is completely different from the man who, moments before, had tried ardently to convince me to leave with him. "You're not...sincere, then?"

"Me?" He barks a laugh. "I'm not the marrying kind. I thought only your mother-in-law was too dense to figure that out."

"But you have a wife in England," I say stupidly. "Harry told me."

"Who turns a blind eye." He straightens his cuffs, rubs a heavy gold cufflink with his thumb. "The same as I do for her. It's a very convenient arrangement, and she would not have been heartbroken if I had left her for another, similar arrangement." Gardiner smiles. "We'd make a good team. Harry doesn't value you."

"I value him." I nod to Hedges, who has been watching all this with careful expressionlessness. "Hedges will see you out."

Why are difficult conversations always best held after dinner? I have made certain Max will be at Ava's until bedtime before I lead Harry into the living room. "That will be all, Katie," I say as we leave her to clear. "Tell your parents we'll have no further need of them tonight."

"What if Teddy wakes up grousing and wants warm milk?" Harry asks, amused, as I close the door.

"Then I'll make it. I'm not incapable."

He mixes our drinks and when he sits, I tell him about my afternoon visitor, leaving out the bits I have difficulty wrapping my head around.

"I'm glad he's decided to go." Harry takes a sip of his drink. "I actually feel sorry for the fellow. He's gone a bit seedy."

I take a deep breath. "You might not feel so charitable when I tell you that he asked me to go with him."

The glass hits the table, hard enough to leave a mark on the wood. "How did you respond to that invitation?"

"By saying no, of course!" Gardiner flattered me, but his main attraction had always been his helpfulness with the clinic. "I'd never leave you."

He covers his face with one hand. "You have no idea how much I needed to hear that."

"Darling"—I slide over and sit on his lap—"how can you even question it? You and Teddy are my life. I may not have handled things well over this past year, but I value every bit of what we have."

His arms come around me and my last conscious thought is that Teddy had better not wake up needing milk, because it is unlikely we would be in a state to hear him.

34

Ava

"Do you have everything you need?" My sister's tone is delicate, as though we are talking about a simple day trip and not a planned excursion into sin.

"What could I possibly need?"

She shrugs, leaning against the curved edge of her vanity and scuffing her toe on the patterned carpet. "Something to wear?"

"I have clothes, Claire." They might not be fancy, but I am perfectly presentable.

Her cheeks turn pink. "I meant night clothes. Something pretty."

"I have a nightgown."

"It's as old as Toby." Her eyebrows raise. "You can't."

I have wondered how Max will react to such a worn garment, but I do not share that embarrassing thought with my sister. "Don't even think about buying me a present."

She turns away, having clearly been ready to suggest we go shopping, and drums pink-tipped fingers on the back of the chair. "Wait," she says, and darts from the room.

I occupy myself by snooping through her closet, cataloging what is new since my last visit, what I might copy for my customers. My sister could outfit my entire family with what she spends on clothes.

Pulling out a yellow blouse the color of daffodil buds, I admire the delicate lace set across the bust and think how nice it must be to wear tiny, lacy underthings, the kind that would pass unnoticed under a silken confection like this. A quick clatter of heels alerts me to her return and I shove the hanger onto the rail and dive back to my spot on the bed.

Claire's arms are filled with a large cardboard box, which she puts on the bedspread beside me. "Open it!" she urges.

There is a thin film of dust on the box; whatever this is, she's fetched it down from that treasure trove of an attic. I lift the lid, discover layers of tissue. Beneath, a glow of something pink. I fold back the first layer.

"Oh, for Pete's sake!" She pulls the garment out, impatient with my slow unwrapping. "It's not new, so you can't complain. I got it in Paris after the war."

It's a robe...no, a kimono. The word floats into my mind. I didn't even know that I knew what a kimono looked like, but this is certainly one. "It's beautiful." The word seems inadequate for such a garment.

It is a dusty pink, a color once called ashes of roses. I don't know if that's the right name now. Without thinking, I rub the fabric between my fingertips, judging. Silk crepe, the best quality I've ever felt. Embroidered flowers spill over the shoulders and down the open front of the kimono, with pale tendrils ending right above the hem. The inside is a darker pink, making me think again of roses, though that's not what these flowers are.

"Cherry blossoms," Claire says, reading my mind. "It's Japanese."

"I thought you said it was French?" I take the kimono from her, spread it across my lap. It is simultaneously weightless and substantial. The embroidery is heavier on the back, pink-and-white flowers massed across the shoulders, interspersed with vivid green leaves. The silk thread has texture under my fingers, while the flowers are so lifelike I almost expect them to have a fragrance.

"We bought it in Paris," she says patiently. "It's from Japan. Stand up, let's try it on."

"It's too nice—" I try to fight her off but I'm afraid she will damage the kimono in her enthusiasm to dress me up. "Fine."

Putting it on, I look at myself in the triple mirror I normally avoid. The dampness outside has loosened my hair, and it falls in waves to my chin. My cheeks are flushed, my eyes bright. But for the telltale tightness around my mouth, I am almost unrecognizable.

"I can't wear this." I slip it off regretfully, trying not to think about how it felt. How I looked.

Claire bundles it up and thrusts it into my hands. "You have to." She reaches into the box and throws the sash—pink on one side, green on the other—on top of the pile. "If you don't take it, I'll put it in the rubbish."

"You wouldn't." In spite of myself, I clutch it to my chest.

"I would, and I will." She laughs delightedly.

It is the most beautiful thing I have ever touched. I want it so badly I can barely breathe. I think of the skill and the hours devoted to the embroidery of all those blossoms, the many thousands of miles it has traveled to reach my hands; I can't let her destroy it, and she would, to prove her point.

"Fine," I mutter. "I'll take it."

Claire

I wake the sound of Teddy's laughter. Not in my room, but in the adjoining nursery, where Katie is getting him ready for the day. I look at the empty side of the bed, then at the clock: I have overslept. Pulling on my robe, I stumble into the nursery. Katie is on her knees, wrestling Teddy into his shorts as he repeatedly lunges toward the train set on the floor nearby.

"Now Mr. Teddy," she croons, "you hold still and let me dress you. The sooner you have clothes on, the sooner you can play."

He swings around, a train car in his hand, and she ducks neatly. "Kay-Kay!" he crows. "You play too?"

"Maybe later." She stretches the word, meanwhile whipping his shirt on and doing up the buttons. "But not if you clock me with that car again."

He falls back on the floor, dissolving into giggles. She rests one hand on his stomach, then digs in, tickling, and he springs up and throws his arms around her.

Something hurts in my chest. When was the last time I was the one to do battle with Teddy in the morning?

"Hello, you two!" I advance into the room, and Katie rises, slinging Teddy onto her hip. "Is it time for breakfast?"

"Kay-Kay?" He looks at her for confirmation.

"Good morning, ma'am." She kisses Teddy's cheek. "Of course it's time for breakfast, Mr. Teddy. Why else would I have gotten you out of your bed?"

When was the last time I had done that, either? Katie has transitioned from housemaid to nursemaid and I've been too preoccupied to notice—as I've also failed to notice, as Harry accused, that he's almost stopped asking for me.

I offer my hand. "Since Mommy's been a sleepyhead today, why don't we all go down to breakfast together?"

Katie sets him on his feet and he looks from me to her, torn. At her nod, he takes my hand and smiles up at me, the same sunny, endearing boy as ever, more willing to forgive his mother's neglect than I am myself. I draw him close for a quick hug, and experience another shock. He no longer smells like a baby. The underlying scent of diaper is gone, but so is the sweetness; he smells like a little boy, though not as strongly as George or Toby.

On the stairs, I slow my steps to accommodate his short legs. When we arrive in the dining room, he makes a face. "Kitchen."

I glance quizzically at Katie.

"He eats downstairs most mornings," she explains. "So I can get to my chores while my mother watches over him."

I have disrupted the entire household with my selfishness. "Well, we're going to eat up here today," I announce, pulling his high chair up to the table. "And then maybe after that, we'll go to the zoo."

She drops him into the chair, ruffling his curls. "Would you like that, Mr. Teddy? Go and see the monkeys?"

His lip comes out. "You come too?"

I wait, breathless, but Katie is as smart as she is kind.

"Not today, Mr. Teddy." She sets the table rapidly. "Katie has work to do, see? But you and your mama are going to have a wonderful time."

"We are," I vow. We'll have such a good time that Teddy will be reminded who his mother actually is—as I have been reminded.

Ava

We start early on Saturday morning. When Max and Claire arrive in her car, Dan bounds down the steps and puts my case in the back before shaking Max's hand. I flinch; it feels as if my son is giving his blessing to my illicit activity. Issuing last minute instructions, I distribute kisses all around and get into the roadster.

"I'm so sorry I can't loan you the car this time. I have a meeting outside the city tomorrow and Harry needs the Packard." Claire goes on and on until I want to strike her with my fists, or the cardboard suitcase sitting next to Max in the back seat. It is humiliating enough that she knows my plans; to insist on driving us to the station, when we could have simply walked or taken a taxi, is too much.

"You've made your point," I finally mutter, as she turns down Market Street. "There's no need to stab me with it."

She looks wounded, and I regret my harsh words. Despite the sharper edges acquired from dealing with a wide variety of people, Claire is soft inside, and takes such things badly.

"Well, I am sorry." She says no more until she pulls in before the main entrance. "Enjoy your trip."

"We will, I'm sure." I am stiff with her because as soft as she is, I can be hard and not know how to bend. "Thank you for the ride."

After I get out, Max follows with our bags. His thanks to Claire are more effusive, but at last my sister is gone. We go inside and he purchases tickets for the Seashore Line.

Despite the weather not being warm enough to swim, the waiting area is crowded with young couples furtively holding hands; clusters of giggling schoolgirls; harassed mothers with groups of children and lunches packed carefully into shoeboxes.

We merge with the crowd, but I feel like there is a bright light shining over my head, marking me as some sort of scarlet woman who would deliberately ask a man to go away overnight for the express purpose of sleeping with him.

"Maybe this is a mistake."

Max tightens his grip on my arm. "It's no mistake," he says quietly, "and if you think I'm letting you run out those doors, you don't know me very well."

I exhale slowly. "Was she unbearable this morning?"

"Just...excited," he says.

Claire and Teddy will spend the night at my house. It's easier than shifting all the kids to Delancey Place, and I will not allow Max to volunteer his rooms for their use. Despite Dan and Pearl's protestations, I would not leave them in full charge. What I'm doing is bad enough without leaving my kids home alone.

Within a few minutes, the rattling flipboard announces our train and the crowd surges toward the platform. Our tickets are standard coach, not the fancier parlor car. Though I am curious about it, I appreciate that Max hasn't spent extra money on unnecessary luxuries when there is a hotel room to be paid for.

"I haven't been in this station since I went home without Teddy and Thelma," I tell him when I settle into my perfectly comfortable seat. "Almost two years."

"A hard day." He deposits our cases in the overhead rack and sits beside me. "Your strength has been tested so many times."

This is not the conversation I intended to have, but something about Max Byrne always makes me talk about myself. It's also what makes me keep him at arm's length, even when I don't want to; sharing my thoughts is more difficult than deciding to share my body.

"That's in the past," I say, hoping he will let it rest.

And he does, remaining silent other than pointing out that our first stop, Penn Station, had recently opened. I remember it being under construction when I brought Teddy to Philadelphia; it has grown, as everything in this city seems to do, all the time.

From there we go north, and then across the river to New Jersey. I stare out the window so I don't have to talk; our intention sits between us like another passenger. I didn't know it was possible for Max to be quiet this long. After the second stop in Camden, he settles his hat over his face and goes to sleep.

I close my eyes, letting the train's movement lull me into a calm I do not feel. When I open them again, much later, we are within sight of another train track, and the ground outside looks marshy, the way it did when we drove down before and he told me to open the window. I stand, and tilt the window slightly. The air is sharp and I taste salt on my lips.

Straightening my hat, I risk another look at Max. He is awake and smiling. Anticipation? Nerves?

"Okay?" he asks.

Shoving the window closed, I say, "Okay."

The silence has been broken. He turns to watch a large family across the aisle, saying, "You surprised me, you know."

"With this?" I'd surprised myself, but I also knew it was necessary.

He nods. "That you'd want—that we should—"

I put a hand on his tweed sleeve. "It's an important part of marriage," I say simply. "We should know if it works before we make a commitment."

Pearl

May 12, 1934

Mama and Dr. Max have gone away overnight. Aunt was more excited than they were, but then she wants them to get married even more than I think they do.

Long before we left Scovill Run, Mama told me what married people do together. I wonder if she and Dr. Max are going to do that, and if that means they really will get married? I was going to ask, but I couldn't get Mama alone. She answers any questions I have, even if they make her uncomfortable. It's like when she told me about the curse, she said she'd rather I know too much too early than not enough and too late.

Of course, I'm no closer to finding a boyfriend than I was when we were back home. Tommy treats me the same as Thelma or the boys. But I'm still glad to know. I can't imagine getting surprised by something like that.

35

Ava

The hotel on Tennessee Avenue is a few blocks from the boardwalk. Its lobby is nicely decorated but a bit rundown—nothing fancy or off-putting here. As we check in, I put my arm through his, showing my well-worn wedding ring to the young desk clerk. Will he realize we're not married?

He pushes the register across the desk, barely looking at us. Max signs it, *Dr. and Mrs. M. Byrne*, and it is done.

A similarly disinterested bellboy takes us to the second floor in a rickety elevator, opens our door with a flourish, and puts our suitcases on the gray floral carpet. "Will that be all?"

Max hands him a coin. "Yes, thank you."

I stand with the suitcases as if rooted to the floor, my eyes darting around the small, comfortable room. Two windows with net curtains let in a flood of light. From what I can see, our room faces the street. I hope it will not be noisy. Between the windows is a white-painted dresser with two drawers; a piece of furniture intended for short stays or people with few belongings. I fit both categories.

Like a child, Max investigates, opening one door to find a shallow closet with a few hangers. The second door leads to a bathroom, and the sight of the high-sided tub stops me cold. Bathtubs are forever tied to Daniel in my mind. I hadn't expected elaborate facilities in a modest hotel.

I turn away. That is no better, because now I'm facing the wide bed, covered with a light yellow chenille spread. There is a slight sag in the middle. Two pillows with homely embroidered cases lean against a spooled maple headboard. Small tables stand on either side, each with a shaded lamp and an ashtray bearing the hotel's name.

"Is it all right?" Max comes back. "You haven't moved."

"Just getting my bearings," I say. "They didn't even look at us."

His eyes crinkle. "I don't think we're anyone's idea of a typical couple sneaking away for a night of passion."

I can't help myself. I fold double and laugh until my stomach hurts. Max joins me. Somehow we are sitting on the edge of the bed, laughing uncontrollably, and part of me relaxes. It can only be so bad if we can laugh together.

Finally, we stop, and the awkwardness descends again. I stand up, brushing my hands over my thighs. "We should unpack. And I'd like to tidy up."

Glad of something to do, Max spins his case onto the bed and opens it. I get a brief glimpse of socks and underwear, a badly folded shirt. "You tidy, and I'll unpack," he says, "and then we'll swap."

With the bathroom door safely closed, I take off my hat and pull a comb from my bag. There are days when I miss my hair; a well-pinned knot would withstand the ocean breeze in a way that my short curls will not. I wash my face and hands, dab powder on my nose, and apply a light coat of lipstick.

I don't even know what we're doing next—are we going to the boardwalk? Will he want to sleep together now, to get it over with? I don't think I'm ready to be seen in daylight without my clothes, and if I have to worry about keeping the sheet over me, I'll never be able to relax.

"He's a good man," I murmur. While Mama would approve of Max, she would most definitely not approve of me taking him out for a drive like he was a car I was thinking of purchasing. "He's a good man."

Max is silhouetted against the window, his case stowed neatly out of sight. Mine rests on the foot of the bed, unopened.

While he uses the bathroom, I hang up my other dress and Claire's kimono and put my underwear in the top drawer, Max having considerately taken the lower one. There is little else to do, and I am sitting on the bed, ankles crossed, when he finally rejoins me.

"I wanted to give you time." He is having trouble meeting my eyes. "I don't know the rules for this situation."

"Well, neither do I," I say with a laugh. "I've been married most of my adult life." I do not mention this is my second time in a hotel, the first having been my one-night honeymoon.

He holds out his hand. "It's after twelve. Why don't we grab something to eat and walk on the boardwalk?"

Hot dogs are not the food of love, but by the time we have chosen a stall and ordered, and then organized our condiments, the awkwardness has evaporated. We find a bench facing the ocean and sit down. I tuck my skirt in tight around my legs, while Max props his feet on the rail and takes an enormous bite of his hot dog.

I tackle mine more slowly, worried that I will dribble mustard on my dress. It's the green print again—perhaps I should have saved it for tonight, in case we go out. We'll have to eat at a restaurant, won't we? I don't think the hotel has room service, and if we're uncomfortable eating on a bench, what would it be like alone in our room?

Max crumples his napkin and tucks it into his jacket pocket. "That fit the bill," he says with satisfaction. "How's yours?"

Swallowing hastily, I start to respond and choke instead. My face reddens as I try to speak and I cover my mouth with my napkin.

"Put your arms over your head." I look at him, eyes streaming. "Raise your arms," he says again. "It'll help."

It does. Within moments the cough subsides, and I wipe my eyes and stare out at the gray ocean until my face stops pulsing with heat.

"It's delicious," I say, but I put the rest aside, unable to face eating more.

"Shall we walk, then? Or would you rather sit?"

"Let's sit." I tuck my skirt again and put my feet on the rail beside his, no longer self-conscious about the state of my shoes. "Are you uncomfortable that I asked you to do this?"

He is quiet for a long moment. "Fine time to ask," he says, "now that we've come a hundred miles so you can have your way with me."

My laugh is so sudden that I snort, and we both laugh harder. He takes my hand, lacing his fingers with mine.

"I was a bit surprised," he says. "But I love you. Of course I want to go to bed with you."

His bluntness is somehow comforting. Because of the stiff breeze, there are very few people in the water. The sand lifts and swirls, dusting us lightly even as we sit high above the beach. The hypnotic sound of the waves drags words from me.

"I've only ever been with Daniel. I don't want you to think I asked because…" I trail off. I don't know how to put my fear into words—that he will think me too forward or sluttish for wanting to know that the sex between us will work before linking myself to him until death us do part.

"Whatever you're afraid of, I'm not thinking it.' Max puts his hat on the bench and scrunches his fingers through his hair. "I'm grateful, honestly. I wouldn't have had the nerve to ask you."

"Because I'm so fearsome." I've grown accustomed to his softer hand, knowing he works as hard, in his way, as Daniel ever did. "What are you thinking, then?"

Max tips his head back, addressing his next words to the sky. "That it's been a long time."

I squeeze his fingers. "For me, too."

"Not as long." He looks at me. "Dare I assume your sister has told you I was once engaged?"

"Yes."

"I thought as much." He sighs. "Do you really want to hear all this?"

Did I? If we are to be married, I will learn about his past eventually; if it makes today's events even a little easier, I will listen.

"If you want to tell me," I say. "You don't have to."

"I don't talk about it—about her—very much." He rises, shoving his hands in his pockets. "Can we move? I don't think I can do this sitting down."

We walk along the boardwalk. Ahead of us is a pier, jutting out into the ocean like a long, accusing finger. Windows glitter along its sides, and colorful placards tempt wanderers inside out of the breeze. I keep step beside him, letting him wrestle with his thoughts without the distraction of my hand through his arm.

"I met her during my third year at college," he says. "It was love at first sight, at least for me. My parents had died of the flu the summer before, and when my roommate found out I had nowhere to go for the holidays, he invited me to spend Christmas with his family in New York.

"Jack had talked about his younger sister a lot, but he didn't have a photograph, so I expected someone like him. When we picked her up at the train the next day, coming in from Vassar for the break, I felt like I'd been struck by lightning." His voice is distant, remembering. "She was...perfect."

"And her name was Daisy?" I stop short, not wanting him to realize that Claire has told me her name, but he seems not to notice.

"Marguerite Finch-Rappaport," he says. "I called her Daisy."

"Why?"

"It's French for daisy," he explains. "Marguerite."

I recall the silver-framed studio portrait Claire showed me of the young woman with her creamy, flawless skin and severe black bob. A proper flapper, by the look of her, but one with an expensive college education. If Max loved a girl like that, what does he see in me—a woman who'd barely finished eighth grade, who doesn't know the French names for flowers?

"She was perfect," he says again. "She accepted me right off, teased me the way she teased Jack, didn't seem to care I was a scholarship student with a background her parents couldn't possibly approve."

I try to imagine a young Max, uncertain of his worth. Is that what is concealed beneath his aggressive charm? "And?"

The brim of his hat shades his eyes. "Somehow I worked up the nerve to kiss her on New Year's Eve. Two nights later she came into my room." He stops, and people walk around us. "She was the first girl I was ever with. If I thought I'd been struck by lightning at the train station, I didn't know what to think after that."

"Did her brother know?" How had they managed, as roommates, if Max and his sister were lovers?

"Jack knew we liked each other, and that we wrote letters." He begins to walk again. "If he'd known we were meeting in New York, he'd have probably killed me."

I listen to the details of their relationship, of Max's unworthiness of the perfect Daisy Finch-Rappaport. Unable to cope with lying to her brother, he found a room in Philadelphia at the end of the school year and took on two jobs, to avoid the risk of being found out if he spent an entire summer with their family.

"I still saw her," he says. "We couldn't meet where I lived, obviously, but she took the train in whenever I had saved up enough money from waiting tables to afford a room where we could be together."

It was a very different story from the way Daniel and I had come together, the only similarity their physical craving for each other. I couldn't pass judgment on that, nor for not waiting until marriage. If Daniel and I had been certain we wouldn't get caught, we wouldn't have waited, either.

"I got sick that fall," he says slowly. "My landlady's kids had the mumps, and I caught them. I didn't think anything of it at the time, other than it was damned inconvenient to have to keep away from her for so long." He sighs again, heavily, and looks at me. "Have you had enough yet?"

I'd had enough of letting him relive this alone. I tuck my hand through his arm. "Keep going."

We reach the Steel Pier, and turn to walk along its length, weaving our way through all the people who had taken refuge there. Music comes and goes in bursts as doors are opened. It is all very gay, the complete antithesis of Max's story.

"That Christmas, we got engaged. A long engagement, that's what she asked for—until I had completed medical school." He stops to stare up at a poster for the General Motors exhibition and shakes his head. "I didn't want to wait, but it was for the best. If she'd found out what was wrong with me after we were married, she would have hated me, and I don't think I could have stood that."

Dan's revelation. "Is it because you can't have kids?"

His eyes cut toward me. "She wanted four—it was something she talked about often, her dream of us with a perfect family. And then I found out I couldn't give her what she wanted." He stops for a moment, his expression closed, remembering. "I took the train to New York and invited her out to a restaurant. Steak, candlelight, the whole works. Set me back a week's pay. And then I told her." His voice is thick. "She asked if I was certain. Science doesn't lie, I said, trying to make a joke of it. Then she took off my ring, put it on the table, and left the restaurant."

That bitch! It is my first reaction and I keep it to myself, but I had already taken against her for breaking their engagement, even before I knew the shallowness of her reasoning. "Then she didn't love you."

"She loved me," he says. "Just not enough."

"You're making excuses," I tell him. "I'm sure she was shocked, or disappointed, but you don't walk away from a relationship like that. Claire spent twelve years trying to give Harry a child, and he never stopped loving her."

Max stops abruptly. "Do you want to see the cars?"

"No." I have little interest in cars on a good day.

"What about a show?" He gestures at another poster, listing the entertainments available at the pier. When I shake my head, he turns to a set of wooden stairs leading down to the beach. "Would you like to…?"

I can't refuse a third time. The thought of sand in my shoes and my hair and my mouth is unappealing, but he's so tentative, so unlike the man I'm accustomed to that I follow him down the steps without objection. He immediately leans against a piling, takes off his shoes and socks and rolls up his pant legs. "I didn't bring another suit," he says. "I don't want to embarrass you when we go out later."

The news that we are going out makes me so happy that I forgive him for wearing one of his worst suits. "Turn your back," I say, and duck beneath the pier, removing my shoes and reaching under my skirt to unfasten my stockings from my girdle. I slip them into my purse—I've just the one pair and I can't afford to lose them.

When I venture out, Max gives me a smile. "You look different," he says.

"You've seen me without shoes before."

His eyes dip down. "But not with bare legs. It makes you look younger, somehow."

"Watch it." I take his hand. "I'm already feeling dumpy and middle-aged because that desk clerk didn't suspect we were up to no good."

Max puts one arm around me and pulls me close, ignoring the hoots and whistles from a group of boys up on the pier. "You are not dumpy and middle-aged," he says against my neck. "You are delicious."

The touch of his lips against my throat sends a tremor through me. I stand very still, registering that my body is giving in to Max more quickly than my mind. "Why don't you finish telling me your story?"

"Not a lot left to tell," he says, stepping away. "I tried to get her back. I made a damn fool of myself, if you want the truth. But she wanted a family more than she wanted me. End of story."

One of the reasons I can allow myself to want Max is that he will not bring up the thorny issue of children. Perhaps I should bless Daisy Finch-Rappaport for her bad manners and worse judgment, for dropping Max so he would be here when I needed him. "Did you want a family?"

"I wanted a house full." He calms himself with some effort. "But it wasn't possible, so I made do."

"Yes, by proposing to a woman who already has a house full." I don't doubt his feelings are genuine, but it strikes me, then—is it me he wants, or the ready-made family I can provide?

This time there is nothing romantic about his grip on my upper arms. "Of course I want the kids," he says roughly, "but I want their mother more."

"You don't look like you've been struck by lightning this time," I say sulkily. I had wanted to know about Daisy, but now I feel vaguely dirty for having listened and I take it out on him.

"Number one, I'm not a boy anymore, and I try not to show when I've been struck." He shakes me lightly. "Number two, when we met, you were married *and* you had spines like a porcupine to keep me at arm's length."

My mouth curves in spite of my best efforts. "You loved Thelma at first sight."

He drops his hands to my waist. "She was available," he jokes. "And she was a way to spend time with you." Scuffing his feet in the sand, he turns toward the water. "Ask your sister how long it's been. She'll tell you, if she hasn't already."

The sand is cool and loose under my bare feet. As we get closer to the ocean, it turns chilly and firm and my feet leave prints on the surface. I try to stay away from the water, but eventually an ambitious wave washes over our feet and we both shriek and run to the safety of dry sand.

"Cold!" I rub my arms, suddenly chilled through. Max takes off his jacket and drops it over my shoulders. It holds the heat from his body, and I slide my arms into the sleeves and hug myself. "It shouldn't be this cold."

"I think we're both a bundle of nerves," he says. "What about a movie? We passed at least one theater on the way to the pier."

A movie sounds good—we will be indoors, and I can pretend to watch the film and more closely examine the feelings he's stirred in me.

"Lead on." I abandon the thought of putting my stockings back on and simply dust the sand from my soles before stepping into my shoes.

The Apollo Theater, at New York Avenue and the boardwalk, is playing a double feature that would be of more interest to my sons than it is to me. I shake my head and peer around the corner, at a tall neon sign visible from where we stand. "How about that one?"

"Let's see what they're showing. I'm not a fan of cowboys and Indians, either." He takes my hand as we walk and it feels natural, even as the remaining grit between my toes works its way free and fills my shoes.

A block away, the Colonial theater shows less current pictures—the second feature, *It Happened One Night,* had come and gone in Philadelphia in March. But it's a comedy, and Clark Gable and his mustache seem attractive enough.

The movie was not at all what I'd expected. It *was* a comedy, but the plot made it very difficult to take my mind from the events to come. Claudette Colbert was wonderful as the dizzy heroine who knew what she wanted until she found someone better. Gable's streetwise reporter was a revelation, and now I understood the comments I'd heard about men's undershirts soon becoming a thing of the past—when he took off his shirt to reveal his bare chest, gasps and giggles erupted all over the theater.

I did not look at Max, but I wondered whether or not he had jumped on the no-undershirt bandwagon, and whether he would look like Clark Gable without his shirt.

Afterward, we went to the same small restaurant we'd gone to on our first trip. Max ordered beer, but I shook my head when asked if I would like one. "Coffee for me, thanks."

"You drank champagne at Claire's," he reminded me.

"I need a clear head," I said, and watched as the color mounted to his face.

I remember this as we return to our room, a few minutes past nine. The desk clerk—a different one, but similarly disinterested—wishes us a good night as we cross to the elevator, and this time, I am the one to blush.

The room is dark, and I bend to turn on one of the bedside lamps, then stop. Do I want light?

"Is something wrong?" He drops his jacket on a chair and comes to stand beside me. "Ava?"

"I don't know." I hide my face in my hands. "This was my idea, but it feels so sudden!"

He laughs. "It's been the only thing on both our minds this entire day, and you know it."

Letting out a breath, I sit on the edge of the bed. "Not the only thing," I remind him. "You told me about Daisy."

The light from outside our window reveals a somber expression. "I don't like talking about that part of my life. Thinking about it, even." He sits beside me and gently takes my hand. "But I thought you should know."

I look at his hand, the frayed shirt cuff, the glint of cufflink barely visible. "You know enough of my past."

He lowers his head, presses his lips to my knuckles. "And I don't want to take any of it away, Ava. I want to build a future with you, and that means all of you. That means Daniel." His breath is warm on my chilled skin. "Never be afraid to speak about him. He's part of who you are."

"It doesn't seem fair," I murmur, waiting for Daniel to appear, summoned by his name. "If I'm going to be your wife, how can I think about another man?"

"Well, I hope I keep you busy enough that you don't think about *another* man," Max says with a smile in his voice. "But I don't want to take away your memories—not yours or the kids'. That's not my purpose."

His earnestness does what it always does, breaks down my defenses. I close my eyes and let him kiss me, and when his mouth dips to my throat, and then to the neckline of my dress, I do not push him away. My hands find his curly hair, but only to guide him closer. When he unbuttons my dress, I am grateful for the dim lighting that disguises the substandard condition of my slip.

He nudges the straps off my shoulders and buries his face between my breasts with a sigh of contentment. A warmth spreads through me, borne of his genuine appreciation. Max is not seeing me as a mother, or a woman past her prime. His hands and his lips only know who I am, in this moment, and it allows me to let Daniel go—at least for now.

36

Claire

It is mid-afternoon when a shout goes up from George. The children stream out the door and down the steps, making so much noise that I am unable to hear the quiet words exchanged between Max and Ava. Max hands her bag to Dan and waves off the taxi, leaning against my car with his arms crossed, looking for all the world like a man who has been given the moon.

"Thank you for staying with them." Ava takes Grace smoothly from my arms and kisses the baby on both cheeks. "I hope they didn't drive you crazy."

"Do I look crazy?" I wink at George and Toby, who had been bribed into good behavior by a promise of a ride in my roadster. "They were perfect. Did you have a good time?"

Her tight-lipped smile reveals nothing. "It was quite chilly."

I look at Max, give a tiny shrug. He studies his nails. "I hope you managed to keep warm." I lower my voice. "How did the kimono go over?"

Ava ushers the children into the house. "I never got around to wearing it. Do you have a coat, Claire? You shouldn't keep Max waiting."

I reach past her to catch up my hat and coat, and Pearl brings my bag. "He'll cope," I murmur as I pass. "You made him wait long enough."

Ava

I wake with my thoughts full of Daniel. He was so real, so briefly there, that for a moment I can smell him. The dream was about that last difficult year, after we lost Mama, when we were so often at odds. It hurts to think about, even now. I never regretted leaving Thelma in Philadelphia, even though it caused one of the ugliest scenes in our marriage. It was the right thing to do; I wish he'd lived to see her with her braces off, keeping up with the other kids. Taking dance lessons.

Loss returns as I remember the future we could have had. The children we will not raise together. The life we will not make. The moments we will not have, because he is under a mountain and I am here. My commitment to my husband goes beyond his mortal life. There is some spiritual plane where Daniel and I still exist together. How will that work if I marry Max? Will a part of me always belong to Daniel?

How is that fair to Max? There is no way to restore what has been lost. Medicine cures ills, stops pain, but grief is a bruise that does not fade—always tender when pressed, lurking under thin skin to remind me, at the slightest touch, of what is gone.

What am I going to do? As I drink my coffee on the bench in the yard, my thoughts turn to Max. He is very different from Daniel, both physically and in the way he touches me. I'm glad—if he had approached me with Daniel's casual, proprietary manner, I might have broken down, and I wanted very much to be present. Laughter in bed is as important as passion, but there had been a surprising amount of passion. I might not be thoroughly convinced that marriage is the right choice, but Max has at least convinced me that *he* is the right choice.

Still, it feels wrong to care about someone new. Needing to move on with my life is like losing Daniel all over again. I didn't want to move on, not at first, but I can't drag the kids through this eternal swamp of grief. And once Grace was born, it became even more difficult to spare the time to mourn him the way he deserved. She was his last gift: grace. When she was born, I said we needed it, but I don't think I realized how much.

After a morning of sewing, I take her out of her basket and transfer her to the coach. "We're going to see your cousin Teddy," I tell her. Her eyes light up, though it's mostly because she likes going outside.

Claire is out and Katie has a few days off to visit her sister. Esther and her husband are at home, but they shouldn't be saddled with taking care of Teddy while my sister is out and about. I have lunch with him in the nursery, fending him off as he keeps trying to feed Grace bits of his meal. "She's not old enough for big boy food," I tell him. "You eat that and get big and strong, so you can take care of her someday."

Soon they both go down for a nap and I am at loose ends. I peruse Claire's bookshelves and wonder how, with her schedule, she finds time to read. Nothing strikes me, and I sink down in her sitting room and put my feet up for a few minutes.

The sound of the front door startles me awake. Can it be Claire already? I spring up and plunge through the door, straight into Max.

"Well, this is a lovely surprise!" His tie is crooked and his cheeks are flushed, as if he's ridden his bicycle all the way from the clinic.

"I thought you were Claire." I shake my head to clear it. It doesn't do to talk with Max if I am feeling foggy.

"She won't be home until six," he says. "It's a little after three."

"Then why are you back so early?"

He grins. "Forgot something. Again. I'll pop upstairs, get it, and be out of your way."

"You don't need to rush." I trail him to the rooms I'd once shared with the kids. "Teddy and Grace are napping and I was reading."

"You were, were you?" He cocks his head and reaches out to fluff my hair on one side. "Looks to me like you were napping, too."

I watch from the doorway as he rummages in a drawer and stuffs something in his jacket pocket. "You're tidy," I say. "Or is it Katie?"

"It's all me, I'm afraid," he says. "She's allowed in to run the sweeper, but I've always looked after myself."

"You haven't made the bed," I point out, going over to straighten the sheets.

"Another thing I forgot this morning." He pulls the sheet taut from the other side, then reaches for the spread. "This is wonderfully domestic."

He might as well add mindreading to his list of talents. Blood warms my cheeks and I duck my head, not wanting him to see that I had imagined him getting out of that rumpled bed. What did he wear when he was alone?

His hands are on my shoulders, making me jump. He's also too stealthy for his own good. "Don't look like that," he says, close to my ear. "Just because the house is empty doesn't mean I expect anything."

"Oh, don't you?" I turn and find myself up against him, so close I can smell his soap under the faint whiff of disinfectant that clings to him after he leaves the clinic.

"You read me like a book." His smile is rueful. "A man can dream, can't he? Of course I want to take you to bed again, but I won't rush you into anything you're not ready for."

He's curious why I've withdrawn, after our night in Atlantic City, when I had given in with no argument. Not given in, but instigated the whole thing. I certainly gave him the impression then that I was ready.

"I dream about Daniel." Max deserves my honesty, though I wish I could be kinder. "All the time. It makes me wonder if I'm ready to turn my back on him."

"You're not turning your back on him." He twines his fingers through mine and I lean against his chest. "He's with you every day, through your children."

"And you don't mind?"

"Not so long as there's room for me, too." He kisses the side of my neck. "Now about that proposal I made a while back…"

Pearl

May 16, 1934

They're getting married! Mama deserves to be happy, and I'm happy for her. But I'm sad, too, because of Daddy. Which doesn't make sense. He's gone, so why shouldn't she get remarried? It's been a year and a half, which is forever and no time at all.

If I'm confused, how does she feel? It's the one question I can't ask her.

Aunt is over the moon, of course. And Dr. Max looks like somebody lit off fireworks in him. Dan is quiet, but I think he's pleased. I remember the night we talked about Mama, and him not wanting to feel like he had to stay here to be the man of the house. I wonder if he'll leave now, or if his job and Tommy are enough to keep him here?

Ava

My life has become an avalanche, gathering speed, and sweeping me along with it. Nothing I can do will stop it, or the proposal I accepted in Max's rooms the other afternoon. It makes me short of breath if I think about it for too long. When Claire pries or Thelma asks an innocent question, I shrug them off and get on with whatever I'm doing.

That doesn't work with Max.

"Do you want to go down to Sansom Street this Sunday?" He runs his thumb over my knuckles. "Spencer's got the clinic in the afternoon."

"What for?" I can't think of anything in that part of town.

"For a ring." His eyes are bright. "I have a little money put aside. I want to buy you a diamond." Leaning forward, he kisses me quickly. "I'd like to buy you a diamond mine, but I'll settle for a ring."

"No," I say, too harshly. "No diamonds." *No mines.* I look down at my worn wedding band, which I will switch to my right hand once we marry. "I don't need an engagement ring."

His face falls. "Are you sure?"

I nod. "It's not necessary."

"It's not," he agrees, "but why does it have to be necessary? I can't give you everything I'd like to, but let me do this."

"No." There is another conversation in my head now, Daniel's voice drowning out Max, promising to buy me a diamond if he got his army bonus. He hadn't gotten it, and that disappointment sent him down into the bootleg mine with our son, and to his death.

I squeeze my eyes shut until the voice recedes. "No," I say again. "I don't want a ring. A wedding band is more than enough."

"It's to do with him, then?"

Max's perceptiveness brings hot tears to the corners of my eyes and I blink them away. "Yes. And I don't want to talk about it."

Claire takes up the crusade a few days later, because of course it couldn't end that easily. "I'm free on Saturday," she says. "We can take the girls with us. I'm sure they'll want to be there."

"For what?" I look up from the skirt I'm hemming.

"For your dress." Her eyes light up with the anticipation of spending Harry's money. "I'll make sure to get the Packard, so we all fit."

"What dress?" I'm surrounded by dresses.

"Your wedding dress." Her tone is the same one Toby uses with George when his younger brother is being particularly thick.

"I don't want to buy a dress." I've been expecting—dreading—this conversation. It was hard enough telling Max I didn't want a ring, but he already knows when to stop asking questions; Claire never learns.

"If you're making it yourself, you're leaving it a bit late."

A wedding dress is the last thing I want to make—for me or anyone else. I stick my needle back into the tomato cushion and wind the excess thread back on its spool. "I'm not making a dress for the wedding and I'm not buying one, either."

"Are you sure?" The doubt is clear on her face.

"I'm sure." The idea of a wedding gown at my age and stage of life is ridiculous. "You don't wear white for a second marriage anyway."

Claire takes a sip of coffee. "You wear whatever makes you feel good. You've taught me that."

I refill her cup and shove it across the table. "A wedding dress wouldn't make me feel good. I would be playing a part."

She closes her eyes. "Do you have any aspirin?"

"Why?"

"You've given me a headache." Pushing the cup away, she stands. "I have to get moving. I promised to meet Stella for lunch." She hugs me quickly, but can't resist one more attempt. "It doesn't have to be white, or even look like a wedding dress. You're welcome to come over and go through the attic again. Look what you did with that black dress."

That black dress is the nicest thing I own, aside from the gown I made for her gala, which will likely never get another outing. It's a shame I can't wear the black, but it would be as wrong as white, and anyway, it's far too formal.

"I'm wearing the green print," I say. "Drop it, Claire."

Her mouth falls open. "You can't wear that. It's more than two years old." After a pause, she says carefully, "It looks...shabby."

"Then I'll put a new collar on it." I push my chair back, the subject closed. I've said yes; we're getting married. We've set a date, and I will be there. But I will not have the circus my sister thinks necessary to seal a man and woman.

Daniel and I got married without any extravagance, and we never felt the lack. I wore a dress that I continued to wear for the next ten years, far longer than my green print, and we almost had to put the wedding off because he hadn't saved enough for the ring. He worked extra shifts to earn money, causing me to worry that he would be killed before we could finally scratch the itch that had plagued us for years.

"—can't believe you're acting like this."

I snap out of my memories, vaguely aware my sister has been lecturing me. "Leave me be."

"I will not." She crosses her arms, and for a moment, Mama's face flickers over hers.

Shaking my head—there are too many ghosts around today—I tell her, "It's my wedding, Claire, and I'll do as I damn well please."

"But it's not logical," she argues, unwilling to give in. "You made a new dress to promote your business but you won't wear something special to honor the man you're marrying?"

"It's not like that." It isn't, but I'm not certain I can explain to her *why* it isn't. "Max doesn't need all that from me, anyway. He knows who I am."

"He might not need it, but I'll bet he'd like it." She opens the workroom door to the spring breeze, still grumbling. "You're such a hardhead."

"It runs in the family," I call after her, and she waves from the car. She's stopped pestering me for now, but if I know my sister, she's not going to drop it any time soon.

37

Claire

Ava's intractability is infuriating. I would buy a dress myself and present it to her, a fait accompli, except she would throw it at me and show up at her wedding in that drab green print anyway. It was fine when it was purchased, but that was in May of 1932, back when she gave Teddy to us. When she met Max for the first time. When Daniel was alive and she had a different life to return to.

But now her life is here, with Max, and he deserves more than what she's willing to give. She cares about him, that much is obvious, but there are times when she almost seems to begrudge the idea of getting married.

When Max comes in from the clinic, I'm alone in the living room.

"Harry not home yet?" he asks, dropping his hat on the hall table and coming to join me.

"Soon. He called to say he'll be late." I glance at the drinks cabinet. "But I'm sure he wouldn't mind if we started without him."

He sets to making a pitcher of martinis. "Today went well," he says over his shoulder. "Ten patients—one from last week, who needed a dressing changed, and three new migrants from West Virginia. Brothers. From what I was able to glean, it's far worse down there."

"I can imagine." I accept the glass and take a welcome sip. I'm glad the clinic is doing well, but I don't need a blow-by-blow description of the patients. "Were they miners?"

"Two of them," he says, sitting on the sofa beside me. "The other is lame and hasn't worked in several years. But the mine closed down and they hopped a train north to see if things were any better."

As Max chats about the clinic, I revisit my earlier conversation and interrupt, asking, "Does it bother you that Ava is so insistent about having everything her way, as far as the wedding?"

Something shifts behind his eyes and he takes a slow, deliberate sip of his drink. "Ava is who she is," he says equably. "We can't change her, and I don't want to."

"But—"

He holds up a finger. "Getting married is the important part, not what she wears or where it's done. You're her sister, Claire. We both love her. Let's not say anything we'll regret."

The sound of Harry's key in the front door rescues us from further embarrassment, but I can't help wondering what Max was thinking before he stood up for her. This isn't how he wants things to be, I'm sure of it. He simply has no better plan than I do for how to change Ava's mind.

I bring it up again after dinner, when Max has gone out, and find my husband's sympathies are with Ava. "You shouldn't push, darling."

"Aren't you happy for them?"

"Of course." He stubs out his cigarette. "But I wonder, sometimes, if they aren't rushing into this."

"Rushing?" That makes no sense. "Max has adored her since they met."

He raises his eyes. "Ava lost her husband in the worst way possible, and since then, she hasn't stopped—moving, building a business, raising her children. Giving birth." Flexing his hands, he adds, "Even though she's accepted Max's proposal, do you really believe she's ready to marry again?"

I have never questioned Ava's constant busyness, except to sympathize with how little rest she allows herself. Is it keeping her from moving forward into the next phase of her life?

"But she needs him," I say. "She needs a husband."

Harry laughs. "I've never met a woman who needed one less."

Ava would probably agree, but I hate the idea of my sister being alone. "It's not natural," I say violently. "I have never imagined being single."

"And that's you." He catches my hand across the small table between our chairs. "You and Ava are very different people."

"She married the first man who asked her."

"So did you." There is something in his voice I don't understand.

"That's different." I'm not sure how, but I have to follow through with something. "I met you. She never even looked at anyone else."

"Have you?"

"Of course not." Not seriously, anyway.

He fumbles with his cigarettes. "I don't know, sometimes, how to love you, or Teddy," he says, looking down. "You act as if love is easy, but I've never found it to be so."

I want to gather him into my arms, but I let him speak.

"It's why I fell in love with you. You were so different from everything—everyone—I knew. I thought if I could love you, properly, I wouldn't end up like the people who raised me."

"Cold," I say, before I can stop myself. My loathing for Irene and what she has done is bigger than my care for his feelings

"Yes." Harry raises his glasses and rubs the bridge of his nose. "I loved my father, but he was distant. He never stopped trying to be what she needed him to be. He was never himself. And that's how I was raised, to meet those expectations and never to trust my feelings. You were like a light in the darkness, showing me I didn't have to live their life."

"You weren't living their life." I think of the forty-year-old bachelor I'd married. "You escaped their expectations."

"Not all of them. I escaped the society wedding to the well-bred debutante of my mother's choosing, but I didn't escape *her*. Not even when you came along." He puts his hand over mine again. "Not until Teddy."

It all comes down to my lack of fertility. "If I'd given you a baby, it would have happened sooner."

"Maybe." He cocks his head. "Maybe not. Maybe neither of us were ready to stand up to her."

"I tried to find common ground with her this year," I say. "For your sake. I thought the clinic was a cause she would finally see as acceptable."

He pushes up from his chair, goes to stand at the fireplace, hands braced on the mantel. "It would never have worked. You wanted to be accepted, and she saw it as an opportunity to turn you into the sort of woman I never wanted to marry."

"She nearly succeeded." She nearly succeeded in other ways, but I don't want to bring all that up again.

The light glints of his glasses, obscuring his eyes. "She nearly succeeded in coming between us, pushing Gardiner at you as your savior, because she knew I'd be bound to say something to upset you."

Did Harry know how close it had come—Irene's plot? If I'd given Francis Gardiner even the slightest encouragement, she would be comforting him after a scandalous divorce. And if it had come to that, where would I be? With a healthy settlement but only occasional contact with my sister's child, who is, legally, my husband's son.

It does not bear thinking about.

"You did not get your capacity for love from them," I say. "The miracle of grace is you have learned to give what you've never received."

Pearl

June 4, 1934

It's not fair that Dandy gets to go everywhere, because he's a boy, and I get to go to school, and to Aunt's, and to the store, and that's it, because I'm a girl. George and Toby have more freedom than I do. Last week, I said something in front of Tommy, and he shrugged and said, "Bring her along next time."

So yesterday morning Dan asked if he could take me to a baseball game. The little boys started yelling, but he told them to pipe down, because they've gone with him and Uncle Jake both. He told Mama I deserved a treat because of how hard I work. That made her feel guilty, especially with the wedding coming so soon.

We walked with Tommy all the way to his house. My legs were tired, but I got to rest while his mother fed us. I've never had spaghetti and I wasn't very good at eating it. His little sisters laughed, but they showed me how to twirl it on my fork and get it into my mouth without it all ending up on my front.

Afterwards, Tommy handed me a pair of pants and told me to get changed. I was wearing my daisy blouse, so I thought it would look funny, but he reminded me that poor people wear what they have. Which was better than saying I don't have much of a bust. So I put on the pants and tucked my hair into Dan's cap.

I don't care about baseball, so I won't write about the game. We snuck in by climbing over a fence, which was fun, and at the end of the night a guard chased us. We ran for two blocks before he gave up and I laughed so hard my chest hurt. Then we walked home. Tommy said Dan could bring the pants back tomorrow. I'd like to keep them. It felt so free, being able to climb and run and not worry about showing my drawers and what people would think, or what they would do because I'm a girl.

It was nearly eleven when we came in, late for a school night. Mama was upstairs, so I changed into my skirt real fast and told her I'd tell her all about it in the morning. And I will tell her about part of it.

Ava

I have maintained my insistence on a simple wedding. Since I'm Catholic and Max is what he calls an unenthusiastic Lutheran, it can't be a church wedding. When Harry suggests a judge who can marry us at City Hall, it seems like the perfect solution. "Just the words," I said, "in front of someone who can legally say them."

When he asks about a reception, I agree to a restaurant lunch after the ceremony—their gift to us—but I make it clear that it will be no extravagant affair, with no fancy cake or champagne toasts. I do not consult Max, knowing he will agree with me. He has been amenable to every suggestion. I am grateful for his understanding, though I myself don't quite know why I'm being so difficult about everything. I am more contrary than my kids, but if I try to examine my reasons, they slip away from me and I am left with Claire's words ringing in my head, that I am somehow disrespecting Max by not choosing to be married in a way that, to me, feels unnatural.

Instead of a honeymoon, we are spending the night in Claire's guest room while she and Harry stay with the kids. It will be an opportunity to finally wear that beautiful kimono. It had been a nice gesture on her part, but that night at the hotel had been about removing things—my clothes, my excuses. It's been sitting in tissue ever since.

"Wouldn't it be nice to make a bit of a fuss?" Pearl asks. "Have a party or something? That way it wouldn't be like Daddy. You could keep that memory separate."

Those memories *are* separate. My life with Daniel is complete, a world contained inside my head like one of those snow globes Thelma loves. Whether my wedding to Max is as elaborate as a princess's or as bare bones as my first won't touch that world, and I can't make myself believe an elaborate ceremony would be anything other than a waste of money. It certainly isn't necessary to make a happy marriage.

"Not even a new dress?" She looks at anywhere but my face, and I know Claire has been talking to her.

"I don't need a dress," I snap. "I don't need a dress or a diamond ring or a party. Your father and I couldn't have been happier, and we didn't have any of that."

We could have been happier, of course; every couple could be, but we did the best we could with what we had. Money might not buy happiness, but it relieves worry, which is very nearly the same thing.

The line appears between Pearl's brows. "But we have more, so what's the harm in it? We eat better now, because we can afford better food. We keep the house warmer—the downstairs, anyway. Why shouldn't you have something nice?"

I remain silent, unable to explain my reasons to my too-adult child. I was glad, the other day, to see her go out with Dan and his friend. She's got a bit of a crush on Tommy, but he's like Dan, not interested in girls yet, so I don't have that worry.

"Don't save it all for us, Mama," she pleads. "You deserve it, too. And Dr. Max deserves it."

I pull the discarded muslin off the table and fold it roughly to hide my shaking hands. "Why not let me decide what I need?" My tone lets her know that discussion is at an end.

Claire

"Burt Grafton is coming over this afternoon," Harry says, carrying his plate back to the table.

It is early on a Sunday morning. Katie has set out breakfast on the sideboard and slipped upstairs to dress for church.

"Should I come back early?" I calculate when the Hedges family gets back from their service and whether I should ask Katie to stay behind. "Ava won't care if I skip out after mass."

"Not at all." He holds up a hand. "As a matter of fact"—he hesitates—"you might want to go to Ava's after church."

"Why?" Mr. Grafton is far from an exciting luncheon guest, but he helped set up the clinic charity, organized building permits, and, for all I know, used his considerable powers of persuasion to make my dream a reality. I should be here to welcome him, even if the men disappear into Harry's office immediately after.

"He's bringing Mother." Harry smiles grimly. "There's no need to put yourself through that."

I take his advice, and Teddy and I spend the day with my sister's family. We play games in the street, and then I help Thelma make a cake while Ava and Pearl sew, calling back and forth through the open workroom door. Max comes in at five, kissing Ava and greeting each of the children in turn: a handshake for Dan, a kiss on the cheek for Pearl, shadowboxing with the boys, and spinning Thelma until she squeals. He gives me a quick kiss, tweaks Teddy's nose, and then addresses himself to the high chair, where Grace sits, waving a spoon.

Looking to Ava for permission, he scoops up the baby and sits at the table, gazing down at her with an expression only slightly less dazed than when he looks at my sister.

"Teddy and I should be on our way," I say. "Did you happen to stop at the house first, Max?"

"I did indeed." He loosens his tie, the very picture of a man at home, and smiles guilelessly. "The coast is clear."

Ava

I want to ask what Max means—why Claire willingly spent the day playing with my kids—but there isn't time.

"Aunt helped me make a cake," Thelma tells him. "With chocolate icing."

Claire mostly watched, as my girl, now seven, has found something she enjoys more than sewing. "And it looks delicious," I add, kissing her head in passing. "Come upstairs, Max, while the girls get supper ready."

"And the boys," Pearl says, grabbing Toby's collar as he tries to skin past. "You can set the table."

He follows me to the second floor bedroom where the girls and I sleep. "Dan's going to put up a dividing wall for this room the way he did with the downstairs." I wave my hand at the pile of building supplies, filling a space already crowded with two beds, two dressers, and Grace's cradle. "So we'll have one side and the girls will have the other."

"It'll be a bit tight," Seeing my face, he adds quickly, "But I'm sure it will be fine." He puts an arm around me and backs me up against the bed. "You can't get away from me in such tight quarters."

"Who says I want to?" I stop thinking about the wedding and let him kiss me in the room that will soon be ours.

Drawing back, he says, "Your sister, but only just." He sits on the mattress and brings me down onto his lap. I slide off; I don't want the kids catching us together like that, not yet. "Don't give her too much grief, she's worked up because you're not doing this *her* way."

I sigh. "She is going to drive me crazy before this is over."

"She feels responsible," he says against my neck. "Introducing us and all that."

A chill runs over me at his warm breath. "And all that," I say irritably. "Introducing us, interfering with Thelma, luring you away from a perfectly good job..."

Max reaches over and turns on the bedside lamp. "A perfectly good job that didn't make me happy," he says. "This clinic is more than I ever dreamed of. You know how I loved working at the camp. Claire's given me that again, in spades, but with the security of knowing it won't vanish tomorrow. You aren't jealous, are you?"

"Of course not." Too sharp, too quick. "Not exactly. It's just sister stuff."

"Good." He squeezes me to him. "Because I don't want you to be jealous of the other woman in my life."

"I'm not." I kiss him again to stop him from talking.

It's not jealousy, not in a way he would understand. I have no fear they would ever become involved—if Gardiner's slickness wasn't to Claire's liking, Max's rumpled amiability would hardly turn her from steadfast, loving Harry—but I do envy the involvement they have in something in which there is no place for me. My sister, who I've always thought of as beautiful but without ambitions beyond marriage and motherhood, created this clinic out of a desire to accomplish something, and she has done everything short of giving it to Max, along with a salary that allows him to support a wife and family.

There is nothing I can do to advance this project so near to his heart, nor can I bring anything to our relationship that will change his life in a positive way. A half dozen children and their tired, prickly mother should be no inducement to a man in his position, but he is stubbornly in love, not just with me, but with the idea of our family.

I can't tell him how scared I am. I can't tell anyone, because there is no one in my life who wouldn't tell me I'm a silly, overreacting woman. Yet I'm not overreacting. Marrying Max will be a change beyond anything I could have imagined for myself. In the last two years I've gone from the wife of a coal miner to a self-employed widow to—what next? A doctor's wife?

Max is not what I imagine when I think of doctors: he's not stiff and highbrow and wealthy, but even in his softness, his love of everyone, he is an educated man with the potential to make far more money than I've ever known. I am not equipped to be the wife of someone like that. I will never be accepted by the kind of people he socializes with. When I meet them at Claire's, it's as her dressmaker sister, which is something they understand. But as his wife, how would that work? Will they be able to respect me after I've knelt at their feet, pinning a hem? Knowing they've made unreasonable last-minute demands, with the unspoken threat of the loss of future business if I don't comply?

It scares me, the thought of living in that world. For all that Claire and Max manage with little effort, part of me wants to hide in my workroom and lock the door from the inside rather than attempt it. When I am alone, in the tub or in the early morning hours, I probe my thoughts, looking for Daniel or Mama to give me answers, but my dead are stubbornly silent. Or maybe I've stopped putting words in their mouths but haven't yet figured out how to solve my own problems.

Claire

Katie meets me at the door and I relinquish Teddy into her hands. "I'll take him downstairs to eat," she says. "Mr. Warriner is in his office. I think he could use a drink."

"Noted." How bad was it that Katie would speak out of turn?

I pause, then knock softly, not wanting to startle him if he is enjoying the peace restored by his guests' departure.

"Come in." He looks far from peaceful, standing at the window with his jacket off. His fine cotton shirt glows in the late afternoon light. The bronze ashtray on the desk is littered with cigarette butts and another Chesterfield smolders in his fingers. There is something strained in his expression, a shadow of an emotion Harry rarely shows. I skirt the desk and put my arms around his waist. He raises the hand with the cigarette out of the way and pulls me close with his other arm.

"Was it bad?" I ask, when he shows no sign of letting go.

"Atrocious." He steps back, takes my hand. "Drink?"

We cross the hall to the living room, where the tall front windows are open to the cooling air. Voices carry from down the street: a burst of laughter, the sound of a car door closing, then the purr of a motor as it drives away.

"Sit." I push him toward his chair and make the martinis myself. "If it was that bad, I'm surprised you waited."

He takes the glass. "If I'd started when I first had the urge, I wouldn't have been sober enough to greet you."

I take a sip. The gin burns the back of my throat. "What was so awful?"

He is silent, then a sound makes me look up. He has removed his cufflinks, dropped them on the table as if that is the proper place for them, instead of the little silver tray on his dresser. His watch follows, and he folds his cuffs back, precisely, to his mid-forearms.

"I've worked out a settlement with Mother," he says. "Burt drew up the paperwork and we signed everything today."

"What sort of settlement?" His martini is already half empty but I hesitate to refill it before we eat.

He drains his glass and fetches his own refill, topping off my barely-touched drink. Dropping back hard into his chair, he says, "A settlement that will allow her to remain in this family—just."

He lays it out for me, everything Irene has done: the finding—and funding—of Francis Gardiner; the article in the *Inquirer*, meant to disgrace me and sink the clinic; her intention that Gardiner should lure me away from my marriage, or at least tempt me sufficiently that Harry would divorce me. Most were familiar, but there are new details, and by the time he finishes, I am shivering. How could anyone hate me so deeply, and with so little reason?

"I didn't need to know all that." I wet my lips, and realize it's my turn to wipe away the taste of betrayal with gin.

"Sorry." He reaches across and takes my hand. "You did ask, and now it's done and dealt with, I wanted you to know everything. No more secrets."

I nod, understanding that his accounting was for my benefit. "No more secrets. So what's the settlement, then?"

His features change, and for a moment another Harry is visible, the hard-edged man I've glimpsed at occasional dinners where the conversation has veered to business. "The price Mother has agreed to pay to continue to be acknowledged as my parent," he says simply. "She will fund the clinic until her death, and in her will, she leaves a further one hundred thousand dollars, which, suitably invested, will keep the clinic running far into the future."

It isn't the gin making me dizzy. I clutch his hand. "How did you get her to agree?" That the clinic is not only safe, but funded in perpetuity—with Irene's money—is something I will think about later.

"Easy." Harry's smile reminds me, suddenly, of Francis Gardiner. Wolfish, and not at all pleasant. "I reminded her that she is not the only member of this family with access to the press. There are more than a few unsavory stories out there about Father which were kept quiet while he was alive." He sighs and takes another drink. "Since her reputation is all she really values, having everyone in Philadelphia know he was serially unfaithful, and that I have several illegitimate siblings, would be a blow from which she would never recover."

In all my years in the Warriner household I've never heard a whisper of scandal. "Is it true?"

He tips his head back and addresses his words to the ceiling. "Every bit of it," he says, "and if it weren't, I would have still told her it was." He looks straight at me. "We've got her, Claire. At last. She can't hurt you anymore."

There is a cost, I learn over dinner, to be paid mostly by Harry. One Sunday lunch per month, two escorts to the orchestra or the opera—box seats, a prominent soloist—and an invitation once a year, on her birthday, to the house which had been hers for almost fifty years.

"That's not too awful." I can manage one meal, considering his part of the bargain. "Will you do it?"

"I signed a contract," he says. "But if you want to serve her one of those jellied horrors, I wouldn't object."

When we go upstairs, I check on Teddy and then fold myself onto the edge of our bed, dropping my head into my hands. The worst is over—Irene's fangs have been drawn, at minimal cost, and the clinic is safe. Harry is better, too, having lanced the boil that has been their relationship since I entered the picture.

Everything is better—I know it is—but as a couple, we're not there yet, and I don't know how to get us there. I stare across the room at the Renoir, letting my eyes lose focus until the colors blur in the golden light of the bedside lamps. Then it comes to me.

We could go back to Paris.

Not for a short trip, but to live, until we are ourselves again. Teddy can come with us. He's old enough now to travel. We can rent a house or an apartment and stay there until we are healed.

When Harry comes in from the bathroom, he sits beside me. "It's over, so I have no idea why I'm so exhausted."

"Because she's your mother," I point out. "For good or ill, and in this case, very ill." I kiss his cheek, smile at the scratch of stubble against my lips. "This hasn't been easy for you."

He sighs heavily, and his body sags against mine for a moment. "What comes next?"

"We do," I tell him. "You and me and Teddy." One hand crosses the space between us, to rest over his heart. "I have a lot of lost time to make up for."

"You're not the only one." Harry raises my fingers to his lips. "I should have dealt with her sooner. I was just confounded—I couldn't believe she would actually take it that far."

I slip my hand free, and turn down the bed. "I have an idea."

Sliding under the covers, he turns on one side to face me. "What's that?"

"France," I say. "Paris, specifically. We were always happy there."

There is a long silence. I would think he slept except for the warm hand, definitely awake, that rests on the curve of my hip.

"Well, it's France," he says reasonably. "Who wouldn't be happy there?"

I cover his hand with mine, slide it along my satin-covered thigh. "Then why don't we go back? Once Ava and Max are settled, let's take Teddy and go to Paris." I lean forward and kiss him, letting him know I do not wish to sleep. "We can pretend we're on *our* honeymoon."

38

Ava

After supper, while the kids clear up, Max and I take Grace out for a walk. It gives us time alone, time for me to reconcile myself toward what is coming and to determine why some part of me still resists my fate.

"You don't mind how cramped the house is?" I stop to lean over the coach. Grace is fussing, but when I reach for her, she bats my hand away and stretches her arms toward Max.

"I'd live in a shoe," he says, hoisting her to his shoulder, "if it meant I got to wake up next to you every day."

He seems to mean it. I'm glad. I can't bear to think of moving again. The house is mine, something I never thought I'd be able to say. It is nothing more than bricks and mortar, but it has been a refuge and a place of healing, and I'm not ready to let it go, not even for Max.

"One thing," he says. "I can live with the house, but can we please replace the sofa? That thing has it in for me."

That thing, as he calls it, has stood us in good stead since my mother's days, but even I have to admit it's falling to pieces. "What, you don't like ending up on top of me every time you sit down?"

"I like ending up on top of you in bed," he says with a grin. "But not in the living room. And if those springs grab me one more time, you'll be mending my pants."

I smile in return. "As if the ruin of one of those suits would be the end of the world." I will never not jibe at him about his wardrobe. "Fine."

Grace squawks and he jounces her soothingly, never missing a step. "I'll make you a deal."

"What?" Mention of deals makes me suspicious.

"You agree to that new sofa, and I'll buy a suit for the wedding."

"I'll believe that when I see it."

We continue our walk, a quick circuit through the Rittenhouse Square neighborhood, avoiding Claire's block by unspoken agreement.

"My sister says I'm hard-headed." We round the corner and turn on to Ringgold Place.

"And so you are." He gives me a glance like a caress, both his hands being occupied with the baby. "How would you have survived any other way?"

After the younger children have gone to bed, I sit a while in the kitchen with Pearl and Dan, talking about nothing. When Dan heads out for a final smoke and Pearl turns eagerly to her books, I go up to check on Grace. I pause in the living room, looking at the shelf of family photos between the front windows. Impulsively, I take down the square metal framed photograph of my first wedding and stare at the tiny black-and-white faces.

How young we were, and even in that stiffly posed photo, how clearly we loved each other. Daniel leans over me, boyish and unformed, his curling hair momentarily tamed. He wears the same suit our son now wears, and looks as uncomfortable. I appear older than my eighteen years, my hair in a fashionable pompadour, wearing a dark, high-necked dress Mama made over for me. I am looking up at him, my chin tilted so I'm not directly facing the camera.

I let myself remember that moment: the strength of his hand on my shoulder, my fingers woven with his. His breath warm on my neck. The knowledge that soon we would be together in a room at the Mansion House Hotel to—finally—to satisfy the curiosity of years.

We hadn't slept much.

I shake off the memory and hastily replace the photo. My gaze lingers on the only other picture I have of my husband, the one Dan took on Christmas, 1931, the day Daniel lost his job and I gave birth to Teddy. The kids and I are seated on the same davenport that Max decries, while Daniel stands behind with his hands on my shoulders. He is smiling—they all are, except me, because I was in labor—but the tightness around his eyes betrays the worry that had already set in.

A squawk from Grace jerks me from the past. I hurry to quiet her before she wakes the house. As I lift her from the cradle and retreat to the bathroom, bouncing her gently to soothe her, I close my eyes and say a prayer to the God who hasn't often listened to me. *Let me do the right thing. Let me keep my family safe.*

It comes down to one simple thing: I can't choose the dead over the living. It would hurt everyone if I let this opportunity for happiness slip past because I can't release myself from a vow to a dead man. Daniel wouldn't want that. Jealous as he was, he wouldn't want me with someone else, but he would want what was best for the kids. And what is best for them is Max Byrne, a mother not mired in grief, and a chance at a normal life.

Pearl

June 10, 1934

For a woman who's coming up on the happiest day of her life, Mama's not sleeping at all. Whenever I wake up because of Thelma's kicking or Grace crying in the night, she's just by the window. Dan framed the wall between our rooms but he hasn't hung the door or put up the plasterboard yet. It will be finished by the time Mama and Dr. Max get back from Aunt's, which is all they're doing for a honeymoon.

I wonder if that was her idea, too, only one night, like she had the one night with Daddy.

I wish she would let herself be happy, but it doesn't feel like she remembers how. Aunt keeps going on about the dress, and while it's a shame she won't buy something new, it's more than just Mama's usual refusal to spend unnecessary money. I don't think it's Dr. Max, though. I saw them kissing the other night, so that seems to be working out okay.

When I tried to talk to her, she asked if I didn't have something better to do with my time. I didn't roll my eyes because she would clip me around the ear for being disrespectful, but I feel helpless when I see her there, staring at nothing. Not even crying.

Claire

As we discuss it over the next few days, I come to understand that Harry is ready to leave for Paris immediately. I had been joking when I suggested going after the wedding, but the day after our initial conversation, he came home with tickets which he handed me at breakfast.

"The *Île de France* is departing from New York in two weeks," he says. "Can you be ready by then?"

Two weeks? I think quickly: there is packing to be done, the house to be closed up, preparations made for traveling with a child—not to mention clothes. Any travel wardrobe will have to be acquired without Ava's help, as she is far too busy to take pity on me and would laugh and accuse me of sailing to France to get away from Irene.

"I'll manage," I say shakily. It was, after all, my idea. "Somehow."

Then there's the issue of Pixie. I hate being separated from my little dog, but he's a creature of habit and I don't think life aboard ship would suit him. Also, he would miss Thelma. If I left him with Mr. and Mrs. Hedges, he could stay in the house, with his basket and his toys, and Thelma could take him for walks after school.

Or...I could leave him with Thelma. I imagine my sister's reaction if I suggest adding a dog to her crowded household and restrain a smile. She will hate it, but she'll give in because the children adore him.

Teddy is easier. Other than clothes and a few favorite playthings, he will travel light. He's growing so quickly, he'll need new things by fall, anyway. It will be fun to shop for him in Paris, to go to the Galeries Lafayette and find perfect little sailor suits or miniature tweeds, so he and Harry can dress alike as we stroll the boulevards.

I pause. Not that we won't want to spend time with our boy—I am ashamed at how I have neglected him—but every moment of every day is unrealistic. This trip is as much meant to rebuild our marriage as it is a vacation. For it to work, Harry and I will need significant time alone.

For the first time, I wish we had a proper nanny, but we have always made do with Katie and, later, Pearl. Two weeks doesn't give me time to find someone, and I don't want a French nursemaid. Teddy will pick up the language while we're there—children are sponges at his age—but I want the person he sees most, aside from us, to speak English with him.

If only Pearl could come along. She would be in her element in Paris; a book lover like my niece deserves to spend time in the City of Light. If we leave at the end of June, we're not likely to be home before April; Harry and I both hate winter crossings. Ava would never allow Pearl to miss months of school.

Katie knocks, and I tell her our plans. Instead of being excited for us, her face falls.

"What is it?"

"Nothing, ma'am." She rolls her lower lip between her teeth. "How many of the trunks should I have brought down?"

"Oh, I don't know. All of them?" I throw open my closet doors and stare at the abundance within. What should I take? I'll need at least two changes for each day of the voyage; if we eat in the dining room, I'll need evening dress, as well. Gowns, wraps, jackets. My furs, for when it gets cold in Paris. Shoes and bags and hats and gloves...I can't stop smiling.

"You'll have a good time, ma'am," Katie says sadly. "I'll miss you."

I squeeze her arms. "And I'll miss you, but you and your parents will be staying on here while we're away."

She blinks. "What will we do in an empty house?"

"Houses fall to pieces when they're left unattended." I open and close my jewelry box; best to take it all. "And I'm hoping to convince Ava to stay here while we're gone. It would give them so more room."

"She'll never leave her little house, ma'am," Katie says, "but maybe you can convince her to come for dinner on Fridays, give my mama someone to cook for besides us."

I remember this when I see Ava later in the day and explain we will be taking the train to New York a few days after the wedding. "I was wondering if you and Max would like to use the house while we're gone."

"Live there, you mean?" Her brow creases. "We couldn't."

"Why not? You'd have more space," I coax. "Wouldn't it be nice to not be packed in like sardines?" Her expression reveals this is a sore point. "You could use our room—or the guest room, whichever you choose—and the children could take Max's rooms. Sort it out however you like."

"No." She shakes her head decisively. "It's too much. We're fine in our house."

I pass along Katie's suggestion about Friday nights, and she accepts, grudgingly. "It is Max's early night. It would be nice not to cook."

"And Harry's letting him use the car." Before she can object, I add, "It'll keep him off that dreadful bicycle. He can pay for the gasoline, but otherwise it's sitting there, unused. Like the house."

I get no further, and accept such victories as I am allowed. I'll bring up the subject of Pearl after the wedding; there's no point stirring the pot prematurely. Let Max get her in a good mood first.

Pearl

June 15, 1934

I overheard Aunt talking to one of her friends today, Mrs. Foster, the red-haired lady with the large bottom Mama sewed that first dress for. She and Uncle are going to France after the wedding. For several months, at least. It sounds like she feels bad about not paying attention to Uncle and Teddy for so long, and she should.

But if they're in Paris, they won't want Teddy around every moment of the day. They'll need someone to watch him.

There's no reason that someone can't be me. No reason at all.

Mama's going to take some handling. She won't want me to miss school, and normally I wouldn't, either. But France? If I can convince Aunt to take me, how can she say no? I've got four days until the wedding to come up with a plan.

Ava

The radio forecast had been for warm, cloudy weather, but I open my eyes to rain lashing the front windows. After a week of wakefulness, I have finally slept but I do not feel refreshed, and would like nothing more than to put the pillow over my head and go back to sleep. I blink and yawn, thinking to do just that, but Thelma and Pearl are at the bedside, smiling expectantly, already wearing their Sunday best.

"Grace is washed and fed," Pearl says, "And Thelma made coffee. Why don't I bring you a cup and you can start getting dressed?"

How have I missed all this activity? I'd taken a bath and set my hair the night before, to save time in the morning, but now I wonder why I bothered. I sit up, rubbing the unaccustomed pins at the back of my head. All this rain will make it collapse. It's just as well I didn't make an effort with my clothes.

"Look at the weather," I say, as if acknowledging it will make it disappear.

"Maybe it'll stop before ten." Pearl hands me my robe and yanks the curtain back. "Get up now, Mama, while I go deal with the boys."

A look at the window reveals a sky as gray as I feel. The street is pockmarked with puddles. Someone hurries past with an umbrella, and as I watch, the wind pulls it inside out. Briefly, I wonder if it would be possible to push the wedding off to a nicer day, but then I come to my senses. The judge made room for us on his calendar, and the clinic is closed until two so Dr. Spencer and his wife can attend. If I even mention delaying, Claire will fall into a tizzy and then I will say something cutting and our relationship will take weeks to recover.

There are no excuses. I said yes, and I meant it, at the time. Max is a good man. I love him. He'll be a good father. There is no reason in the world for me to not want to go through with this, other than the pain in my chest that says I'm betraying Daniel's memory.

Until he died, I'd never been one to look back; it's the biggest difference between me and Claire. Lately, I've looked over my shoulder so much I'm at risk of turning into a pillar of salt, like Lot's wife. I am crystallizing, becoming harder, when I'd finally allowed myself to soften over the last year.

Is it wrong that I can't cry when this overwhelming sadness presses in on me? When I told the kids that Max and I were getting married, Thelma and Pearl both cried—tears, I think, of sadness *and* joy.

An ending *and* a beginning.

But I am not yet ready for the end, so how do I begin again? There is no one to ask. Claire is so invested in our wedding she might as well be the one walking down the aisle; my kids, for all their maturity, are kids;

Esther Hedges is a friend, but she thinks the sun rises and sets on Max, so I can hardly reveal my second thoughts to her.

My husband-to-be is the closest I have to a confidant, but that doesn't mean I can sit him down and say I'm not ready, not after I've slept with him and invited what feels like half of Philadelphia to our wedding. No, I am well and truly stuck in a situation of my own making.

The floor squeaks above my head and soon footsteps pound past the door—the boys, on their way to breakfast. I pull the robe around my shoulders and contemplate moving.

"You okay, Ma?" Dan leans in. He is dressed in Daniel's suit and a clean shirt. "Anything I can do?"

At the sound of his voice, all the tears I haven't been able to find spring to my eyes. "I'm fine."

A pause, then the door closes and he comes to sit on the bed, putting his arm around me so my head rests on his shoulder. For a moment—just a moment—I let the tears come.

"I'm fine, really." I wipe my face on my sleeve. "A touch of nerves."

He rubs my back. "I don't wonder. You let yourself feel things now."

All those feelings I've suppressed have begun to circle, like wolves, and I make a sound—a sob or a laugh—and sit up straight. "Right now I'd rather not feel anything."

The doorknob rattles. "Mama? I've got your coffee."

"Leave it by the door," Dan calls, continuing to rub. "It's going to be all right, Ma, if that's what you're worried about. I'll get the room finished tonight, and when you come back tomorrow, everything will be perfect."

I look around at the chaos of construction. "It's not the room," I manage to say. "I know you'll do a fine job."

"Then what is it?" He goes still in that way that reminds me of Daniel. Neither of them were much for words, but I've always taken comfort in their silence. "Is it him?"

I think of Max, getting ready in his room at Claire's, whistling as he does up the buttons on one of his terrible suits. "No. It's not Max."

He fetches my coffee, closing the door firmly against his eavesdropping siblings. "Tell me what it is."

The rich scent clears my head. I take a sip and try to put my feelings into words. "I worry it's too soon to come right. That I'm not over your father and Max will end up feeling like he's second best, trying to step into shoes that are too big for him."

"Let Max worry about Max." Dan takes the cup from my fingers and drinks from it. "He knows you, Ma. He understands."

"That's what I keep telling myself." I let him keep the mug and push myself to my feet, pacing the room between the uprights of the framed wall. "But I don't know..."

"Then call it off." He puts the cup onto the dresser and turns me to face him. "You don't have to do it, if it's not right. I can take a note to Aunt Claire's."

"I couldn't." Even thinking about it feels impossible. "They would think I'd lost my mind."

"They wouldn't. We all just want you to be happy, Ma."

"And I will be." I shake my head, and begin to remove my pins with numb fingers. "I think I needed to hear myself say it, that's all."

"Glad I could help." He wraps me in an embrace that lifts me up onto my toes, then leaves. "I'll send the girls up to help you get ready."

The car arrives at half-past nine and Hedges comes to the door with an umbrella to escort me down the front steps. The rain is relentless. By the time I reach the car, my skirt clings wetly to my stockings and my shoes are full of water. Claire slides across the back seat so I can join her and the kids pile onto the other seat, except for Toby, who insists on sitting up front with Hedges. This causes George to clamber over the seat, landing in his brother's lap.

I block out their mounting argument and ask, "Where are Harry and Teddy?"

"With Max," she says calmly. "They left early, to talk to Judge Bradfield. You two can take my car after, and Harry and I will ride with the rest of the family."

I nod, trying not to think about *after*. "Is Esther coming, too, Mr. Hedges?"

"Already there, ma'am," he says. "Katie is keeping an eye on Mr. Teddy and my missus is having a conversation with the Lord about your future happiness."

"That's good of her." I rub my cold hands together and clamp them between my knees so Claire doesn't see their shaking.

Inside City Hall, we cram into an elevator to the second floor and the kids stream ahead when Claire gives them the number of the judge's chambers. She and I walk more slowly, and as we come up on the glass-paned door, she takes my hand.

I catch a glimpse of my reflection in the glass. As I feared, my hair is limp, all the curl ruined by the damp. "I look a fright."

"You do not." Claire straightens my new white collar and touches the gardenias she pinned to my shoulder in the car. "You look lovely."

She bought corsages for herself and for the girls, too, so I can't complain her extravagance is directed solely at me, but flowers make my dress look even worse. I half-wonder if that was her intention.

Max is on the other side of the door, with the others. I wish he'd come out for a moment; seeing him would bring me back to myself.

"Remember," Claire says, "remember how we stood together outside the courtroom before my wedding?"

"I remember." She had been a beautiful bride, all gold and white, her satin and lace gown making everything around her look dingy. "You were so excited."

"I was so scared."

I hadn't been scared to marry Daniel. It wouldn't have made sense to be scared of him. We'd known each other since we were tiny, when our mothers penned us on the porch so we wouldn't run off and get into trouble. Am I scared now? Not really. Just deeply uncertain. I love Max—it would be difficult not to—and marrying him will make the kids happy.

So why does it feel like I'm making a huge mistake?

Claire

Ava is the last person I would have never expected to have a case of nerves. When she makes a decision, she sticks with it. She was the one who said yes. She even slept with Max before agreeing to the marriage. I haven't decided if that was foolish or the wisest thing she could have done, but it's pure Ava, either way. I can't imagine what's gotten into her, but as the door opens and I cross the threshold, she takes a deep breath and I know she will be a step behind me. Because Ava doesn't back down.

The rows of seats in front of Judge Bradfield's bench are surprisingly crowded. Dr. Spencer and his wife; George Howe; Lucille Gordon, the clinic's nurse; Prue Foster, smiling hugely; a tall, dark boy with two little girls; some shabby women who might be Ava's neighbors; an elderly Jewish man in a fur-trimmed hat, with a small woman by his side; a tall man in some kind of uniform; even Aunt Honora, blessedly alone.

Max stands to one side, peering around me to get a look at Ava, and my eyes slide past him to Harry.

When I mentioned my wedding, it wasn't only to distract Ava; that day has been on my mind since I woke up—how frightened I had been, frightened even of Harry. I had never dreamed, in those innocent days, how many things could go wrong in a marriage, how easy it was for something solid to nearly disintegrate in my grasp. I stare at my husband until he meets my eyes. Smiles, eventually, but it's not the smile from before. Not yet. Something to work on in the days ahead, when we are alone in the middle of the ocean.

The children have turned to watch their mother's approach. Pearl holds Grace in her arms. Her eyes are shining with tears. Thelma, on Dan's lap, is crying outright. The little boys grin.

So much water under the bridge. So much has happened to them—to all of them—in the last few years. Max feels like a reward for surviving it all.

Though knowing Max, he wouldn't think of it like that. Ava is his reward: for his experience with Daisy, for all his good works, for his patience in getting to this day.

I step aside and sit next to my husband. Teddy clambers from Katie's lap onto mine, and Harry takes my hand. As Ava pauses beside Max, I pray everything will work out. For all of us.

Ava

I can't breathe. I stood in that echoing hallway and had a conversation with my sister, then walked into a room filled with people who love me—so many people—and yet I can't breathe. How am I even standing up? I should be out cold on the floor, everyone clustered around, fanning me, but no, I'm upright and conscious. Apparently I'm capable of walking, too, because when I stop and turn toward Max, he smiles at me with his whole heart in his eyes. I concentrate until my expression matches his. His hands are warm; mine are cold, as befits a woman who might actually be dead and too numb to fall down.

"Hello," he says softly.

"Hello." He is wearing a gray, double-breasted suit—a perfectly normal pinstriped suit like Harry would wear. Or a doctor. "You look...nice."

"Don't sound so surprised. I want that new sofa."

Max may not look like a traditional doctor, but Owen Bradfield is like a judge from a movie. His face is pale, marked by strong, iron-gray brows and a matching mustache over narrow lips. He doesn't look as if he smiles often. His collar, high and tight around his neck, is from another era. According to Harry, he is marrying us on a day when he has no court appearances, but he wears his black judicial robe.

The walls of the chamber are lined with dark wood. Between the panels, high, dirty windows streaming with water look north up Broad Street. A pair of flags stand at lazy attention on either side of portraits of George Washington and Herbert Hoover. Our current president is nowhere to be seen.

Judge Bradfield begins to speak, and the words of the ceremony flow over me, but I don't listen. I won't have to say anything for a few minutes, and the respite gives me time to remember how to breathe and deal with how surprisingly handsome Max is when he's not dressed like a vaudeville comedian.

There is a pause, and Judge Bradfield asks, "Does anyone present know of any reason that this couple should not be joined in matrimony?"

I look up, and Max smiles at me, a heartbreaking smile. I know what he's going to say before he says it. "I do."

Gasps from behind me: Claire, Pearl, Esther.

"You?" The judge glances quizzically at him. "And what objection could you possibly have, Dr. Byrne?"

Max squeezes my hands. "I think the bride is doing this for all the wrong reasons." His fingers tighten on mine, but I look only at the hazel eyes that see straight into me. "For her kids, maybe for me. Not for herself."

"Max…" I don't know what I want to say, and the pressure in my chest won't allow me to form words properly.

"I'm not saying you don't care—"

"I do!"

He winks. "Be careful throwing those words around, you might end up married after all." There is a ripple of laughter. Everyone, despite what he is doing, is with him. "But I don't think it should be today."

Something in me wilts, even as I take my first deep breath in what feels like days. After everything that's happened, does he not want me? Then something else, stronger, makes me straighten again. This is right. *Max* is right. He is giving me permission to grieve my husband, my old life, and to become fully independent before joining myself to him. It's a gift, and Mama always said to accept gifts with grace.

"I won't say it, then." I look over his shoulder at the pale oval of Claire's face, and I don't even care right now if this is the ruination of all her plans. "Not today. But until that day comes, there's no one I'd rather keep company with."

A wide smile breaks across his face and he pulls me to him, squashing my gardenias and giving me a smacking kiss. "That's something worth celebrating. Harry, does that invitation to lunch stand, even without a wedding?"

Harry rises, one hand resting lightly on Claire's shoulder. "We'll be a bit early, but the restaurant won't refuse to serve us because you've called things off."

I turn into Max's embrace. "Thank you," I whisper against his cheek. "Thank you."

"For what?" He backs away far enough to see my face.

"For knowing." I rest my forehead against his. "For knowing what I didn't know how to say." The tension has drained away, leaving me so tired I can't imagine sitting through a long restaurant lunch in the same way I can't imagine not sitting beside him. "For loving me."

"Like I had a say in any of it." His mouth quirks at one corner. "I'm not letting you off the hook, though. You did say yes."

I kiss him, smiling against his lips. "And I meant it. I'm not going anywhere."

Max clasps my hand and raises it in the air, as triumphant as if we'd just won a boxing match. "Then let's go and celebrate that we're not getting married." He looks at me, eyes twinkling. "Today, anyway."

This is the fun part for an author. In *Coming Apart*, I mentioned how much I enjoyed exploring my city, trying to find what remained of 1930s Philadelphia, but I got to dive deeper this time around and I hope that my affection for—and fascination with—old Philadelphia comes through.

For those wondering, Chippy (or Chiffy) Patterson was a real person, and a legal legend in the city, if somewhat of an embarrassment to his family. If you can lay hands on it, there's a biography called *The Worlds of Chippy Patterson* that is an absolute delight.

Another real person is Lenny Sharamatew, Pearl's friend at Girls High. She's the mother of my dear friend, Dianne Dichter, to whom this book is dedicated. When Di read part of the early draft, she mentioned that her mother would have been a contemporary of Pearl's, and that was enough for me to include her because Lenny—or Helen, as I knew her—was a lovely woman and I'd like to think that Pearl would have had a friend like her. The parts about Lenny being interested in horticulture and the nursery on the school roof are true. Thanks to Dianne, and her daughter Alex, for letting me borrow Lenny's high school yearbook to flesh out Pearl's world.

When I understood in *Coming Apart* that Ava was a seamstress, I was excited. Sewing has been a lifelong love, and the idea of all those 1930s dresses made my heart beat faster. But other than a dress each for Claire and Prue, there was no place for glamorous fashion in that first book. I've remedied that in *Coming Closer*, and I hope all my sewing friends (who requested more clothes, more sewing) are gratified.

Claire's side trip into philanthropy and the clinic were unexpected, but when I realized that FDR's first inauguration was the last one to be held in March, and it would therefore fit into the timeline of this book,

I could easily see her being swayed by the can-do spirit of the age and interacting with those powerful, independent women.

Inaccuracies (that I know of): the intense bout of winter cold that caused Max to warn Ava about the pipes freezing actually happened in February, 1934, not January, but it would have made for an action-packed shortest month of the year, and the story simply lined up better with that slight change. If we can still get weather forecasts wrong, weather in the rearview can also be slightly off. That's my story, and I'm sticking to it.

Also, an unknown. Despite digging, I was unable to find out when the migrants were moved on from their art museum Hooverville, so I chose a date that fit my story. It may have been earlier or later; knowing how the world works, it was probably earlier.

Thanks, as always, to my husband for his unwavering love, support, and patience, and for asking what happened to Jake. I hope I've answered that question, and I'm sorry he turned out to be an opportunistic jerk.

The third (and I believe final?) book in the *Ava and Claire* series, *Coming Together*, is scheduled for release on October 18, 2023. Please keep an eye out. The sisters look forward to seeing you again, and so do I.

About the Author

As an only child, Karen Heenan learned early that boredom was the ultimate enemy. Since discovering books, she has rarely been without one in her hand and several more in her head. Her first series, *The TudorCourt,* stemmed from a lifelong interest in British history, but she's now turned her focus closer to home and is writing stories set in and around her native Philadelphia.

She lives in Lansdowne, PA, just outside Philadelphia, where she grows much of her own food, makes her own clothes, and generally confuses the neighbors. She is accompanied on her quest for self-sufficiency by a very patient husband and an ever-changing number of cats.

One constant: she is always writing her next book.

Follow her online at karenheenan.com and sign up for her newsletter to receive a free novella and updates on what's next.